# KISS
# ME
# KILL
# ME

J. S. Carol is the author of *The Killing Game*, which was short-listed for the CWA Ian Fleming Steel Dagger Award. As James Carol, he has also written the bestselling Jefferson Winter series. *Broken Dolls*, the first of these, was published in 2014 to rave reviews and reached #1 on the Amazon fiction and thriller charts. In addition James is writing a series of eBooks set during Winter's FBI days. *Presumed Guilty* is the first of these.

James lives in Hertfordshire with his wife and two children. When he's not writing he can usually be found in a pair of headphones, recording and producing music.

# KISS ME KILL ME

J. S. CAROL

ZAFFRE

**For Nick Tubby. A good friend and one of life's true gentlemen.
Thanks for everything buddy.**

First published in Great Britain in 2018 by
ZAFFRE PUBLISHING
80–81 Wimpole St, London W1G 9RE
www.zaffrebooks.co.uk

A CIP catalogue record for this book is available from the British Library.

ISBN: 978–1–78576–394–6
eBook ISBN: 978–1–78576–395–3

1 3 5 7 9 10 8 6 4 2

Typeset by IDSUK (Data Connection) Ltd

Zaffre Publishing is an imprint of Bonnier Zaffre,
a Bonnier Publishing company
www.bonnierzaffre.co.uk
www.bonnierpublishing.co.uk

# Prologue

Everything looked perfect.

Zoe did another circuit of the kitchen table, just to be sure. Today was their third anniversary, so this was important. She straightened a spoon, just a fraction of an inch, but it made all the difference. The bowls were bone china, the glasses crystal, and each place setting was finished off with a neatly pressed white linen napkin. Small details, perhaps, but those small details showed how much you cared. The box of Raisin Bran was for Daniel, the cornflakes for her. Orange juice for Daniel, a jug of mineral water for her.

She did one more slow circuit, but couldn't see anything she wanted to change. Daniel was moving around upstairs, which meant he was out of the shower. He had a big meeting today, so he would be wearing his best suit, and probably the new red silk tie. Whichever tie he chose, it would definitely be red. He claimed that red was a power colour. On that basis, all his ties were red. Zoe wasn't sure if this was an actual fact or something he had read on the Internet.

The bedroom door rattled open. This was her cue to put on the toast and pour his coffee. The combination of smells was like heaven. Daniel appeared a short while later. Like she'd thought, he was wearing his best suit and the new tie. The combination was impressive. He had been handsome when they first met; if anything, he was even more handsome now. Zoe suspected that Daniel was one of those men who would get better looking with age, like George Clooney. And there was a definite passing resemblance: both had brown eyes and dark hair, and that easy way of smiling that made you feel as though you were the only person in the room. Daniel stopped at the work island and looked at the table, eyes moving from his place setting to hers, then back again. Zoe walked over to join him.

'Happy anniversary,' she said.

'It doesn't seem like three years, does it? Where does the time go?'

Daniel wrapped his arms around her and pulled her into an embrace. A kiss for the top of her head; a long, lingering one for her lips. He broke away, then took her by the hand and led the way to the table. The chair gave a small screech when he pulled it out. She sat down and he guided it back into place with another screech. Then he walked around the table and took his own seat.

'Carmichael's is booked for eight. So we can celebrate. I think you should wear the blue dress. Do you know the one I mean?'

Zoe nodded.

'The diamond earrings I bought for your birthday would go nicely with that, don't you think?'

She nodded again. And they would. The earrings were from Tiffany's, eighteen carats and inlaid in white gold; the dress was a Dolce & Gabbana. Carmichael's was one of Portland's most exclusive restaurants, a place for being seen. Appearances were important. Whenever there was something to celebrate, this was

Daniel's first choice of venue. The toast popped and Zoe went to get it. She put it in the rack and carried it over to him, then took her seat again, carefully because she hated the way it screeched against the tiles. The sound reminded her of fingernails on a blackboard, and had much the same effect; the disquieting itch that ran the length of her spine got right into her bones.

Daniel picked up the cornflakes box and carried it to her side of the table. He tipped some into her bowl, glanced at her stomach, then took some out. He placed the packet back beside the Raisin Bran and reached for the water jug. Zoe watched the water splash into her glass; she watched it splash on top of her cereal.

They ate in silence. Daniel finished the last of his toast, then wiped his hands on the napkin, rolled it into a ball and tossed it on top of his plate. He walked to Zoe's side of the table and glanced in her bowl to make sure she had eaten everything.

'I've left lunch in your refrigerator. And remember, dinner's at eight, so you'll need to be ready to leave by seven thirty.'

He kissed the top of her head and walked out of the kitchen. His footsteps echoed along the hallway, the front door opened and closed, then silence. Zoe did a slow count inside her head and stopped when she reached twenty-three. A second later, the Porsche Boxster roared three times in quick succession. The noise was loud and obnoxious. This happened whenever Daniel got behind the wheel. He turned the key and punched the gas pedal three times. Once, twice, then once more for luck. The behaviour had an OCD quality, like if he didn't do it he might crash.

Zoe sometimes wondered if he loved that car more than he had ever loved her.

Sometimes she wondered what would happen if he did crash and die.

# PART I

# ROSE-TINTED SPECTACLES

*Those who are faithful know only the trivial side of love;
it is the faithless who know love's tragedies.*

Oscar Wilde

# Chapter 1

## THEN

'Are you sure you haven't been smoking grass, Zoe? You know it makes you paranoid.'

Lizzy was talking behind her hand like they were back in high school. The whispering was for the benefit of the customers. It was a slow Tuesday at the end of the month and there were only two, a woman and her grown-up daughter, who were currently occupying a table in the middle of the dining area. The scene being played out there smacked of obligation rather than enjoyment. Zoe hated shifts like this. Waiting tables was no one's idea of fun, but at least when you were busy the time passed more quickly.

'Waiting for an answer,' Lizzy prompted. She might have been whispering, but she was still too loud. Everything she did was too loud; that was just who she was. Her hair was currently dyed bright red, there were piercings in her tongue, nose and ears, and last week she had gotten yet another tattoo. Zoe wished she could be so reckless, but that wasn't going to happen, not in this lifetime. Instead of red hair, hers was a boring preppy brown, and the only thing she had pierced were her ears. They were opposites in so many ways, yet somehow they fit. Lizzy Slater was the loud to her quiet, the confident to her crippling viper's nest of insecurities.

'I have not been smoking grass,' Zoe whispered back.

Lizzy shot her a cynical look.

'I have not. Because you're right, it does make me paranoid. That's why I don't smoke it anymore. So, if we take grass out of the equation, where does that leave us?'

Lizzy sighed and shook her head. 'We've already had this conversation. Popeye has not been sneaking around our apartment.'

'And I'm telling you he has. Who ate those Pop Tarts?'

'Ah yes, the Pop Tart conspiracy.'

'I didn't eat them, and you didn't eat them. Unless you were lying about that.'

'Which I wasn't. I told you, Mike probably ate them.'

'He said he didn't.'

'And men never, ever lie.'

They stared at each other for a moment.

'Then there's the fact that he's been in my room going through my stuff,' Zoe said.

'No, you *suspect* that, which is a totally different thing.'

Zoe kept staring and Lizzy let out a long sigh.

'Okay, so what has he done this time? No, don't tell me. You got home and discovered the front door had been broken down?'

'He doesn't need to break it down. He's the building superintendent. He has a key.'

'I'm still waiting for the piece of evidence that's going to put him away for life.'

Zoe hesitated, then whispered, 'The toilet seat was up.'

'Seriously?'

The mocking smile made Zoe feel as though she might actually be crazy after all. But she knew she wasn't. Popeye had been in their apartment. Again.

'Maybe I left it up,' Lizzy said.

'That would be a first.'

'Maybe you left it up.'

'Not going to happen.'

'Mike stayed over last night, and he's always leaving it up.'

'It was down when I went to my lecture this morning, and that was after you guys had left. When I got back from my lecture, that's when I found it up. Popeye has been in our apartment, I'm telling you.'

Before they could get any deeper into this, chef called over to tell them the meals were ready to go. Lizzy gave Zoe a look then shooed her towards the plates. Giovanni's was one of those places where the kitchen opened into the dining area. Some people liked that; Zoe didn't. She preferred life to have a little mystery.

Lizzy was winding her up, but this was nothing new. Zoe had figured she would react like this and almost hadn't said anything. Now she was wishing she hadn't. It would be a different story if Lizzy suspected Popeye was going through her room. If that happened she would probably punch him out first and ask questions later. She wouldn't just let it go, that was for damn sure.

As infuriating as Lizzy could be, Zoe found it impossible to stay mad at her for long. They had shared a dorm room in their first year, and it had been a blast. They were both new to Portland so they got to discover the city together. Lizzy was currently in the final year of a fashion degree, while Zoe was on the home stretch of her creative writing course. One of these days Lizzy would be ruling over a New York fashion house like it was her own personal kingdom. That was inevitable. And while she was out there making things happen, Zoe reckoned that she'd probably be shivering in an attic, starving for her art.

'Okay,' Lizzy whispered when Zoe got back. 'Judging by the fact the seat was up, are we to assume that he actually used the toilet?'

'That's what I'm figuring.'

'That's crazy.'

'Is it? Popeye's a total creep. You've seen the way he looks at us, right? Don't tell me you haven't noticed.'

'He looks at everyone that way. There's something wrong with his eyes. That's why we call him Popeye.'

'He's a psycho.'

'And you're qualified to make that diagnosis, Dr Chapel?'

'You don't need a degree to work that out.'

'Well, my psycho detector isn't going off, and it's usually pretty accurate.'

'We need to move to a new apartment.'

Lizzy shook her head and let loose with another sigh. 'You know why we live there, right?'

'Because it's cheap.'

'No, Zoe, because it's the *cheapest*. We can't afford to live anywhere else, so before I even start to think about moving I'm going to need something more than your paranoia.'

'I am not being paranoid.'

Lizzy put a hand up, stopping Zoe in her tracks. 'Popeye is strange, no arguments there. He's from eastern Europe, and he doesn't speak English so well, and he has this weird way of looking at you where it's like his eyes are going in different directions, but that doesn't mean he's going to murder us in our beds. *Vive la difference*, that's what I say. Okay, changing the subject. What are you up to this weekend?'

Zoe hesitated. She wanted to push further, but what was the point? 'Working. I've got an overdue assignment, and a couple of shifts here. What about you? What are you up to?'

'I'm back in Chicago dealing with the human zoo that's my family. It's my parents' silver anniversary so everyone will be there. All the mad old folks. And of course, my mom is organising everything so she's going to be an absolute stress-head, which means she'll be the maddest one of all.'

Zoe laughed and Lizzy's face suddenly fell.

'Jesus, Zo, I'm sorry. Here I am bitching about my family. I completely forgot.'

'Are you kidding? I love hearing about your messed-up family. I get to live the fun stuff vicariously, and I don't have to deal with the stress. It works for me.'

'Even so.'

'There's no "even so". Tell me more.'

Before Lizzy could respond, the door swung open and two businessmen walked in. Zoe barely noticed the guy on the left because something about the guy on the right made her do a double take. He was in his early thirties, and handsome. Not quite model-handsome, but not far off it. That wasn't what made her look twice, though. After all, this wasn't the first guy who looked like they should be on the cover of *GQ* who'd walked in here. He was wearing a suit that was so neat it must have been tailored to fit; his shirt was dazzlingly white, his black leather shoes were shone to a high gloss, and the tie was made from red silk. And that wasn't it, either. Again, well-dressed businessmen weren't exactly font-page news around here.

No, the thing that made her look again was the way he seemed to own the room the second he stepped through the door. Some people could do that. Presidents, movie stars, pop stars. It wasn't as though they were trying to draw attention, they just did. Part of it was confidence, but a bigger part was an absolute certainty about where they fitted into the universe. Zoe reckoned she stood at the opposite end of the spectrum. When she walked into a room she doubted anyone noticed.

'Close your mouth,' Lizzy whispered into her ear. 'You're going to catch a fly.'

Zoe turned to face her. 'I don't know what you're talking about.'

'Don't you? So why have you gone bright red?'

'I have not,' Zoe replied, even though she knew she had. Her cheeks felt as though they were on fire and her stomach had that freefall sensation you got when you were caught in a lie. Lizzy started pushing her towards the two men.

'Stop it, Lizzy! What the hell are you doing?'

'I'm playing Cupid. What does it look like?'

Zoe dug her heels in and came to a halt. 'I said quit it. And anyway, why would he be interested in someone like me?'

'No, the question is why *wouldn't* he be interested?' Lizzy looked at her. 'Tell you what, I'll go and get them seated. It'll give me a chance to check him out. You know, make sure he's not a psycho.'

Before Zoe could say anything else, Lizzy was off.

# Chapter 2

## NOW

Zoe watched the second hand ticking slowly around the face of her Rolex and wished it would move faster. It had just turned twenty after one, so there was still another forty minutes to go. The last twenty would be like torture; the last five would be the worst of all. They always were. Those were the minutes where the hunger was so pronounced it seemed to eclipse everything else; the minutes where all she could think about were the plastic containers waiting in the refrigerator.

Experience had taught her to wait until two. It was all about pacing herself. Daniel had told her to be ready for seven thirty, but he might call just before that to tell her their dinner reservation had been moved to nine. It wouldn't be the first time. That extra hour and a half of hunger would be hard, but she could manage it. Usually she was ready for lunch by ten, but if she had eaten it then that extra hour and a half later would be unbearable.

To start with she had kept the cravings at bay by shoplifting food. Candy bars, bags of chips, anything to fill the empty space in her stomach. The way she looked had worked to her advantage. Who would suspect someone so well dressed of stealing a

Hershey bar? Her overconfidence had been her downfall. The store owner hadn't called the police, but Daniel was a regular customer and he'd had a quiet word. Her punishment had been two days without food, just so she could understand what real hunger felt like.

After that she had stopped shoplifting food. What was the point? Somewhere along the line she would get caught again, and this time she might not get off so lightly. Maybe this time the police would be called. If that happened, she hated to think what her punishment would be. Instead, she had been forced to get creative. Eating toothpaste, but not so much that Daniel might notice; stealing sugar and ketchup sachets from fast food restaurants; keeping a small Ziploc bag hidden at the bottom of the trash can for scraping Daniel's leftovers into. On one occasion she had been so desperate she had eaten dirt from the backyard, but that made her throw up. Some of the things she had been forced to do left her feeling ashamed, but the short respite she got from her hunger made up for the humiliation. You did what you had to in order to survive. When you got down to it that was all she was doing here, just trying to survive.

Cooking Daniel's dinner was its own kind of hell. Standing at the stove, all those mouth-watering smells wafting around her, it was too much. On the few occasions where she dared to steal some, the guilt and paranoia had almost killed her. She had sat there at dinner slowly driving herself crazy, because he must have known what she had done. How could he not have? But he hadn't said a word, and she had breathed a silent sigh of relief and promised herself it would never happen again. Except that was a lie, because eventually it would reach the point where she couldn't help herself and the cycle would start all over again, need battling guilt like she was a junkie.

The big hand moved slowly past the nine, and the ten, and then the eleven. She wanted to eat, wanted to eat now, but she made herself wait. Five minutes today would be ten tomorrow; by this time next week it would be an hour. It just wasn't worth it.

Zoe counted the second hand through the last thirty seconds then got up from the table. *Her* refrigerator was the small under-counter one. On the top shelf were two plastic containers containing her lunch. Usually everything she needed to prepare Daniel's dinner would be on the middle one, but because they were eating out tonight this was empty today. This was the smallest of mercies, but when hope was in such short supply you took what you could get. Seeing the ingredients sitting on the shelf, being able to look but knowing that was all she could do, was a whole other circle of hell.

Lunch was the same every day, just like breakfast was always cornflakes and water, so, even without looking, she knew what she would find. In the first container there would be five sticks of cucumber, a two-inch square of chicken and ninety-nine grains of brown rice. The soup was in the second container, although to call it soup was a stretch. It was thin and watery, and totally tasteless. Daniel made a new batch every Sunday evening and split it into seven containers, each marked with a day of the week. The Monday one was left in her refrigerator; the rest were locked in the freezer.

She put the food onto a plate and there was more white china than food, like nouvelle cuisine, albeit a twisted version. The temptation was to hurry, but she made herself take it slowly, chewing each mouthful properly before moving on to the next. She ate the two-inch square of chicken first. It had been boiled, and it was as though the process had leached all the flavour away. Next she moved on to the sticks of cucumber, eating them one at a time to make the meal last as long as possible.

Before eating the rice, she counted the grains. She had watched Daniel put them out onto the kitchen island yesterday evening. He did it the same way each time. When he was finished there would be nine neat piles containing ten grains each arranged in three rows of three. Off to the right there would be a single lone pile of nine. She had considered asking him why he did this, but she wasn't sure she wanted the answer.

Zoe heated the soup in the microwave, poured it into a bowl, then sat back at the table. She ate a spoonful and it was like eating boiled water. Even though it was disgusting, she knew that she would finish every last drop. It might not be filling, but it warmed her stomach, and that was something at least.

As she ate her soup, she wondered how she had ended up here. It was a question she must have asked a thousand times, usually during those long hours when sleep seemed to have deserted her altogether. Like all the really tough questions there was no simple answer. In hindsight she could see how her path had been set back in Montana when she was still a kid. She had never been one of the popular girls at school. She would try to fit in, but then it got to the point where it just wasn't worth the effort. It didn't matter what clothes she wore, they were never going to be cool enough; it didn't matter what she said or did, it was never quite going to be the right thing. Her parents would tell her she was amazing, that she could be anything she wanted, that she could do anything, and for a while she believed them. She had this whole future mapped out for herself, one where she would escape from Great Falls and become rich and famous, and that would show everyone.

Except it hadn't worked out the way she imagined. Life never did. First her mom died, and then her dad, and somewhere between those two events her dreams shrank to the point where she lost sight of them. And then Daniel Barton had entered her life and encouraged her to dare to dream again, and for a short time her dreams had burnt brighter than ever, like fireworks. The trouble with fireworks, however, was that they always burned out too quickly. If she had been a stronger person she would have found some way to leave him, but who was she trying to kid? There was no way to get away from someone like Daniel, not when they'd gotten their hooks into you.

Zoe shut her eyes and ate another spoonful of soup. With them closed, she could almost imagine she was in a restaurant, maybe even Giovanni's, eating a late lunch with Lizzy after the last customers had left. When she opened them again her life was the same as ever; the same as it would always be from now until the day she died. The kitchen really was beautiful, like something you might see in an interior design magazine. Until you looked a little closer. How many of those perfect kitchens had a padlock on the pantry door? Or the refrigerator? There might not be any bars on the windows, but this was still a prison. She finished eating and for a while just sat there staring into space. Three years of marriage. How had that happened? It felt like three hundred.

She tidied away her lunch things then went upstairs to change. Daniel had left her gym clothes on the bed. Today he had chosen the black leggings with the pink waistband, and a black Nike top. She got dressed and went downstairs. Her car key was on the board that hung above the ornamental table at the front door; her cell phone was in the dish. The bright red Mercedes SLK on the driveway was a guilt present, one of many. She put her gym bag in the trunk, then climbed into the driver's seat and started the car. This was the sort of day her mom would have called a Goldilocks day. Not too hot; not too cold. The sun was shining and, aside from the occasional wisp of cloud, the sky was an endless blue. They were halfway through April. This had once been Zoe's favourite time of year. She had loved the colours, and the way everything felt so optimistic. These days she felt so distanced from that person; it was as though she had no concept of what optimism was anymore.

Their house was on Fairfield Boulevard, one of Portland's more exclusive streets. The neighbourhood was made up with large clapboard houses that had spacious, well-kept yards front and back. The street was wide, the trees tall, the air clean and fresh. Today it was as quiet as ever. The soccer moms had already dropped their kids at school and gone off to the gym or a coffee house; their husbands had gone out to work. In some respects she wasn't that different from those women; in others, her life was about as different as it was possible to get.

Driving past Carmichael's, the reality of her situation suddenly caught up with her. Here she was driving an expensive sports car, and living in a beautiful home, and tonight she would be eating here, and for a short while the ache of hunger deep in her belly would abate. But what about now? Because the reality was that for most of the day that ache would constantly be there.

Any other person would go to a store or a diner and buy something to eat, but she couldn't do that because she had no money or bank cards. Daniel controlled the finances, just like he controlled every other aspect of her life. A homeless person could beg a few dollars for a McDonald's, but she couldn't even do that. Why would anyone give her money? She clearly had plenty.

Daniel had taken her to Carmichael's on their first date. It had been a complete disaster. The second she sat down, she knew she shouldn't be there. Her clothes were all wrong, and it felt as though everyone was staring. She had been totally overwhelmed and out of her depth, and Daniel had been so understanding. He had noticed her discomfort and offered to take her somewhere else, anywhere, she just had to say the word. They ended up at the Marrakesh, which was her favourite coffee house in Portland. This was her secret place, somewhere she went when she needed to get off the merry-go-round. It was also a place she had never shared with anyone. That was how sure she had been about Daniel back then. They might only have just met, but she had known that he was the one.

She pressed the gas pedal and drove on. Carmichael's shrank in the rear-view mirror, and that seemed like an appropriate metaphor for her life, because that too had shrunk and disappeared to nothing. As she drove, she wondered what had happened to the man she had fallen in love with, the one who had laughed and joked over lattes and muffins, the one who, for a short while at least, had made her feel as though she was the bright star at the centre of the universe.

And then she wondered what had happened to that naive young girl who had once believed that a happy-ever-after might actually have been possible.

# Chapter 3

## THEN

Zoe glanced at her cell phone then moved the drape aside so she could see the street. Daniel had said seven thirty, and it was now seven thirty-four, and she needed to ease herself back from the cliff edge, because the fact that he was four minutes late did not mean that she had been stood up. She looked at her cell phone again. No texts, no missed calls.

'Would you relax!' Lizzy called from the sofa.

'I am relaxed.'

'If that's relaxed, I'd hate to see what you're like when you're tense.'

'I want tonight to go well, that's all.'

'In that case you need to take a chill pill. Just be yourself.'

Zoe shot her a sceptical look.

Lizzy closed her magazine and placed it on the sofa. 'I'm serious, Zo. If Dan sees you for the amazing, beautiful, talented person you are, he's not going to be able to resist. And anyway, if it doesn't work out there are plenty more men out there.'

'Maybe for you there are. But this is me we're talking about.'

Lizzy shook her head. 'Zoe, Zoe, Zoe. You have no idea, do you? You need to have more confidence in yourself. Maybe you should take a self-assertiveness course.'

'Ha ha.'

'I'm serious. Go through life with the expectation that people are going to walk all over you and that's exactly what's going to happen. Are you a lioness or a doormat? Let me hear that roar.'

'Roar,' Zoe replied, deadpan and without any real feeling.

'Just be yourself, and you'll be fine. That's all I'm saying.'

'He doesn't like being called Dan, by the way. He prefers Daniel.'

'Whatever.'

Lizzy went back to her magazine and Zoe looked out the window again. Droplets of rain had collected on the glass, and the street had been washed clean. She was about to let the drape drop back when Daniel's Porsche turned the corner. By the time it had pulled up at the kerb, she was already reaching for her coat.

'Not so fast,' Lizzy told her. 'You don't want to appear desperate. Let him come to the door to meet you. Make him work a little.'

Zoe glanced out the window just in time to see Daniel walk across the sidewalk. He disappeared into the building. Less than a minute later there was a knock on the door. It felt like ten.

'Remember,' Lizzy said. 'No hurrying. You're in control here. You're calling the shots.'

Zoe forced herself to walk along the hall; she did a slow count to five and opened the door. When Daniel saw her he smiled his amazing smile, and all her stress evaporated in an instant.

'Sorry I'm late,' he said. 'I had a meeting that went on longer than it should have. I thought I'd get here in time but the traffic was a nightmare. And, of course, my cell phone battery died.'

'Don't worry about it. You're here now. That's the important thing.'

Zoe's fingertips brushed the back of his hand and the touch was as electric as the kiss they had shared in the cab after their first date. There had only been the one, but it was a kiss that promised a lot more. She heard footsteps behind her and glanced over her shoulder. Lizzy was walking towards them.

'Hey there, Dan.'

Zoe noticed the way Daniel winced before he returned the greeting. Rubbing people up the wrong way was one of Lizzy's less endearing traits. Like the red hair and the piercings, she did it to get a reaction.

'By the way,' Lizzy said. 'I'm meeting up with Mike for a drink later. I'll probably stay at his place tonight.' She paused. 'I'm just saying.'

Zoe felt the burn rising in her cheeks. Being annoyingly embarrassing was another of those traits. Before Lizzy could do any more damage, she headed out into the hall, pulling the door closed behind her.

'I'm sorry about that,' she said. 'Lizzy can be a bit much at times.'

Daniel waved the apology away. 'Don't worry about it. So how long have you two known each other?'

'Since I arrived in Portland. We started college at the same time.'

'That's the same as me and Josh. He's the guy I was having lunch with the other day. I met him during my first week here and now he's my business partner.'

'With Lizzy and me, I guess it's a case of opposites attract.'

Daniel thought this over for a second then nodded. 'Same for me and Josh. If we were too alike it just wouldn't work. We'd probably end up killing each other.'

They drove up to Nob Hill and parked outside the Marrakesh. When Daniel asked where she wanted to go for their second date, she had suggested coming back here. She had meant it as a joke but he thought she was being serious, and before she could tell him otherwise, the arrangements had already been made. Daniel got out and walked around to the passenger side. He opened her door and they ran hand in hand through the rain to the entrance.

The coffee house was owned by a guy called Roy who originally came from London. He dressed like it was still the Summer of Love. Kaftans, beads and plenty of tie-dye. The decor reflected his personality. There were rugs on the walls and an impressive collection of hookahs. The place was painted in sunburnt yellows, oranges and reds. Daniel paid for their lattes and muffins, and carried them over to a booth at the back of the room. They had their very own Woodstock on the stereo. Since they arrived they'd had tracks from Santana and Hendrix. Nothing post-1970 ever got played in here; it was like the clock had stopped when the sixties ended. Zoe sat down and sipped her coffee. Daniel was studying her from the other side of the table.

'What?' she asked. 'Have I got a booger hanging from my nose?'

Daniel laughed. 'You're okay. No boogers. I was just think-ing that you look more relaxed than you did that time at Carmichael's.'

'That's because I'm feeling more relaxed.' She smiled. 'Okay, last time we went out you managed to dodge all the personal stuff. That's not going to happen this time.'

'Okay, so what do you want to know?'

Zoe leant forward. Her elbows were on the table top and her head was propped on her hands. 'Everything.'

He laughed again. 'Such as?'

'How about we start with where you're from and who you are, and what you do for a living.'

'Is that all?'

Daniel took a sip of coffee and started talking. He had been born and raised in Prophetstown, a small city a couple of hours out of Chicago. Good grades; captain of the little-league team; no brothers, no sisters. He moved to Portland to go to college, and majored in business studies. After graduating Daniel and Josh had started a software company called Myriadian Solu-tions. Josh dealt with the programming side of things, while Daniel made the deals. The company currently had a staff of twelve and offices down near the Willamette River. It was doing well. So well, in fact, that Daniel was in the process of putting together an expansion plan.

His enthusiasm was infectious, and that was obviously one reason the company had been so successful. He had a very clear vision of what he wanted, and how he was going to achieve it.

That came shining through in the way he talked. He made a refreshing change from the college boys she usually dated. Zoe just hoped that he wasn't looking at her and seeing a silly little college girl playing at being a grown-up. She was twenty-two; he was thirty-one. There were nine years between them but she was sure they could make this work.

'Okay, enough about me,' he finally said. 'It's your turn. I want to know all about Zoe Chapel.'

Zoe took another sip of coffee, then started talking. She had come from Great Falls in Montana, which was probably the most boring place on the planet. She was an only child, and for the most part she'd had a pretty amazing childhood. Her parents had all but given up on having kids, then she came along. She was a complete surprise, but a good one. Needless to say, they had doted on her. Things started to go wrong shortly after she turned twelve. Her mom was diagnosed with stage-four breast cancer; six months later she was dead. A few years later her father died from a brain aneurysm. That had been a rough time for her. Being a teenager was challenging enough; being an orphaned teenager was in a whole different league. What she failed to mention was how bad it had really been. She had become withdrawn and her confidence had hit an all-time low. Somehow she had found the strength to eventually pick herself up and move on, but looking back, she wasn't sure how.

'Jesus,' Daniel said when she finished talking. 'I'm sorry.'

'Why? It's not your fault. Shitty things happen.'

'This goes beyond shitty.'

The way he said this, Zoe had the impression he wasn't talking about her. She waited for him to speak, but he didn't. There was a faraway look on his face. 'What?' she prompted gently.

He looked across the table and smiled sadly. 'I know exactly how shitty this all is. I was sixteen when my parents died. It was a house fire. I only escaped because my bedroom was at the back. I had to climb out my window.'

'My God, Daniel, that's terrible.'

'It was a long time ago.'

'Even so. How did you cope?'

'I didn't. Not really. I went off the rails for a while. By the time I eventually got my act back together I'd missed a lot of school. My grades suffered. Before it happened, I was heading to Stanford.'

'Instead you ended up in Portland.'

'Things happen for a reason. I've got no complaints. My life here is pretty good.'

Daniel suddenly laughed, and for a split second Zoe was convinced he was laughing at her. The shame burning through her was as familiar as it was unwelcome.

'Look at us,' he said. 'Could this get any more depressing? Okay, I want to hear a good memory. And don't overthink it. Just say the first thing that springs to mind.'

Zoe's mind suddenly went blank. It was always like this when she got put on the spot. She reached for her coffee to buy some time, took a sip, then put the mug back down. 'Whenever there was anything on at school, like the Christmas play or field day, my parents were always there. I can't remember them missing a single event. It didn't matter that I never won a single race and that I always forgot my lines, they would always be the proudest parents there. God I miss them so much sometimes.' She smiled sadly. 'That's the problem, I guess. I have a lot of good memories from my childhood, but ultimately they're all going to be tainted by what happened. Losing my parents so young, well, something like that is going to define you.'

The way Daniel was staring across the table made her feel self-conscious, like she had said too much. 'What?'

'I was just thinking about my own dad. He used to come to all my ball games. When we were playing at home he always had the same seat on the bleachers. That way I knew exactly where to look for him. So what happened after your father died?'

'My dad had remarried by then, so I carried on living with my stepmom and stepbrother. She was incredible. I don't know what I would have done if she hadn't been there to help me pull things back together again. It was around that time that I got into writing. That helped, getting my thoughts and feelings down onto paper.'

'I'd love to read something you've written.'

'You're just saying that.'

'I'm not. Look, I'm just a businessman. All I do is make deals. To create something from your imagination, that must be amazing. The truth is, I'm jealous.'

'Bullshit.'

'It's not. Hand on heart. So, have you written any novels yet?'

Zoe nodded. 'Two. And they're both crap.'

'But you haven't given up, have you? Please tell me you'll keep going.'

'No, I haven't given up. In fact, I've recently been playing around with some ideas for a new story.'

'You've got to write it. I'm telling you, it'll be a bestseller.'

Zoe laughed. It was hard not to get swept up in his enthusiasm. In some ways it was a bit much, though. Writing was something she did; it wasn't something she shouted about. Sure, she had dreamt about having a *New York Times* bestseller, but that was all it was, a dream. Everyone knew that dreams rarely came true. If life had taught her anything, it was that.

'How can you say that when you've never seen anything I've written? For all you know I might suck.'

'Anything you write is going to be amazing. I just know it.'

'I wish I shared your faith.'

'You should believe in yourself, Zoe. If you don't, who will?'

Daniel waited for her to look at him, then reached out and placed his hand on top of hers. His skin was soft, his touch warm, and she was glad they had come here again tonight. This might have been her secret place, but some secrets needed to be shared.

They had their second kiss in the entranceway of her apartment block, sheltering from the rain. That second kiss led to a third, and a fourth, and at some point Daniel suggested they might be more comfortable upstairs, and Zoe found herself agreeing. They had just started making out on the sofa when the front door banged open. A second later, Lizzy was standing in the doorway of the living room, shaking her head, a bemused grin plastered over her face. By that point Daniel and Zoe had fled to separate ends of the sofa.

'*Yeah*,' Lizzy said, drawing the word out. 'Well, Mike stood me up, so I decided to meet up with Angie for a couple of drinks, and don't mind me, because I'm out of here.'

'You don't have to run off because of us,' Zoe said quickly. 'Look, I need to pee. Why don't you keep Daniel company? It would be a good opportunity for you guys to get to know each other better.'

She hurried out into the hallway and for a moment just stood outside the bathroom door. She felt guilty, but didn't know why. It wasn't as though Daniel was the first guy she had brought back to the apartment, but it was the first time Lizzy had walked in on her, and maybe that was the difference. She pushed the door open and froze.

'Lizzy,' she called out. 'I need you to come here.'

Zoe heard Lizzy making her excuses. A couple of seconds later she appeared at the end of the hallway.

'Is everything okay?' she asked.

'Not really.'

Lizzy stopped at her shoulder and followed her gaze into the bathroom.

'You can see that, right?' Zoe said. 'You can see the seat's up?'

Lizzy sighed. 'Maybe it was Dan.'

'Daniel has been with me the whole time.'

'Look, I've had a long day. I really don't have the energy for this right now.'

'Is there a problem?' Daniel asked.

Zoe turned and saw him walking towards them. He stopped when he reached the bathroom door.

'Well, I don't think there is,' Lizzy said. 'But Zoe would beg to differ. She thinks our building supervisor has been breaking in so he can use our toilet.'

'We keep finding the toilet seat up,' Zoe added. 'And neither of us is doing it.'

'Maybe I'm doing it in my sleep.'

'So what? You fell asleep at work, sleepwalked here, put the seat up, then sleepwalked back to Giovanni's?'

'Okay,' Daniel said, and they both turned to look at him. 'If your building supervisor has been doing this, then you should call the police.'

'With all due respect, Dan. What's this got to do with you?'

Daniel put his hands up. 'Hey, I'm just playing peacekeeper here.'

'Well, don't.'

'I think calling the police is a good idea,' Zoe said.

'No, it's not. As soon as you tell them about the toilet seat they're just going to write you off as another hysterical female.'

'No, they're going to have to investigate further.'

Lizzy gave her a sceptical look. 'Because they don't have anything better to do?'

'Why are you so reluctant to call them, anyway?' Zoe nodded to herself as the penny dropped. 'You're worried they might find your stash, right?'

'Zoe!' Lizzy glanced at Daniel and he responded with a shrug.

'Your secret's safe with me.'

'Anyway,' Lizzy went on. 'That's not what this is about.'

'So what is it about?'

'*I* think you're acting hysterical. Not to mention paranoid and a little crazy. To be honest, Zoe, right now I'm more worried about *you* murdering me in my sleep.'

'There might be another way to deal with this,' Daniel said, and they both turned to look at him again. 'What if I talked to him?'

'And say what, exactly? No, don't tell me: you're going to make him an offer he can't refuse?'

Daniel smiled. 'No, what I'll do is tell him is that you guys are worried that someone has been breaking into your apartment. Then I'll ask him if he's seen anyone suspicious hanging around the building. He's probably going to say no, in which case I'll ask him to keep an eye out. If it is him, then that should be enough to scare him off. What do you think?'

'I think it sounds like a good idea.' Zoe said. 'Lizzy?'

'If it stops you running to the police and embarrassing your-self, then I say go for it.'

'In that case I'll be right back.'

Zoe watched him disappear out the door, then turned to Lizzy.

'This was not how I imagined tonight going.'

'But up until now it had been going fine, right?'

'Better than fine.'

'And better than my evening, judging by the way you two were going for it on the sofa.'

Zoe felt the heat rising in her cheeks.

'Jesus, Zo. If anyone needs to get laid, it's you.'

'So what happened with Mike?'

'He had a ton of college work to catch up. I even offered to go over to his place to help ease his stress, but he declined. Which is his loss. By the way, you don't have to worry about me. I plan to make myself scarce as soon as Dan gets back.'

'Would you stop calling him that? You know he doesn't like it.'

Lizzy smiled. 'Yeah, I know. Have you seen the way his mouth goes all tight. It kind of reminds me of Ben Stiller in *Zoolander*. You know, when he does Blue Steel.'

Zoe sighed. 'Just stop doing it, please. For me.'

'You know Zo, I like Dan and everything, but don't you think he kind of takes himself a bit too seriously? I mean, getting all uptight over a name. What's that all about?'

'Yeah, and you just love it when people call you Elizabeth.'

'That's different.'

Daniel reappeared five minutes later. Zoe was on him the second he stepped through the door. 'Was it him?'

Daniel shrugged. 'Maybe, maybe not. But I can guarantee that if it was him, then he won't be doing it again.'

'Thanks, Dan,' Lizzy said in a high-pitched Valley Girl voice. 'You're our hero. Okay, I'm out of here. You kids have fun, and try not to make too much noise.'

Zoe watched her walk off to her bedroom, then turned to face Daniel.

'I'm sorry about that.'

Daniel put his hand up, stopping her there. 'It's fine. You don't need to apologise.'

'So, what now?' she asked.

'If it's all right with you, I'm going to head home. I've got a big meeting tomorrow and I'm figuring that if I don't go now then I might not be getting much sleep.'

'You wish.'

'Yeah, I do wish. Look, I'll call you tomorrow.'

He smiled his great smile, and that almost made up for the disappointment. 'You'd better,' she told him.

'I will. That's a promise.'

# Chapter 4

## NOW

Zoe took her dinner smoothie out of the refrigerator and carried it across to the table. Last night she had been at Carmichael's for their anniversary and for a short while she had been able to remember what it was like to be a normal person. As usual, Daniel had ordered a salad for her, while he had something more substantial. That didn't matter, though. It was the first proper meal she'd had in over a month. Forcing herself to eat slowly had been the biggest challenge. She wanted to bolt down her food, but that would have drawn the wrong sort of attention. On a couple of occasions Daniel had reached across the table and gently touched her hand. Anyone looking over would have seen a husband and wife sharing a tender moment, but the reality was that he had been reminding her to take it easy.

Daniel was working late tonight, so she was having dinner on her own. She sat down and booted up her laptop. He had given her the computer when she moved in. It was fitted with a spyware program that monitored keystrokes. Should she be tempted to surf the Internet, he wanted to know exactly what she was looking at. The program had been on there from the start, but she only found out about it much later.

At seven thirty on the dot the Skype alert sounded and Daniel's face appeared on the screen. He was sitting at his large, ultra-tidy desk. During all the times they had eaten dinner like this, she had never seen so much as a stray pen on there. Tonight he was having McDonald's: a quarter-pounder, fries and a chocolate shake. The food was lined up in front of him, and the sight of it made Zoe's mouth water. It had been years since she last had a McDonald's.

Daniel bit into his burger and nodded for her to start. She lifted the glass to her mouth and her stomach clenched in anticipation. The recipe was the same every night: whole milk, oatmeal, Greek yogurt, almond butter, coconut oil, a banana, and protein powder. Saturday was weigh-in day. If her weight was off by even so much as a couple of ounces, then the amounts would be altered accordingly. The ideal weight for a five-foot-seven woman was one hundred and thirty pounds; Daniel preferred her at one hundred and ten. To maintain that weight she needed eighteen hundred calories a day. Most of those calories came from these smoothies.

They ate in silence. At the end of the meal, she showed him the empty glass and a second later the screen went dead. There was no goodbye. One second he was there, the next gone. If only it was that easy, she thought as she shut down the laptop.

For a long time she sat at the table, staring into space. She could feel the smoothie sitting heavily in her stomach and was tempted to go through to the bathroom. But if she did that once she would be tempted to do it again, and at some point Daniel would notice she was losing weight and want to know why. Any fluctuation from that magic figure of one hundred and ten pounds, either up or down, and Daniel wanted to know why.

She sat there until her stomach settled. Then, because there was nothing else to do, she went to bed. There was a TV in the living room that she could watch. Technically. The living room was a minefield; just one thing out of place and that would be enough to set him off. Other than when she cleaned it, she avoided going in there. She liked to be tidy, but Daniel's standards went way beyond that. Although thinking about it, she wasn't sure if this was less about his standards and more about having another way to exert his control over her.

Reading wasn't an option either. Her book privileges had been revoked eighteen months ago. They had been out for dinner and, according to Daniel, she had been taking too much interest in one of the men on the next table. She hadn't, but pointing that out would have made a bad situation ten times worse, so she had kept quiet. Of course, Daniel had taken her silence as an admission of guilt. The last book she had read was *The Storyteller* by Jodi Picoult, but she had no idea how it ended, because Daniel had burnt it. As she watched the pages go up in flames, her heart had shattered. How could anyone burn a book? It might not have been the worst thing he had ever done, but it was one of the things that had hurt the most. He knew how much books meant to her.

She left the bedroom door open so she could listen out for him. It had gone one o'clock by the time he got home. It took three attempts before he got the key into the lock; he shut the door much louder than usual. Zoe rolled onto her side and willed her breathing to slow. She followed the sound of his heavy foot-steps up the stairs, and along the landing, and into the bedroom. He undressed noisily and slowly, like he was having trouble coordinating himself. She followed the sound of his footsteps as he walked through to the bathroom, followed them as he came back less than ten seconds later. The bed creaked to accommo-date his weight. He moved closer and stopped at her shoulder. She could feel his warm breath on her cheek; she could smell the beer on his breath. Her heart was hammering so hard he must have been able to feel the vibrations through the mattress.

'Zoe,' he whispered.

Her blood froze and she fought to keep her breathing long and relaxed. She wanted him to believe that she was asleep.

She needed him to believe.

'I know you're awake, Zoe.'

The whisper had taken on a sing-song quality that sent shivers through her bones. Her eyes were shut tight. Like a frightened child, she would do anything to make the monster go away.

'LOOK AT ME!' he screamed.

Zoe's eyes snapped open. She sat up quickly and scurried away from him, her back sliding up against the headboard. Daniel was kneeling there in his boxer shorts. His eyes were blazing, his face twisted with rage. The light sneaking out from the bathroom painted him with sinister shadows. There was nothing left of the man she had fallen in love with. Nothing at all. Zoe's insides had turned to water. She wanted to yell at him to get away from her; she wanted to cry, but that would have made things worse. He was holding a toilet roll in his hand.

'What is this?' he screamed in her face.

'It's a toilet roll,' she stammered.

'That's right, it's a toilet roll.' His voice had become calm and reasonable, and somehow that was worse.' And which way round does it go on the holder, Zoe?'

'I put it on the right way.'

'That's not what I asked.'

'The end goes away from the wall,' she said quietly.

'So, why was the end next to the wall?' He waved the toilet roll in her face and the loose end flapped against her cheek. 'Well, what are you waiting for? Take it.'

Zoe reached out and he pulled his arm back. His smile was cruel. It was nothing like the smile she remembered from their early days. He held it out again, and this time let her take it.

'So, what? You're just going to sit there looking dumb?'

Zoe got up and went through to the bathroom. She felt as though she was here but not here, like she was sleepwalking through a nightmare. Daniel got up from the bed and followed her. She didn't dare turn around because right now any reaction would be interpreted as defiance. Her hands shook as she put the toilet roll back on the holder. The end was definitely away from the wall.

Just like it had been the last time she did this.

Just like it was every time.

'Haven't you forgotten something?' he asked in that calm, reasonable voice.

Zoe reached out and folded the end into a point. She didn't dare turn around. Instead, she stared at the wall tiles. She heard him moving behind her and a second later something splashed on the floor. A few stray drops landed on her legs, but she kept staring at the wall, following the lines of grout like they were the most interesting things she had ever seen.

'I'm going to sleep in the spare room,' he told her. 'I can't bear to be anywhere near you right now.'

Zoe waited until she heard the bedroom door slam shut then started to clean up the mess he had made. This time she had gotten off lightly, and for that she was grateful. That was how low the bar was currently set. She wondered if there was a way for it to get any lower. If there was, then Daniel would find it. She finished cleaning up and walked back through to the bedroom. Daniel might have been drunk but his suit jacket was hanging neatly on the back of the chair, the pants were folded neatly onto the seat and his shoes were paired neatly underneath. The bulge in the back pocket of the pants caught her attention. Now that she had noticed it, it was all she could see.

Zoe opened the door and peered out onto the landing. She wasn't sure which room he was using, but all the doors were closed and everything seemed quiet enough. She tiptoed back to the chair, picked up his pants and slid the wallet out. There was a bundle of hundreds and fifties inside, more than a thousand dollars. Her heart sped up and her head filled with thoughts of escape. A thousand dollars would get her a thousand miles away from here.

But then what?

She was thinking about Seattle again. She couldn't help it. This happened whenever she started dreaming about escaping.

Daniel had taught her many lessons over the years, but that one had been the hardest. Zoe pushed the money into the wallet, slid it back into his pocket and folded the pants onto the chair. She was careful to make sure that everything was left the way she had found it. She climbed into bed and pulled the covers over herself. It was a long time before she finally fell asleep.

# Chapter 5

## THEN

Daniel was talking with Al at one of the window tables. The bottle of Chianti they were sharing was already past the halfway point, which went some way to explaining their cheery mood. Al was a man of two stories. Behind the scenes he was a stress-head who obsessed over every last detail; out front he was Mr Jovial. That said, he was a good boss, strict but fair, and he always made sure there was a bowl of pasta waiting when they finished their shifts. There were times where Zoe reckoned that she and Lizzy would have starved to death if it hadn't been for Al.

Daniel looked over and caught her eye. He smiled then waved her back to work. Zoe picked up the glasses from the table she was clearing, and she was smiling too. Today was their four-week anniversary, not that she was keeping track. A full-blown relationship hadn't been on her agenda, but she hadn't counted on someone like Daniel walking into her life. Very occasionally you met someone you clicked with; rarer still were those times when you stumbled across someone you felt like you'd known forever, even though you had only just met. Daniel fell into that second category. He just seemed to understand her, and this was an understanding that went beyond words. They liked the same things; they shared the same opinions and ideas; from the start they had been able to finish each other's sentences like they were mind readers.

The fact that they were both orphans must have had something to do with it. This was something you could only truly understand if you had lived through it. Zoe had had her tragedies to deal with, Daniel had had his, and although those experiences were unique there was enough common ground to create a bridge that only they could cross. Then again, maybe it was fate, and, if that was the case, who the hell knew how that one worked? Maybe she had been subconsciously looking for him, and he had been subconsciously searching for her, and now that they had found each other didn't they owe it to themselves to see how far this thing would actually go? Because from where she was standing this was the real deal, and she strongly suspected that he felt the same way.

Things in the restaurant were winding down, which was a relief. The handful of customers still here were relaxing over their coffees, and wouldn't stay much longer. Giovanni's had been busy tonight. To make matters worse, Carol, the other waitress, was new, so she was still trying to find her way, which meant that Zoe had to pick up the slack. She had hit the ground running and hadn't had a second to catch her breath.

She glanced at Daniel again. Only, it wasn't just him looking at her. Al was looking too. The way they were both staring, it was obvious that they had been talking about her. This time it was Al who waved her back to her work.

It was after eleven before the last customer le
her into her coat, shouted a cheery 'goodnight'
his arm around her and led the way outside. It m
June but the night was chilly. Zoe huddled deepe        ner coat
and pressed up against Daniel, stealing his warmth. Just having
him here made her feel so much safer. The apartment was only
a ten-minute walk away. Fine in the daylight; not so fine for a
woman on her own late at night.

'Thanks for walking me home,' she said. 'You've saved me a
cab fare.'

'My pleasure. And, anyway, hasn't it occurred to you that I
might have an ulterior motive?'

'It has.'

'And does that cause you a problem?'

Zoe laughed. 'Nope. So what were you talking to Al about?'

'I was telling him that you wouldn't be working this weekend.'

She pulled Daniel to a stop and they turned to face each
other. 'Why would you do that? I need the money. My rent's
due.'

'Don't worry I'll cover your rent.'

'I can't let you do that.'

'Yes, you can. And no arguments.' He smiled like this was a
done deal. 'You know how you're a massive Stephen King fan?'

She nodded.

'Well, I've booked us a suite at the Timberline Lodge on
Mount Hood. Stanley Kubrick filmed some of *The Shining* there.
Except I doubt I need to tell you that.'

Zoe was shaking her head. 'That's not going to work. I'm supposed to be going out with Lizzy on Saturday night. It's her birthday.'

'You said her birthday was next Tuesday.'

'It is. But a bunch of us are going out on Saturday for drinks. I'm sure I told you.'

'If you did, it must have slipped my mind.'

'Could you move the booking to next weekend?'

'Probably not at such short notice. Look, if you can't go, I'll just have to take the hit on this one.'

'You said a suite, right? How much did that cost?'

'Look, don't worry about the money. Honestly.'

Zoe sighed. 'This puts me in a really awkward position, you know.'

'No, it doesn't. If you told Lizzy that you were going out with her, then you should go. We can do this another weekend.'

'But what about the money?'

'I already told you: don't worry about it.' Daniel shook his head. 'I've really screwed up. I was sure you told me that you guys were doing something special on Tuesday.'

'We are. Well, kind of special. We're having a girls' night in, eating pizza and watching *America's Next Top Model*.' Zoe sighed again. 'Please don't think I'm being ungrateful.'

'It's okay, we'll just do it another time. It's no big deal.'

'But that's the thing, it is a big deal. No one has ever done anything like this for me before. Never.'

'There will be other weekends. I promise.'

'That's not the point.'

Zoe looked at Daniel. He was putting on a brave face but she could see how disappointed he was. And who could blame him? If she had been able to see her own face, she would no doubt have been wearing a similar expression. And then he smiled, and everything was okay again.

'I love you, Zoe.'

For a moment she was speechless. Sure, she'd had this conversation in her head, but to hear the words out loud, well, that was another matter altogether. They might only have been together for a month, but she had known she loved him pretty much from the start. She only hoped that he had been hit as hard.

'That's what this weekend was all about,' he added. 'I wanted to take you somewhere romantic and tell you that I loved you. I wanted the first time to be special, but I guess I'm not cracked up for all this romantic stuff. So, are you going to say something? Because by my reckoning I've said "I love you" twice now, well, three times actually, and I'm starting to wonder if I called this one wrong. And I'm rambling, so please say something to shut me up.'

Zoe laughed. 'Of course I love you.'

'And you have no idea how relieved I am to hear that.'

He pulled her close and they fell into a kiss. By the time he broke away, she had made her decision.

'We're going,' she said.

'To the hotel, you mean?'

She nodded.

'What about Lizzy?'

'Lizzy can have me all to herself on Tuesday. And you can have me all to yourself for the weekend.'

'If you're sure.'

'I'm sure.'

They kissed again then carried on walking. The living-room light was on in the apartment, which was a problem. Zoe had been hoping that Lizzy would be in bed. This was one conversation she wasn't looking forward to. Putting it off until morning would have been much preferable.

'I don't want you to take this the wrong way,' she told him. 'But it might be better if you stayed at your place tonight. I'm going to need to smooth things over with Lizzy.'

'No problem. I totally understand.'

'Are you okay to drive?'

'I'm fine. I only had one glass of wine, and it wasn't a particularly big one. Al enjoys a drink, though, doesn't he?'

Zoe laughed. 'Yeah, you could say that.'

They kissed goodnight and Zoe watched the Porsche pull away from the sidewalk. The car turned the corner, and then it was gone. She took a moment to psyche herself up then went inside.

The second she opened the apartment door, she knew that a bad situation was about to get a whole lot worse. *The Very Best of The Smiths* was playing, and that was never a good sign. Zoe had never heard of The Smiths before she met Lizzy. The band was from the UK, and had been big during the eighties. Their lead singer sounded as though he was permanently contemplating suicide. She found Lizzy curled up on the living-room sofa, hugging a pillow. She was enveloped in a cloud of marijuana smoke, and there was a bottle of wine open on the table. Her eyes were red and puffy from crying. She looked up, saw Zoe, and immediately burst into tears.

'Mike broke up with me.'

# Chapter 6

## NOW

The stench of vomit mingled with the cloying aroma of cleaning products, the two smells conspiring to make Zoe feel sicker than ever. The taste of puke coated her tongue, her throat felt raw, and her stomach muscles ached. Lunch had stayed down for all of twenty minutes. Even though it would be hours until she next ate, she didn't care. She retched again, but all that came up were a few strings of bile. She wiped her mouth then sat down with her back against the cool wall tiles. Her hands travelled down to her stomach and she smiled to herself.

The first time she had been sick, she thought she had stomach flu; the third time it happened she started to wonder. When she counted back and realised she had missed her period, she still didn't want to believe. So she had driven to a pharmacy in a part of the city she never visited and stolen a pregnancy test. Even when the pink cross appeared she still couldn't believe it.

Her smile faded as reality hit home. She could see the future unravelling in front of her, and none of it looked good. A life filled with fear was no life for anyone, let alone a child. She knew she should be angry with herself for getting into this situation.

She was twenty-six, a grown woman; it wasn't like she was a teenager anymore. She really should have known better. But she couldn't be angry because the truth was that she wanted this baby more than anything in the world.

In the early days Daniel had made out that he wanted children. Not only had she believed him, she had actually convinced herself that he would make a good father. She had brought the subject up before they got married, and he had made all the right noises. He loved kids and couldn't wait to start a family; he had told her that he wanted four, two of each, maybe even five, or hell let's make it six for the round half-dozen. Zoe had laughed and told him that they needed to see how they got on with one first. But he had been adamant: he wanted a house that was alive with the laughter of children.

Like so much of their relationship this had been a lie. The day he had sat her down and told her they wouldn't be having children was one of the most heartbreaking days of her life. He hated babies because all they did was puke, shit and cry; and he hated kids because they were such high-maintenance little bastards. When she started to cry he had actually smiled. He had been so calm when he was telling her this. In that moment, he had never looked uglier.

And now she had a big problem, because she had to escape. If Daniel found out she was pregnant he would either force her to have an abortion, or he would find a way to induce a miscarriage. And then he would come up with a suitable punishment. The thing he would never understand was that losing this baby would be the worst punishment he could ever inflict on her.

The thought of what she had to do terrified her. That said, there was a small part of her that felt like it was coming awake after being asleep for a hundred years. Everything was foggy and indistinct, but there was a definite sense of reclaiming something precious and long forgotten. Right now she had no idea what she was going to do, but she would work something out. She had to. For the baby's sake.

Her hands travelled down to her belly again. She imagined the baby growing inside her. Those tiny fingers and tiny toes. The tiny heart. She imagined looking into those perfect eyes for the first time, and the way those perfect little fingers would curl around her imperfect ones. And then she imagined the baby lying in her arms, curled up tight and sleeping.

'Don't worry,' she whispered, 'I'll keep you safe.'

# Chapter 7

## THEN

The woman staring back from the bedroom mirror looked like a stranger, and maybe that was a good thing, because part of Zoe liked what she saw. This woman was confident, sophisticated and in control. She might even be described as beautiful, although this was something Zoe would never have admitted out loud to anyone. Of course, there was another part of her that thought the stranger in the mirror looked like a silly little girl who was playing dress up in her mom's clothes.

When Daniel had suggested going back to Carmichael's, her first reaction had been a kind of horrified disbelief. She could still remember their first aborted date, and how awkward it had been. Daniel must have read the panic on her face, because he had gently prodded and poked until he had the full story. The next thing she knew, she was in the sort of high-end boutique that would normally have turned her away at the door, trying on dresses while Daniel looked on, and feeling like Julia Roberts in *Pretty Woman*. The dress she ended up with was a red strapless Gucci number that cost more than her entire wardrobe. It was beautiful, though, and so elegant. The problem was that she was neither of those things.

Zoe walked through to the living room and stood in the doorway waiting to be noticed. Lizzy was on the sofa, laughing at a rerun of *Friends*. She was dressed in her work clothes, and Zoe would have traded places in an instant. She told herself to get it together. She wasn't even out of the door and she already had tonight written off as a disaster. Zoe coughed into her hand and Lizzy turned around.

'Look at you,' she said, still laughing. 'All dressed up with somewhere to go. You know, all you need are some pearls and you could be one of those women you see standing next to their politician husbands in Washington. Make-up to hide the worry lines, a fake smile to hide the sadness, and Prozac and Pinot Grigio to stabilise your mood.'

Zoe's face fell. 'Thanks, Lizzy. Like I don't feel self-conscious enough as it is.'

'It was meant as a joke. You look great. You really do.'

'And I really believe you now.'

'Seriously, you look amazing, and I love that dress on you. The colour suits you.'

'It's Gucci,' Zoe said miserably.

'And that's a reason to slash your wrists?'

Zoe sank down on the sofa beside her friend. 'I don't know if I can do this, Lizzy.'

'Do what? Go to Carmichael's?'

Zoe nodded.

'Of course you can. It's just dinner, for Christ's sake. You've eaten dinner before, right?'

'You don't get it. I won't fit in. Everyone's going to take one look at me and know I'm a fraud. To make matters worse, Daniel's partner Josh is going to be there with his wife, so I'll be expected to make small talk with complete strangers.'

'Take it from me, fitting in is highly overrated. Wave your freak flag high, that's what I say.'

'You're not helping, Lizzy.'

'So why are you smiling?'

Zoe did her best to look as though the world had ended, but the kooky face Lizzy was pulling made it impossible.

'It's going to be fine, Zo.'

'If you say so. By the way, I'm really sorry, I can't do drinks this Friday.'

Lizzy's smile faded. 'And what's Daniel got planned this time? Dinner at the White House?'

'Don't be like that.'

'Why not? We hardly ever go out anymore.'

'We went out last Friday.'

'Lucky me.'

'Lizzy!'

'Sorry, it's just that you always seem to be out with Dan, or you're staying at his place, and, well, I miss you. You might be a bit of a geek at times, but you're my geek. At least you used to be.'

'Are you working Saturday? I'm doing an evening shift, but I'm free during the day.'

Lizzy shook her head. 'I'm doing the lunchtime shift.'

'Sunday?'

'I've got nothing planned.'

'Me neither. So, let's do something fun together. Just you and me. How does that sound?'

'It sounds good.'

The doorbell rang.

'Look,' Zoe said. 'I've got to go. Are we good?'

'Yeah, we're good.'

They hugged and Zoe ran along the hallway and pulled the door open. Before she could say anything, Lizzy called out a 'Hey Dan, how's it going?' from the living-room door. She fired a dirty look at her friend over her shoulder.

'Sorry,' Lizzy said brightly. 'I meant to say Daniel. My bad.'

Daniel's smile didn't quite reach his eyes. 'And how are you doing, Lizzy?'

'Things here on Planet Slater are just peachy.'

'That's good to hear.'

Daniel laughed and this time the emotion was real and heart-felt, and that was good. Zoe needed them to get on together. The last thing she wanted was to be forced into a situation where she had to choose between them.

'Okay,' Lizzy said. 'I'm going to go and leave you two lovebirds to it. Have fun.'

With that, Lizzy was gone. Zoe walked quickly out into the hall, pulling the apartment door closed behind her. Daniel took one look and smiled. 'Wow,' was all he managed.

'That's a good thing, right?'

'The best.'

He kissed her, then wrapped her up in his arms like he was never going to let go. Not that she wanted him to. She could feel his smile, soft on her cheek.

'How did I get so lucky?' he whispered.

'I've been asking myself the same thing.'

'And?'

'And nothing.'

'What does that mean?'

'It means that if you over-analyse things there's a risk that the magic will be lost.'

'Don't worry, that's not going to happen to us.'

'Promise?' she whispered.

'I promise,' he whispered back.

He let go and took a step back so he could look at her again. The smile turned into a frown and Zoe felt a wave of anxiety rise through her. It had taken him less than a minute to see her for the fraud she was.

'What's wrong?' she asked.

'There's something missing,' he said, more to himself than to her. 'Something that would make this particular picture absolutely perfect.'

He pulled a jewellery box from his jacket pocket and held it out. Zoe hesitated, then plucked the box from his fingers. The lid opened with a sharp snap. Inside was a necklace. The chain was made from spun gold, and she was pretty sure that the stone wasn't zirconium. The way it caught the light, it was like there were a dozen rainbows trapped in there.

'Is that a real diamond?'

Daniel answered with another smile.

'I can't accept this. It's too much.'

'No, it's not.'

Before she could argue, he took the necklace from the box, spun her around so her back was to him, and fastened it around her neck. His hands were gentle on her neck, his breath soft. She could smell his aftershave. One of the things she loved about him was the fact that he always smelled so good. He kissed her neck, turned her around so she was facing him again, then stepped back to admire her.

'Now you look perfect.'

# Chapter 8

## NOW

Her meals for the next two days were arranged neatly in the refrigerator. Breakfast on the top shelf, lunch on the middle, dinner smoothies on the bottom. Each one was labelled with a yellow Post-it. Written neatly on each was the date and time they were to be consumed. When Daniel got back from his trip he would be expecting to see photographs of her sitting at the kitchen table with her meal. He had bought an instamatic camera for this purpose, and an analogue clock that he had modified so she couldn't alter the time. The clock had to be in the picture too. He had also bought an album to keep the photographs in.

Daniel never Skyped when he was away on business, which made her wonder what he got up to, particularly during the evenings. He didn't even call. The second he left, it was as though she ceased to exist. Zoe was fine with this. These days she seemed to spend most of her time trying to be invisible.

She closed the refrigerator and went upstairs. Her outfits for the next two days were hanging in plastic see-through dry-cleaning bags in her bedroom closet. These were labelled and dated too. Clothes for the gym, clothes for cleaning, clothes for wearing around the house. Zoe found the hangar that held today's gym outfit and removed the plastic. She scrunched the clothes up to make it look as though they had been worn, then dumped them in the wash basket.

The T-shirt she wanted was buried right at the back of her bottom drawer. It was old and faded, and completely tasteless. There was a picture of a palm tree on the front; Venice Beach was written underneath in swirly green writing. She had kept it because of its sentimental value. One summer, Lizzy had hired a car and they had taken a road trip down the Pacific Coast. They managed to get as far as Venice Beach before they ran out of money and had to turn around. Lizzy wanted matching tattoos as a memento of the trip; matching T-shirts was Zoe's compromise. Right now, she felt as though she could do with some of Lizzy's attitude and fearlessness. This T-shirt was all she had left of her, so it would have to do.

She found an old pair of jeans that she hadn't worn in years and pulled them on. Daniel preferred it when she wore her hair down, so she tied it into a ponytail. It took a second to recognise the woman staring back from the mirror. She looked totally different from the person she usually saw in the mirror, like an old friend she hadn't seen for years.

Zoe was halfway down the stairs when the front door rattled. She froze to the spot, her heart thundering. Any second now the door was going to swing open and Daniel was going to come in, and he would see what she was wearing, and he wouldn't be happy. The door rattled again, then something landed on the mat. Relief washed over her. It was just the mailman. Zoe took a deep breath and carried on down the stairs. She scooped the mail from the mat, placed it on the table beside the door, then grabbed her coat and car keys and headed outside.

Fifteen minutes later she arrived at JB Fitness Studio on Halsey Street. Daniel had installed a GPS tracking app on her phone, so she left it in the glovebox to create the illusion that she was at the gym. She walked the first block, but by the time she reached the second she was jogging. Ten minutes later she was in a part of the city she would usually avoid. This was the sort of neighbourhood where you could buy things and still maintain your anonymity. Drugs, prostitutes. An abortion.

The clinic was based in an old warehouse. The brickwork was filthy, the paintwork on the doors and window frames cracked and peeling. For the best part of five minutes Zoe hovered in the shadows on the opposite side of the street. A girl walked up to the clinic entrance. She was young. Nineteen or twenty, perhaps. She was at that stage where you couldn't tell for sure if she was pregnant. The building swallowed the girl up and all Zoe could do was stand there stuck in the shadows, watching the now empty street. *It's now or never.* Despite how freaked out she was, she couldn't help noticing that the voice in her head belonged to Lizzy. When things got tough, Lizzy could always be relied upon to give her that final push.

Before she could change her mind, Zoe crossed the street, pushed open the tatty door and went inside. The signs led her to a reception area on the second floor that smelled like every hospital she had ever been in. The girl she had seen earlier was at the desk, filling out a form on a clipboard. Zoe walked over and stood behind her. The girl finished doing her form and went to sit on a chair to wait. She offered a small smile as she walked over, and Zoe did her best to smile back.

'Can I help?'

The receptionist was black and middle-aged. Her eyes were tired, her face kind. For a moment Zoe just stood there staring dumbly, her mind a complete blank. For the life of her, she couldn't remember the name she had given when she made the appointment. The receptionist was staring and waiting patiently, and all Zoe could think of was running.

'Have you made an appointment?' she prompted.

Zoe nodded.

'What's your name?'

All she could do was stare. Her tongue and stomach were tied in knots. Everything was in knots.

'What time was the appointment?'

'Eleven,' she whispered.

'Eleanor Sanders?'

Zoe nodded. Sanders was her mom's maiden name; Eleanor was her paternal grandmother. The receptionist handed her the clipboard and she filled in a form. Her hand was shaking, but the writing was just about legible. The receptionist took the clipboard and told her to have a seat. It didn't take long to work out that the room she wanted was directly opposite where she was sitting. A teenage girl who was well into her third trimester waddled out, and the girl who was ahead of her went in. By the time it was Zoe's turn, she had read the posters a dozen times and still not taken in a single word.

The nurse doing the ultrasound was younger than her, and not long out of college. The clinic was a free one, so she might even still be at college. She was making small talk, but when she saw how nervous Zoe was, she stopped. She ripped off a long length of paper towel, arranged it on the examination table, then told her to lie down and roll up her T-shirt.

The table was cold, but nowhere near as cold as the gel on her stomach. The nurse used the scanner to smear the goo in, then went searching for the baby. To start with she couldn't find anything. Zoe's first thought was that there must have been a mistake with the pregnancy test. Both of them. Her second thought was that the baby was dead. And then the nurse smiled, and everything was okay again.

It took a moment to see what the nurse was seeing. At first the picture on the screen was just a monochromatic mess of grey and black. There was no cohesion, no order. And then she saw it, a gentle, steady throb no bigger than a nickel. It pulsed through a dozen different variations of grey, and each beat of that tiny heart was the promise of a future.

'She's okay?' Zoe whispered.

'Your baby's fine,' the nurse said. 'Although you might want to consider the possibility that *she* is actually a *he*. We'll be able to tell by twenty weeks. If you want to know, that is.'

'She's going to be a girl.'

The nurse laughed. 'Judging by what I'm seeing here, and what you've told me, I'd say you're about eight weeks, which puts your due date somewhere around the ninth of December. Congratulations.'

The nurse turned her attention back to the screen and started talking through what she was seeing. Zoe barely heard a word. She was transfixed by the fluttering heartbeat on the screen. It was so faint, yet so strong. She had tried to tell herself a million times that she was pregnant, but just hadn't believed it. Not in her own heart, and that was where you needed to believe something like this. She believed it now, though. That tiny heartbeat made it real.

Outside, Zoe headed back into the shadows on the opposite side of the street. For a long time she hid there, staring at the scan picture, studying it, memorising it. She had known what needed to be done since she'd taken the pregnancy test, but her ideas now needed to be replaced with action. Because this was really happening. She was going to have a baby, and if they were going to survive, they had to get away from Daniel.

Zoe took one last look at the scan picture, then ripped it in two and went searching for a trash can. She wanted to keep it, but it was too dangerous. This was not what she had imagined it would be like to be pregnant, but then again, nothing in her life ever worked out how she imagined. She had learnt the hard way that there was no such thing as happily ever after. That was just a lie you told at the end of the fairy tale to make sure the children slept.

The problem with that particular lie was that it didn't stop the nightmares.

For Zoe, the nightmare always ended the same way: on a bus in Seattle, with rain lashing against the windows, and the sound of Daniel's footsteps moving slowly up the central aisle. Almost two years had passed since then, but there wasn't a single day that went by where she didn't wonder what might have been if she hadn't screwed up.

The nightmare always started the same way too, with her driving Daniel to the airport. By this point the honeymoon period was well and truly over. Things weren't as bad as they would become, but they were bad enough for her to know exactly what sort of monster she was married to. For once she hadn't minded taking him to the airport. This way she could make sure he got on the plane. So she had followed the signs to the drop-off area and pulled into an empty space and they had gotten out, and Daniel had retrieved his suitcase from the trunk and told her that he loved her, and Zoe had repeated the words back, and then he was gone, swallowed up into the crowd of people heading for the terminal.

She stopped at the house to pick up the bag she had packed the day before. It was hidden in the garage, buried behind a pile of boxes that hadn't moved in years. Her next stop was a pawn shop, where her wedding band, engagement ring and Rolex netted twelve hundred dollars. They were worth more, but her heart had been in her mouth, making it impossible to haggle.

Two hours later she was driving around Eugene, looking for the rougher neighbourhoods. She left the car with the keys dangling from the ignition. It took twenty minutes to walk to the Greyhound station, where she bought a single ticket to Seattle. If Daniel tracked her this far, he would never expect her to head north again. Carrying on south made much more sense.

The only downside with Seattle was the forty-five minute stopover in Portland. She spent the whole time counting off the minutes and checking the faces on the other side of the bus window. She saw Daniel everywhere. She saw him in the way that guy was walking, and she saw him in the jacket the man disappearing around the corner was wearing. And that other guy over there was the same height and build, and it was only when he turned around that she saw it wasn't him.

By the time Zoe reached Seattle the day was pretty much done. She checked into a cheap hotel and crashed into bed. She was so exhausted she slept for ten hours straight. It was the most sleep she'd had in years.

Her new name was Emily Slater. Emily after her mother, and Slater because she needed some of Lizzy's strength. Zoe had been so tempted to call Lizzy. She probably still hated her, and with good reason, but Zoe was pretty sure she would forgive her after she heard what Daniel was really like.

Except she couldn't call her. For this to work both Zoe Chapel and Zoe Barton needed to completely disappear. That meant severing all ties with her old life, like going into witness protection. It wasn't that difficult. Daniel had done a thorough job of making sure she had no friends, and she had no family that she was still in touch with. All Daniel ever wanted was to be the centre of her universe. All it took to achieve this was six months of marriage.

Her first priority was finding somewhere to live. She would have preferred an apartment of her own, somewhere she could come and go without having to explain herself. Somewhere she could add extra locks to the front door. Unfortunately, all she could afford was a room in someone's house. And maybe that was for the best. What was the point of escaping from one prison just to end up in another?

The classifieds yielded a couple of dozen possibilities. Most were already taken, but by the end of the day she had found somewhere. The house she ended up in was owned by a woman called Mary whose husband had passed away earlier in the year. Mary had three cats and a streak of eccentricity a mile wide. She didn't need the money, she just wanted someone in the house in case she died suddenly. She hated the idea of being found a week later, bloated and stinking the place up. Her words. She got up at seven every morning. If Zoe got up and she wasn't around she had permission to come into her bedroom to check she was alive. Otherwise she had to stay the hell out.

After paying a month's rent and the deposit, Zoe only had a hundred dollars left. Finding work proved easier than finding somewhere to live. By the end of the second day she had already completed her first shift in one of Seattle's thousand and one coffee houses. Tradewinds was small and privately owned. The woman who ran it was happy to pay her in cash. She was even happier about the fact that she was paying less than minimum wage.

By the fourth day she was starting to remember who Zoe Chapel was. This was the person who liked blueberry muffins, even if they didn't agree with her waistline. This was the person who listened to eighties rock, even if it was crappy big-hair dinosaur music. This was the person who cried at romantic movies even if it was pathetic. This was the person Daniel had failed to see even though he had her up on a pedestal and was scrutinising every single inch.

He would have arrived back from Oklahoma City yesterday, and he would have been furious that she wasn't at the airport to pick him up. How many times did he call her cell and end up getting bounced to voicemail? And how many times did he call the house only to get the answering machine? What did he think when he got home and found the house empty? Did he search it from top to bottom looking for evidence that she had been kidnapped? Did he go through the messages on the answering machine, searching for the one made by the kidnapper? Or did he jump straight to the conclusion that she had run off with another man? That was more likely since it played into his paranoia and jealousy. He wouldn't have gone to the police because this was his business; it had nothing to do with anyone else. And Zoe was fine with that. She had been careful, but she doubted she had been careful enough to fool the police.

The one thing she was absolutely certain of was the fact that Daniel wouldn't rest until he found her. For the rest of her life she would be looking over her shoulder, but even that was preferable to staying with him. Her plan was to stay in Seattle for as long as it took to get some cash together, then move on. Hopefully she would be here no longer than a couple of weeks, three max. The more she moved, the harder it would be for him to find her.

The cats were howling for their breakfast when Zoe got up the next morning. She immediately thought the worst. She couldn't help it. Daniel had stolen what little optimism she ever possessed. Mary's bedroom was the first door off the landing. Zoe knocked once. No response. Shit. She'd had a heart attack. Or a stroke. She knocked harder and this time there was a noise from the other side. The rustle of covers. A squeak of bedsprings.

'Mary, it's me, Emily.' In her panic, she had almost used her real name. 'I'm just checking you're okay.'

'I'm still alive, darling. What time is it?'

'Just gone eight thirty.'

'Goodness, how did that happen? I never sleep this late.'

The coffee had brewed by the time Mary got downstairs. Zoe poured her a mug and put it on the table. Mary's hair was a crazy mess and her dressing gown was decorated with random scraps of coloured material, like a patchwork quilt made by a hyperactive five-year-old. She fussed the cats, gave them their breakfast, then sat down opposite Zoe and sipped her coffee.

'It's good to be alive,' she announced.

Zoe laughed. 'And I'm very glad that you are.'

'Not as glad as I am. Any idea when you'll be back from work?'

'I'm doing the ten-to-six shift, so probably around six thirty.'

'Good. I'll have dinner ready.'

She said this like it was a done deal. And in her head, maybe it was. They'd had dinner together every evening since Zoe moved in. 'You don't have to do that, Mary. That wasn't part of our agreement.'

'I know I don't have to, but I want to. I like the company, and I like cooking. Unless, of course, you have other plans. You don't have other plans, do you? A date, maybe?'

'No, I don't have a date.'

'Shame. A pretty thing like you should have a boyfriend.' She paused. 'Or a girlfriend. I'm not one to judge.'

Zoe smiled. 'Okay, you make dinner tonight, but I'll cook tomorrow.'

'You've got yourself a deal. And I'm assuming lasagne is okay. I make a mean lasagne.'

It was raining hard when Zoe got to work a few days later. Tradewinds was as busy as she had ever known it, which suited her. When you were busy, you didn't have time to think. Things quietened down after the lunchtime rush and she was able to take five to grab a sandwich.

Lunch breaks were not part of the deal. That had been made clear at the start. This job sucked, no doubt about it. Unfortunately, until Emily Slater existed on paper, her options would be seriously limited. As to how she might achieve that, right now she had no idea. Her first priority had been getting away from Daniel. Her second priority was finding a way to earn some money. Now that had happened she could start thinking about what came next. What did she want to do with the rest of her life? That was the question. She could go anywhere. Do anything. Be anyone. In some ways it was exciting; in others, it was terrifying.

It was raining as heavily as ever when her shift ended. Her umbrella had a large canopy and was as colourful as Mary's dressing gown. Zoe had bought it on her second day in Seattle. It had been a long time since she had bought something just for herself. In the grand scheme it was such a small thing, but it felt huge, like she was finally moving in the right direction. The bus stop was a five-minute walk from the coffee house; she had to wait another six before the bus finally arrived. The doors folded open and she climbed on board. The umbrella left a trail of drips all the way down the central aisle.

She picked a seat halfway along and got settled. The doors folded closed, but before the bus could pull away there was a sharp knuckle rap on the window and they concertinaed open again. The man who got on had his face turned away, but Zoe recognised him straightaway She would have recognised him anywhere.

Daniel paid for a ticket and came down the aisle towards her. He was walking as though he had all the time in the world. Zoe felt sick. She wanted to run, but there was only one door. To reach it she needed to get past him. His gaze was fixed on her and it was like she was the only person in the universe. His smile was terrible. It looked friendly enough, but this smile had teeth. Daniel slipped into the seat beside her and placed a gentle hand on top of her shaking ones.

'Hi, Zoe,' he said brightly. 'It is so good to see you again.'

Zoe looked down at their hands, feeling dumbstruck and devastated. From the corner of her eye she saw him reach into his coat pocket. The wedding band went back on first, then the engagement ring, then the Rolex. Daniel tilted her head up with the tip of his index finger. He might as well have been using a gun.

'If you ever try to leave me again, remember one thing: wherever you go, I will find you.' He smiled his terrible smile. 'You belong to me, and don't ever forget that. Together forever, sweetheart. Together forever.'

# Chapter 9

## THEN

The drive to the airport was quiet and uncomfortable. Because Zoe was shorter, she had offered to squeeze herself into the back of the Porsche so Lizzy could have the passenger seat. Big mistake. It was so damn uncomfortable back here. Daniel followed the signs to the short-term parking lot and found a space. He turned and offered a smile, and it helped just knowing he was there. The way he was so sensitive to her needs was just one of a dozen reasons why she loved him. Daniel fetched Lizzy's suitcase from the trunk and put it down in front of her. For a couple of seconds they stood around it in a loose group, nobody really knowing what to say or do. It was Daniel who broke the silence.

'I'll wait here. You guys need some time to yourselves. Take as long as you want.'

Zoe took hold of his hand and gave it a quick squeeze. 'Thank you.'

'And thanks for the lift, *Dan*,' Lizzy added.

For once this didn't seem to bother him. It actually provoked a smile.

'Good luck with the new job,' he said.

'I'm going to need it.'

'Lizzy, you're going to slay them.'

She pulled him into a tight hug and her lips found his ear. Zoe couldn't hear exactly what she whispered, but it sounded a lot like, 'You see and look after my girl.'

'I will,' he promised.

This scene made Zoe miserable and happy in equal measure. She was here with the two people she loved most in the world, but this would be the last time for God knows how long. Lizzy pulled out the handle of her suitcase and they trundled towards the terminal. Zoe waited with her in silence while she checked the suitcase in. There just weren't any words to say all the things she wanted to say. It had been like this since Lizzy broke the news that she had got an internship with a fashion designer and was moving to New York. She was going to be three thousand miles and three time zones away. She might as well have been going to the moon. Now their college days were behind them, there was an inevitability to this. College pulled you together for a few short, intense years, then you were sent spinning off into your own separate futures. Zoe knew all that but it didn't make what was happening here any easier.

That said, she was happy for her friend. How could she not be? Lizzy had worked so hard for this, and it was such an amazing opportunity. An internship might only be one small step away from slavery, but that step would get her onto the first rung of the ladder. Lizzy would be racing to the top in no time. If Zoe had had half her drive and ambition she would already be number one on the *New York Times* bestseller list.

'We'll see each other soon,' Lizzy promised as they joined the security queue. 'I'll fly out in the fall. And maybe you can come visit in December. We could go Christmas shopping together. You know, that's one thing I'm definitely looking forward to. The stores. Portland has its moments, but when it comes to shopping, it can't touch New York.'

'Make sure you save some money for that airfare.'

'Of course I will. Nothing will stop me getting on that plane. You better believe it.'

That provoked a sad laugh. 'I believe it.'

They shuffled forward a couple of steps. Zoe could see the security post up ahead. She reckoned they had another five minutes, max. Five minutes, and then Lizzy would be gone. Despite all the promises they had made to each other to keep in touch, Zoe couldn't help feeling as though she was losing her best friend forever.

'Are you going to be okay, Zoe?'

'I'm going to be fine.'

'I worry about you, you know.'

'You don't need to.'

'Here's an idea, maybe you could come and live in New York. We could get a place together. You could wait tables and write your book.'

'Sounds idyllic. I particularly like the part about waiting tables.'

'I'm serious, Zo. New York's full of writers. It's the perfect place to launch your career.'

'But I like Portland. There are lots of restaurants to work in.'

'And let's not forget Dan.'

'We've already had this conversation, Lizzy.'

'I'm just worried that things are moving too fast, that's all.'

'I'll be fine.'

'And this is where I point out that you don't have the best track record when it comes to men.'

'That's a bit harsh.'

'Harsh but true. Remember Stuart?'

'Daniel's not Stuart. *He* was a total douchebag.'

'At the end he was. But up until the point where he cheated on you he was your knight in shining armour. Then there was Kevin. Remember him? Remember the restraining order?'

'There was no restraining order. Stop exaggerating.'

'Only because I threatened to kick his ass if he didn't quit stalking you.' She paused and took a deep breath. 'Look, all I'm saying is be careful. Your problem is that you lead with your heart and before you know it you're in too deep.'

'And your problem is that you worry too much.'

'Because it's a best friend's prerogative to worry.'

'Well, you don't have to. Not this time. Daniel is totally different from the other guys I've dated. That's what I like most about him.'

'Like?' she said, eyebrows arched.

'Okay, okay. I love him.'

'And that's what I'm talking about. You just be careful, okay?'

They shuffled forward, getting ever closer to the front of the queue. And then it was time. They stood to one side to let the people behind past while they said their final goodbyes. There were lots of hugs and lots of tears. Zoe had expected it to be bad, but this was horrendous. She felt like she was losing a limb. Lizzy showed her passport and boarding pass to the security guy and got waved through. She turned and blew a kiss from the other side. 'See you soon,' she mouthed, and then she was gone.

As far as Zoe was concerned 'soon' couldn't come around quick enough.

The apartment had never felt so empty.

Lizzy had only been gone for two days, but in some ways it felt like forever. Last night they talked on the telephone for almost two hours; the night before it had been an hour and a half. But it just wasn't the same. It didn't matter that Lizzy was the untidiest person in the world, or that her taste in music could best be described as dubious, and nor did it matter that she would play it too loud. Right now, Zoe would have given anything to have her back.

The door to Lizzy's room had been closed ever since she left. All her pictures and posters were gone, all her clothes and CDs, her stuff and clutter. It was like the room had been raided by tomb robbers. Zoe hurried through the living room, because that was just as bad. All she could see was the blank space on the wall where Lizzy's Picasso print had hung. The kitchen was tidier than Zoe had ever known. There wasn't a dirty plate or cup in sight, and all the surfaces gleamed. Even a sink full of dirty dishes wouldn't be a problem right now. In fact, she would have welcomed it.

She had advertised for a new roommate, and was meeting someone this evening. They had sounded really nice on the phone; they probably were really nice. The problem was that they weren't Lizzy. Zoe knew that she had been taking Lizzy for granted, and if she could go back and change that, she would. But it was too late now, and that realisation just made her feel worse than ever.

Zoe switched on the kettle and went through to the bath-room. She opened the door and all she could see was the raised toilet seat. Her heart froze and she had to grab hold of the door frame to steady herself. She blinked, but when she opened her eyes it was still up. She closed the door and fumbled her cell phone from her pocket. Her hands were shaking so much it took three attempts to call Daniel. He answered on the second ring.

'Hi, Zoe. Look is this important? I'm right in the middle of something here.'

'He's been in the apartment again,' she sobbed, the words coming out in a rush.

'Who? Your super?'

'Yes.'

'Are you there now?'

'Yes.'

'Okay, just stay where you are. I'll be there in five.'

It was actually sixteen minutes. Zoe counted them off in her bedroom, huddled on her bed, hugging her pillow for comfort. Daniel knocked on the door and she ran to answer it. She checked the spyhole to make sure it was him, then unhooked the intruder chain, unlocked the door, wrenched it open and threw herself into his arms.

'Hey, it's going to be all right,' he soothed as he stroked her hair.

And now the tears came, partly from the trauma and fear, and partly because she was missing Lizzy so much. Daniel whis-pered reassurances and stroked her hair, and let her cry. At some point he manoeuvred her back along the hall to the bathroom. He pushed the door open, saw the raised seat, then closed it.

'Do you want me to go and speak to him?'

Zoe shook her head. 'What good is that going to do?'

'Should I call the police, then?'

'Yes. No.' She shook her head in frustration. 'I don't know. Do you think they'll be able to stop him?'

Daniel shook his head. 'Maybe. Maybe not.'

'What am I going to do?'

'Well, for starters, you can't stay here on your own. How about you stay at my place for a few days until we get a plan worked out?'

'If that's okay.'

'Of course it's okay.'

'I'll need to pack some things. And I'm going to need a new toothbrush. I don't want to go in the bathroom.'

Daniel smiled. 'I'm sure we can buy you a new toothbrush.'

Zoe wiped her eyes then walked through to her bedroom. She found a bag and started throwing clothes into it. She wasn't sure what was actually going in there and didn't really care; she just wanted to get the hell out. Daniel walked over with her jewellery box.

'You probably don't want to leave this here.'

Zoe reached out to take it, but it slipped from her hands and crashed to the floor. The lid sprang open and the contents scattered across the rug. She knelt down and started collecting everything back into the box. Daniel was kneeling beside her, helping. The last piece went in and she shut the lid.

'You'd better make sure it's all there,' he suggested. 'Just in case something rolled under the bed or something. I didn't see anything when I looked, but it might be a good idea to check.'

Zoe opened the lid and rummaged through the contents. Aside from her mother's rings and the things that Daniel had bought, there was nothing particularly valuable. She paused, frowning. The frown quickly gave way to panic.

'The diamond necklace you gave me is missing.'

'Are you sure?'

'Positive. I kept it in the box it came in, and that's definitely not here.'

They had another look under the bed, but couldn't see it. They tried all the less obvious places too, but it wasn't there. Not that she had expected anything different. They would have heard the box hit the floor. The only explanation was that Popeye had stolen it. Daniel was shaking his head and looking furious. Zoe had never seen him angry before. He was usually so calm and in control. He took a deep breath, and when he looked at her again his emotions were back in check. He waited for her to meet his eye.

'What would you think about moving in with me permanently?' he asked.

'Are you being serious?'

'Totally. Look, I know we've only been going out for three months, but that's long enough. At least, it is for me. And, anyway, what's the alternative? Living here on your own, knowing that your creep of a superintendent is sneaking around your apartment while you're out?'

'I won't be alone. I've advertised for a new roommate. I'm supposed to be meeting someone tonight.'

'And you know how long it took to get Lizzy house trained, and I'd argue that you weren't particularly successful there.'

Zoe shook her head. 'I don't know, Daniel. It just seems so fast.'

'Maybe so, but that doesn't cause me a problem. Does it really cause you that much of a problem?'

Zoe said nothing.

'Don't you want to live with me? Is that it?'

'Of course I do. One day. And what do we do about the necklace? Should we go to the police?'

'Forget the necklace. I'll buy you another one. And anyway, I don't want it anywhere near you after that creep's touched it.' He paused. 'Look, I love you, Zoe. I want your face to be the last thing I see at night and the first thing I see in the morning, and call me selfish, but I want that every day. I want us to be together forever. So what do you say? Is it a yes, or is it a no?'

Zoe glanced around the bedroom and realised that the decision had already been made. This apartment was filled with memories of the good times she had shared with Lizzy. The tears and drama too, and there had plenty of that. But with Lizzy gone there would be no new memories. Those were going to be made with Daniel. He was the future; Lizzy was the past.

'Yes.'

Daniel had insisted on renting a U-Haul truck for the move. He said it would be fun, and it was. Riding in a truck through the city gave Zoe a whole new perspective. You saw things you wouldn't normally see. The whole way to Fairfield Boulevard she was like an overexcited kid, pointing things out and giving a running commentary. They pulled up at the sidewalk and got out. The house was a Dutch colonial with four bedrooms and three bathrooms. According to Daniel, there was four thousand square feet of space. The clapboard was painted grey and the windows were shining. It was gorgeous. Back when she was growing up in Montana, Zoe had never dreamt that she would end up living in a place like this. Not for a second. She had to pinch herself to make sure she wasn't dreaming now.

The back doors of the truck let out a horror-movie screech when they opened. Her collection of belongings barely took up half the floor space, and it wasn't piled particularly high. Considering this represented twenty-two years on the planet, it was a bit pathetic. It only took twenty minutes to get everything into the house. The cases containing her clothes went into the main bedroom; everything else went into one of the spare rooms to get sorted through later.

'I've got something to show you,' Daniel said. 'It's a surprise.'

'What?'

'If I told you, it wouldn't be a surprise, would it?'

He took her by the hand and led the way upstairs. By the time they were halfway up, Zoe had a good idea what the surprise might be. When they walked straight past the bedroom door without stopping, she realised she was wrong.

'What's going on Daniel?'

'You'll see.'

'Please tell me you don't have a Red Room of Pain.'

He stopped walking. 'Would it cause you a problem if I did?'

She gave a non-committal shrug and he laughed. 'Jesus, Zoe, you're going to be the death of me.'

'So what's this big surprise?'

He took her hand again and led the way to a closed door at the end of the landing. 'Open it.'

Zoe opened the door. At first she didn't get it. Or rather, she didn't want to get it in case she was wrong.

'What is this, Daniel?'

'What do you think it is?'

'It looks like your new study,' she replied carefully.

'No,' he corrected. 'It's *your* new study. If you're going to write the great American novel, you'll need somewhere to work.'

Zoe was momentarily lost for words. This was too much. She walked slowly into the room. It smelled of paint and cut wood, and it was bigger than her old bedroom, maybe half as big again. One wall was taken up with empty bookshelves that were just crying out to be filled. The window overlooked the back yard and let in plenty of light. There was a desk positioned beneath it. At first she thought it was a replica. It wasn't. It was antique mahogany, at least a century old. The leather blotter was green; the gold leaf at the edge had worn away. On top of the desk was a brand new MacBook Air. Next to that was a bottle of champagne and two glasses.

'Well, say something,' he prompted. 'You like it, right?'

She turned and looked at him. The smile on her face was so big it was a wonder her face hadn't split in two. 'Like it? I *love* it.'

He breathed out a dramatic sigh. 'You have no idea how much of a relief that is. I was worried you might hate it. So, would you like some champagne? It's Bollinger. Your favourite.'

She actually preferred Moët, but didn't want to spoil the mood by pointing this out. 'Maybe we should hold off on the champagne,' she suggested.

'But we're celebrating.'

'Damn right we are.'

Zoe moved the MacBook to the bookcase; the champagne and glasses went next to it. Then she walked slowly back to the desk. Daniel's eyes were on her the whole way, following her every move, and that gave her a real kick. Her hair was a mess, her face was filthy, she was wearing old clothes that did her no favours and she probably needed a shower. Despite all that she knew he wanted her and that just added to the thrill. She perched on the edge of the desk and beckoned him forward with a little wiggle of her index finger.

# Chapter 10

## NOW

Zoe arrived early for her hairdresser appointment, which wasn't unusual. This was one of the highlights of her week, because for a short while at least she could imagine she was a normal person. Marilyn had her iPhone out, thumbs flying across the screen as she typed out a text. She hit send, then switched off the phone and placed it on the shelf beneath the mirror.

'Sorry about that, Mrs Barton. My friend is having a crisis.' She rolled her eyes. 'Or should I say that she's having yet another one?'

Zoe smiled. 'No need to apologise.'

Marilyn took her coat and went to hang it up. By the time she returned, Zoe was settled in the chair.

'So, how is that handsome husband of yours?'

'Busy, as always.'

'I wish I could say the same about mine. I tell you, he must be about the laziest man on the planet.'

'I take it he hasn't found a job yet?'

'Not yet, but he's got another interview tomorrow, so fingers crossed. He better get this one. I tell you, I'm getting fed up with him being under my feet all the time.'

Marilyn started fussing with her hair, and Zoe tuned her out. The conversation was much the same from week to week, so she could do this on autopilot. Daniel was perfect, while Marilyn's husband was a lazy no-good waste of space. So long as she stuck to that script everything would slot into place just fine. The thing was, they were both liars. Marilyn clearly loved her husband and would do so until the day she died, and Daniel was anything but perfect.

Zoe had worked out long ago that her marriage was nothing but one huge lie built on a foundation of smaller ones. The lies had started during their second date at the Marrakesh. Daniel had told her that his parents died in a fire. They hadn't. Looking back, Zoe felt she should have known, or at least been suspicious. Every time she asked about his family he would change the subject. As their relationship got deeper and darker, the need to discover who she was actually married to increased. The logical place to start was with his family. It took one phone call for the lie about his parents to unravel. This was back when she still had phone and Internet privileges; back when her world was still in the process of shrinking.

A quick Google search had given her the number for the *Prophetstown Echo*. The woman who answered had put her through to the editor. Back when Daniel was a teenager, he had been the news editor, and he had no recollection of the fire that Daniel's parents had supposedly died in. Zoe had asked if he was sure. 'I'm positive,' he replied, laughing. 'If something that exciting happened around here, I'd remember. You'd better believe it.'

Zoe believed it.

She had dug some more and discovered his mother had a Facebook page. She didn't use it very often but there was enough information on there to establish that both his parents were alive and well and still living in Prophetstown. One look at the photographs was enough to dispel any doubts as to whether she had the right account. The physical similarities between Daniel and his father were undeniable.

Zoe had been curious to know what had happened to cause the estrangement, but there was no way to find out. Had she contacted his parents directly there was no telling how they might have reacted. Maybe they would have hung up on her. Then again, maybe it would have prompted them to reach out to Daniel, and if that had happened, how would he have reacted to the idea that she had been sneaking around behind his back? In the end she had decided that it was enough to know that they were alive and leave it at that.

The reason Daniel lied was disturbingly obvious. One of the things they had bonded over was the fact that they were both orphans. He had been manipulating her from the very start. Every time she showed a vulnerability, he would find some way to use it against her, and he would do it in such a way that he became either her saviour or an ally. Like the time he discovered she was in debt, shortly after they moved in together. She had inherited some money after her father died; that was what she had used to pay for college. The problem was that it hadn't been anywhere near enough. The fees were crippling, and then there were all the day-to-day expenses; it didn't help that she had wasted her first year studying law because that felt like the proper, sensible, grown-up thing to do.

When Daniel found out, he had offered to pay her debts off. All of them, almost twenty thousand dollars. There had been no hesitation. He'd just sat down at his computer and with a couple of keystrokes she was debt free. Zoe had offered to pay him back, but he told her there was no hurry. Once she sold the rights to her book, that would be soon enough. Or the TV rights. Or the film rights. What's more, she had believed that that was what was going to happen. She would write her book and sell it for a million. Back then, anything seemed possible.

After settling her debts, Daniel had offered to help get her finances in order. First they worked out a budget. Her estimated earnings went at the top of the spreadsheet, her expenses underneath. The list of expenses was short. Zoe had offered to contribute to the household bills but Daniel just laughed and told her not to be silly. He had taken one look at the meagre list of expenses, then pulled the laptop towards him. The additions he made included allowances for clothes, hair and a gym membership; he increased her miscellaneous figure to five hundred dollars. The changes added up to double her income. When she queried this he just shrugged and told her he would make up the difference.

Within three months she had stopped working at Giovanni's because Daniel wanted her to concentrate on writing her book. At the time it didn't occur to her that there might be another reason. The fact that she was now financially dependent on him was just another means of control.

Marilyn had moved on to her nails, and this week's gossip. One of her neighbours was pregnant, and the baby wasn't the husband's. The woman's husband was white, her lover was black, and this was the talk of Marilyn's apartment block. For Zoe, this was a glimpse into a world that could have been a movie. There was a part of her that wanted to tell Marilyn everything. It was a conversation she'd had in her head dozens of times. She'd had similar imaginary conversations with the staff at the gym, and the clothes stores she shopped at. In braver moments, she had imagined going to the police and requesting sanctuary.

The reason she hadn't said anything was rooted in Marilyn's first question. *So, how is that handsome husband of yours?* Marilyn and Daniel had never actually met. They had talked on the phone a couple of times, yet from the way she spoke you would think they were best friends. This was the effect Daniel had. He charmed and mesmerised people. Even Lizzy had been fooled to start with.

And what would she say anyway? Marilyn would have no trouble believing that one of her neighbours was married to a monster, but she would struggle to see Zoe that way. It just wouldn't add up. Marilyn thought Daniel was one of the good ones, and that Zoe was one of the lucky ones. Zoe could see it in her eyes; she could hear it in her voice. When Marilyn looked at her she saw someone who had a handsome, rich husband and a fancy sports car, and lived in a big house; she saw someone who didn't need to work because her husband picked up all the bills. In short, she saw someone who had won the lottery of life.

And Marilyn wasn't alone there. Virginia and Kathleen at the gym wouldn't have believed her either. Hell, even Josh wouldn't have believed her, and he knew Daniel better than anyone. That was what she was up against. Another problem was that when those secrets started coming out, they would just keep coming. The abuse, the baby, everything. Daniel would conduct a major damage-limitation exercise. What would happen if he managed to contain things? What would happen if he was able to make it look as though she was some sort of crazed fantasist? Because it was possible. Things were bad, but if that happened how much worse would they be? It just wasn't worth the risk. In his mind she would have betrayed him, and for this level of betrayal he would make her suffer like she had never suffered before.

Marilyn finished her nails then went to get her coat. The iPhone was still on the shelf beneath the mirror. Zoe glanced over her shoulder. Marilyn had got sidetracked by one of her colleagues and was looking the other way. By the time she returned with her coat, the phone was pushed into the leg of Zoe's boot.

Marilyn walked her to the door and they said their goodbyes. The bill would be sent to Daniel, so there was nothing to pay. He would settle up at the end of the month, promptly, like he did every month. Marilyn held the door open.

'Have a good day, Mrs Barton.'

'You too. And I'll see you next week.'

Zoe walked away quickly. The stolen cell phone was burning against her skin, branding her. The lie she'd just told felt as though it was burning her too. If her plan worked, then with luck she would never see Marilyn again.

# Chapter 11

## THEN

Breakfast was set out on the table, just waiting for Daniel to appear. Cereal, toast, orange juice, coffee. It was nothing special, but it showed she cared. Like he kept telling her: the little details were the ones that mattered. The door opened and he walked in. He was dressed for work and his hair was damp from the shower. His hands were hidden behind his back.

'Close your eyes,' he said. 'I've got a surprise.'

'What sort of surprise?' she asked carefully.

'Well, if I told you that it wouldn't be a surprise, would it? So are you going to close them or not?'

'What are you going to do if I don't?'

'Zoe,' he said, exasperated.

She grinned then shut her eyes.

'Hold your hands out.'

She held out her hands and something fluttered down onto her outstretched palms. She opened her eyes. The sheet of paper she was holding was an email confirmation for a hotel booking. Seven nights at the Bellagio. Checking in tomorrow.

'We're going to Vegas?'

'We're going to Vegas, baby,' he confirmed. 'Just you and me for a whole week.'

Zoe let out a squeal then smothered him with kisses. She broke away just long enough to check that he was real, then kissed him again. Her mind was whirring with the hundred and one things that needed to be done before they boarded the plane. She picked up her cereal bowl and coffee and headed for the kitchen door. She could eat breakfast while she packed.

'Zoe,' Daniel said, and there was an indulgent tone in his voice.

'Sorry.' She put her cup and bowl back on the table. He was funny about having food and drink upstairs, but she understood where he was coming from. The carpets had cost a small fortune.

'Before you run off, there's something else.'

'Do I need to shut my eyes again?'

She was joking, but Daniel seemed to be giving the question some serious thought. He also looked nervous. She wasn't used to seeing him this way, and that made her nervous too.

'Is everything okay?' she asked.

'Everything's fine.'

'Are you sure?'

'Everything's fine. I promise.' He was trying to be reassuring, but had missed by a mile. 'Look, maybe it would be better if you did shut your eyes. You might want to sit down as well.'

This time she didn't stall. She sat down and shut her eyes. Then she waited. She could hear him moving around in front of her.

'Okay, you can look now.'

Zoe opened her eyes, and for a moment she was speechless. Daniel was down on one knee, his arm outstretched. The engagement ring he was holding out was decorated with diamonds and rubies.

'I love you, Zoe Chapel. I've loved you from the first moment I set eyes on you. Will you do me the honour of being my wife?'

The words were clichéd, the delivery wooden; he sounded like he had gone over these lines in his head a hundred times. Zoe realised she was nodding but not actually saying anything. 'Yes. Of course I'll marry you.'

She slid down onto her knees and they locked eyes. This was the face she would be waking up to for the rest of her life; this was the man she would have and hold until death parted them. There was a time when that idea would have terrified her. Not anymore. She held out her left hand and he slipped the ring onto her finger. It fitted perfectly. His lips found hers, then moved around to her ear.

'Together forever,' he whispered.

'Together forever,' she echoed back.

Lizzy was at work when she called with the good news. It was just after nine in Portland, so it had already gone noon in New York. She should have worked this out before she picked up the telephone, but she had been too wrapped up in her own drama.

'Is this important?' Lizzy asked. No "hello"; no "how you doing"? She was talking in a harsh whisper and sounded stressed.

'Yes, it is.'

'Okay. I'll call you back in five.'

Before Zoe could say anything else the line went dead and she was left staring at the receiver. Daniel had gone to work, and she was all alone with her excitement. If she didn't get it out there, and soon, it was going to suffocate her. This house was big, but today it felt even bigger than usual. Emptier too. What she wanted more than anything was for Lizzy to be here so she could share the news in person. These were the moments when Zoe missed her most. She was pacing back and forth across the kitchen when Lizzy called back. She could hear running water in the background.

'Are you hiding in the restroom?'

'I'm not supposed to take personal calls at work.'

'Couldn't you just take an early lunch?'

'Zoe, I'm an intern. I don't do lunch. That's for the grown-ups.'

'I'm getting married,' Zoe blurted out.

Silence on the other end.

'Are you still there, Lizzy?'

'Yeah, still here. You just kind of took me by surprise, that's all. So when's the big day?'

'Wednesday.'

'As in this Wednesday? Like two days from now?'

'Exactly like two days from now. We're getting married in Vegas.' She paused for a second, then ploughed on. 'Look I know it's mega-short notice, but I really want you there. And don't worry if you can't afford the airfare. I'll get Daniel to pay. So, what do you say? Will you come?'

More silence.

'Say something, Lizzy.'

'I'm sorry, Zoe. There's no way I can get the time off. We've got a big show coming up, so I'm working flat out at the moment.'

'What about if we moved the wedding to Saturday? You could fly out Friday evening, right?'

'I guess that could work,' she replied carefully.

'What's wrong?'

'Nothing's wrong.'

'Yes, there is. I know what you're like, and this isn't what you're like.'

'Look, I don't want to be the one to burst your bubble.'

'But?' she prompted.

'You know what I'm going to say.'

'Maybe so, but I still need you to say it.'

'Isn't this happening a bit fast? You haven't even known him a year.'

'It's almost a year.'

'This isn't like buying shoes, Zoe. If you wake up on Thursday morning and decide you don't like him anymore, you can't just return him to the store. And you've got to admit, Vegas doesn't have the best record when it comes to long-lasting marriages. Remember Britney Spears?'

'I love him, Lizzy. This isn't some teenage infatuation, this is the real thing.'

'In that case, wait a while.'

'And how long should we wait? Six months? A year? And if we do wait, is that going to change the way we feel?'

'All I'm saying is that if this is the man you're going to be spending the rest of your life with, then you're going to want to be sure.'

'I am sure.' Zoe sighed. 'I thought you'd be happy for me.'

'I am happy for you.'

'In that case, say you'll come.'

'Okay, okay. Move the wedding to Saturday and I'll see what I can do.'

'I'm going online right now to book your flight.'

'I said I'll see what I can do. No promises.'

'Sorry, can't hear you. The signal's breaking up.'

Lizzy laughed. 'You're calling from a landline.'

'I'll speak to you later.'

'Missing you already,' Lizzy replied, and then she was gone.

Twenty minutes later Lizzy texted to say she could make it. By that point Zoe had already ascertained that there was a seat on the 8 p.m. Delta flight from JFK on Friday. Five minutes later it was all booked.

Next, she hit the stores. By the time she got home she had enough outfits for a week in Vegas, and her card was buckling under the strain. Daniel had told her to go wild and that was exactly what she had done. The wedding dress she bought was simple, elegant and white. The store assistant told her she looked amazing. Then again, she would. This was one of those moments when she really needed her mom or her best friend there. Zoe had sent a selfie to Lizzy, and she had texted back saying all the right things, but it just wasn't the same.

♦

Zoe was upstairs packing when Daniel got home. 'Up here,' she shouted down.

She heard him climb the stairs; heard his footsteps on the landing. He came into the room and walked over to the bed. They hugged and kissed and said 'I love you'. The suitcase was lying open on top of the bed. Two thirds was taken up with her stuff, one third with his. She caught him looking.

'I know what you're thinking,' she said. 'You're thinking that I don't need all these clothes.'

He laughed. 'I didn't say a word.'

'I've got some really good news. Lizzy can make it to the wedding.'

His face fell. 'I was looking forward to it being just the two of us. I wanted this to be romantic and special.'

'It'll still be special if Lizzy's there. In fact, that's what will make it even more special for me.'

'Is she coming on her own?'

Zoe nodded.

'So we're going to have to entertain her. How's that going to work? Tables for three in restaurants? Don't you think it's going to be a little awkward?'

'We're going to Vegas. Believe me, there will be plenty to keep her entertained. Chances are we'll hardly see her. And anyway, she's only coming for the weekend. The rest of the time it'll just be the two of us.'

'And how does that work? We're getting married on Wednesday.'

'We need to move the wedding to Saturday. I tried to call, but you've been in meetings all day.'

He frowned and shook his head. 'I don't know, Zoe. Everything's already booked and paid for.'

'You can try, though.'

'I can, but I doubt it'll do much good. It took weeks to organise this. It's just too short notice.'

'There must be something we can do. I really want Lizzy there.'

Daniel sat down on the edge of the bed and took her hand. 'It's okay to have second thoughts, you know. I realise I've kind of sprung all of this on you. It's a lot to process.'

'I'm not having second thoughts.'

'So let's go to Vegas and get married.' Zoe said nothing and Daniel sighed. 'Look, I love you and I want to spend the rest of my life with you. Most of all, though, I want you to be happy. If having Lizzy there means so much to you, I'll cancel the wedding. We can get married in Portland later in the year. And we can give Lizzy plenty of notice so she can get some vacation time. In the meantime, we go to Vegas and have a blast. Just you and me. I know it's not exactly conventional, but who cares if we have the honeymoon before the wedding?'

Zoe could tell from the look on his face that he meant every word. She could also see the hurt behind those words. He had spent ages planning this. He just wanted to make her happy. When you got down to it, this was about her and him, and the fact that they were going to be spending the rest of their lives together.

'Okay,' she said. 'Let's go to Vegas.'

'How was your party?' Zoe asked. She was using the bedroom phone because she wanted some quiet. Daniel was downstairs watching TV, something with guns and car chases. The surround sound was on and the volume was deafening. She could feel the thud of the explosions through the mattress.

'It wasn't a party. I was working.'

'Was there alcohol? Were there any hot guys?'

She laughed. 'The answer to both questions is yes.'

'You're not home alone, are you?'

'No.'

Zoe smiled. It was like being back at college. 'What's he like?'

'Horny. As am I. So we're going to have to cut this short. Did you manage to get a hotel booked? If you didn't, it's not a problem. I can make the booking myself. It's going to be so good to see you again. It feels like it's been forever. What am I saying? It has been forever.'

'Actually, there's a problem. Daniel can't get the wedding moved.'

'Ah.'

'What's that supposed to mean?'

'You're going to Vegas, right? As in *the* Las Vegas? As in Sin City? As in the one that's in Nevada?'

'So?'

'So, there are a million places to get married in Vegas. They even have drive-thrus, for Christ's sake.' Lizzy paused and took a deep breath. 'How difficult do you think it would be for Daniel to move the wedding? Not difficult at all. Worst-case scenario, the place he's booked doesn't have any space on Saturday. No problem, he goes elsewhere.'

'But he's already paid for it.'

'So he loses a few hundred bucks. Big deal. It's not like he can't afford it. Look, if he wanted to move the wedding to Saturday, he could do it easily.' She stopped again and let out a long sigh. 'Can't you see what's going on here? I mean, what's really going on? He doesn't want me at the wedding, Zoe.'

'You're wrong. Totally and utterly wrong. He even offered to cancel the whole thing and move it to later in the year, just so you could be there.'

'And how guilty did he make you feel? Zoe, he's playing you. He's been playing you since the moment you met.'

'Bullshit.'

'Is it? After you hooked up with him, I hardly ever saw you, and when I did see you, he was always there. What about your other friends? When was the last time you saw them?'

'That's because they've all moved away from Portland.'

'Not all of them. And what about your book? How much work have you done on it since you moved in with him?'

'What's that got to do with anything?'

'Everything.'

'You've never liked him, have you? Admit it.'

'Okay, I admit it. I don't like him. Look, *please* don't marry him, Zoe. I'm begging you. It'll be the biggest mistake you ever make.'

'You don't know anything about us.'

'I know enough to see the danger signs. You want to know what I think? I think you should pack a bag and get the hell out of there. Tonight. Mark my words, the guy is toxic.'

Zoe opened her mouth to say something then closed it again. She had been angry, but not anymore. It was suddenly obvious what was going on here. 'You're jealous, aren't you?'

'Excuse me?'

'You heard me. You're jealous. That's what this is really all about. You can't stand to see me happy.'

'Seriously, you're going to put this on me? God, Zoe, will you just listen to yourself?'

'I'm not hearing any denials.'

'That's because there's nothing to deny. You're talking like a crazy woman.'

'Yeah, maybe I am crazy. Crazy for ever thinking that you're my friend. A friend would be happy to hear I was getting married to the man I love. They would be supportive.'

'No, that's what acquaintances do. That's what your neighbours and work colleagues and virtual strangers do. A real friend has the balls to tell you that you're making the worst mistake of your life, and they'd keep telling you until you actually listen.'

'Do you want to know what the worst mistake of my life was? It was meeting you.'

'Okay, I'm going to say this one more time. And I'm going to say this slowly and in words of one syllable, because maybe then you'll actually hear me. Leave. Him. Now. Not tomorrow. Not next week. Just pack a bag and get the hell out of there *tonight*.'

'I need to go.'

Zoe dropped the receiver back into the cradle. What the hell was going on? This morning Daniel had proposed, and now this. How could the best day of her life turn so quickly into the worst?

She had no idea how long she sat there staring at the wall. It felt like a long time. The door opened and Daniel came in. He took one look at her and asked, 'What's the matter?'

'I've had a fight with Lizzy.'

He came over and sat down on the edge of the bed with his arms wide open. She pressed herself into his body, looking for comfort but not finding any.

'Whatever this is about, it'll blow over,' he said as he stroked her hair. 'Give it a couple of days and it'll be like it never happened.'

'Do you think so?'

'I know so. You guys will work it out.'

He helped her to her feet, then gathered up the quilt.

'What are you up to?' she asked.

'What do you think? I'm looking after my wife.'

'I'm not your wife yet.'

Daniel laughed. 'That's just a detail. Okay, here's what's going to happen. I'm going to take this downstairs and get you comfy on the sofa. I'm even going to let you have the remote so you can watch whatever crap you want. Once you're settled I'm going to order pizza because that's your go-to comfort food.'

He started walking to the door and turned around when he realised she wasn't following.

'Thank you,' she said.

'Zoe, there's nothing to thank me for. Nothing whatsoever. I hate to see you hurting. If there's anything I can do to help you feel a little better, then of course I'm going to do it.' He paused, smiled. 'Things will work themselves out. They always do. Just you wait and see.'

'I hope you're right.'

Daniel smiled, and for a moment Zoe truly believed that everything would be okay.

'Of course I'm right.'

But he wasn't.

To start with Zoe had been too angry to even think about making up with Lizzy. She ignored her calls, ignored the Facebook messages. Then she was too preoccupied with the wedding. Then she was too preoccupied with writing her novel. Whenever the subject came up, Daniel had been quick to tell her that it would probably be best to give it a little longer.

Time would sort everything out.

You'll see.

She almost called a hundred times, but always found an excuse not to. Eventually the calls from Lizzy had gotten further apart, then stopped altogether. Lizzy had a brand new life in New York, and she had her life here in Portland with Daniel. Even if they did make up, it was never going to be like it used to be, so maybe a clean break was for the best.

And all the time her world carried on shrinking without her noticing, until eventually it had shrunk to the point where reaching out to Lizzy was no longer an option.

# Chapter 12

## NOW

'I'm going to Tucson,' Daniel announced over breakfast.

The spoon of cornflakes was halfway to Zoe's mouth. All of a sudden she didn't feel hungry. Her stomach swirled and she willed her breakfast to stay put. Thankfully, the morning sickness hadn't been too bad. Most days she had bouts of nausea but she could count on one hand the number of times she had actually thrown up. She put the spoon back into the bowl and watched it slide into the watery cereal.

'When do you leave?'

'Tomorrow morning. My flight's at nine, so I need to be at the airport for seven.'

*Tomorrow.* Tomorrow was Monday. Six days had passed since the scan. She had made plans but so far she hadn't put any of them into action because she thought she would have at least a week's notice. Another wave of nausea hit and she did her best to ignore it. Her stomach was in knots, her nerves stretched to breaking point. She hoped that none of this was showing.

'My suit needs to go to the dry cleaner's,' he added. 'Have you got time in your packed schedule to make that happen?'

'Which suit?'

'The grey Armani.' He said this like it was the most obvious thing in the universe, and she was the stupidest. 'I'll need it back today.'

'No problem. There's a place over on Sandy Boulevard that offers a same-day service.'

He gave her a look as though he was about to explode and she wondered if a tiny bit of attitude had somehow slipped through the cracks. If he wanted to, he could easily take the way she had said 'no problem' and turn it into a dismissive 'whatever'. It wouldn't be the first time he had done something like that. And maybe this time he would actually have a point because that's what had been running through her mind. It didn't matter how careful she was, very occasionally something sneaked through. She prayed this wasn't one of those occasions. That said, those sparks of attitude were like precious jewels. Zoe Barton might be the face she showed to the world, but Zoe Chapel was still in there somewhere.

'When are you back?' she asked quickly.

'Wednesday evening.'

They finished breakfast in silence, the only noise the clinking of spoons against china. Zoe had to stop herself from cringing when he kissed her goodbye. After he left, she sat at the kitchen table for a long time. It crossed her mind to wait for his next trip. Myriadian had customers all over the US, which meant there would be another. The problem was that there was no pattern to them. Sometimes they would only be a week apart; at other times it could be a month, even two. She could hide her pregnancy for a couple of weeks, but two months was out of the question.

Zoe made herself sit there a little longer while she went through everything she needed to do. There was only twenty-four hours to get everything together, and that just didn't seem long enough. The second Daniel's plane took off tomorrow, she had to be ready to leave; by the time he landed back in Portland on Wednesday evening she needed to be somewhere he could never find her.

If Seattle had taught her anything, it was that she couldn't underestimate him. Her car had ended up a burnt-out wreck on a stretch of wasteland on the outskirts of Eugene. That much of the plan had worked. Where it went wrong was that the police were able to track the owner through the number stamped on the engine block. Daniel was the registered owner. The private investigator he hired had bribed a guard at the Greyhound station to let him watch the security camera footage. He saw her buying a ticket, saw her board a bus bound for Seattle. It took the investigator three days to follow the bus route north and ascertain that she had indeed gotten off in Seattle. The next four days were spent visiting restaurants, coffee houses and bars. Daniel had told him that she had once worked as a waitress. Since that was the only work experience she had, and she would need money, that was the logical place to start searching.

Zoe knew all of this because Daniel had told her. It was an opportunity for him to show how clever he was; it also reinforced the idea that if he could find her once, he could do so again. He wanted her so defeated that she gave up trying, and until she discovered she was pregnant, it had worked.

Zoe's first stop was the dry cleaner's on Sandy Boulevard; her second was the gym. She put her cell phone in the glovebox, then retrieved Marilyn's iPhone from its hiding place beneath the driver's seat and switched it on. There were dozens of missed calls and unanswered texts, which was a good sign since it meant the phone hadn't been disconnected yet. She switched it off to conserve the battery and got out of the car.

It took ten minutes to walk to Knott Park. The whole way, she kept glancing over her shoulder. She found an empty bench and sat down. She knew Lizzy's number by heart; she should do, the number of times she had almost called it. She connected the call and pressed the iPhone to her ear. There was a moment of silence where she was convinced Marilyn must have had the phone disconnected, and then a robotic voice declared that *the number you have dialled has not been recognised.*

Zoe's stomach went into freefall. Up until this point, she hadn't realised how much she was relying on Lizzy. Her whole plan hinged on Lizzy's forgiveness, but to get that she need to talk to her. Zoe checked the screen. Definitely the right number. Just to be sure, she punched it in again. And got the same result. Her hands found their way down to her belly and came to rest there. She was clutching the cell phone so tightly her knuckles ached.

Focus.

The cell number had been changed, but that was no reason to panic. People changed their numbers all the time. The obvious thing was to call Lizzy at work. Unfortunately, Zoe couldn't remember the name of the fashion house she worked at. It was named after the designer who founded it; the first name began with an A. Adam, Alan, Alexander, Arthur. No, it was Andrew. She was sure of it. The surname sounded French, or maybe Italian. Desjardins, Defrie. Demarco. Yeah, that was it. Andrew Demarco. Zoe got the number from the operator and dialled.

'Andrew Demarco, can I help?'

'Can you put me through to Lizzy Slater, please?'

'I'm sorry, she doesn't work here anymore.'

'Do you know where she's gone?'

'Sorry, no.'

'Is there someone there who does know, please?'

Zoe could hear the desperation in her voice, but there was nothing she could do about it. The line went quiet, then the receptionist said, 'Who's calling?' There was suspicion in every syllable. Any second now she was going to hang up.

'I'm an old friend,' Zoe said quickly. 'Lizzy went out with my brother back at high school. I'm trying to get hold of her because he was involved in a traffic accident at the weekend. He's in a coma and it doesn't look like he's going to make it. We're going to switch the life support machine off and I thought Lizzy might want to say goodbye before we do.'

She had no idea where this lie came from. Probably the same place she got her story ideas. The receptionist went quiet, then, 'Let me put you through to Dee Dee. He heads up the department she worked in. If anyone knows where she's gone, it's him.'

'Thank you.'

'Hold on and I'll see if he's there.'

The hold music went on long enough for Zoe to become convinced that Dee Dee must be on vacation, then, 'Oh my God, that is so awful about your brother. Alicia was just telling me. You want to know where Lizzy went, right?'

'Yes. Please.'

'She got a job at Ralph Lauren. I'm not sure who she had to sleep with to get it, but there you go. I tried to persuade her not to leave, but my pleas fell on deaf ears. I told her she was going to end up being the tiniest of fish in the biggest of ponds, but she just wouldn't listen to the voice of reason. What did you say your name was again?'

'Zoe.'

'Not *the* Zoe? She was heartbroken when you guys fell out. Absolutely bereft. Funny, she never mentioned anything about your brother.'

'That's understandable. She was devastated when they broke up. My brother was the first guy she fell in love with. She never got over him.'

'Yeah, I'm hearing you. I don't talk about my Ground Zero either. Anyway, have you got a pen?'

She told him she did and he reeled off two numbers. The first was for Lizzy's new cell; the second was the direct number for the department she worked for at Ralph Lauren.

'Thanks. I appreciate this.'

'My pleasure, but do me a favour. When you speak to Lizzy, tell her that I love her and miss her, and that she needs to call me so we can go out for drinks. And sorry again about your brother.'

Zoe tried Lizzy's cell phone first but it went straight to voicemail. It was two thirty in New York; her cell was probably off because she was at work. She tried her work number next. It rang three times before someone picked up. The woman who answered sounded seriously harassed.

'I'm trying to get in touch with Lizzy Slater. Is she there, please?'

'Yeah, sure. Hold on a second.' There was a short pause, then, 'Lizzy! Telephone!'

Zoe had to jerk the phone from her ear so she didn't end up deafened. Her mouth had gone dry, like it was full of sand. This was what guilt tasted like. She knew exactly what was going to happen next. The second Lizzy heard her voice, she was going to tell her to go to hell then hang up. What's more, it was nothing less than she deserved.

'Hello.'

Lizzy's voice was unmistakeable. Chicago, with airs and graces. Zoe had heard it happy, she'd heard it sad, and she had heard it like it was now: questioning, hassled and pissed. Just hearing it was enough to make her heart light up. With that one word, the last three years disappeared. It could have been yesterday when they last talked. Zoe tried to speak, but nothing came out.

'This better not be some crank call.' Lizzy sounded more pissed than ever. 'I'm way too busy for that shit.'

'Lizzy, it's me. It's Zoe.'

Silence on the other end. In her wildest imaginings Zoe had never envisioned a situation where Lizzy would be rendered speechless.

'Well, say something,' she prompted.

'Jesus, Zoe, is that really you?'

'Look, I know you probably hate me, and it's nothing less than I deserve, but I just want you to know that I'm sorry. I am so, so sorry.'

'There's nothing to be sorry about. Nothing at all. It's so good to hear your voice again. How are you doing?'

'Not good. Look, Lizzy, I'm in trouble. Big trouble. I need your help.'

'It's Dan, isn't it?'

'Yes.'

'Give me your cell number. I can't talk here, but I'll call you back in five. Whatever that bastard has done, we can fix it.'

Zoe was staring blankly across the park when the phone rang. She connected the call.

'Okay,' Lizzy said, 'I've only got thirty minutes, so we need to be quick. How bad is it?'

Zoe's first instinct was to tell her that it wasn't too bad. Unbelievable. Even after everything that Daniel had done, she still had this inexplicable need to defend him.

'It's bad,' she said, and it was so hard getting the words out.

'I'm going to kill him.'

Zoe almost laughed. The comment was just so Lizzy. 'I'm pregnant. That's why I need to get away. I can't let him hurt the baby.'

'Does he know?'

'No. And he's not going to. Not ever.'

'Everything's going to be okay, Zo. You've got to believe that.'

She wanted to believe, but it was just so hard. She had been running uphill for so long she didn't know how to do anything else. 'I hope you're right.'

'I'm always right, and don't you forget it.'

'Is this the part where you tell me "told you so"?'

'Never. Okay, start talking.'

Zoe took up twenty of the thirty minutes giving Lizzy the condensed version of the story. She started at the wedding and brought her right up to the present day. She told her everything, nothing was left out. It was a relief to finally be talking about all of this. That was the thing with secrets. They kept piling up on top of each other until you ended up crushed beneath them.

'Can I stay with you for a couple of days?' she asked when she was done talking.

'Zo, you can stay as long as you want.'

'This is just temporary.'

'If you're worried about what's going to happen when the baby comes, don't be. I was thirteen when my brother was born, so I know about living with babies.'

'That's not the problem. Daniel is going to come looking for me. I couldn't live with myself if he hurt you.'

'Hurt me? Just let him try.'

'You don't know what he's like.'

'He doesn't frighten me.'

'Well maybe he should. Look, don't underestimate him, Lizzy. That was my big mistake.'

Lizzy didn't say anything for a moment, and that was good because it meant she was thinking about it. 'Maybe you could get a restraining order,' she suggested.

'That won't stop him from hurting me and the baby. What's going to happen? He turns up on my doorstep and I call the police. By the time they get there it'll be too late, we'll already be on the way to the hospital. Or the morgue. The only way for this to work is for me to disappear somewhere he'll never find me.'

'We need a plan.'

'Yeah, I've been working on that. First I need to get out of Portland, then I need a couple of days so I can work out my next move. The problem at the moment is that I just can't think straight living in the same house as him.'

'Okay, how about this? One of my friends owns a cabin in the Catskills. If I smile sweetly, he'll let us stay there. And I've got some vacation time due. It's short notice, but I'm sure I can get time off if I pull the family emergency card. There's no way that asshole will be able to find you there.'

'Okay, I'm going to need you to book a flight. From Seattle, not Portland. The last thing I want is to bump into Daniel in departures because his flight's been delayed. It's a three-hour drive. If you book one for early afternoon, that'll work. Text the flight details to this phone.'

'No problem.'

'I'll pay you back for the ticket when I get to New York.'

'Don't sweat it,' Lizzy said. 'All that matters is that you get away from that bastard, and soon.'

'Ralph Lauren. I'm impressed. You've finally made the big time, just like you always said you would.'

She laughed. 'Believe me, it's nowhere near as glamorous as you might think. I'm still just a glorified coffee girl.'

'It's a foot in the door, though. A step up the ladder.'

'Any more clichés you want to throw at me?'

'No, that's all I've got for now. I'll see you tomorrow.' It felt weird saying that. Weird but right.

'I can't wait. And be safe, Zoe.'

The line went dead. Zoe looked at the iPhone for a second. She had one more call to make, but wasn't sure she could do it. Before she could change her mind she punched in the number and hit the connect button.

# Chapter 13

## THEN

It hadn't taken much to make the study her own. The first thing she had done was buy some framed movie posters. *The Shawshank Redemption*, *It's a Wonderful Life*, *Amélie*, *Good Will Hunting*. Great films, great stories. Whenever she was short on inspiration all she had to do was turn around, and there it was on the walls. Fresh cut flowers brightened up the desk and added some colour to the day. Zoe hated that desk. It was too old-fashioned and stern. It just wasn't her. She wasn't about to complain, though. That seemed petty. When she told Daniel she liked to listen to music while she wrote, he had surprised her with a state-of-the-art speaker dock for her iPod.

She stuck to his work hours. That way they could still spend plenty of time together. Mornings were for doing the actual writing; afternoons were for research; evenings and nights were just for him. Zoe couldn't remember a time she had been happier. She was living the life of a writer, and she had the man she loved at her side. There were moments where she had to pinch herself to make sure she wasn't dreaming.

As soon as Daniel left the house in the morning, she would head upstairs and start work. Most days she got two thousand words down; on a really good day it was closer to two and a half thousand. The novel was completed in a three-month frenzy. Lizzy had always been her biggest cheerleader, and even though they were no longer talking, it was as though she was still cheering her on. That comment about neglecting her writing had stung more than Zoe was prepared to admit, because it was true. Finishing the book was her way of proving Lizzy wrong.

The story was told from the perspectives of a Jewish mother and daughter who ended up separated when they were sent to the camps. The narrative followed their efforts to find each other after the war. The twist was that Lila, the daughter, was actually a ghost, something you didn't find out until right at the end. Unsurprisingly, there was plenty of herself in Lila. What was interesting, though, was how much of Lizzy there was in the mother.

It took another month to redraft the book, and by the time she finished Zoe felt as though she had run a dozen marathons back to back. There was a real whirlwind of emotions going on inside her. On the one hand she was elated. She had done it. She had finally written a book she could be proud of. Sure, there was plenty of work that still needed to be done, but it was nothing a good editor couldn't help with. The book wasn't brilliant, but she was confident that it was okay. Better than some she had read; worse than others.

On the other hand, she couldn't get over how depressed she felt. She had been warned about this on her writing course. Writing a novel was an intense process. Day in, day out, you were communing with imaginary people. Except it got to the point where those imaginary people started taking on a life of their own. When that happened they became as real as your family and friends. More real, in some ways. Completing the book meant saying goodbye to them, and that hurt. Crazy as it sounded, Zoe felt like she was grieving.

'Close your eyes. I've got a surprise.'

Zoe had her hands behind her back and a smile on her face. Daniel was sitting at the kitchen table nursing a bottle of Budweiser. His tie was crooked and the top button of his shirt was undone. He looked a little roguish, and sexy as hell. It was a look that worked for him.

'What's the surprise?' he asked.

'If I told you that it wouldn't be a surprise, would it?'

He grinned and took a long pull on the Bud. That was usually his line. It was fun turning the tables on him.

'Look,' she said, 'just close your eyes. Please. This is getting heavy.'

Daniel put the beer bottle down and shut his eyes. The manuscript landed in front of him with a solid thump. It was four hundred and forty-eight pages long. Zoe had used up a whole printer cartridge and most of a ream of paper printing it out. She had tied a red bow around it. Partly to keep the pages together; partly because it was a present. *The Day of Stones* was printed on the title page in large letters.

He opened his eyes. 'You've finished it.'

'This morning.'

He pulled the manuscript towards him and tugged at the bow until it came undone. His smile turned to a frown. 'You've used your maiden name. What's wrong with Zoe Barton?'

'There's nothing wrong with it. It's just that I've always written as Zoe Chapel.'

'There were a lot of things you used to do as Zoe Chapel, and now you do them as Zoe Barton. Why should this be different? Plus there's the added bonus that it comes earlier in the alphabet. It's only one letter away from the 'A's, which puts you right at the front of the book stores.'

'I never thought about it like that.'

'It's your call, but I think you should at least consider changing it.'

He lifted up the title page and placed it face down on the table. The dedication was printed in italics. *For Daniel . . . Together Forever.* He looked up at her and his smile was back.

'Together forever,' he whispered, more to himself than her. He reached for her hand and gave it a squeeze. There was a kiss for each of her fingertips.

The dedication page went on top of the title page. He squared them up, checked to make sure they were neat, then squared them up again. She watched him pick up the first page and told herself this was no big deal. Except it was a big deal. Daniel was the first person to see the book. His eyes moved from side to side as he read through the first page, and she forced herself to look away. She had gone over the first paragraph so many times she could recite it by heart. Every time she opened the Word file, there it was, right up at the top of the document. This wasn't the only section of the book she could recite. There were whole chunks of text seared into her memory. She had heard the term labour of love, but up until now she had never really understood what that meant.

Daniel stopped reading. He put the manuscript back together again, squared it up, then retied the bow. 'I'll read this later.'

Zoe felt a small flash of disappointment and told herself not to be silly. What had she expected? That he would just drop everything and read it there and then? He took another long pull on the bottle of Bud and smiled that amazing smile, and that almost made everything okay again.

'So now the novel's finished, does that mean you'll start going to the gym again? I mean, when was the last time you went?'

She made a face. 'Yeah, it's been a while, hasn't it? I don't think I've been since before we got married. Mind you, we've still been getting plenty of exercise.'

Daniel smiled. 'We have, but not quite enough to work off the calories from all those cookies and muffins you've been eating while you've been writing.'

'You know about that?'

'You're not very good at hiding the evidence.'

Zoe grimaced. 'I guess I've put on a couple of pounds.'

'And I'd still love you if you put on three hundred.'

She laughed. 'Tell you what, today I'm going to pack myself full of junk food to celebrate, and tomorrow I'll start a diet.'

'Sounds like a plan. If there's anything I can do to help, just let me know.'

Zoe reached out and gave his hand a quick squeeze. 'Thanks, but unfortunately this is one of those things you have to do on your own. And don't worry, I will start going to the gym again. I promise. I refuse to be one of those people who has a gym membership that never gets used.'

He smiled. 'Again, if you want me to help motivate you, just say the word.'

# Chapter 14

## NOW

After picking up Daniel's suit from the dry cleaner's, Zoe had left her phone in the glovebox of the Mercedes and started walking. She knew about the GPS app on the cell. What she wasn't so sure about was whether there was a tracking device attached to her car as well. That was why she wasn't taking any chances. If Daniel checked in on her she didn't want him to think that she was doing anything other than the things he was expecting her to do.

There were numerous dry cleaners in Portland offering a same-day service but only one that was within easy walking distance of Spies Like Us. She must have passed this place a thousand times without ever going in. Up until now she had never needed to. The store sold surveillance equipment, everything you needed to spy on your fellow man. It had a shady feel, like this was a place that existed beyond the law. Just walking through the door was enough to make her paranoia levels jump up.

The owner was pushing seventy and looked like a war vet. His left arm ended just above the elbow, and the sleeve of his army surplus shirt was rolled up and fastened with safety pins. There was a look in his eye like he hadn't made it all the way back from whatever war he'd fought in. There was no 'hello', no 'can I help?', just a ton of suspicion that oozed off him in waves. His gaze followed her all the way to the counter. She told him what she wanted and he answered with a bemused smile, like he had seen it all before.

'How many kids have you got?' he asked.

'One,' she lied. 'A two-year-old boy.'

He nodded like this answer was nothing less than he expected. 'You'd be surprised how many women like you we get in here.'

The comment made her wonder what he was actually seeing. A soccer mom? One of those women who spent her whole life shopping and working out at the gym? She caught her reflection in the smudged counter top and had to wonder how this had happened. How had she become this woman she barely recognised? And how would he react if he could see her as she really was?

She was on the point of walking out when he suddenly turned and headed towards the back room. He returned a couple of minutes later with the item she had requested and laid it on the counter. She looked at it. This one small thing had the power to end her marriage forever.

'Shall I run through how it works?'

'Please.'

The more the old guy talked, the more Zoe warmed to him. He was nowhere near as creepy as she first thought. Strange, yes, but a long way from being a psycho. He told her to call him Brett; she told him that her name was Eleanor. Brett finished talking and Zoe took off her Rolex. She laid it on the counter and held her breath. She just hoped that Daniel would be too preoccupied with his upcoming trip to notice she wasn't wearing it. And if he did notice, she just hoped he wouldn't get too angry when she told him she had left it in her gym locker. If pushed, she would tell him that she had gone back to the gym but someone must have stolen it because it wasn't in the locker and it hadn't been handed in. The story was thin, and all she could do was pray that things didn't go that far.

'I don't have any money,' she said quietly.

Brett looked at the watch. 'Is that real?'

Zoe nodded.

He looked at the watch again, closer this time. 'Tell me to mind my own business, but this isn't about your kid, is it?'

Zoe shook her head.

'Do you actually have a kid?'

'Not yet.'

'You're pregnant?'

She nodded.

Brett picked up the Rolex, studied it for a moment, then held it out. 'I can't take this.'

'You've got to. Please.'

Brett leant across the counter and crushed the watch into her hand. 'Let's class this as one of those IOU kind of situations, eh? Once you're back on your feet, pay me then, okay?'

'Thank you.'

'Don't mention it. Again, tell me to mind my own business, but is there anything I can do to help?'

'You've already done more than enough.' She paused. 'I will pay you back. I promise.'

'Yeah, I know you will.'

Back in the car, she checked for texts. There was one from Lizzy: a seat had been booked on tomorrow's 13.17 flight from Sea-Tac to New York. Zoe pushed Marilyn's iPhone back into its hiding place beneath her seat and put the car into drive. Five minutes later she turned onto Fairfield Boulevard. Even though it was too early for Daniel to be back, she still expected to find his Porsche on the driveway. It wasn't, but she couldn't quite shake the feeling of impending doom that hung over her. She parked in her usual spot, then grabbed her stuff and hurried inside.

The collection of toy bears on the bedroom bureau dated back to the days when things had still been good between them. The ones with hearts on were Valentine's presents; the rest were bought to commemorate unnecessary anniversaries. One week together, one month, three months. At the time Zoe thought it was harmless fun, yet another way for him to show how much he loved her. And she had liked the attention. She wasn't going to deny that. It had felt good to be wanted.

There were eight bears in the collection. She was hoping he wouldn't notice a ninth. She spent a long time positioning the bear so it looked as though it belonged with the others. If Daniel glanced over there couldn't be anything to make him suspicious. On one wall there was an impressionist painting of a horse. Zoe stood in front of it and looked back at the bureau. The bear was staring directly at her with its blank eyes. If she hadn't known it was there, she doubted she would have noticed it.

♦

Just before seven the Porsche pulled up on the driveway. The engine died; the door opened. Zoe couldn't get over how nervous she felt. How scared. They'd had dinner together more than a thousand times, but those were just rehearsals. This was the only performance that mattered. The kitchen door opened and Daniel came in. He looked slightly dishevelled from being at work all day.

'It's chicken risotto tonight,' she said.

'How long until it's ready?'

'Another five minutes.'

'Well, what are you waiting for? Less talk, more action.'

Daniel unlocked the main refrigerator and pulled out a bottle of Bud. He twisted off the lid, took a long drink, then started preparing her smoothie. Zoe finished making the risotto and carried his plate to the table. The smoothie was ready and waiting for her when she sat down. Her heart was beating hard and fast; every sip of the smoothie sat like lead in her stomach. This would be their last evening together. Their last night. All going well, twenty-four hours from now she would be in New York.

Safe at last.

The silence that enveloped them while they ate was unbearable; counting the minutes until bedtime was even worse. It was almost impossible to act normal. She was convinced that Daniel would notice the bear on the bureau. Every time he looked at her she was convinced he could see right through her.

They got into bed. The light went off.

'I love you, Zoe.'

'I love you too.'

'Together forever.'

'Together forever,' she replied. Back at the start this was their promise to each other. Now it was her curse.

She knew what was coming next, because the same thing happened whenever he went away. It didn't matter what she said, or what excuse she made, it wouldn't make any difference. There was a rustle of covers as his hand snaked towards her. His fingertips brushed her belly, and she hated him for being so close to the baby. His hand lingered there, and for a heart-stopping moment she was sure that he must have noticed something. And then it was moving again, heading lower. At least this would be the last time, she told herself. She tried hard to find comfort in this but there was none to be found.

# Chapter 15

## THEN

The first thing Zoe saw when she walked into the kitchen was the manuscript. It was still on the kitchen worktop, untouched and unread. It had been there for over a month now. In her fantasy, Daniel had dropped everything and disappeared into his study, desperate to read it. The fantasy ended with him reappearing at breakfast the next morning, bleary eyed from being up all night reading, and telling her how much he loved it. More than once, she had almost asked him why he hadn't read it, but she couldn't face the answer. Because the truth was that he had started it, and then he had stopped. And the reason he stopped was because he hated it.

She was prepared to accept that her overactive imagination might be at work again. After all, Daniel had been really busy recently. Really stressed too. A big contract had fallen through, one that he had been working on for the last three months. If that wasn't enough, a couple of evenings ago someone had broken into his car while he was at the gym. He had come out to find the driver's window smashed, and some of his CDs missing. The police had been useless. He'd had to push hard to get them to send someone around to run fingerprints. Zoe reckoned they probably sent someone around just to shut him up. It was highly unlikely they would be pursuing this any further. The theft of a couple of greatest hits compilations wasn't exactly the crime of the century.

The whole thing had left him really pissed off. She couldn't think of a situation where she had seen him so angry. He'd ranted about how useless the police were, and what the hell do they pay taxes for anyway, and God help the thief if he ever got hold of him. She had tried to make light of things by pointing out that no one had died. Big mistake. He had looked at her and all the hate and anger he'd felt for the thief had been momentarily focussed on her. This only lasted a split second but it seemed much longer. The fact he had acted this way was totally understandable. He had come from nothing and worked hard for his success. The Porsche wasn't just a car to him, it was a symbol of what he had achieved. The same went for this house. It was more than just bricks and mortar, it was a constant reminder that the poor days back in Prophetstown were far behind him.

So yes, if she looked hard enough she could find reasons why he hadn't started reading the manuscript. Unfortunately, each of those reasons led to another two for why her book was a pile of shit.

It had gone eight before she heard him moving around upstairs. A short while later he came into the kitchen. He walked over to the table and planted a kiss on top of her head.

'I woke up and you weren't there,' he said. 'Trouble sleeping again?'

She nodded. 'I didn't want to wake you, so I got up.'

'Shame. I was hoping for a lazy Sunday morning.'

'We could go back to bed,' she suggested. 'Technically it's still morning.'

'I can't, sorry. I've got a busy day ahead of me.'

She frowned. 'I thought you didn't have anything on today.'

'No. What I said was that I didn't have anywhere to go.' He walked over to the manuscript and picked it up. 'See you later,' he said, and then he was gone.

It was late afternoon before Daniel finally emerged from his study. He came over to the kitchen table and placed the manuscript in front of her. The pages were all neatly squared up. If she hadn't seen him reading when she took him some lunch she would have wondered if he had looked at it at all.

'Well?' she asked.

'It's not what I expected,' he replied carefully. 'Don't get me wrong, it's not bad.' He paused, searching for the right words. 'It's just a bit dark, that's all.'

'Daniel, one of the main characters is a little girl who was killed in the Holocaust. Of course it's dark.'

'Look, maybe I'm not the right person to do this.'

'Why not? You read books.'

'Yeah, but not books like this.'

'And what's that supposed to mean?'

'It's just a bit pretentious, don't you think? I mean, what do you know about being in a concentration camp?'

'If you hate it, just say so.'

'I don't hate it, Zoe, I just don't get it.' He paused again. 'I guess I expected more from you, that's all.'

'*You expected more.* Now who's being pretentious?'

He sighed and softened his voice. 'Like I said, maybe I'm not the right person to do this. I prefer thrillers, Zoe. Books with murders in.'

Anger bubbled up inside her. Daniel was entitled to his opinion; at the same time she was entitled to protect her baby. 'And there weren't any murders in my book? Like six million murders wasn't enough for you.'

'Why are you being like this anyway? Why do you want to turn this into a fight?'

'I can't think. Okay, how about this? Maybe this is important to me. Maybe I expected my husband to be more supportive.'

Daniel laughed, but there was a sharp edge there that Zoe had never heard before. 'I haven't been supportive? Are you kidding me? You live in my house. You eat my food. I put clothes on your back. How is that not being supportive?'

'Fine, if that's how you feel, I'll leave. And you can keep the clothes. I hate them anyway.'

'Do you know what you are, Zoe? You're nothing but an ungrateful little bitch.'

'Fuck you.'

She picked up the manuscript and turned to leave but only managed two steps before he grabbed her arm. His fingers dug into muscle. He was gripping hard enough to leave bruises. She tried to shake him off, but he just tightened his grip.

'Let go. You're hurting me.'

The first slap didn't really register. She heard the sound of skin on skin, and felt the burning in her left cheek, but somehow it didn't seem real. Daniel would never hit her. He loved her. The second slap sent her crashing to the floor, the pages raining down all around her like giant flakes of confetti. Her head was throbbing and her shoulder felt like it might be dislocated. Daniel had his foot pulled back as though he was going to kick her. She curled into a ball to protect herself. She could hear the air reverberating through her chest, hear the blood whooshing through her ears in time with her thundering heart. And then she heard the sound of his footsteps as he walked away.

That was the day everything changed.

That was her Day of Stones.

Once Daniel had calmed down, he came looking for her. He found her in the bedroom, packing a bag. He begged her not to go and told her he was sorry. He was so, so, so sorry. It would never happen again. Never. He had no idea what happened, or why. It was a moment of pure madness. Things were going to get better. Just wait and see. Better than they had ever been. *I promise I promise I promise.* There were even tears, something she would never have expected to see from him.

Daniel was utterly relentless in his apology. He just kept going until she eventually caved. There were gifts and meals, and romantic weekends away, and for a while things were almost like they had been at the start. Almost. It was never going to be exactly the same, because some things could never be undone. No matter how much you might want to, or how hard you tried, you couldn't turn the clock back.

The warning signs had always been there, but she had chosen to ignore them. She had caught glimpses of his temper, but everyone got a little bit angry every now and again; she had caught glimpses of his controlling nature, but everyone had their little peculiarities and eccentricities; she had caught glimpses of his jealousy and possessiveness, but didn't that just prove how much he loved her? For everything he did, there was always an excuse.

She should have left him then; she should have just walked out the door and never looked back. But his words got right under her skin. He could be so damn convincing when he wanted, and he'd had all of his powers of persuasion turned up to full. She believed that he was sorry; she believed he could change. She believed him when he told her that he loved her more than life itself. She believed him because she thought that she knew him better than he knew himself.

She believed because she loved him.

And it wasn't as though he had to change much. All she wanted was the man she had shared a coffee with on that first date at the Marrakesh, and for a while, it seemed as if that was what she had got.

Then he hit her again.

This time she didn't believe him.

# Chapter 16

## NOW

Breakfast was laid out neatly on the kitchen table. The toast was in the toaster, the coffee was brewing, and the smell was pulling the knot in Zoe's gut tighter and tighter. One way or another, this would be the last time she prepared his breakfast. When Daniel finally appeared he was dressed for flying. Jeans, a T-shirt, a zip top, sneakers. Everything was designer. He wanted to be comfortable, but he still needed to make a statement. He took one look at the table and wrinkled his nose.

'You know I can't eat breakfast before I fly.'

She did. She also knew how angry he had been the one time she hadn't made it. On that occasion, she had hurried to get something prepared. By the time it was ready he had lost his appetite. Her fault, of course.

'Sorry,' she said.

'I don't need apologies, I just need you to be more considerate.'

He rolled his eyes, and Zoe prayed that things wouldn't escalate. These days he went straight for the body, and she couldn't afford a kick or punch to her stomach. It had been five months since he'd last hit her. That was a long time, but she knew the next beating could happen at any time. She gazed down at the table top. Anything to avoid eye contact.

'Maybe next time you'll think about how your actions impact on other people,' he said. 'Then again, probably not. You never learn.'

Zoe heard him walking away and breathed a sigh of relief. She had expected him to rant on about how pathetic she was, and how he couldn't understand why he'd married her. She was surprised he had backed down so quickly.

As usual, he complained about the Mercedes on the way to the airport. This always happened. The car was too small, too uncomfortable. The thing was, he had bought it. It was one of the guilt presents he'd got for her after Seattle, bought to replace her old car. Zoe followed the signs to the drop-off area and found a parking space. Daniel retrieved his suitcase from the trunk, then leant back into the car. The passenger seat was between them, but he was still too close for comfort.

'You know what time my return flight lands?' he asked.

She nodded. 'I've got the details written down at home.'

'Don't be late.'

'I won't,' she promised.

There was no kiss, no hug, no 'I love you'. He just turned and left. Within two steps she had been completely forgotten. Zoe watched him tow his suitcase towards the terminal building, and prayed she never saw him again.

A short while later she was driving past the big houses that lined Fairfield Boulevard. The day was just getting started. The early risers would have already gone to the office, but it was still too early for the school run. She wondered how many of these front doors hid lives that appeared perfect on the outside, but were actually living nightmares. Because that was the thing: everyone had something to hide.

Daniel would have passed through security by now and gone into the departures lounge. He would have bought a coffee from Starbucks, and probably a cookie. Then he would have bought a magazine and gone to find a place to wait where he could watch the planes taking off and landing. Zoe had flown with him enough times to know his behaviours and patterns by heart. If nothing else, Daniel was, and would always be, a creature of habit.

She parked on the driveway and for a moment just sat staring at the house. It seemed like a hundred years had passed since she pulled up here in a rented U-Haul truck that had her few meagre possessions in the back. That day was like a dream that had happened to someone else.

She made herself sit there a moment longer while she went over her plan again. She must have gone through it a thousand times, but you couldn't be too careful. After Seattle there had been a month where Daniel treated her like a princess, then another three where they slowly slid back into the old ways. When he eventually snapped, she had genuinely thought she was going to die. What's more, a part of her had wished for that to happen, because then the nightmare would have finally been over.

Afterwards there had been more apologies, and more gifts. There had been more promises, too, but these had proved as empty as all his previous ones.

The key for his Porsche was hanging on the peg board by the front door. There was a good chance that he had fitted the car with a GPS tracker, but that shouldn't be a problem. He would have no reason to check where the car was until he came back from his trip and found it gone. He would eventually discover it had been left in the long-term parking at Sea-Tac, but by then she would be long gone,

On the other hand, there was no telling when he might check up on the whereabouts of her Mercedes. If he saw that she was heading up the I-5 he would want to know why. And if his plane hadn't taken off then you could bet that he would walk straight out of the departures lounge and come looking for her. Knowing how much he loved the Porsche, stealing it didn't sit comfortably with her, but she didn't see that she had any other option. It wasn't like she had the cash to hire a car.

Zoe went through to the living room and switched the TV on to NWCN. If there had been any major terrorist incidents at the airport, she needed to know. The reporter on the screen was looking intense, while the police were getting busy in the background. The excitement was happening in Salem, though, which was far enough from Portland not to affect her. According to the news crawl at the bottom of the screen a bank robbery had gone wrong and turned into a hostage situation.

It took five minutes to transfer the nanny cam film to her laptop. Every time the house creaked, she was sure it was Daniel. Even when everything went quiet again, she could still feel him sneaking up behind her. The picture was every bit as good as Brett had promised. Zoe fast-forwarded until Daniel appeared.

He took down the horse painting and laid it gently against the wall. The code for the safe was six numbers long. Zoe caught the first five easily enough. Two, five, nine, four, four. She couldn't see the last digit because he had stepped in front of the camera in anticipation of the door opening. Once she stopped panicking she realised it wasn't a problem. She could work out the last number through trial and error.

Zoe watched the film again to make sure she had the correct numbers, then went back through to the bedroom. She kept repeating them to herself, turning them into a chant, searing them into her memory. The horse painting was heavier than it looked. She propped it against the wall and punched the first five numbers into the keypad. It took four attempts to work out the final digit. There was a rumble and a click as the lock released. The door fell open an inch. She pulled it all the way open and peered inside.

Bundles of bank notes were piled up behind the large lockbox that contained her jewellery. She lifted one of the bundles out. According to the paper band wrapped around the middle it contained fifty one-hundred-dollar bills, which added up to five thousand dollars. There were ten bundles in total, which added up to fifty thousand dollars. That was enough for a new identity and the rent on an apartment, even a car. It was enough to give her and her baby a brand new start. Common sense kicked in with her next thought. How was she going to get fifty thousand dollars through airport security?

The stairs creaked and she froze, listening hard. She couldn't hear anything, but nor could she shake the feeling that Daniel was out there. She ran to the door. No one on the landing. No one on the stairs. She stood listening for a second. The house was as quiet as she had ever known it. No sounds upstairs; nothing downstairs. She hurried over to the safe and quickly stuffed the money back inside. Her hand brushed against a jewellery box hidden away in the back.

Her first thought was that Daniel had bought this for her birthday. It was only when she was able to see it properly that she realised how wrong she was. This wasn't a present for the future; it was one from the past. The last time she had seen this was back at the apartment she had shared with Lizzy. She opened the box. The necklace was exactly as she remembered it: the chain made from spun gold, and the diamond with a dozen rainbows imprisoned inside it. She closed the lid and put the box back in the safe. Yes, she could pawn it. The problem was that it was cursed. She didn't want it anywhere near her.

For a moment Zoe was convinced her passport wasn't there. She eventually found it buried beneath some documents at the right-hand side of the safe. She pushed it into the back pocket of her jeans, then locked the safe and hung the painting back on the wall. She paused at the door and scanned the room. It looked exactly the same as it had done when she came in.

The sound of quiet footsteps stopped her dead. They were coming from behind, getting closer. Her brain came grinding to a halt. She knew she should be sprinting for the stairs, but she was rooted to the spot. A part of her had always known it would end like this. It didn't matter what she did, Daniel would always be one step ahead. The footsteps stopped, and still she couldn't move. Silence crept around her, freezing her heart. Out of the silence came two bright words that echoed with the promises made on that rainy day in Seattle.

'Hi, Zoe.'

# PART II

# THE DEVIL IN THE DETAILS

*From my rotting body, flowers shall grow and I am in them and that is eternity.*

Edvard Munch

# Chapter 17

## THEN

'There's a parking space over there, Daniel.'

Josh was pointing to a spot between a BMW and a Lexus. It was tight, but doable. Daniel stamped on the brakes, came skidding to a halt level with the Beemer, found reverse, and backed the Porsche into the space. And got it first time.

'Admit it,' he said. 'You're impressed.'

'You think?'

'So where's this restaurant?'

Josh pointed again and Daniel followed his finger to a small glass-fronted property wedged between a tattoo studio and a clothes store. Giovanni's was written on the sign above the door. It was tricked out in the colours of the Italian flag: green, white and red. The lack of imagination was a serious concern. On first glance, Daniel had assumed this was a coffee house.

Josh must have read his mind because he started laughing. 'Yeah, I know it doesn't look much, but trust me, the food's amazing.'

'It better be.'

They got out and Daniel double-checked the car was locked before crossing the street. The waitress who greeted them at the door had bright red hair and multiple piercings. She was in her early twenties, and attractive, but she wasn't his type. Even before she opened her mouth it was obvious she had way too much attitude.

'Table for two,' Daniel said.

The red-haired girl shrugged like a teenager and nodded towards the dining area. 'Take your pick. As you can see we're rushed off our feet.'

The sarcasm aside, she had a point. There was only one table taken. A twenty-something woman and an older lady were part way through their main courses. This did not bode well. Empty tables equated to crap food. Daniel fired a dirty look at Josh, and he replied with a shrug that was almost as annoying as the waitress's. If he hadn't been starving, he would have suggested eating elsewhere.

'We'll have the corner table, please,' Josh said.

'Sure.'

The waitress picked up a couple of menus and led the way across the room. They got settled and ordered the wine. Daniel watched her walk away. It was a shame she had so much attitude. That was one hell of an ass. He turned back to Josh. 'This table-cloth is plastic.'

'It is. But can you smell that?'

Josh took an exaggerated sniff, and grinned. Daniel hated to admit it, but the food did smell good. The waitress came back with their wine and a basket of bread. She scribbled their orders onto her pad and walked away. Daniel took a sip of wine and watched her moving across the room. There was one other waitress working today, a brunette. She was hanging out by the kitchen counter, looking bored and waiting to be useful. The red-haired waitress leant in to her and they started whispering. There was an easy camaraderie between them, but it was clear who the alpha was.

The brunette glanced over. Her hair was tied back into a ponytail, and she was dressed in black pants and a white blouse. The clothes were unflattering but she wore them well. It was obvious there was a great body hidden beneath them. She looked fresh and vital and alive. She also looked as though she was happy to hide in the shadow of her friend, and that offered a whole host of possibilities. Alphas might promise a good time, but ultimately they ended up being high-maintenance bitches. Betas tried harder.

Josh was talking about his latest project, but Daniel was only half listening. He kept glancing over at the brunette. She was still talking with her friend. Until someone put their hand up, there wasn't a lot else for them to do. Josh stopped talking and followed his gaze.

'I know what you're thinking,' he said.

'And you're not? She's brunette and cute. Just your type.'

'Maybe so, but I'm married, remember?'

'Since when has that stopped you?'

'I'm not going to dignify that with a response.'

'So, are you still seeing Charlene or Crystal or whatever her name was?'

'It's Carmine, and it's none of your business.'

Daniel laughed. 'And how is the lovely Pamela?'

'Still spending all my money, and still screwing her personal trainer and thinking I don't know. At some point it'll be cheaper to divorce her, but until that day comes I guess I'm stuck with her. One day,' he added wistfully.

Josh stated this like it was one of those things, which was just as well since he wasn't getting any sympathy. He had hooked up with Pamela a couple of years ago. She had seen him as her meal ticket, and played him good. Two months after they met, she was pregnant; one month after their whirlwind wedding she miscarried. Daniel doubted she was ever pregnant; Josh maintained she had been. He had to say that, though, otherwise he ended up looking a fool.

The food arrived, only it was the brunette who brought it over, which got Daniel wondering. He glanced over at the counter. The red-haired waitress was trying to act casual, but she was definitely watching them. Up close, the brunette was even more attractive than he'd first thought. She was one of those girls who didn't have a clue how beautiful they were, something that made her all the more attractive. If she had known, there was no way that she would have worn her hair like that. It was flat and lifeless; the style was completely wrong for her.

'Spaghetti carbonara?' she asked.

Josh raised his hand and she put the plate down in front of him; the lasagne went down in front of Daniel. She asked if they wanted pepper or parmesan, and both of them declined. She told them to enjoy their meals, then smiled a smile that made her whole face light up and headed back to the counter where her red-haired friend was waiting and watching.

'Man, you've got it bad.'

Daniel tore his eyes away and looked at Josh. 'And you're talking crap. This is business as usual, my friend. Nothing more, nothing less.'

Josh grinned. 'Yeah, if you say so.'

Josh left first to give him some alone time with the brunette. The sacrifices we make for our buddies, Daniel thought. Under different circumstances, it could easily have been Josh sitting here. The fact that she had managed to turn both of their heads without really trying made her all the more desirable in his book. Having a woman on your arm that made other men envious had always given him a buzz. He swirled the wine around his glass while he considered his next move. The initial approach in any deal was crucial. Make a good impression and you at least stood a chance of closing it; make a bad one and you would be fighting a losing battle.

On this occasion he was pretty sure he had made a good first impression. The next stage was the sell. He swirled the wine one last time, then finished it in a single gulp and waved for the bill. The brunette brought it over and Daniel handed her his card. The easiest way to get someone on your side was by faking an interest in them, so he started by asking her what she did when she wasn't waiting tables. He listened carefully to her responses and used these to inform his questions. They were just getting into a decent rhythm when she suddenly slammed the brakes on the conversation.

'It's been good talking to you,' she said. 'Maybe we'll see you in here again.'

'Maybe you will,' Daniel replied. This wasn't going how he had planned. He held out his hand because he couldn't think what else to do. She hesitated, then shook it and her touch was electric.

'Would you like to go out for dinner sometime?' he asked, figuring what the hell.

'Sure.'

And that was that.

Deal closed.

Their first date was a disaster. He had taken her to Carmichael's, and from the way she reacted it was like he had asked her to kill a baby. At her suggestion they ended up in a coffee house that was kitted out like a dope den. It wasn't Daniel's idea of a good time, but it seemed to work for her. They went back to the same coffee shop for their second date. Her idea, not his. There was lots of talk, and lots of sharing, and afterwards they went back to her place. They were just getting comfortable on the sofa when her red-haired friend burst in and everything turned to shit. Seemingly, the building superintendent had been wandering around their apartment uninvited.

Daniel had found the superintendent down in his basement apartment. The guy really was a sad sack. Mid-fifties, balding, short. It was clear why the girls had nicknamed him Popeye: he had to tilt his head to the side to make eye contact. Daniel explained why he was there, and the way the guy's face blanched was as good as any confession. He told him that if he had to come back he would be bringing a hammer. And he would break his fingers. All of them. One at a time. Back upstairs, he made his excuses and headed home. There was no way he was getting laid tonight. Not after that.

For their third date they went to an upscale burger joint. It was down on the waterfront, one of those trendy places that disappeared as suddenly as they appeared. Again, this was Zoe's choice. After dinner they caught a cab. The driver asked where they wanted to go and Daniel gave Zoe a hopeful look. She answered with a nod and a smile, and he was quick to give his address before she changed her mind. The sex was mind-blowing. It was four in the morning before they finally drifted off to sleep, exhausted, satiated and sore. They awoke three hours later, and started all over again.

Josh was hard at work when he got to the office. He knocked on his door and went in.

'You're late,' Josh said. 'What happened? Did you sleep in?' He gave Daniel a hard, inquisitor's stare, then shook his head. 'There wasn't much sleeping going on, was there?'

'I don't know what you mean,' Daniel replied with a grin.

'So who was the lucky girl? Anyone I know?'

'Do you remember that waitress at that crappy restaurant you took me to last week?'

'The brunette?'

'That's the one.'

Josh said nothing. He was still staring like an inquisitor from the other side of the desk.

'What?' Daniel asked.

'I'm just waiting, that's all.'

'Waiting for what?'

'For all the gory details. Usually this is the point where you feel the need to overshare.'

Daniel said nothing.

'Okay, so no oversharing, then.' Josh laughed. 'So when are you guys getting married? Because from where I'm sitting, that's where this one's headed.'

It was Daniel's turn to laugh. 'And end up like you? Read my lips, Josh: not going to happen. Like I told you back at that God-awful restaurant, this is business as usual.'

# Chapter 18

## NOW

'Could Daniel Barton please come forward?'

Even though Daniel had been expecting this, the announcement still came as a shock. It seemed too soon. Five hours had passed since he had left Zoe at Portland airport. An hour and half of that had been spent waiting in the departures lounge, then there was the two-and-a-half-hour journey, and an hour spent hanging around at LAX waiting for his connecting flight. Another thirty minutes and he would have been in the air, heading for Tucson. He had resigned himself to the idea that nothing was going to happen until he got there. If it was going to happen at all.

He pushed through the queue and walked towards the desk. The other passengers didn't know it yet, but they were going to be delayed. First so his case could be removed from the hold; then they would need to wait for a take-off slot to become available. LAX was one of the busiest airports in the world, so that second delay was likely to be longer.

The short walk gave him time to decide how to play this. Anyone in this situation would be worried. Guilty or innocent, it was only natural. Daniel went through the times he'd been in unnerving situations, looking for an appropriate frame of mind, and found one. When he was nine he got caught stealing a T-shirt from a store. He could clearly remember standing in the security office at the mall, scared out of his mind. It wasn't the thought of the police getting involved that worried him, it was how bad the beating from his father would be. In the end, the police weren't called, and his father never found out. His worries might have been unfounded, but the fear was real. That was the memory he used now.

The three women gathered around the desk could have been clones. Identical airline uniforms, identical blank-faced airline smiles. Two security guards were at the side of the desk, watching him. Both looked like ex-cops. They might have been dangerous once, but age had made them soft. Daniel stopped in front of the oldest one.

'I'm Daniel Barton.'

'We need you to come with us, sir.'

'Why? What's going on?'

'If you could please just follow us, sir.'

'Not until you tell me what's going on. I'm supposed to be flying to Tucson.'

The security guard stepped to the side and motioned for him to start walking. Daniel glanced at the airline women, looking for support, but just got more of those blank smiles. Anyone else, this was where they would comply, not unless they were a real hard-ass, and that wasn't the game he was playing today.

The guards led him away from the gate, and all he could do was follow like a little lost sheep. He was moving reluctantly on heavy legs. There was no acting involved. Not this time. He had a rough idea of how things should play out, but there were a dozen unforeseen factors that could come into play. The security guards took him to a small room well away from the airport's public areas and told him to wait. The walls were too white, the lights too bright. Four chairs surrounded the cheap table, two on either side. Five minutes later two LAPD detectives appeared. One male, one female. They sat down in the chairs opposite his and introduced themselves as Thompson and Harris. Their faces were grim.

'Can we see some ID, please?'

The question came from Thompson, the female detective. She was younger than Harris, but since she was taking the lead Daniel assumed she must be more senior. He took his passport from his laptop case and handed it over.

'Can someone please tell me what's going on?'

Thompson handed the passport back. 'There's been a fire at your house, Mr Barton. I'm afraid it's been totally destroyed. Firefighters found a body. There's no easy way to say this, but we believe it's your wife's. I'm sorry.'

Daniel nodded. This was the point where he had thought he would have to fake being dumbstruck. There was no faking going on, though. Out of everything that had just been said, only one word registered: fire. He looked at Thompson to make sure he had heard right. The detective wasn't saying anything, but that was a bad-news face if ever he saw one. The anger burning through him was sudden and red hot. Things were not supposed to go down like this. Not once had there been any mention of his house being burnt down. That was the sort of detail he would have remembered. No way would he have signed off on something like that.

What the hell was going on?

The foundations shifted again and he told himself to get his shit together. This was unfamiliar territory, and it wasn't comfortable. Daniel took a deep breath, squashed down the anger, and forced himself to focus. He had to deal with the here and now; everything else could wait. He was anticipating a deluge of questions, but that hadn't happened. Then he got it. These two were messengers. As far as they were concerned this was the Portland PD's problem.

'Can we get you anything, Mr Barton? Some water, perhaps?'

He shook his head. 'No. I'd just like to get home, please.' He realised what he had said and tried again. 'What I mean is that I want to get back to Portland.'

The detective waiting at Portland airport introduced himself as Tommy Wang. He was in his late thirties. Asian, black hair, dark brown eyes. He smiled easily, but he was a cop, and you could never trust a cop, no matter how friendly they might appear.

'When can I see my wife?' Daniel asked.

Wang shook his head. 'It's okay, you won't have to.'

Daniel gave him a puzzled look. 'Don't you need me to identify her?'

'We do, but that's not how this works. It's not like you see on the TV, Mr Barton. Everything's done using photographs these days. It's easier on the families that way. What's going to happen is that I'm going to take you to the station and a grief counsellor will walk you through the procedure. Afterwards, I'll need to ask a few questions.'

'Questions? I don't understand. This was an accident, right?'

'That's how it looks, but we're still not sure exactly what happened. The fire department is carrying out its own investigation. We'll know more once that's concluded.'

That second part left Daniel cold. He had to wonder what they might find. He had been assured that nothing would come back to haunt him. Then again, he had been assured of a lot of things.

'I realise this must be a huge shock,' Wang continued. 'I can't even begin to guess what you're going through.' He paused, then delivered a line that Daniel would hear a lot in the coming days. 'I'm sorry for your loss, Mr Barton.'

Daniel followed Wang to his car and they drove to police headquarters in silence. The building took up a whole block. It was made from concrete and glass and shaped like a bloated triangle. Wang parked the car and they took the elevator to a room on the eighth floor that had comfortable padded seats, bright lights and no personality. The walls were painted white and there was a rough brown work carpet on the floor. The bright green cheese plant supplied the only colour. There was a box of tissues on the table.

The woman who stepped forward to greet them introduced herself as Serena Robinson. She was in her mid-forties, black and tall, almost six feet. Given the touchy-feely nature of her job, Daniel had been expecting hippy clothes and bangles, but she was wearing a sober grey pant suit. They shook hands and she guided him to a seat. Wang made his excuses, then left.

Serena spent the next couple of minutes putting him at ease. Her voice was gentle and sympathetic. She must have done this a thousand times, yet there were no signs of boredom in her delivery. They had managed to retrieve some jewellery from the body. This was what they wanted to use for the actual identification. The implication was clear and hung uncomfortably between them: Zoe's body must have been in a pretty bad state, otherwise they'd be using pictures of that. This was just the first stage, Serena explained. In addition they would also be checking dental records, but that could take a few days.

'I'm going to pass you a clipboard,' she said. 'There's a photograph attached to it, face down. In your own time, I'd like you to turn it over. Take as much time as you need, Mr Barton. There's no hurry.'

'Okay.'

She passed the clipboard and Daniel rested it on his lap. What would constitute a normal reaction? Would you turn the picture over straightaway because you wanted to get this over and done with? Or would you hesitate because you didn't want to face the truth? Daniel decided that both reactions were appropriate. This was a situation where everyone's response would be unique.

Serena was sitting patiently. She gave the impression that she could wait all day.

Daniel did a slow count to twenty then turned the photograph over. There was a watch and two rings in the picture. All three items were blackened and heat damaged. He remembered getting down on one knee and giving Zoe the engagement ring; he remembered sliding the wedding band onto her finger in Vegas and promising that they would be together forever; the Rolex had been a birthday gift.

When Daniel was six he found a stray dog roaming the streets and persuaded his mom to let him keep it. She wasn't keen to start with, but she'd had a dog when she was growing up, so it hadn't taken much to wear her down. He named the dog Galahad. For the whole summer they were inseparable. Shortly after the new semester started his father ran Galahad down on the driveway. He claimed it was an accident, but Daniel didn't believe him. He cried when he heard what had happened, and his father had hit him until he stopped. Daniel hadn't been allowed to bury Galahad in the yard. Instead, his father had made him toss the dog's corpse in the trash. Daniel could still remember how devastated he'd been when the garbage truck pulled away from the house. He had cried for the rest of that day, right up until his father got home from work. On those rare occasions when he needed tears, this was his go-to memory.

It never failed.

Serena left after making sure he was going to be okay, and a couple of minutes later Wang came in carrying two cardboard cups.

It was just about long enough for Serena to have filled him in. Wang handed him a cup.

'I thought you might like a coffee.'

'Thanks.'

The detective dug into his suit pocket and brought out some milk pots, sugar sachets and a plastic stirring stick. He held them up and nodded a question.

'Just sugar, please.'

Wang passed the sugar sachets and the stick; he dropped the milk pots in the waste basket. Daniel stirred one of the sugars into his cup and took a sip. The coffee tasted like crap.

'Are you okay to answer some questions?' Wang asked.

'I think so.'

Daniel kept his answers short. All the same, he was careful to make sure he didn't come across as evasive. The type of questions Wang was asking, it sounded as though he was just going through the motions. Daniel didn't get the sense he was under suspicion. After ten minutes he'd had enough.

'I'm finding this really difficult,' he said.

'That's okay. I'm pretty much done here.' Wang folded his notepad closed. 'Have you got anywhere to stay tonight?'

The question caught Daniel by surprise. Originally, he had been planning on staying at the house. Obviously that was no longer an option. 'I guess I'll book into a hotel.'

Wang shook his head. 'You really shouldn't be on your own, Mr Barton. Do you have any relatives in the city you can stay with?'

Daniel shook his head.

'A friend, perhaps?'

'Josh Wilson. He's my business partner. I can stay at his place.'

'Do you want me to call him?'

'No, I'll call. It would be better if he heard about Zoe from me.'

Josh picked him up in his Tesla and they drove in silence. They detoured via Fairfield Boulevard so Daniel could assess the damage to the house. It was only a fifteen-minute drive, but it was a long fifteen minutes. Josh was in shock. He was doing his best to process this, but he was struggling. Death happened when you were old; it didn't happen when you were in your twenties. Daniel was in shock too, but his shock was tempered with the disbelief that came from the knowledge that this was not how things were supposed to have played out.

The next left took them onto Fairfield Boulevard. Daniel could clearly remember driving along here to meet the realtor. Even before he got out of the car, he knew he was going to buy the property. He had been brought up in a tiny row house in one of Prophetstown's poorest neighbourhoods. This wasn't the mansion he had dreamt of, but it was a definite step in the right direction.

The house was unrecognisable. You could make out the rough shape, but it was as though a giant hand had smashed down on top of it. The roof had completely gone and there wasn't a single window left intact. The wood cladding was black and ruined. All his belongings would have been destroyed in the blaze, all his clothes. This house had been proof of everything he had achieved, and now it was gone. Looking at it brought on a fresh wave of anger. What the hell had that dumb bastard been thinking?

They got out, and the first thing Josh did was light a cigarette. His hand was shaking, the flame jerking and jumping. He put the lighter away, took a long drag, and together, they walked slowly up the driveway. Zoe's Mercedes was pretty much undamaged, but the Porsche was a write off. A section of the wall had fallen on top of the hood, scorching and bending the metalwork. Both front tyres had melted. Josh stopped alongside him and looked at the wrecked Porsche.

'This is messed up,' he said. 'Totally and utterly messed up.'

There was no response to that, because Josh was right. This was totally screwed up. Daniel walked to the front of the house. The smell turned his stomach. Burnt wood, melted plastic, old smoke. He thought he could smell charred meat, but maybe that was his imagination. The front door was unlocked. He pushed it open and stepped into the hallway. The walls were blacker in here, the stench of the blaze overpowering. The stairs had been destroyed, along with most of the landing, which caused him yet another headache. The safe was fireproof, so the money would be okay, but it was up on the second floor. How was he supposed to get to it?

The key for the Mercedes was hanging on the hook board next to the front door. The plastic had melted and the electronics were probably shot to hell, but Daniel was betting the metal part of the key still worked. Josh was hovering in the doorway.

'How safe do you think it is?' he asked.

'Not very.'

'Maybe you should get out.'

'Yeah, you're probably right.' Daniel didn't move. He was staring, transfixed, at the devastation.

Josh took a long shaky drag on his cigarette. 'Did they tell you where they found Zoe's body?' he asked uncertainly

Daniel shook his head. 'They didn't say.'

Another hesitation. 'Do you think she suffered?'

'She burned to death. Of course she suffered.' Daniel glared at Josh, annoyed at his stupidity, annoyed by his questions. Annoyed by him, period. Mostly he was annoyed at himself, though. This was affecting him more than he had imagined it would. His emotions were getting the better of him and that wasn't good. He sighed. 'I'm sorry, buddy. This is hard.'

'For you and me both.' Josh took another drag on his cigarette, and then he started to weep.

Daniel punched the gas pedal three times and reversed the Mercedes off the driveway. He didn't look back as he drove away. The sight of the ruined house broke his heart.

Josh's apartment was in downtown. He had bought it during the early days of his marriage. Back then he was still going out of his way to impress Pamela, and it was definitely more her taste than his. They parked side by side in the underground lot, then headed up to the tenth floor.

The apartment wasn't anywhere near as clinical and cold as it had been when Pamela lived here. The walls were still white, and there was still too much glass and steel, but Josh was finally putting his stamp on the place. Framed music posters had replaced the modern art. Bob Marley, Nirvana, Radiohead. They looked tacky and cheap and reminded him of those stupid movie posters Zoe had hung in her study. The large red leather La-Z-Boy recliner in front of the TV was brand new, and just as tasteless. It would have been a cold day in hell before Pamela signed off on that one. The window gave a good view of the Willamette flowing northwards to the Columbia River. Darkness had fallen and the water looked like obsidian.

Josh poured two straight bourbons, three inches in each. He handed a tumbler to Daniel, then took a drink and contemplated his glass. His sigh started in his heart. He looked as though he might start crying again.

'I can't believe she's gone. What the hell is going on?'

Daniel shrugged. He had been asking himself the same question.

'And to lose your house as well. That's just messed up.'

'Don't worry. I'll book into a hotel tomorrow.'

Josh looked suddenly mortified. 'That wasn't what I was getting at. You can stay here as long as you want. It'll be just like the old days.'

Daniel smiled and nodded because that was the appropriate response. It was clear how hard Josh was trying, how much he was hurting. It wouldn't be like the old days, though. Too much water had flowed under the bridge since then. Way too much.

It seemed like a lifetime ago since they first met. Daniel's first college lecture had been a marketing one. He had gotten there early, keen to impress and eager to learn. Josh had appeared just before the lecture started and crashed into the empty seat next to his. He looked as though he'd been partying hard. Afterwards they got talking. It turned out that Josh's degree was in computer science. Basically, he'd taken a wrong turn and ended up in the wrong lecture theatre. The only reason he stayed was because he'd seen a girl he liked.

Even though they were complete opposites, they'd hit it off. And they worked well together. Daniel was logical, Josh creative; they each brought something unique to the table. It really was a case of the whole being bigger than the sum of its parts. Josh was a hard guy to dislike. He had one of those faces you just had to trust. It was almost impossible to believe that he would ever screw you over.

Their first business venture together was selling weed. Back at college, Josh had loved getting stoned; Daniel didn't. He hated the way it left him feeling foggy headed and stupid, but he could appreciate a sound business opportunity when he saw one. College campuses were made up of people just looking to have a good time, and if you could provide that good time, then you were going to make money. Josh had the contacts; Daniel had the marketing know-how. Their business partnership was formed with a handshake and an agreement to split everything fifty–fifty. It was an agreement that still stood to this day.

Daniel glanced over. Josh was holding his tumbler in both hands, the edge resting on his lower lip. He was staring out of the window and looking utterly devastated, like his whole world had come crashing down. The thing that struck Daniel most was the fact that this was exactly how he himself should look.

# Chapter 19

## THEN

Daniel walked into the foyer and shook the rain from his coat. This building had definitely seen better days. The stonework was filthy, the floor tiles were worn, and the buzzer panel looked like it had never worked. There were businesses based on all four floors. According to the jumble of mismatched plaques fixed to the wall these included a couple of accountancy firms, and a law practice that clearly dealt with the less lucrative end of the law.

Chuck Mayweather Associates was on the second floor. Daniel knocked and waited. He had to knock a second time before Mayweather answered. The private investigator was in his early fifties, balding, skinny and anonymously bland. He looked more like an accountant than a PI. It was a look that worked for him. If he was following you, you'd never know.

'We have an appointment,' Daniel said.

'We do indeed, Mr Barton. Come on in.'

Mayweather sounded more like a lawyer than an ex-cop. His was a voice that would carry through a courtroom and inspire the confidence of a jury. Not that Daniel needed his confidence inspired. It was Mayweather who had found Zoe when she ran away to Seattle. The PI stood to one side and waved Daniel into the reception area. There was a computer and telephone on the desk, but no sign of a receptionist. There had been no receptionist last time either. Chuck Mayweather Associates was very much a one-man show.

Mayweather led the way to his office. Nothing had changed. It was neat and tidy, and the desk was identical to the one in reception, like he'd gotten a discount for buying two. The computer was a laptop, and the tall filing cabinet next to the window had a plant on top that had died months ago. There was a basset hound in the basket next to the desk. The dog looked up at Daniel with sad eyes, then turned around, flopped back down and got settled again. Mayweather waved Daniel towards the seat in front of the desk.

'Can I get you a coffee?'

'Not for me, thanks.' He nodded towards the dog. 'I'm guessing that's your associate.'

'The best associate there is. Oreo never makes a fuss. Nor is he ever going to want a share of the profits. So long as I keep him in kibble he's happy.'

Mayweather's seat huffed out a puff of air as he sat down. He studied Daniel across the desk. 'So how can I help this time?'

'I think my wife is having an affair with my business partner.'

'And this is based on what, exactly?'

Daniel took the cigarette lighter from his pocket and placed it carefully on the desk. It was cheap, plastic and pink. Mayweather glanced at it, then looked back at Daniel. His eyes were wide, eyebrows slightly raised. He didn't say anything, just waited for an explanation.

'I found this in my house a couple of days ago. It was beneath the table by the front door.'

Mayweather leant across the desk and picked up the lighter. He spent a while examining it, turning it this way and that, then flicked up a flame. He stared into the fire for a second, then put the lighter back down.

'How do you know this belongs to your business partner?'

'He's always losing his lighters, so he uses cheap disposable ones. Like this.'

'Are you sure that this is his?'

Daniel nodded. 'I've seen him using it and made a joke about it being pink.'

'Maybe it belongs to your wife. There must be millions of lighters like this one in circulation.'

'She doesn't smoke. It's Josh's. I'm certain of it. I was away on a business trip a couple of weeks ago. I'm figuring that must have been when he lost it.' He paused. 'You know, things actually seem to be okay between me and Zoe at the moment. It's like she's trying harder than usual to please me.'

'Maybe the reason he came by the house was completely innocent.'

Daniel shook his head. 'One, Josh isn't in the habit of just dropping by out of the blue. Two, if the reason had been innocent, he would have said something to me. Three, he knew I was away, so he must have gone there to see Zoe.'

'You're building this whole thing on an assumption that might prove false.'

'Which is where you come in. I want proof. Solid, hard proof.'

'You said that things are going okay between the two of you at the moment. And we know that things weren't going so okay a couple of years ago, otherwise she wouldn't have run off to Seattle. But what about between those two points?'

'It's a marriage. You get good times and bad.'

'Yes, you do. Any more meaningless platitudes you wish to share?'

Daniel had a sudden urge to slap the smug expression off of Mayweather's face. 'Look, what do you want me to say?'

Mayweather leant back in his seat and put his hands up in surrender. 'All I'm trying to do is establish the state of your marriage. In my experience people in happy marriages do not have affairs.' He paused. 'Okay, let me ask you a hypothetical. Let's say I discover that your wife is having an affair, what are you going to do with that information?'

Daniel didn't respond, and Mayweather nodded. 'See, that's what I'm talking about. People spend so much time focussing on whether or not their spouse is having an affair, they forget to consider the impact that the truth will have on their lives. My mother, God rest her soul, used to have this saying. What's done can't be undone. Once you know the truth, you can't *unknow* it.'

'You want to know if I can *handle the truth*. Is that it?'

Mayweather smiled. 'Something like that.'

'Look, all I want is confirmation that they're having an affair. Is that something you can help with, or am I wasting my time here?'

Mayweather nodded. 'Yes, that's something I can help with. If she is having an affair, I will find out.' He paused and waited for Daniel to meet his eye. 'The question is, do you want to know? Sometimes ignorance is bliss, Mr Barton.'

'Only if you're an idiot.'

Mayweather smiled again, then took a spiral-bound notepad from his desk drawer. He opened it to a clean page and found a pen. 'Okay, let's get started.'

Two weeks later Daniel was back in Mayweather's office. The PI took a brown manila envelope from his desk drawer and handed it over. Daniel didn't open it straightaway because that would make everything real. He wanted to know; he *needed* to know. At the same time, he didn't want to know. Mayweather wasn't saying anything. He'd been here before. Daniel was betting he had seen all sorts of reactions in this situation. Tears and fury and everything in between. Oreo looked up momentarily, then settled back down to sleep. Daniel took a deep breath and opened the envelope. Inside was a printout of a bank statement. One of the transactions had been circled in red, a payment to the Holly Tree Inn.

'That's Mr Wilson's bank statement,' Mayweather said. 'The Holly Tree is a motel in Beaverton.'

Mayweather might have said something else, but if he did Daniel didn't hear. Up until this point, he'd been holding on to the slim hope that there might be another explanation as to why that cigarette lighter had ended up in his house. Beaverton was only a fifteen-minute drive from the centre of Portland. Why had Josh needed to book a motel room so close to home? Daniel glanced at Mayweather for confirmation that he was reading the situation correctly. Anyone except Josh, he thought, but the evidence was right there in his hand, and in the sorry-for-your-loss expression on the PI's face.

'The receptionist recognised a photograph of your wife,' Mayweather said, and that was the final nail in the coffin.

For the longest time Daniel didn't say anything. He couldn't speak; he could barely breathe. The anger was all-consuming. Josh's betrayal killed him. After everything they had been through together, everything he had done for him, how could he? Daniel was holding the printout tight enough to crumple it. He wanted to destroy, and to keep destroying until the whole world was cinders and ash. He took a deep breath, then relaxed his grip on the printout, smoothed it out and placed it gently on the desk. Mayweather was watching from the other side of the desk. Daniel looked up and met his eye.

'Tell me everything.'

The Holly Tree Inn was just off Highway 217. The main building had two floors and looked like an oversized rustic cabin. The walls were faced in stone and the metal roof was painted brown to look like wood. The trees and bushes created the illusion of a forest glade. The woman at reception was called Trina. She was in her early twenties, pretty but plain. Daniel recognised her name from the conversation he'd had with Mayweather. According to the PI, Josh and Zoe had used room 106; according to Trina, the room was currently vacant. Daniel paid in cash, and Trina gave him the key.

The walk to the room dispelled any illusion that he was at a secluded forest lodge. The hum of traffic from the nearby highway was constant, and the skyline was dominated by Portland's skyscrapers. He unlocked the door and went inside. Everything was either beige or brown. Bedding, drapes, walls, carpets. Daniel switched the light on and closed the drapes. The bulb was a low-wattage one, and the dim light struggled to penetrate the shadows. It shouldn't have been possible to make this place any more depressing than it already was, but somehow he'd just managed it. He walked over to the bed and pressed his hand on the mattress. This was where they had done it.

Daniel rearranged the pillows then lay down. With his eyes shut he could imagine Zoe and Josh in here, screwing each other's brains out. He'd made love with Zoe often enough to know the sort of noises she must have made. All he had to do was substitute his name for Josh's and he had the perfect soundtrack to the porn movie playing inside his head.

He lay there for a long time, those images repeating over and over and driving him insane. He lay there until they finally began to fade and he could think a little straighter again. Mayweather had asked him what he would do if he confirmed the affair. By the time Daniel walked out of that motel room, he knew exactly what he had to do. Sure, he could divorce Zoe and wind up his business partnership with Josh, but both those actions would leave him out of pocket, and neither one of those traitors was getting so much as a single cent from him. No, there was only one way to deal with a betrayal of this magnitude, and that was permanently. At the end of the day Zoe belonged to him. If he couldn't have her, then no one was going to have her. It really was that simple.

Two nights later the three of them went to Carmichael's for Josh's birthday. The dynamic was weird, and it wasn't just because he knew that Josh was screwing Zoe. This was the first time the three of them had been out for a meal since Josh's marriage ended. Daniel and Zoe were just getting settled at their usual table when he turned up. The hug Zoe and Josh shared was completely innocent. The kiss was just a quick peck on the cheek, lips barely grazing skin.

'We've got something for you,' Zoe said.

She handed Josh a present that was wrapped in silver paper and tied neatly with a red bow.

'Guys, you shouldn't have.'

He tore the wrapping away to reveal a plain white box. There were no markings to indicate what might have been inside, or who had made it, or even which store it was from. He removed the lid, rustled through the tissue paper and lifted out a Hawaiian shirt that was heavy on the reds and oranges. Daniel was looking for subtext in the gift, but couldn't find any. There was nothing particularly special about it; no hidden messages were being swapped here. As gifts went it was quirky, and that made it the sort of thing Josh would get a kick out of. He might wear it once, if at all; within no time it would be forgotten about and consigned to the back of his closet.

'Happy birthday,' Zoe said.

'Yeah, happy birthday, buddy,' Daniel added.

Josh smiled. 'Another year older, another year wiser.'

'And another year closer to the grave.'

'You're such a goddam pessimist, Daniel. Anyone ever tell you that?' Josh laughed and held the shirt up. 'Thanks for this, guys. I love it.'

The meal was an exercise in multitasking. Daniel had to work hard to make it look as though he didn't know; at the same time he was studying Zoe and Josh carefully, just waiting for one of them to slip up. By the time the main course was finished, he was seeing them both in a brand new light. The way they were acting, he could almost have believed he had imagined the whole thing.

While they were waiting for the coffees and brandies to arrive, Daniel excused himself to use the restroom. He didn't go straight back to the table afterwards. Instead, he hovered in the shadows, watching. There was still nothing in the way they were behaving that made him suspicious. He could understand Zoe being so careful, but he was surprised at Josh.

He was just about to rejoin them when Josh made a mistake. As he was putting his wine glass down he reached out and touched the back of Zoe's hand. It was a gesture that could never be mistaken for friendship. Zoe hissed something and his hand jerked back. He bumped his glass and just managed to catch hold of it at the last second. There was fear on Zoe's face.

Daniel give them a minute to get back into character before making his way over. The coffees and brandies arrived and Josh started telling a joke. Even though Daniel didn't feel much like laughing, he managed to conjure up a smile. Zoe and Josh weren't the only ones who knew how to act.

# Chapter 20

## NOW

The next morning they took separate cars to the office. Josh was in his Tesla and Daniel was behind the wheel of Zoe's Mercedes. Five minutes after leaving downtown they were pulling into their respective parking slots. The office building they leased was on Barbur Boulevard, not far from the Willamette. It was two storeys high and faced with silver and glass. MYRIADIAN SOLUTIONS was written in large black letters above the door. Josh had wanted to shut the office down for the day; Daniel had argued to keep it open. The last thing he wanted was to be stuck with Josh moping around like a heartbroken schoolgirl.

They climbed the stairs to the second floor. Their offices were to the right; the door on the left led to the bullpen where everyone else worked. Instead of turning right, Daniel turned left. Josh gave him a puzzled look.

'People need to know what's going on.'

'Yeah, I guess. But is this a good idea?'

'Are you going to do it?'

Josh's face turned white. The fact that he hated public speaking was no big secret.

'That's what I thought.'

Everyone stopped what they were doing when they entered. Phone calls were quickly wrapped up, and chairs turned in their direction. The expressions ranged from devastated to expectant. The only person who wasn't there was Catherine, their PA. She would be at her desk at the other side of the building. Daniel cleared his throat.

'For those of you who haven't already heard, my wife Zoe died yesterday.' He paused as though he was uncertain what to say next. In his mind's eye he saw the garbage truck carrying Galahad away. Tears pricked the corners of his eyes and he wiped them away. 'I'm sorry, I just wanted you to know, that's all.'

He walked away quickly, leaving a stunned silence in his wake. Josh caught up with him by the stairs.

'You don't have to be Superman, Daniel. If you go to pieces, nobody's going to think any less of you.'

'You think I'm not going to pieces. I'm falling apart at the seams here. It's like up and down have swapped places and I'm about to face-plant on the sidewalk.'

'Well take today off.'

'And do what?'

Josh had no answer for that. Not that Daniel expected one. Your wife died suddenly, what were you going to do? Pack up the car and head to the coast for a vacation? Hit the clubs and party? This was one of those life events where there were no guidelines. It was unique and unprecedented, and the expectation was that you muddled through as best you could. Because that was what he was doing here. Making it look as though he was muddling through. Things might be turning to shit, but he still needed to keep up appearances. If anything, he needed to do that more than ever.

'We've already talked about this, Josh. Right now, it's best if I keep busy. Chances are I won't get any work done today, but that doesn't matter. Anything's got to be better than hanging around your apartment, staring at the walls.'

Josh reached out and gave his arm a friendly pat. He was looking guilty. And so he should. This was his fault. If he had kept his dick in his pants they wouldn't be here now. Fact.

'Anything you need, anything at all, just let me know.'

'Thanks, buddy. I appreciate it.'

Catherine burst into tears when she saw them. It took almost a minute before she had pulled herself together enough to speak.

'I am so sorry for your loss, Mr Barton. If there's anything I can do.'

'Thank you, Catherine.'

'I've already cancelled your meetings. I hope that's okay.'

He nodded. 'Can you hold my calls as well?'

'Of course.'

As Daniel walked into his office he could hear Catherine bringing Josh up to speed. He closed the door and sat down. The blinds were open and the desk glowed where the sunlight touched it. The burner phone was pushed right down at the bottom of his pants pocket. He dug it out and went to the log. There was only one number. He hit the button to connect the call. Seven rings, then the line went dead.

♦

Daniel spent the next three hours catching up on paperwork. It was boring and mindless and required minimal thought, but at least it meant he wasn't completely obsessing over the Zoe situation. He was playing for time here. The further they moved away from yesterday's events, the less chance there was of something coming back to bite him on the ass.

Just before lunch there was a commotion outside the office. Daniel stopped what he was doing and tuned in to what was happening on the other side of the door. Catherine's voice was raised, and that never happened. He recognised the voice of the person she was arguing with, but couldn't quite place it. The arguing stopped and the door burst open.

Three years had passed since he last saw Lizzy, but she hadn't changed. She still dressed entirely in black; she still had piercings and tattoos; and she still wore her attitude like a suit of armour. The only difference was her hair. It used to be dyed bright red, now it was cut into a sleek, raven-black bob. Catherine appeared in the doorway, full of apologies for letting Lizzy through.

'It's okay, Catherine, I've got this. Close the door on your way out, please.'

She looked at him for a second longer, then backed out of the office, closing the door behind her. Daniel kept his mouth shut and waited for Lizzy to make the first move. As far as he was aware, Zoe had broken off contact with her when they got married. Clearly that wasn't the case.

Lizzy stalked over. She placed her hands on the desk and glared down at him. 'What did you do, Dan?'

'I'm sorry, I don't understand.'

'To Zoe. What did you do to Zoe, Dan? It's a simple question. Zoe's dead and I know that you had something to do with it. So I'm asking again: what did you do?'

'Excuse me?'

'Don't play dumb. You know exactly what I'm talking about, *Dan*.'

Lizzy looked furious, like she was just looking for an excuse to rip him to shreds. Daniel figured that righteous indignation would be the appropriate response. That's how an innocent person would act when confronted with something like this. He got up and leant across the desk. Standing, he was three inches taller. 'How dare you come in here and accuse me like this? If you think I had anything to do with Zoe's death, you're crazy. I *loved* her.'

Lizzy's laugh was dry and brittle and filled with scorn. 'Yeah, loved her to death.'

'I'd like you to leave now.'

'I bet you would, *Dan*. Does it make you nervous, me appearing out of the blue like this? Are you worried that I'm going to tear down whatever alibi you're building? So what role are you playing this time? The grieving, heartbroken widower would be my guess. Because that's what you do, isn't it, Dan? You only let people see what you want them to see.'

'If you don't leave, I'm calling the police.'

'Good. That's where I'm heading next, so it'll save me a cab fare.' She leant across the table and lowered her voice. 'You really want to hit me right now, don't you? That would teach me a lesson, right? That would put me back in my place. So where would you start? The body, right? I mean you wouldn't want to leave any marks on my face.'

Daniel realised he was gripping the desk and forced himself to relax. She wasn't just trying to needle him, she was succeeding. The anger burning through him was white hot and vicious and demanding a way out. But if he lost it now, he lost everything. 'You don't know anything about my relationship with Zoe,' he said calmly. 'Nothing at all.'

'I know she was terrified of you, and that's all I need to know.' She paused, eyes blazing. 'I'm going to keep coming at you until the truth comes out, Dan. That's a promise.'

Lizzy stormed from the office, slamming the door behind her. A second later, Catherine knocked and entered.

'I am so sorry, Mr Barton. I couldn't stop her.'

'It's okay.'

'Is there anything I can do? Anything I can get you?'

'No, I'll be fine.'

Catherine gave him the sorry eyes again, then left. Daniel walked over to the window in time to see Lizzy climbing into the back of a cab. He was already thinking about damage limitation. Discretion was Catherine's middle name, so she wouldn't say anything; Josh had gone out to get some lunch, so he wouldn't have overheard them arguing; and the rest of the staff was in the main office, out of earshot. To all intents and purposes, this confrontation never happened.

But it had happened, and now he had a major problem. What was Lizzy going to tell the police? Based on what she'd said, she knew things about his marriage that would be best kept quiet. At the moment, the police had no reason to suspect him, but that could all be about to change. Once they got hold of a potential motive, they kept hold. He needed to find out exactly what she knew, and what she thought she knew. But how?

Then there was the question of whether Zoe had talked to Josh about her marriage. He was certain she hadn't. Josh was totally transparent. He was one of those people where what you saw was what you got. If Zoe had said anything there was no way he'd be able to keep that to himself. Then again, he'd managed to do a good job of hiding the affair, so maybe he wasn't totally transparent.

He spent the next five minutes going through his options. The only thing he knew for sure was that a knee-jerk reaction would be a mistake. He took Detective Wang's business card from his pocket and tapped it against the windowsill. He could call Wang and tell him about Lizzy's visit. It wouldn't take much to paint her as a crazy woman with a vendetta. The motivation was there. She blamed him for the fall out with Zoe; she had never liked him; she wanted to use Zoe's death to get revenge. The problem was that it would be too easy for him to end up looking like the crazy one.

The best course of action was to do nothing, but that didn't sit well because he preferred to instigate events rather than react to them. He thought he had everything under control, but he didn't. Not really. The truth was that this situation had been spiralling out of control ever since the detective at LAX had told him that his house had burnt down.

Daniel sat down at his desk and drank some coffee. It was stone cold and he ended up spitting it back into the mug. The screensaver had kicked in. A quick tap of the trackpad brought up Outlook Express. There were three new emails, all with Zoe's

name in the subject line. These emails were the electronic equiv-
alent of sympathy cards, and as such they were the last thing he
needed to see right now. He glanced at the screen one last time
then hit delete.

It was late afternoon before Wang turned up. They shook hands
and got seated.

'How are you holding up?' Wang asked.

Daniel shook his head and sighed. 'I don't know how to
answer that. None of this seems real.'

Wang looked around the office, cataloguing what he was seeing. He seemed amiable enough, but it would be a mistake to
underestimate him. Daniel had to keep reminding himself they
wouldn't be doing this here if he'd been under suspicion.

'I'm surprised you came to work,' Wang said eventually.

'What else was I going to do? Stay home?'

The detective caught his smile before it got too far. 'I guess
not.'

'I thought that coming here would distract me.' Daniel shook
his head again. 'But how are you supposed to distract yourself
from something like this?'

There was nothing Wang could say to that. At least nothing
that wouldn't be better suited to a sympathy card.

'So what can I do for you?' Daniel asked.

'The fire department has concluded its initial investigation. It
would seem that the fire wasn't an accident. It was arson.'

Daniel's stunned expression was one hundred per cent genuine. The fact that this was arson wasn't a surprise; the fact that

the fire department had worked it out was. One thing he had been very clear about was that this had to look like an accident. Then again, there seemed to be a whole load of things he had insisted on that had been ignored. It was as though he'd signed off on a plan, only for it to be totally disregarded. The implications hit all at once, making him reel. If this was arson, then Zoe's death couldn't be an accident. It didn't matter what Lizzy said, or didn't say, this was now a murder investigation.

'Are they sure it's arson?'

Wang nodded. 'They found traces of gasoline. That's what the perpetrator used as an accelerant. The fire started in the living room. Once it got started, it quickly spread to the rest of the house.'

'If this was arson, that means Zoe was murdered.'

Wang nodded again. 'That's correct.'

'Jesus, who'd want to kill her?'

'That was going to be my next question.'

Daniel shook his head. 'I can't think of anyone who would want her dead. She didn't have any enemies. Everyone liked her.' His face twisted into a pained expression. 'Did she suffer much?'

'It's possible she was already dead before the fire got to her. At least, I'm hoping that was the case. We'll know more after the autopsy.'

'What exactly are you doing to find the guy who did this?'

'Mr Barton, we're doing everything possible. You can rest assured of that.'

After Wang left, Daniel sat staring blankly out the window and wondered what the detective knew, and what he suspected.

His alibi was solid. He had been thirty thousand feet in the air when Zoe was murdered. There would be security camera footage showing him going through Portland airport, and there would be footage showing him disembarking at LAX. There would be an electronic record of him being on the flight, and there were more than a hundred witnesses on the plane who could attest to the fact that he had been the passenger in seat 17C. None of that would help if this turned into a charge of conspiracy to murder, though.

And why hadn't Wang mentioned Lizzy? Had she been bluffing about going to the police? If so, why? Bluffing made no sense. There was nothing to be gained. If she had gone to the police then the fact that Wang hadn't asked about the state of his marriage was worrying. The detective would want to verify Lizzy's story, and the obvious way to do that was by talking to him. So why hadn't he?

It was too soon to start panicking. That would qualify as a knee-jerk reaction. It wasn't too soon to start formulating a Plan B, though. Vancouver was only three hundred miles away. If things turned to shit, that was where he was headed. Canada was huge. A person could well and truly lose themselves up there.

Fairfield Boulevard was busier than he had ever seen it. In addition to all the police vehicles there were two news trucks. The bigger of the two had the NWCN logo all over it. Camera operators and sound guys were getting busy beside it, unspooling cables and setting up their equipment. A police truck with

FORENSICS UNIT written on the side was parked directly outside the house.

Daniel parked as close as he could and climbed out of the Mercedes. The route to the house took him past the news crews. His coat collar was up, his head down, and nobody paid him any attention. In the daylight, the house looked even worse. There was nothing worth saving. It needed to be razed to the ground and rebuilt. Crime scene tape fluttered in the breeze and there were cops everywhere. Two forensics investigators in white boiler suits were hovering near the front door. Daniel kept walking until he got stopped. The cop who stopped him was in his early twenties, a real eager beaver.

'Sorry, sir, you need to go back.'

Daniel nodded towards the burnt-out building. 'This is my house.'

'Even so, I still can't let you through.'

'Where's your superior officer? I'd like to talk to him.'

The cop tipped his head and said something into the radio attached to his jacket. Two minutes later a forty-something guy in a cheap suit appeared. He held his hand out and waited for Daniel to shake it.

'Sergeant Jim Scott. I'm sorry for your loss.'

'How bad is the damage?'

'Bad. The few things that weren't destroyed in the blaze are smoke damaged. Basically you're going to be starting from scratch, I'm afraid.'

'When will I be able to get access?'

'That'll depend on how long it takes us to investigate this.'

'Sorry, that came out wrong. I'm not trying to hurry you. Take as long as you need. Please. All that matters is that you find out who did this.'

'Don't worry, we'll find them.'

'Have you got any leads?'

'We've got a couple of things we're following up on.'

'Anything you can tell me at this stage?'

Scott shook his head. 'Not at this stage.'

Daniel wanted to push harder. It was natural for him to be curious; however this needed to be balanced against the fact that he was supposed to be grieving. What he really wanted to ask was what would happen when they found the safe? It wasn't illegal to have fifty thousand dollars lying around your house, but it would definitely raise questions. Not mentioning it brought its own problems. What would happen if they found the money and he hadn't said anything? It was a tough call. Daniel decided to keep quiet for the time being. He would phone Wang about it in the morning. That would also give him an opportunity to question the detective about how the investigation was going.

'Thanks for your time,' he said to Scott.

'No problem. I just wish I had some better news. Don't worry, though, Mr Barton, we will catch the guy who's responsible for this.'

Daniel walked away, hoping he was wrong.

His hotel room was on the eleventh floor. The drapes were open and he could see the city lights stretching into the distance. Josh had wanted him to stay at his place again, but he had pulled the need-to-be-alone card. The truth was that he didn't want to be anywhere near Josh. Zoe's death had hit Josh hard. Given the circumstances, it was hard to be sympathetic. It would be too easy to say or do the wrong thing.

Daniel had already drunk a quarter of a bottle of vodka, but he was feeling as sober as when he cracked the seal. Sometimes getting drunk was the only solution. Unfortunately those were the days where no matter how much you drank, it didn't have any effect. It felt as though he had turned his back for a split second and the whole world had gone crazy. He was used to being in control, used to calling the shots. Forty-eight hours ago he had been a man with a plan. What was more, he had truly believed it was a good one.

He drained his glass and went through to the bathroom to pee. As he was washing his hands, he caught his reflection. Only it wasn't his face staring out from the mirror, it was his father's. *You're never going to amount to anything, Dan. You realise that, don't you? You're just a waste of good air.* Before he could stop himself, he punched the mirror, fracturing the glass. He blinked and his own face was back, staring out from behind the spiderweb of cracks. His father's words still hung inside his head, though.

*You're just a waste of good air, Dan.*

That had been one of Daniel Barton Senior's favourite lines. And maybe he was a waste of air. Maybe the old bastard had been right all along. Daniel had built his world from nothing and it all seemed to be crumbling before his eyes, and what did he expect? People like him never amounted to anything. Thinking otherwise was just an exercise in self-delusion.

It was all Zoe's fault. Her and Josh. He was glad she was dead. Unfortunately he couldn't say the same for Josh. He should be dead too. Then again, wasn't that just another example of how the plan had imploded?

Daniel went back through to the other room, poured himself a large vodka, and sat down on the bed. His hand ached but there was no blood. The pain helped ground him again, so he welcomed it in. He took a long drink, then shut his eyes and imagined Zoe burning in the flames.

# Chapter 21

## THEN

Daniel's first stop was Mr Fix-IT, a computer repair store on Martin Luther King Boulevard. There were four shelves filled with used laptops displayed in the window. Because the specs were a couple of years out of date, these were being sold at a fraction of the price of the newer models. The fact they were a little slow wasn't a problem. All he needed was something quick enough to surf the net, and there were a dozen machines here fitting that bill.

In the end he went for a Dell and ended up paying twenty-five dollars less than the ticket price. He only haggled because this was the sort of store where that would be expected, and the only reason he bought a used model was because it was going to end up in a dumpster when he was done with it. A brand new laptop, someone might retrieve and sell on. This one just wasn't worth the hassle.

He drove straight past the first coffee house he saw. And the second. And the third. He had once read that the subconscious could influence the decisions people made. If that was true, how many bad guys had found themselves in prison thanks to that? However many it was, he had no intention of joining them.

The coffee house he ended up in was the sort of place he usually wouldn't be seen dead in. The owners were trying too hard to make the place look classy, but scratch away at the surface and the illusion became obvious. The seats were covered with vinyl that had been made to look like leather, and the tables had been artificially distressed to make them look like antiques. The only thing going for it was the free Wi-Fi.

He ordered a coffee and headed for a table tucked away at the back. The laptop screen was angled so no one could see what he was doing. It seemed to take forever for the computer to boot up. Back in college Josh had become obsessed with the darknet. The first time he mentioned it, Daniel thought he was making it up. The darknet was an alternative Internet that existed below the actual Internet, a dark basement where you could find all that bad stuff that needed to be hidden from sight. This was where you went to buy drugs; it was where paedophiles swapped photographs.

And it was where you went if you were looking for someone to kill your wife.

Daniel started by downloading the Tor browser. This looked and acted like a standard browser, with the added benefit that he was now invisible and could access the darknet. Josh had explained how it worked, something about bouncing around different servers to make it impossible to track the user, but Daniel hadn't really been listening. All that mattered was that the Feds wouldn't be breaking his door down any time soon.

The first few websites he tried looked totally bogus. One guy gave a menu of prices that ranged from ten thousand dollars to have your spouse taken out, to a hundred thousand dollars if your target was a top-level politician. Another site claimed to represent a consortium of mercenaries who were prepared to do anything and everything so long as the price was right.

An hour later, Daniel was on the verge of giving up when a site caught his eye. To start with this site wasn't trying too hard, which was why he hadn't noticed it earlier. In fact, it wasn't trying at all. There were no photographs, no eye-catching graphics, no logos or catchy site names. There was just plain text, and an encryption key that needed to be used in any communication. It was the simplicity of the site that appealed. If Daniel had been a contract killer, this was how he would have advertised himself.

He typed a short message, but that was as far as he got. The cursor arrow was hovering over send, his finger was hovering a millimetre from the trackpad, but he just couldn't quite take that final step. He'd convinced himself that the other customers were FBI agents. The second he hit send they would swoop in and slap on the cuffs, and his life as he knew it would effectively end. A quick glance around and he could see how crazy he was being. There were some students, a businesswoman, a couple of moms, and that was it.

No Feds.

No cops.

There was a single strand of reality hidden amongst all the paranoia, though. If he got this wrong then he would end up in prison. Those were the stakes, and that was why he couldn't do it. There was too much to lose. Yes, a contract killer might pick up the message, but it could just as easily be a Fed trying to entrap him. It just wasn't worth the risk.

Daniel shut down the laptop and let out a long sigh. This was going to be tougher than he thought. That said, he would find a solution. That was what he was good at; that was his gift. The ability to solve impossible problems.

Over the next three days he disposed of the laptop. The screen went into a dumpster in the south of the city, the keyboard into a dumpster in the north; he destroyed the hard drive and mother-board with a hammer, scraped the pieces into a bag and disposed of this in a dumpster in the east. This was overkill, but you could never be too careful. He'd done his best to cover his cyber-tracks but it was possible that something was still lurking on the hard drive, something with the potential to put him in prison.

A week later, he found himself back at the Holly Tree Inn. He had told Josh he had a meeting, but the truth was that he just needed to get away from him. Being in such close proximity, breathing the same air, he couldn't trust himself not to do some-thing he might regret. So he had climbed into his Porsche and started driving, and somehow he'd ended up back here. Trina was working reception again. Room 106 was vacant.

He let himself into the room, pulled the drapes and lay down on the bed. The walls were thin enough to hear the couple in the next room talking, but too thick to make out what they were say-ing. And then they stopped talking and everything went quiet. The silence was eventually broken by the sound of the bed mov-ing, quiet and slow to start with, but getting louder and quicker as they found their rhythm. The noise stopped a couple of times, presumably so they could change position, and started up again with barely a missed beat. The banging provided a counterpoint to the noises the woman was making. It was all too easy to imagine that it was Zoe and Josh in there. By the time they'd finished, the acid in Daniel's gut was burning hotter than ever.

Two weeks had passed since he was last here. The thing with time was that it softened the edges of memory. Lying there listening to the couple next door, the edges sharpened again. Zoe belonged to him, not Josh. How dare he? And how could she do this to him, after everything that he had done for her? Their betrayal had ripped him apart. His reconstruction began with their destruction. That was why they needed to die. While they lived and breathed there would always be a reminder of how he'd been fucked over, and that was not going to happen. He needed the slate wiped clean, and that meant removing them from the equation.

Unfortunately he still had no idea how to make that happen. How the hell did you find a hitman? It wasn't as though you could put out an ad in a newspaper. Heading down to South America was one possibility. There would be someone in Honduras or Columbia who'd be willing to do it. The problem was that he would probably end up dead in the process. A rich white guy waving his money around in Bogota, he might as well have a target painted on his forehead. New York and LA were out for the same reason.

He was so desperate he'd even considered doing it himself, just shoot them both in the head and be done with it. Getting hold of a gun would be easy enough too. This was America, after all. Could he pull the trigger? Damn right he could. Of course, if he did that then he might as well march into the nearest police station and turn himself in.

The whole situation was eating him up. He wasn't sleeping; his work was starting to suffer because he couldn't concentrate; it was even affecting his appetite. If this went on much longer then Zoe and Josh would notice that something was wrong. If that happened they might start so suspect he knew something, and then he would lose the element of surprise.

He had always believed that a problem was a solution that was just waiting to happen. He still believed that, but this belief was being sorely challenged. He knew there was a way to do this. The problem was that he was running out of places to look.

After leaving the Holly Tree, he had driven around for hours, taking turns at random with no real destination in mind. It seemed fitting somehow, because that was how his life felt, like it was totally lacking direction. He knew what he wanted to achieve. He had defined the problem. So why couldn't he find a solution? The frustration was just one more reason to hate Zoe and Josh. The sooner they were removed from his existence, the sooner life could get back to some sort of normality.

By the time he eventually reached the office, the lot was practically empty. There were a handful of cars, but no sign of Josh's Tesla, which was probably just as well. He parked in his spot, killed the engine and for a while just sat there staring up at the MYRIADIAN SOLUTIONS sign. He'd built this company from nothing. This was his crowning glory. Only now the crown was tarnished.

He got out of the car and headed for the entrance. Gabriel was working the late shift on the desk. The security guard wished him a good evening as he walked past. Daniel replied with a distracted 'good evening' of his own and kept on walking, heading for the stairs, lost in his problems and thoughts.

'Is everything okay, Mr Barton?'

Daniel stopped with his foot on the first stair. In the time it took to turn around, he had his game face back on.

'Everything's fine.'

Gabriel was staring in a way that made it clear he wasn't convinced. 'Are you sure? It's just that if ever I saw a man who was in need of a drink.'

Daniel managed to conjure up a laugh from somewhere. 'It's been a long day, that's all.'

'Maybe so, but that doesn't change the fact that you look like you could do with a drink.'

This time Daniel's laughter was real. 'Are you buying?'

Gabriel reached into his jacket pocket and pulled out a silver hip flask. He held it up and nodded. Daniel walked back to the desk and took the flask. He unscrewed the lid and knocked back a hit of bourbon. Gabriel was studying him in a way that made him uncomfortable. Scratch away the amiable exterior and there was something unpredictable lurking just below the surface. Daniel had first-hand experience of how dangerous he could be. The guy was like a pet tiger. He might act all friendly, but that could change in a heartbeat.

It wasn't that Gabriel was physically imposing, because he wasn't. He was somewhere around five-eight, and slightly built.

There wasn't an ounce of fat on him, just layer after layer of tight muscle. In that respect he reminded Daniel of a long-distance runner. His hair was short, curly and black, his eyes bright blue. Gabriel claimed that he had been a sniper in the army, and Daniel believed him. There was a stillness to the man, a sense that this was someone who had all the time in the world.

The scar tissue creeping out from the collar of his shirt ran up his neck and onto his left cheek, where it suddenly stopped. The skin was ridged, hard and pink, and looked like melted plastic. The rest of his face was untouched, but you had to wonder how much of his body had been affected. Judging by what he could see, these were serious burns. Gabriel must have got the injuries when he was in the army. Maybe through one of those IEDs he'd heard about, something made from fertilizer that had been cooked up in a local's kitchen.

Daniel knocked back another slug of bourbon and held the flask out. Gabriel plucked it from his hand and took a sip. 'Something's bugging you. Is it anything I can help with?'

The question sparked a flashback to the last time he had 'helped'. The images from that video were not going to be forgotten in a hurry. 'Not this time, no.'

'Are you sure?'

'Positive.' Daniel held out his hand and Gabriel passed him the flask. He wiped the top, took a long sip, then passed it back. 'Thanks for the drink. I think I'm going to head upstairs now.'

'Any time.'

As Daniel walked away he could feel Gabriel watching, but when he turned around the security guard was studying something on his computer monitor. Gabriel had barely registered when he first started working here. Then, about five months ago, he had given him a memory stick. Daniel had asked what was on it, and Gabriel had responded, cryptically, that it contained a film that was best watched in private. Daniel had plugged the stick into his work computer, thinking blackmail. He was partly right.

He recognised Carlos Rodriguez immediately. How could he not? Rodriguez was the company accountant. For years Daniel had been hiring call girls on business trips and putting these payments through as 'entertainment' expenses, which was a pretty creative piece of accounting. Okay, none of his clients were being entertained, but he had been. Thoroughly. Rodriguez had looked into these payments and worked out what they were really for. If he had left it there then it wouldn't have been a problem, but he had threatened to tell Zoe unless Daniel paid him ten thousand dollars. Daniel didn't have a problem with Zoe finding out; nor was it much of a problem finding ten thousand bucks to pay Rodriguez off. However he did have a problem with being blackmailed.

Gabriel had overheard them arguing after everyone else had gone home one evening, and taken the matter into his own hands. He had broken into Rodriguez's apartment and waited for him to come home. Then he had tied him up, doused him with gasoline and threatened to set him alight if he didn't tell him exactly what he was up to. Even after Rodriguez told him that he would back off, Gabriel hadn't put his Zippo away. He had kept waving the flame until Rodriguez had begged for his life.

Daniel had waited until everyone else had left before heading downstairs. 'What do you want?' he had asked. 'Money?'

Gabriel nodded. 'Five grand. Which is a bargain. Rodriguez wanted ten and that would have been the first instalment. Because that's the thing with blackmailers, they always come back for more.'

'And what's to stop you coming back for more?'

'You have my word that that won't happen.'

Daniel had learnt long ago that a man's word meant shit, but he didn't see he had much of an option, so he had shaken Gabriel's hand and paid the money, and, miracle of miracles, that was the end of it.

Upstairs in his office, Daniel sat in the dark for a while, mulling things over. He had destroyed the memory stick after watching the film of Rodriguez being tortured. That didn't matter. With his eyes closed he could remember ever single detail. Most of all, though, he remembered how comfortable Gabriel had looked. How much fun he was having. One reason Daniel had been so successful was that he recognised talent when he saw it, and he knew how to use that talent to his benefit. He would have to tread warily, though. Scaring off a blackmailer was one thing; being involved in a murder was a whole other ballgame.

# Chapter 22

## NOW

Tommy Wang was hovering by the elevators when Daniel got down to the lobby the next morning. There was no smile, no cheery hello. Daniel's eyes were gritty from too little sleep and too much alcohol. This was not a good start to the day.

'Mr Barton, I'm wondering if you could accompany me back to the station. I've got a couple of questions I'd like to ask.'

'Of course. Anything I can do to help.'

'I'm parked outside. If you'd like to follow me, please.'

Wang turned without waiting for a response and led the way outside to an anonymous silver sedan parked at the kerb. He held the rear door open for Daniel, closed it gently behind him, then climbed into the driver's seat and pulled away from the kerb. The seats were leather, the interior clean. No door handles. Those missing handles made this real in a way that it hadn't been thirty seconds ago. Innocent men did not get driven off in handle-less police cars. There was panic in his belly. Daniel did a slow count to ten and tried to squash it down.

He had positioned himself so he could see Wang in the rear-view mirror. The detective was staring silently at the road ahead, his face a mask of studied unreadability. So what did he know, and what did he suspect? Right now Daniel would have given just about everything he owned to have those questions answered. The closer they got to police headquarters, the more nervous he became. Up until now, their interactions had all followed the same script, both of them playing clearly defined roles. Daniel was the grieving husband; Wang was the diligent cop who was trying to piece everything together. This latest interaction was different. Again, he was back to those missing handles.

The room Wang took him to was nothing like the comfortably bland room where he had met with Serena the grief counsellor. The walls and ceiling had once been white, but time and grime has turned them grey. The floor tiles had been scuffed by countless feet and chair legs, and the table was bolted to the floor and had a steel handcuff hoop welded onto it. A digital recorder sat on top of the table, and there was a camera on a tripod in one corner. The large one-way mirror was covered in smudges, like it hadn't been cleaned in years. The room was small and claustrophobic, and even though it had been cleaned recently, it still smelled stale.

Wang sat down and waved him into the seat facing the mirror. Daniel couldn't decide whether the face being reflected back was guilt-ridden or grief-stricken. The detective leant across and switched on the digital recorder. While he was busy reeling off the date, time and names, Daniel glanced over at the camera. There weren't any red lights showing, but he couldn't be certain that it was off. How difficult would it have been for Wang to arrange for it to be switched on before they got here? And how easy would it be to disable the recording light? Paranoia, perhaps, but it felt justified. Wang finished talking and waited for Daniel to look at him.

'Zoe had a relationship with Josh Wilson.'

This statement was only seven words long, but it might as well have been a whole novel. The information must have come from Lizzy. She would have told Wang everything she knew and everything she suspected, and she would have done her level best to paint him as a monster. On the bright side, if Wang had any evidence connecting him to Zoe's death he would have arrested him already.

'Did you know about this?' Wang asked.

'I did.'

'When did you find out?'

'A couple of weeks ago.'

'How?'

'I hired a private investigator.'

'I'll need the name of the PI.'

Daniel gave up Chuck Mayweather's name and address without a second thought. All Mayweather had done was confirm the affair. There was nothing connecting the PI to Gabriel. He glanced over at the mirror. His lips were pressed together hard, his eyes narrowed. He was thinking guilt rather than grief. He forced himself to relax.

'That must have been tough,' Wang continued. 'Finding out that your wife and business partner had cheated on you.'

'It was.'

Wang didn't say anything for a moment. He was staring across the table, waiting for the silence to be filled. 'I'm curious,' he said eventually. 'Why didn't you mention this earlier?'

'Because it was a private matter. It didn't have anything to do with anyone else.'

'And Josh,' Wang pointed out. 'It was his business too. Does he know that you know?'

'I don't think so.'

Wang raised an eyebrow. 'You don't think?'

'I'm not in a position to say what he knows and doesn't know. You'd have to ask him.'

'But you see him most days at work. If he was suspicious, you'd have picked up on something, right?'

'Put like that, I guess he doesn't know. But like I say, you'd have to ask him.'

'We will.'

This statement was followed by another loaded silence. There were a dozen questions he could fill it with, but he kept his mouth shut.

'When did you last see your wife?'

'Two days ago. She drove me to the airport.'

'And what was her mood like?'

'She seemed like her normal self.'

Wang smiled. 'You're going to have to help me out here, Mr Barton. I never knew your wife so I've got no reference point to work from.'

'She wasn't saying much, but that wasn't unusual. Zoe wasn't much of a morning person.'

'Can you think of a reason why someone would want her dead?'

Daniel shook his head again. 'Like I told you the other day, everyone who met Zoe loved her. That's the effect she had on people.'

'Not everyone,' Wang pointed out.

It was a statement that didn't need qualifying. There was another long silence.

'One thing that's puzzling us is motive,' the detective continued. 'Based on the fact that the fifty thousand dollars in the upstairs safe was left untouched, we don't think this was a robbery. However, before we rule that out completely, we'll need you to take a look at the house. Would you be able to do that?'

'Of course.'

Daniel answered the question on autopilot, his mind suddenly reeling. His first instinct was to ask when he could get the money back. The words were almost out there, and he only just managed to stop himself. His wife was dead. How would it look if he started going on about money?

'I don't know how much it will help, though,' Wang added. 'Pretty much everything was destroyed in the blaze.'

'I know. I've been there.'

'When?'

'The day it happened. I went there after leaving here. I visited yesterday as well.'

'Did you go inside?'

'The first time I did, but only into the entranceway. I was worried about how safe it was.'

'So you wouldn't have noticed if anything had been stolen?'

Daniel shook his head. 'Sorry.'

The silence that followed this was as long as the others.

'Fifty thousand dollars is a lot of cash. What was it for?'

Daniel had been thinking long and hard about this. He could claim to be a gambler, but that lie would be too easy to tear apart. Wang would want details of card games that he had attended or bookies he had used, information he wouldn't be able to provide because he wasn't a gambler. Kickbacks were another possibility. That would be more believable. After all, he was a businessman. Unfortunately, paying bribes was illegal, so Wang would be obligated to investigate further.

'The money was for a new car.'

Wang stared across the table. 'Most people would use a wire transfer.'

'But if they used cash they'd get a discount of ten to fifteen per cent.'

'Because the person you're buying from is dodging their tax obligations.'

Daniel shrugged. 'What happens after I've handed over the money is none of my business.'

'Fifty grand will buy a nice car. You know, I wish I had that sort of money to spend on one, but it's not going to happen. Not in this lifetime.' He smiled, but Daniel didn't smile back. 'I'm going to need the name of the car dealership.'

'There is no dealership.'

'Yet you have fifty grand in your safe.'

'That's the budget I had to play with. Once I found a car, I wanted to be able to move fast. I didn't want any delays while I got the cash from the bank. Of course, it goes without saying that the last thing I'm thinking about right now is buying a car.'

'Of course.'

Another long silence.

'Do you know what a nanny cam is, Mr Barton?'

'It's a camera hidden in a child's toy.'

'That's right. You'd use one to spy on your nanny if you were worried that she was abusing your kids. Hence the name.'

'I'm sorry, you've lost me. How is this relevant?'

'We found a nanny cam in your house. At least we found what was left of one. It had been hidden inside a stuffed bear. Did you know that some husbands use these cameras to secretly film their wives?'

'That camera has nothing to do with me.'

'You're sure of that?'

'Positive.'

'In that case, it must have been Zoe who put it there. Any idea why she would do that?'

For a moment Daniel couldn't speak. He caught his reflection in the mirror. The person staring back looked completely baffled. Zoe must have been spying on him. It was the only explanation. Now the initial shock had worn off he was wondering how long the camera had been there, and what might have been caught on film.

'I've no idea,' he told Wang.

'You were married for three years. There must have been occasions where you and your wife argued.'

'Of course there were. All couples argue from time to time.'

'And how heated did your arguments get?'

'They were just arguments,' Daniel replied carefully.

'Did you ever hit your wife, Mr Barton?'

The question might have been expected, but it still struck hard. 'I'm not sure I like where these questions are going. Do you think I had something to do with my wife's murder? Is that what's going on here?'

'Mr Barton, at this stage we need to look at every possibility.'

'Should I be calling my lawyer?'

'That would be your prerogative.'

'Am I under arrest?'

'No, you're not.'

'So, I can leave whenever I want?'

'Again, that would be your prerogative.'

Daniel stood up and walked towards the door. Any second now Wang was going to stand up and start reading him his rights. He heard the detective's chair squeak, heard him getting to his feet.

'Mr Barton.'

Daniel turned around.

'Please make sure your cell phone is switched on. I'll need to arrange a time for you to visit the house.'

'Anything else?'

'Just one thing. If you see Josh Wilson, please let him know that we'd like to speak to him.'

♦

Daniel got a cab back to the hotel and headed straight to the underground parking lot. It was gloomy and filled with the echo of his footsteps. At any second Gabriel could jam a gun into his skull; he probably wouldn't even hear the gunshot. Daniel stopped walking and turned a full circle. The lot was empty, but that didn't stop him seeing danger everywhere he looked. His heart was racing and he was breathing too fast. The paranoia was making him crazy.

He forced himself to take a deep breath but it didn't help. What was going on? It was like the whole world had turned against him. The loss of control was the hardest thing to handle. There must be some way to get back into the driver's seat. If Zoe and Josh had managed to keep their hands off of one another then he wouldn't be in this situation. That was the bottom line. Wang had better hope that he found Josh before he did. Because if he got hold of Josh, he doubted he would be able to control his rage. He wouldn't want to. The cheating bastard needed to pay for what he had done. He needed to pay the same way that Zoe had.

Daniel hurried over to the Mercedes and got in. He tried to put the key in the ignition, but his hand was shaking too much and he dropped it. He reached under the seat and his fingertips brushed the key; he delved a bit further and closed his hand around it. His watch snagged something as he was bringing his hand back out, and that was when he found the iPhone. It was pink with a scratched case, and a generation out of date. How had Zoe managed to buy this? How did she pay the bill?

He switched the phone on and navigated to the log. There were calls and texts from a whole load of people he had never heard of. Zoe must have stolen it. He opened a couple of texts at random and the name Marilyn jumped out. Zoe's hairdresser was called Marilyn. Was this her phone?

Daniel scrolled back down the log until he reached the point where the calls started to go unanswered. In amongst these were six calls he could connect to Zoe. Five were outgoing, one incoming. Two were to cell phone numbers, two to landlines, and one to a 1–800 number. The incoming call was the longest at twenty-seven minutes and forty-one seconds. All six calls had been made the day before Zoe died, and all of them had happened close together.

The first of the unknown numbers was for a cell. Daniel took out the burner phone and punched the number into it. It went straight to a disembodied voice that informed him this was a disconnected number. Which was no great surprise. Zoe's call to this number only lasted seven seconds, long enough to listen to this message then hang up.

The 1-800 number took him through to AT&T's operator assistance service, and the landline number that followed it was answered by woman who said, 'Andrew Demarco.' Daniel hung up. Andrew Demarco was the name of the New York designer that Lizzy had gone to work for. The third number was also a landline, the area code the same. The woman who answered said, 'Ralph Lauren'. Daniel hung up without saying anything. He didn't need to ring any of the other numbers.

Next he checked through the texts. There was one from Lizzy. It was short and to the point, and confirmed all his suspicions.

*Flight booked Sea-Tac 13.17. Can't wait to see you again xxx*

So, Zoe had decided to leave him again, only this time she had enlisted Lizzy's help. Since they last spoke, Lizzy had got both a new cell phone number and a new job.

Daniel called the office from the car to let Catherine know he was on his way. She didn't ask why he was late, and he didn't offer any explanations. He asked to be put through to Josh and she told him that he was working from home today. He tried Josh's landline first. The answering machine kicked in after a handful of rings. *Sorry I'm not in. Leave a message and I'll get back to you as soon as I can.* His cell went straight to voicemail.

Maybe there was an innocent explanation, but Daniel didn't think so. Gabriel had better have made this one look like an accident. There couldn't be any more screw-ups. With luck the hit had taken place while he was being interviewed. He smiled. He liked the idea of Wang being his alibi.

Five minutes later he pulled into the Myriadian parking lot. The white Chevrolet Sonic parked in his slot shouldn't have been there. Everything was clearly signed. He parked in Josh's space and got out. Lizzy got out of the Chevrolet.

'Busy morning?' she called over.

'Whatever this is, Lizzy, I don't have time for it.'

'I thought you'd like to know that I met with Detective Wang. You know, Dan, he strikes me as someone who knows their stuff. If anyone's going to get to the bottom of what happened to Zoe, it's him.'

'Zoe's death had nothing to do with me. I've already told you that.'

'But it's not me you need to convince, Dan. It's Wang.'

'Goodbye, Lizzy.'

Daniel turned and walked towards the building entrance. His hands were curled into fists, the fingers tensing then relaxing, nails digging into his palms. He looked back as he walked into the building. Lizzy was standing with her hand on the Chevrolet's hood. She lifted her hand and gave him a little toodle-oo wave. In his head he could hear every time that she had ever called him Dan. *Dan, Dan, Dan, Dan. Dan.* I'm not finished with you, he thought as he disappeared into the building.

He was halfway up the stairs when his cell rang. Josh's name had flashed up on the screen, which meant that Gabriel hadn't got him after all. The thought was a depressing one. He connected the call.

'Hi, Josh.'

The silence stretched on long enough for Daniel to wonder if the connection had been broken, then Gabriel's voice came on the line.

'We need to talk.'

# Chapter 23

## THEN

Of course, Josh worked late the next day.

This wasn't unheard of, but it was unusual. It wasn't that Josh didn't do his fair share, because he did. It was just that he preferred to put his extra hours in at home, where he could work late into the quiet hours of the night. Josh had always been a night owl. A procrastinator too. That said, he always met his deadlines. This usually involved an all-nighter and copious amounts of caffeine. That was as true today as it had been when he was chasing a deadline for a college assignment. Daniel didn't know how he did it. *His* assignments had always been completed in plenty of time. The first thing he always did when he took on a new project was work out how he was going to manage his time.

The sound of a distant door opening broke into his thoughts. A couple of seconds later Josh was standing in his office.

'I'm heading home now,' he said. 'See you tomorrow.'

'Yeah, have a good evening.'

'By the way, I've emailed that proposal you wanted. Fingers crossed we get this contract. It could be a big one.'

'Fingers crossed,' Daniel said.

'Fingers, toes and anything else you can think of.'

The echo of Josh's laughter lingered long after he left. Daniel couldn't shake the feeling that he was laughing at him rather than with him. He still couldn't get over how good an actor Josh was. They could have a conversation like this and it was as though nothing was going on. Daniel walked over to the window and peered through the blinds. He watched Josh climb into his Tesla; watched him pull out of his parking space and drive off; watched a little while longer in case Josh decided to come back. He gave it another fifteen minutes before switching off his computer and heading downstairs. Gabriel looked up when he heard him approaching.

'How are you doing, Mr Barton?'

'Have you got your flask?'

'That bad, huh?'

'That bad.'

Gabriel pulled the hip flask from his jacket pocket and handed it over. Daniel took a slug then passed it back. It went back and forth again, the silence between them becoming increasingly charged. Daniel had been awake most of the night, talking himself into having this conversation, then talking himself out of it again. One second he was convinced that the security guard held the answer to his problems; the next he was convinced that it was a really bad idea.

At some point he had eventually drifted off. When his alarm shocked him awake, one word was ricocheting around in his head. Insurance. That was why his cell phone's voice recorder was switched on in his pocket; that was why every conversation they had from now until the end of time would be recorded. If Gabriel even thought about turning on him, it would be made very clear that two could play that game. He took another sip of bourbon and glanced at Gabriel. Some ex-servicemen ended up as security guards when they returned to the real world, some ended up as bodyguards or mercenaries; and it was conceivable that a few would end up working as hitmen. After all, when you got down to it, they were in the business of killing.

And if that was the case then it was conceivable that Gabriel might be able to hook him up with one.

'My wife's been cheating on me,' Daniel said carefully.

'I'm sorry to hear that.'

'What would you do if you found yourself in my position?'

'What would I do if I found out my wife was cheating on me?'

Daniel nodded.

'The question's irrelevant. I'm not married.'

'Okay, hypothetically speaking, what would you do?'

Gabriel didn't say anything for a moment. The way he was staring left Daniel feeling as though he was trapped in the cross-hairs. 'What are you actually asking here?'

Daniel said nothing.

Gabriel smiled. 'In that case, hypothetically speaking, I'd respond by telling you that this was neither the time nor place for this particular conversation.'

The next afternoon, Daniel faked another meeting and drove to Forest Park. The park was the largest urban forest in the US. On one side were the Tualatin Mountains, on the other, the city sprawl of Portland. It was more than five thousand acres, which meant there were plenty of places you could talk without being overheard.

Gabriel was waiting in the parking area, standing by the hood of his Grand Cherokee, face to the sun and not a care in the world. Daniel parked his Porsche in the next slot and walked over to join him. With his battered jeans, worn boots and red plaid shirt, Gabriel looked completely at home in the woods. By contrast, Daniel was wearing a thousand-dollar suit, three-hundred-dollar shoes and feeling like a fish out of water.

'Follow me,' Gabriel said.

Daniel looked around the parking area. There were no other vehicles, no other people. Aside from the birds they were completely alone. 'Why not talk here? There's no one around.'

Gabriel walked around to the driver's door of the Jeep and started to get in.

'Where are you going?' Daniel called out.

'Home.'

'Why?'

'You might not value your freedom, but I value mine.'

'There's no one here.'

'Goodbye, Daniel.'

That last statement made it clear what was really going on. Gabriel had never called him Daniel. Not once. This wasn't about whether or not they were alone, it was about Gabriel establishing his status as the alpha male. Fine, if that's what he wanted to believe.

'Okay,' Daniel called out. 'We'll do this your way.'

Gabriel paused with his hand on the handle, the door still half open. He stared for a second then climbed out and headed towards one of the trails. Daniel fell into step behind him and they disappeared into the trees. They walked for maybe a quarter of a mile, heading deep into the woods. The next turn took them into a small clearing. Gabriel walked over to the stump of a felled tree and sat down. Daniel opted to stand. It would be good for Gabriel to understand that he wasn't calling all the shots. He let the silence between them grow, determined not to be the one to fill it. He could feel the reassuring press of his cell phone in his pants pocket. He had set the voice recorder running before he had gotten out of his car.

'If we're going to do this then we need to keep any meetings between us to an absolute minimum,' Gabriel said eventually. 'I was serious earlier when I said that I don't want to end up in prison.'

'Believe me, I have no intention of ending up there either.'

'It's good to know we're on the same page. So, do you want your wife's lover scared, or do you want him put in the hospital?'

Daniel said nothing.

'What do you actually want from me?'

'When you were in the army, I'm assuming you knew people who had killed. Do you know anyone who kept on killing after they left?' Daniel paused. 'For money,' he added quietly.

'Who's your wife sleeping with?'

'Josh.'

'Well, I guess that explains why you want him dead.'

'Not just him.'

Gabriel met his eye, then stared off into the trees. Daniel waited as long as he could, but the silence was just too much.

'Do you know someone who might be able to do this?' he asked.

'Yeah, I know someone.'

'Can you put me in touch with them?'

'No.'

'Look, don't play games. Either you can help me or you can't.'

Gabriel turned and looked at him again. The small smile playing on his lips was anything but reassuring. 'The reason I can't put you in touch with them is because they're sitting right in front of you.'

It was Daniel's turn to fall silent.

'One hundred thousand dollars,' Gabriel added. 'Fifty thousand each.'

According to one of the bogus websites that Daniel had looked at, a hundred grand would have paid for a hit on a top-level politician. That same 'hitman' would only have charged ten thousand to kill Zoe. At the time, the price had struck him as low; that was the reason he decided the site was bogus. Fifty thousand per hit was more in line with his expectations.

'How do I know you're able to do this?'

'Have you had any more problems with Mr Rodriguez?'

'With all due respect, scaring a blackmailer is a completely different thing.'

'You're right. It is.'

Gabriel's smile chilled Daniel to the bone. He looked so relaxed; they could have been discussing the weather rather than murder. There was no doubt in Daniel's mind that the man sitting on the tree stump was a killer. Daniel was suddenly all too aware of how vulnerable he was. What good was a cell phone recording if Gabriel decided to kill him here and now?

'I understand your need for assurances. If I was in your shoes I'd want some too.' Gabriel stared into the trees for a moment, then turned back to Daniel and waited for him to meet his gaze. 'Keep an eye on the news over the next day or two.'

'And what exactly am I looking for?'

'You'll know when you see it.'

Over the next two days Daniel became obsessed with the news. His phone had tabs open for both the local and national stations; the same with his work computer. He was checking every couple of minutes, unsure exactly what he was looking for and driving himself insane with all the second-guessing. He'd more or less reached the point where he was starting to think that Gabriel was full of shit when an update about a house fire in Tigard caught his eye. He turned the volume of his work computer up. This story had actually broken the day he met Gabriel at Forest Park. At the time it hadn't struck Daniel as being that big a deal; it was just someone's bad-luck story. If there was one thing he'd learnt over the past two days, it was that the news was an endless procession of bad-luck stories.

It was the photograph behind the anchor that caught his eye. The last time he'd seen Carlos Rodriguez was in the video Gabriel had made for him. His resignation letter had been sent via email; he hadn't even bothered to clear his desk. And now Rodriguez was dead, killed in a fire at his home.

Sitting there in his office, staring at his laptop, Daniel had to wonder if Gabriel had made Rodriguez beg for his life again. It seemed like the sort of thing he might do. For a brief moment he wondered if this was a good idea, and then he remembered how he'd felt when Mayweather had handed him the envelope that had contained a copy of Josh's bank statement; how he'd felt back at the Holly Tree, listening to the couple having sex in the next room and imagining it was Zoe and Josh. That was the point where his resolve returned. Gabriel wasn't just his best chance to put this right, he might be his only chance.

The next day they were back in the same clearing in Forest Park. Gabriel was sitting on the stump, totally relaxed, while Daniel chose to stand. The security guard was dressed for the outdoors again; Daniel had made an effort and was wearing jeans and walking boots, but he still felt out of his element.

'Relax,' Gabriel said. 'It's all going to work out fine. Back when I was in the army one of my buddies found out that his wife was having an affair. I helped make it go away. The point is, I'm a free man and my buddy's a free man, and I'm afraid that's the only reassurance I've got to give you.'

'Then I guess that will have to do. So when are you going to do it?'

'When you're out of town. That way you'll have a ready-made alibi. The plan is to make it look like an accident. I'm going to need a list of all your upcoming business trips.'

'I can do that.'

'There might be a problem.'

Daniel frowned. 'What?'

Gabriel took an envelope from the inside pocket of his jacket and held it out. Daniel hesitated, nervous where this was headed. Gabriel waved the envelope at him and this time he took it. There was nothing written on the front, nothing on the back. It looked innocent enough, but Daniel felt as though he'd been handed a bomb. He ripped the envelope open and turned it upside down. A folded sheet of paper slid out. Daniel unfolded it and for a long time all he could do was stand there staring at the photocopy of the ultrasound picture.

The original had been torn neatly down the middle and taped back together. The name printed along the edge was Eleanor Sanders. Sanders was Zoe's mother's maiden name. Daniel had no idea who Eleanor was. Maybe the name had been chosen at random, or maybe it was significant to Zoe. He willed his hand to steady, but there was just too much anger burning through him. This was one truth too many. The picture was a mess of grey and black; it was difficult to make anything out. In the middle was a bean-shaped mass of black, and inside that, a tiny grey shape that was presumably the foetus. It must have been early days, because whatever that thing was it looked nothing like a baby.

Murdering your wife was one thing, murdering your *pregnant* wife was another thing altogether. You would have to be a monster to kill your unborn child. Except Daniel knew for a fact that this baby was not his. He'd had a vasectomy at nineteen. They'd had the hypothetical baby talk before they got married. Most couples did. It was all part of the process. Date for a while, move in together, get engaged, have the baby talk, get married. Zoe had made it clear that she wanted children; Daniel didn't, not ever, but had said that he did because he wanted Zoe.

He tore the photocopy in two, then tore the halves into quarters. He kept tearing until he was left with a mound of confetti piled on top of the envelope. Then he tipped his hand and watched the pieces blow away. Out of sight, out of mind, he thought as the breeze scattered them. Except something like this never left your mind, not once it had got in there.

'The baby's not mine,' he said.

Gabriel said nothing. The silence contained one single unspoken question. Daniel reached into his pocket and took out an envelope of his own. Fifty grand. Half upfront; half on completion. That was the deal. He held it out and waited for Gabriel to take it.

'Kill them all.'

# Chapter 24

## NOW

Gabriel's directions took Daniel west on Highway 26. He had to assume that Josh was dead, and that got him wondering about what sort of accident he'd had. The radio was tuned to KXL. So far there hadn't been any news stories that could be connected to Josh. The envelope in the glovebox contained $9,950. Ninety-nine hundreds and one fifty, all neatly bundled up. It was fifty dollars shy of the $10,000 federal limit.

The money was a sweetener. A show of good faith. He wanted Gabriel to be in no doubt that he would get paid; he wanted there to be no doubt that he was playing straight with him. Gabriel could have the rest when he got his money back from the police. He would probably demand the whole fifty thousand, and as far as Daniel was concerned, he could have it.

Forty-five minutes later he drove into Timber. The town was tiny. There was a wooden post office that looked like it dated all the way back to the 1800s, a couple of houses, and not much else. It was situated right on the edge of the Tillamook State Forest. Fir trees stretched as far as the eye could see. The directions took him to a narrow dirt track ten minutes outside of Timber. Daniel turned onto it and bumped along for fifty yards before slowing to a stop.

Tall trees crowded in on either side of the car. The main road had already disappeared from the rear-view mirror. Nobody knew he was here. He was driving deep into the woods to meet a killer. Not only that, this was someone who had killed a pregnant woman. In movies the hitman always drew a line at killing women and kids. But this was real life, and it would seem that those rules and limitations didn't apply.

Daniel pressed the gas pedal gently and the Mercedes rolled forward. The car wasn't built for this terrain and he could feel every rut and bump. The track led to a small wooden two storey-house that looked like it had been here forever. One of the two vehicles parked near the front door was Gabriel's Cherokee; the other was Josh's Tesla. He was surprised to see Josh's car, but at the same time it wasn't a complete surprise. The world he'd woken up to today was one that had been built on shifting sand.

Daniel parked and killed the engine, then leant across the passenger seat and took the money from the glovebox. He got out and climbed the porch steps, the wood creaking softly underfoot. All he could hear were the birds, and the wind shushing through the tall pines, and the thump of his heart as it threatened to rip through his ribcage. He knocked gently on the door.

'Come in.'

The door opened on smooth hinges and Daniel stepped inside. Gabriel was standing at the bottom of the stairs. There was a gun in his hand and a small smile playing on his lips. Josh was sitting on a wooden chair, his hands and ankles bound with duct tape; more tape secured him to the chair, long strips that had been wrapped around his chest, stomach, thighs and lower legs. A four-inch strip was stuck across his mouth.

Daniel walked over, the smell of piss getting stronger with every step. The stain on the front of Josh's pants was so dark it was almost black. His eyes were wide and terrified. There was something else in there too. It took a moment to work out that it was hope. The stupid bastard actually thought he could save him. He looked pathetic. A complete and utter joke. Daniel found it impossible to believe that he had once called him a friend.

He took another step forward and Josh cowered back. That tiny spark of hope had gone. Daniel brought his arm back, getting ready to punch. The anger was unlike anything he had ever experienced. He was going to start punching, and he was going to keep going until Josh was dead.

'Stop.'

One quiet word, one quiet syllable, but it had the power to stop Daniel in his tracks.

'That's not how this works,' Gabriel said. 'You want to walk away from this a free man. Yes or no?'

'Yes.'

'So we need to create a story that the police can buy into. By now, they should have worked out that Josh and Zoe were romantically involved. Yes or no?'

'Yes.'

'And the reason you know this is because you're their number one suspect. Yes or no?'

Daniel hesitated. 'Yes.'

'Did you mention me when they questioned you? And I want the truth. Don't even think about lying.'

'I didn't say a word. I promise.'

'Good, that means the story holds.'

Gabriel stopped talking and tapped the gun against his leg. Once, twice, three times. *Tap tap tap.* The sound was barely audible but it was still deafening.

'Okay, here's what happened. Josh rented this house so he could spend a romantic few days here with Zoe while you were out of town. When the police dig deeper they'll find his name on the rental agreement. The owner of the property left the keys under the mat so there was never any face-to-face contact. With me so far?'

Daniel nodded.

'After dropping you off at the airport, Zoe texted Josh to tell him she wanted to finish the affair. She was tired of the lies and the deception. It would be best if they were just friends. Josh couldn't accept that, though. He rushed around to the house and they had a big argument that turned ugly. Has the autopsy been carried out yet?'

'It's scheduled for today.'

'The pathologist will discover that Zoe died from a broken skull. The injury is consistent with her falling over and smashing her head open on the kitchen floor. What happened was that Josh knocked her down while they were arguing and she landed awkwardly. When he realised she was dead he panicked and burned the house down to hide the murder. Then he drove here and killed himself.'

Daniel glanced over at Josh. His eyes were wider and more terrified than before.

'The police will eventually find this cabin,' Gabriel continued. 'And when they do they'll discover Josh still dressed in his gasoline-soaked clothes. There will be no question that he's their man. He's got a motive, means and, with you away on business, he had the opportunity.'

Daniel almost pointed out that Josh's clothes weren't soaked in gasoline, then he noticed the canister by the front door.

'Things will be uncomfortable for a while,' Gabriel went on. 'But so long as you keep your head, you'll come out of this smelling of roses. Which brings us to the matter of money. I assume you've brought my fifty thousand dollars.'

Daniel took the envelope from his jacket pocket and handed it over. Gabriel weighed it in his hand.

'This feels light. If I count it, how much will it come to?'

'Nine thousand, nine hundred and fifty.'

Gabriel aimed the gun at Daniel's head. 'Are you trying to screw me over?'

Daniel felt his bladder and bowels loosen. 'No.'

'Then why are you trying to cheat me out of my money?'

Daniel tried to swallow but it was impossible. His saliva was like concrete. 'The police have the money. It was in the bedroom safe. They found it when they investigated the fire. I will get it back, though, and as soon as I do you can have it. All of it.' He nodded towards the envelope. 'Hopefully that will compensate you for any inconvenience.'

He had made his pitch. All he could do now was wait to see if the offer was accepted. Gabriel made him sweat it out a while longer, then nodded once and the gun went down.

'You can take the tape off Josh's mouth,' he said. 'I'm sure you two have plenty to talk about.'

♦

Daniel stepped closer. All Josh's fear was focussed on him. The effect was intoxicating. He stopped a foot from the chair, and for the best part of a minute just stood there feeding on the terror. Josh cowered when he reached for the end of the tape; he bit back a yelp when it was ripped off.

'I'm sorry,' he whimpered.

'Sorry for what?'

Josh didn't answer. He was staring at the tape wrapped around his thighs.

'Look at me!' Daniel yelled.

Josh's head snapped up. His eyes were bloodshot and filled with tears.

'Answer the question, Josh. What are you sorry for?'

'Zoe,' he whispered.

'I'm going to need more than that.'

'I shouldn't have slept with her.'

'*Slept.*' Daniel shot him a puzzled look. 'There wasn't much sleeping going on, was there?'

'I shouldn't have had sex with her.'

'Closer, but we're still not quite there yet. You fucked her, Josh. Isn't that right? And Zoe's got a name.'

He nodded weakly. 'I'm sorry.'

'So let me hear you say it.'

'I shouldn't have fucked Zoe.'

'Louder. Yell it from the rooftops, Josh.'

'I shouldn't have fucked Zoe,' Josh shouted.

'No, you shouldn't. But you did, and here we are.'

'There must be something I can do to make this right.'

Daniel shook his head. 'We're beyond that.'

'But we're friends. There's got to be a way to work this out.'

'*Were* friends. *Were*, Josh. The second you stepped over the line our friendship ended.' He paused. 'Did you love her?'

'It wasn't like that, Daniel.'

'Wasn't like what?'

'I wasn't trying to steal her from you.'

'But you were attracted to her, right? You have been from the start. Since we saw her at the restaurant.'

Josh said nothing.

'You've always been jealous that she chose me rather than you. Admit it.'

'You're wrong. I was happy you guys got together. Really I was.'

'So how did it all start?'

'I went around to your house while you were away on business in San Diego. One thing led to another. It was just that one time. It should never have happened. I'm sorry.'

'Liar.'

'I swear, it just happened the once.'

'What about the time you took her to the Holly Tree?'

Josh's eyes widened.

'That's right. I know all about that. I saw your bank statement. It clearly showed that you made a payment to the Holly Tree Inn. Now why would you go and do a thing like that Josh?'

'I booked the room, but nothing happened. All we did was talk. That's the truth. I promise.'

Daniel's laughter was bitter and cold. 'Do you think I'm stupid?'

'All we did was talk.'

'Am I really supposed to believe that?'

'You have to believe me. It's the truth. I swear to God, Daniel.'

'Okay, here's what I'm struggling with. If all you wanted to do was talk, then why not use the telephone like everyone else? Why did you need to meet up in a motel room? And what exactly did you *talk* about?'

Josh said nothing.

'That's what I thought. Because there wasn't a whole lot of talking going on, was there, Josh?' Daniel looked over at Gabriel. 'How does this work?'

'*No*,' Josh screamed. 'Please, Daniel, don't do this.'

The strip of tape was still hanging from the side of the chair. Daniel pulled it off and slapped it back on Josh's mouth, shutting him up mid-plea. Gabriel unscrewed the silencer, put it on the table, then walked over to the chair. He looked down at Josh.

'If you're going to shoot yourself in the head, never fire through the temple. Get it wrong and you'll end up lobotomised. Putting the barrel in your mouth is the best option. But that won't work here. Josh will instinctively clamp his mouth shut. One thing the pathologist will be looking for is broken teeth. That would indicate foul play. Place the gun under his chin and angle it slightly towards the back of his skull. That way the bullet will do the maximum amount of damage.'

'Me?'

'Of course.'

For a moment Daniel was speechless. It was one thing to sanction a murder; it was another thing entirely to pull the trigger.

'Is there a problem?' Gabriel asked.

Daniel thought it over and realised there wasn't. He could do this. What's more, he wanted to do this. 'No, there isn't a problem.'

Gabriel handed him the gun butt first. Daniel weighed it in his hand, getting used to the feel. It was a Beretta, solid and well maintained. He could smell the gun oil. Josh was staring wild eyed, his head going from side to side. Daniel stepped closer and pushed the gun under his chin. Josh was trying to get away, but the duct tape kept him in place. Following the movements of his head was easy enough. All he had to do was keep the end of the barrel slotted into the soft groove of his jaw.

'Goodbye, Josh.'

He squeezed the trigger.

Josh's eyes were open and empty, his face slack. The only thing keeping him upright was the duct tape. It was weird. The lights had been on; now they were off. Permanently. His face was unharmed. He had always been good-looking. That was one of the things he had traded on. His looks wouldn't do him any good now, though.

Daniel's ears were filled with a high-pitched whine, and the stink of cordite stung his nose. Something wet and warm had stuck to his cheek, and when he wiped it, his fingertips came away red. There was too much adrenalin flying around his body. He wanted to yell and scream and whoop; he wanted to run a marathon. He wanted to cry. Zoe was dead. Josh was dead. This was what revenge looked like. For a moment he was back in

Chuck Mayweather's office and the PI was telling him that what was done couldn't be undone. If Mayweather had been here he would have told him that that was fine because there were some things that you didn't want undone.

Gabriel took the Berretta from him, then walked around Josh's body, studying it from all angles. He sucked in a breath and shook his head.

'What's wrong?' There was a note of panic in Daniel's voice. If Gabriel was seeing problems then this was bad. Gabriel stepped closer and dug the gun into the nape of Daniel's neck. The barrel was still hot.

'Give me your car keys.'

'Please don't kill me,' Daniel whispered.

Gabriel dug even harder with the hot end of the gun and Daniel shut his eyes, like that might somehow block out what was going on here. 'Give me your car keys.'

'Please don't kill me,' he repeated, only this time the words were nothing more than air.

'Then do what I ask.'

The gun dug harder. This was his last chance. Either he complied or Gabriel would blow his head off. Here, now – no warning, no more chances. Daniel opened his eyes slowly and rummaged through his pockets for the keys to Zoe's Mercedes. He held them out with a shaking hand and Gabriel took them and pushed them into his pocket. The insistent pressure of the gun eased.

'You've still got a spot of blood on your cheek,' Gabriel said.

Daniel reached up and wiped it away.

'And that's the problem,' he added. 'The police have forensics specialists who are experts at reading blood spatter patterns. When they look at this scene they're going to find an area in front of Josh where there's no blood. It's not going to take long for them to deduce that someone was standing there. When that happens our suicide scenario fails. Which means that we need a new narrative.'

He paused. Daniel's mind was racing but he had nothing to add. Not a single goddam thing.

'I'm thinking that you must have found out about this place and lured Josh here. You bound him to the chair, confronted him about the affair, then killed him. In order to make it look like suicide you removed the restraints and pushed him to the floor. At some point the enormity of what you'd done would have hit like a freight train. Add in the fact that your wife is dead and it all became too much. Ripped apart by guilt and grief, you can only see one way out. You kill yourself.'

Gabriel raised the Beretta and took aim. His finger tightened on the trigger and Daniel felt something warm and wet between his legs. Time suddenly seemed too short, and too long, the microseconds contracting and expanding. His mind was simultaneously a rambling mess and razor sharp. It was a contradiction that should have been impossible, yet here he was, living proof that it was possible. All he could see was the gun. It demanded his complete attention. The mouth of the barrel looked massive. Gabriel suddenly lowered the gun and stepped back.

'Wait here,' he said.

By the time Daniel had worked out that he was still alive, Gabriel was already halfway up the stairs. He looked at the door. It wasn't locked. He was about to make his move when a voice from the floor above stopped him in his tracks.

'What the hell is going on, Gabriel?'

The voice was female, and it was one he knew only too well.

# PART III

# TOGETHER FOREVER

*He who saves a life is responsible for it forever.*

Chinese proverb

# Chapter 25

Zoe glared at Gabriel. He was standing next to the bed, rolling the used duct tape into a ball. Thirty seconds ago that tape had been stuck to her. The skin on her wrists still itched from being bound to the bed frame. Her face was itching from the strip of tape he had used to gag her

'I asked you a question. What's going on?'

'There will be time for explanations later. For now, I need you to go downstairs.'

'You drugged me!'

'*Please,* go downstairs.'

That emphasis on *please* showed how far things had come. Zoe's anger faded, replaced with an emotional state that swung wildly between disbelief and despair. She glared again, then stood up and walked across the room. Gabriel stepped aside to let her out of the door and she walked along the landing and down the stairs, her legs threatening to give way, her heart vibrating violently inside her chest.

She saw Josh's feet first. Black patent leather shoes, black socks. His feet weren't moving. Zoe carried on down the stairs and more of him became visible. Legs, waist, body. His legs were bound to the chair with duct tape. There was more tape around his thighs and belly. Zoe was trying to convince herself that this was the reason he wasn't moving. She took another step and stopped dead. No amount of denial could prevent her seeing the truth now. Josh's head had tipped forward and was resting lightly on his chest. There was a hole in the top of his skull where the bullet had exited. All Zoe could see was the blood. There was so much of it. She didn't want to look, but it was impossible not to.

Gabriel stepped past her and motioned for her to follow. Somehow she managed to start moving again, one slow uncertain footstep after the next. And now she could see Daniel. He was sitting on a chair that was identical to Josh's. His hands were resting on his lap and his pants had a dark stain around the crotch. The smell of warm ammonia intensified the closer she got. She stopped in front of him. He was staring at his hands and refusing to meet her eye. He looked pathetic. It was hard to believe she had ever been scared of him.

'Why?' she asked.

Daniel tilted his head towards her, but didn't say anything. There was hatred in his eyes. Fear too. Plenty of fear.

'Why?' she asked again.

Gabriel stepped beside her and levelled the gun. 'I think Zoe deserves an answer. It's a fair question.'

Daniel's gaze swung from Gabriel to the gun, then back to Zoe. 'I love you.'

She shook her head and for a moment her anger overcame the disbelief. She wanted to hurt him for all the hurt he had caused her. She wanted to keep hurting him until there was nothing left to hurt. 'No, you don't. You never loved me. You tried to own me. I was just another possession. Like your house or your Porsche. The idea that someone might try to take one of your things away from you was just too much for you to bear. That's why you tried to kill me. Admit it.'

'It wasn't like that.'

'Wasn't it?'

'I'm sorry.'

This provoked a laugh. She couldn't help it. How many times had he told her he was sorry? The difference was that he genuinely meant it this time.

'Is there anything else you want to say?' Gabriel asked.

Zoe shook her head. This was a lie. There was so much she wanted to say, but Daniel just wasn't worth the effort. She was suddenly more tired than she had ever been. If she could turn back the clock and make it so they'd never met, she would. She couldn't, though. Gabriel walked over to the table and picked up the roll of duct tape. He held it out to her. She hesitated, then took it.

'Secure him to the chair.'

'Wait,' Daniel said quickly. 'I recorded our conversations. They're with my lawyer. If anything happens to me, he has instructions to give them to the police.'

Gabriel smiled. 'Where's the trust, Daniel? Where's the love?'

'They'll know my death wasn't suicide. They'll come for you.'

'By the time that happens I'll be long gone.' He turned back to Zoe. 'Tape him to the chair.'

Daniel cowered back as she walked towards him. The fear now eclipsed everything else; there was no room for any other emotions. This was a complete reversal of roles. For once she had all the power. Except even that was an illusion. Only one person in this room held any real power.

Gabriel stepped forward and used the gun to push Daniel upright. He didn't say a word; he didn't have to. Zoe worked as quickly as her shaking hands would allow. Ankles first, then thighs, then body, then wrists. She went to step back and Gabriel stopped her. He held out the gun, handle first, and motioned for her to take it. She was about to tell him that she didn't understand, and then she got it. She shook her head.

'This is how you set yourself free, Zoe. Forever. He won't be able to hurt you anymore.'

'No,' she whispered.

Gabriel stepped behind her and pressed his body into hers. The forced intimacy made her cringe. She wanted to get away, but there was nowhere to go. He slid the gun into her hand and curled her fingers around the handle.

'Put your finger here. On the trigger.'

The words were hot and gentle inside her ear. She shook her head.

'Please put your finger on the trigger, Zoe.'

She wanted to argue, wanted to tell him that she couldn't do this, but her finger had already slid onto the trigger. It felt as though her whole universe began and ended with that small curve of metal. Daniel met her gaze. She had never seen him look this desperate, or this pathetic. How could she ever have been scared of him? Looking at him sitting there, it was impossible to believe that this was the man who had terrorised her every waking moment.

'Please don't do this, Zoe.'

Daniel's words were rushed out on a series of sobs; the tears were flowing freely down his cheeks. Gabriel moved Zoe's arm into a firing position, his gentle hand absorbing all her shakes and trembles. His lips found her ear.

'He wanted you dead. You and your baby. Don't forget that.'

She looked at Daniel, searching for confirmation, searching for the truth, but he had disappeared too far into his fear to offer either.

'You can do it, Little Sis,' Gabriel whispered. 'You can set yourself free. Just squeeze that trigger.'

'No,' she whispered back.

Zoe was vaguely aware of Daniel. He was screaming now, yelling and pleading for his life. All pretence of cool had fled. *Zoe please don't do this please please please I don't want to die.* He was wasting the few precious breaths that he had left.

Gabriel's finger tightened around hers.

Ounce by ounce he increased the pressure.

Her marriage ended with a spreading bloom of blood on Daniel's shirt, and a ringing in her ears that would last the rest of the day.

# Chapter 26

The gun tucked into the waistband of Gabriel's jeans provided Zoe with a focus point. When she was looking at the gun, she wasn't looking at the bodies. Right now she was clinging on to whatever shred of denial she could, because this was just too much to comprehend. A part of her understood that Daniel and Josh were dead. She had seen their bodies. And the blood. But this was one of those situations where seeing did not necessarily equate to believing.

'Go and sit in the car. I'll be there in a minute.'

Gabriel sounded so relaxed. It was totally surreal. The way he was talking this could have been a coffee house instead of a room that stank of death. She looked back when she reached the door. Gabriel was pulling on a white forensics suit. There was a large red gasoline can at his feet. He caught her staring, and stared back until she left. Being outside felt alien, like she was stepping into a world she barely recognised. The loamy smells of the forest were sharper than she remembered, the colours bright enough to hurt her eyes. There were three vehicles parked in front of the cabin. Josh's Tesla, Gabriel's Grand Cherokee, her Mercedes.

The last time Zoe had travelled in the Cherokee, she had been hiding in the trunk. She glanced through the rear window as she made her way to the passenger door. The trunk cover was rolled back, making the space look huge. When she'd been in there, the cover had been firmly in place, and that space had been as small and dark as a coffin.

As she climbed into the Cherokee she caught a glimpse of her reflection in the passenger window. She looked nothing like Zoe Barton anymore. Her hair was cut short and dyed blonde and Daniel would never have let her have her hair like this because he thought that all blondes were airheads; the leggings, T-shirt and sweatshirt were the sort of thing that he wouldn't have let her wear in a million years.

Only now it didn't matter what he thought.

Gabriel appeared at the cabin door a couple of minutes later. He took off the forensic suit, rolled it into a ball then tossed it back inside. Zoe could see the flames through the open doorway. There were just a few stray spits of orange and red at the moment, but she could sense the fire's potential. Gabriel climbed into the driver's seat, started the engine and backed out into the clearing. Zoe expected him to put the car into drive and get the hell out, but that didn't happen. Instead, he just sat there with the engine idling, watching as the flames started to lick at the windows.

By the time they finally drove onto the track, the blaze was tearing through the first floor. Jagged shards of yellow and orange were dancing behind the windows and ripping at the drapes; smoke was creeping out through the cracks in the frames. There were no flames in the upstairs windows yet, but it wouldn't be long. Whatever had kept her going up to this point suddenly vanished. The numbness seemed to fill every part of her, and in some ways that was a good thing. She didn't want to feel, because she didn't have the strength to endure the pain that brought. Daniel and Josh were dead, and it was all her fault.

She stared through the windshield as they bumped along the track. She was still staring when they turned onto the road. They passed through a small town that was made up of a post office and a couple of houses, but she barely noticed. When they eventually hit the highway, she couldn't tell if they were going north, south, east or west. She knew she should be paying attention, but it was impossible to think about the present when she was stuck so firmly in the past. She kept finding herself lost in the same two moments of time.

The first was when she came downstairs and saw Josh.

The second was when the gun went off.

Gabriel glanced over from the driver's seat, checking she was okay. Zoe wanted to scream that nothing about this situation was even remotely okay. She didn't say anything because she couldn't trust her anger. If she let it loose who knew what might happen? She could see herself losing control and grabbing the steering wheel and running the car into a ditch. Maybe that would be enough to knock Gabriel unconscious, or even kill him. Then again, maybe it would be her who wound up dead. So she squashed the anger down and stared through the windshield at the road unfurling into the distance.

# Chapter 27

'I need to pee.'

Gabriel glanced over, then turned back to the road. 'Look under your seat,' he said.

Zoe leant forward and rummaged beneath the seat. Her fingertips brushed plastic. She delved deeper and pulled out a large plastic soda bottle. He had to be kidding. She held it up and shook her head. 'This won't work.'

He glanced over, eyes on the bottle then back to her. 'Look again.'

This time she found a large plastic funnel. The implication was depressingly clear. 'Can't we pull over at a rest stop?'

Gabriel shook his head. 'We're on a tight schedule.'

'It would only take a minute.'

'If you're that desperate, use the bottle.'

'Come on, Gabriel, it's not going to take that much time.'

'I said *no*, Zoe.'

She took one more look at the bottle and the funnel, then slid them back beneath the seat. She needed to go, but not that badly. The fuel gauge showed under a quarter of a tank; the car's computer showed sixty-three miles before they needed to fill up; the needle was stuck on seventy. If she had the math right, they would need to stop for gas at some point during the next hour. Zoe was pretty sure she could hold on for that long.

'Where are we headed anyway?'

'The cabin.'

'The one in South Dakota?'

Gabriel nodded.

'That's got to be two thousand miles.'

'From where we are now, it's probably closer to a thousand.'

'And what? We're going to drive all the way there?'

'Unless you've got a better plan.'

She hesitated, then said, 'We need to talk about what happened back there.'

'So talk. We've got plenty of miles to kill.'

'No one was supposed to die.'

Gabriel looked over again. 'If Daniel had lived, then at some point he would have come looking for you.'

'No, he wouldn't. I committed suicide, remember? My car was found next to a deserted stretch of beach, and my clothes were found in a neat pile on the sand along with a suicide note. After all, *that* was the plan.' A pause. 'But none of that happened, did it?'

'No.'

'So what did happen?'

'As far as everyone is concerned you died when your house burnt to the ground. The fundamental problem with your plan was the lack of a body. Even with a suicide note, Daniel was never going to fully accept that you were dead. There was always going to be a tiny bit of doubt. Over time that doubt would have eaten away at him. Eventually he would have convinced himself that you might be alive. That *might* would have been enough to persuade him to come looking for you, and when he started looking he was never going to stop.'

'You don't know that.'

'Even now, the conspiracy nuts will tell you that Elvis is alive.'

Gabriel didn't say anything else. He just kept staring ahead until the uncertainties in Zoe's head had piled up high enough to become certainties.

'Okay,' she conceded. 'Maybe he would have come looking for me.'

'There's no maybe about it, Zoe. For him to truly believe you were dead he needed to see a body. If we'd gone through with your plan you'd be constantly looking over your shoulder just waiting for him to appear. Is that the life you want?'

'And you're just thinking to mention this now?'

'I couldn't say anything earlier. Daniel had beaten you down to the point where you didn't know which way was up and which was down. You were a wreck. A total mess. All that mattered was getting you out of your marriage. I needed you to be safe. That's all I've been doing. Keeping my Little Sis safe.'

'I'm not your little sister.'

Gabriel laughed. 'You're right, but Little Step-Sis doesn't have the same ring. It sounds like a disease.'

Zoe didn't find this funny. Not even a little bit. She stared out the windshield and tried to ignore the ache in her bladder.

◆

Time had dragged before, but now it was crawling by. The further they travelled, the more her bladder preoccupied her. She had heard pregnant women joke about needing to pee every two seconds. Now she was pregnant, she was starting to realise that it was no joke. More than once she'd been tempted to reach for the soda bottle and funnel, and that was no joke either. They were currently on the I–90, somewhere in Washington State. Spokane was fifty miles away. The last town they had passed through was sixty miles ago. Since then all she had seen were mountains and trees and whole vast tracts of empty nothingness.

Twenty miles later they passed through Tyler. The place was no more than a dot on the map, but it was big enough to have a gas station. The fuel gauge was finally showing empty. They must be running on fumes. Gabriel touched the brakes and hit the turn signal.

'There's a baseball cap in the glovebox,' he said. 'Put it on.'

Zoe opened the glovebox and took out the cap. It was black and unbranded. She adjusted the strap and put it on. Gabriel glanced over.

'Pull the cap down lower. I don't want anyone seeing your eyes. You've got the sort of eyes a person might remember.'

Zoe pulled the cap down and he glanced over again.

'That's better.'

They turned onto the forecourt and pulled up at a pump. The gas station was small. There were four pumps and a booth, and no other customers. The old guy manning the booth had a long white ponytail and a bushy mountain-man beard. He was wearing a red cotton shirt that strained to hold his gut in, and black suspenders to keep his pants up. He was sitting next to the cash register reading a magazine.

'Wait here,' Gabriel told her.

'Can't I use the restroom? I'll be back by the time you've filled up and paid.'

He didn't answer. Which meant he hadn't said no.

'Look,' she added, 'I just don't want to have to pee in that bottle with you sitting in the next seat. It's too weird.'

'So it's not the fact that you're peeing in a bottle that's causing you a problem. It's the fact that I might see.'

Zoe said nothing.

'I could close my eyes if that makes you feel better.'

'That's not funny.'

Gabriel glanced at the empty forecourt, glanced at the booth, and he still hadn't said no.

'Okay, I'm going to fill up the car, then I'll escort you to the restroom. Does that work for you?'

Zoe nodded. 'Thank you.'

Gabriel got out and unhooked the nozzle. The old guy in the booth looked up to check which pump they were at, flicked a switch to get it working, then went back to his magazine. Zoe watched the numbers on the pump climb higher. Her mind was spinning just as fast, but no matter how hard she tried she couldn't see a way out of this situation. Her mother used to tell her that you made your own bed. Those words had never seemed truer than they did now. Gabriel finished filling up then headed over to the booth to pay. He took his change then walked back to the car and opened the door for her.

'Shall we?'

He held out his hand and waited for Zoe to take it, then they walked across the forecourt like they were husband and wife. His hand was wrapped lightly around hers, but that was just for show. If she tried to run all he had to do was tighten his grip and she wouldn't be going anywhere.

The signs took them to a door that opened onto a short, narrow corridor. Gabriel pushed it open and peered inside. The corridor was dirty and hadn't been painted in decades. There were two more doors in here. One had a men's sign; the other had a shadow where a sign used to hang. He stepped back and checked the side of the building. There were two windows, one for the men's room, the other for the women's. Neither was large enough to climb out.

'I'll wait here,' he said. 'Be quick.'

Zoe stepped into the corridor and a rusty spring pulled the door squeaking back into the frame. She opened the door without the sign and went in. The toilet might have been filthy, but it was better than peeing in a bottle. She ripped off a long strip of toilet paper and wiped the seat; she hovered rather than sat. She was just finishing when she heard the squeak of the door spring. She flushed the toilet, washed her hands, then opened the door.

The woman waiting in the corridor was in her late forties. She had a flat, pale face, and the complexion and lines that came with a hard life. The suit made Zoe think that she might be a travelling salesperson. The way she smiled it was like she was saying, *Yeah I'm desperate too, but what you gonna do?* They stepped around each other, exchanging places. The woman kept giving her strange looks, and who could blame her? With her ball cap and DIY hairstyle, Zoe reckoned she must look like an asylum inmate. The door squeaked open and she stepped outside.

'There you are,' Gabriel said.

Anyone listening in would think they were husband and wife. He had that air of tired resignation down to a T. At the same time you knew that, no matter how crazy she drove him, he would love her until the day she died. The act was for the benefit of the saleswoman. She would be in the ladies' room by now, and the glass in the window was thin enough to hear what was going on outside. Gabriel took her hand and they walked back to the forecourt. He stopped at the corner. They were out of earshot of the restrooms. Out of earshot of the old guy in the booth.

'Did you talk to her?' he asked in a low whisper.

'No.'

His eyes locked on hers, searching for lies. 'Not even to say hello?'

She shook her head. 'I didn't say a word.'

'You're sure? You've been under a lot of stress lately, and stress can make people do some stupid things.'

'I didn't talk to her, Gabriel. Not a word. I promise.'

Gabriel stared a moment longer, then took her by the hand and led her back to the car. He opened the passenger door, then went around to the driver's side and got in. Instead of driving away, he sat staring through the windshield in a way that made Zoe nervous. A short while later the saleswoman came around the corner. She hesitated for a second, eyes scanning the forecourt.

'Yeah, that's what I figured.' Gabriel was nodding to himself like the pieces were slotting into place. 'So when did you get so good at lying, Zoe?'

'I'm not lying. I didn't talk to her. That's the God's honest truth.'

'Yeah, right.'

The words came out on a resigned sigh. He reached across to open the glovebox and his body brushed up against hers, causing her to sink back in her seat. He dug deep and came out with two pairs of latex gloves. He held one pair out for her.

'Put these on.'

'What are you going to do?'

'Put the gloves on.'

'Why?'

'Put the gloves on.'

She put them on. They felt greasy, cold and restrictive. Gabriel reached under his seat, brought out a silenced gun and climbed from the car. Zoe fumbled at the safety belt, trying to get it undone. By the time it was unclipped and she was out of the car, Gabriel was already taking aim. Zoe opened her mouth to shout a warning, but it was too late. The saleswoman was frozen to the spot, eyes fixed on the gun. She could see how much danger she was in. She might not understand, but she could definitely see.

Gabriel pulled the trigger and the back of the woman's skull exploded in a shower of bone and red blood mist. The effect was brutal and immediate. One second she was upright and breathing, the next she was dead on the ground. Without breaking stride, Gabriel changed direction and headed for the booth. The guy at the cash register had dropped his magazine and was staring at him. Run, Zoe thought, but it was too late. There was a brief moment of horror-stricken realisation. It lasted long enough for Gabriel to take aim and pull the trigger.

# Chapter 28

Zoe sprinted towards the highway. She had to get away. Had to escape. Gabriel was totally out of control. She stopped when she reached the road. There was no traffic coming from the left; nothing from the right. The highway was flat and straight, and completely deserted. She glanced over her shoulder, saw Gabriel running towards her, and started moving again, heading for the woods on the other side of the highway. Trees stretched away from the road as far as the eye could see. Plenty of places to hide.

'Stop, or I will shoot you.'

Zoe ran harder than ever. She didn't hear the gun go off, but she saw the place where the bullet hit the blacktop a couple of feet to her left. It was close enough for her to get hit by a few spurts of grit and dirt. She came skidding to a halt. Her heart was thundering; her body was buzzing from the sudden flood of adrenalin. The trees were only a dozen feet away, if that. So close, but they might have been on the other side of the universe. She heard his footsteps coming up behind her. He stopped at her shoulder.

'I just want to keep you safe,' he said. 'You and your baby.'

'By shooting me?' Her voice was shaking and she was trembling all over.

'I needed to get your attention. The state of mind you're in, if you'd run into those woods you might have ended up lost forever.'

She turned to face him. The gun was gone, tucked into the waistband of his jeans and hidden by his shirt. 'You shot at me.'

'That bullet went nowhere near you. Believe me, if I wanted to hit you, I would have. I don't miss, particularly not from that sort of range.' He smiled. 'Did you really think I was going to shoot you?'

Zoe didn't know what to think. She had no idea who this person was. He looked like her stepbrother, he sounded like him, but there was no way that the Gabriel she had known would have done the things she just witnessed. The Gabriel she had known had protected her from the school bullies. He had looked after her. He wasn't a cold-blooded murderer.

'Maybe we should go our separate ways,' she suggested.

'That's not a good idea.'

'Why not?'

'Because I promised to look after you. How far do you think you'll get before the cops catch up with you? There's going to be questions about what happened here; questions about what happened back in Oregon. Maybe they'll believe you when you say that I'm to blame for everything. Then again, maybe they won't. And if they don't, then you could be looking at serious prison time, and who's going to look after your baby then?'

Zoe said nothing.

'I know this is a lot to take in, but I need you to believe me when I say that I'm going to keep you safe. I need you to trust me. Can you do that?'

At that moment she didn't trust a single word that came out of his mouth, but she nodded anyway.

'Okay, let's hustle. We don't want to be hanging around here any longer than necessary.'

Zoe started moving, one heavy footstep at a time, like her sneakers were made from lead. She was still waiting for the world to start turning again. Maybe it wouldn't. Maybe she was destined to live out the rest of her life trapped in this moment. She tried not to look at the dead woman as she walked past, but couldn't help herself. This was all her fault. She followed Gabriel into the booth.

'Grab one of those plastic bags from over there and empty the cash register,' he said.

She looked where Gabriel was pointing, but didn't move.

'I need you to stay with me here. Can you do that, Zoe?'

She nodded then walked over to the counter. The old guy's chest was still, his eyes unfocussed. A halo of blood was spreading around his head. He was obese, which made it difficult to manoeuver past him. Any space back here was either taken up with his body, or his blood. She found a bag, then opened the cash register and started scooping out the bills. Today's takings didn't add up to much, eight or nine hundred dollars maybe. It hardly seemed worth the effort.

Zoe finished filling the bag and looked down at the body. The bulge in his pants pocket had to be a cell phone. Gabriel had disappeared into the back room. Why, she had no idea, but that didn't matter. Zoe crouched down and started wrestling the phone out, but the damn thing was stuck. She glanced over at the door. Any second now Gabriel was going to appear and find her down here, and how the hell was she going to explain what she was doing?

She eventually managed to fumble the phone out and quickly stood up. She switched it on and the screen lit up. There were nine dots in three rows of three. She twisted her hand and the light fell differently. She could see the dirty smear of the Z that connected seven of the dots. Zoe ran her finger across the screen, following the smear, and she was in. Another glance towards the door. Still no sign of him.

It took a second to find the icon she wanted, and another second to access the number pad. These were seconds she didn't have. She was about to punch in 911 when a noise from the back room made her freeze. She quickly switched off the phone, and only started breathing again when it was tucked safely into the waistband of her leggings and the sweatshirt was pulled down to hide the bulge. Zoe grabbed the money bag and stepped out from behind the counter. Gabriel appeared a second later.

'We've caught ourselves a lucky break,' he said. 'The security cameras were switched off. Have you got the money?'

She held up the bag and he took it from her shaking hand.

'Everything's going to be okay,' he said. 'I'm going to keep you safe. Both of you.'

Zoe met his eye then quickly looked away. Gabriel said something else as they stepped outside. All she caught were two words. 'Cell' and 'phone'. She forced herself to keep moving as though she hadn't heard.

'Zoe!'

She stopped and turned slowly.

Gabriel nodded down at the dead woman lying sprawled on the forecourt. 'I need her cell phone.'

Zoe knelt down and started looking for the phone. Rummaging through the dead woman's pockets made her feel like a ghoul. The cell was stuffed into the woman's jacket pocket. She pulled it out and held it up. Gabriel nodded once then started walking to the car. She gave it a second then followed. By the time she had got herself buckled into the passenger seat they were already moving across the forecourt and heading for the highway.

The speedometer needle hit seventy and Gabriel thumbed the cruise control. The gas station disappeared from the rear window, and Zoe was left wondering what the hell had just happened. If it hadn't been for the money bag in the footwell, and the dead woman's cell phone in her hand, and the dead guy's phone pressing into the small of her back, she would at least have made a token effort at convincing herself that none of this was happening. She removed the ball cap and put it back in the glovebox. Gabriel stopped her before she could remove the gloves.

'Not yet. I need you to check the call log on the phone.'

Unlocking the cell was easy enough. All she had to do was hold her finger on the screen for a couple of seconds. Finding the log took a little longer.

'The last call she made was forty-eight minutes ago,' Zoe said. 'To another cell number.'

'Show me.'

She held the phone up. Her hand was still shaking. Daniel had scared her plenty, but not like this.

'Can you keep your hand still?'

Zoe used her free hand to steady the one holding the cell. It took another three glances before Gabriel was convinced.

'Switch it off and remove the battery.'

She did what he asked. He pressed a button on his door and the passenger window buzzed down. A blast of cool air rushed in and ruffled her hair.

'Toss the battery into the undergrowth. Pitch is as far as you can, like when you used to play softball. Give it a mile, then do the same thing with the phone.'

Zoe wound her arm back and threw the battery, letting it fly. It sailed through the air and disappeared into the long grass. She waited for Gabriel to give her the nod, then threw the phone. She was expecting the window to go back up but it didn't.

'Get the money bag.'

She reached between her legs and retrieved the bag from the footwell. Gabriel looked over.

'Tie a knot in the top, and tie it tight.'

She did what he asked and he glanced over again.

'Now throw it out the window.'

She looked over because she wanted to make sure she had heard right.

'I don't want anything that connects us to the gas station,' he added.

'So why steal the money?'

'Because the cops will think this was a robbery that went wrong.'

She waited for more, but that was all she was getting. She threw the bag out and watched it disappear into the undergrowth. The window buzzed back up.

'You can take the gloves off now.'

Zoe pulled them off and rolled them into a ball. Gabriel did the same with his. He passed them over and told her to put them into the glovebox. The question in her eyes was answered with a question of his own.

'They weigh next to nothing. How far do you think you'd be able to throw them? We'll get rid of them next time we stop for gas.'

She put the gloves into the glovebox.

'There's a bag of food on the back seat. Get me a candy bar, please. Have something yourself, if you're hungry.'

Zoe wanted to ask how he could eat after what happened, but didn't. Just thinking about food was enough to make her feel nauseous. The last time she had eaten was at breakfast. She knew she should at least try to have something, for the baby if nothing else, but she just couldn't face anything right now. She reached for the bag and passed him a Musketeers, watched as he ripped the candy bar open and took a bite. Zoe looked at him for a while longer but he was clearly done talking for now. She settled back in the passenger seat and stared out the windshield again.

# Chapter 29

They kept on the I–90 after Spokane. Nothing was said for the next five hours, and nothing much happened except darkness started to fall. The miles disappeared behind them, each one looking pretty much the same as the last. They were both staring through the windshield, lost in their thoughts and the silence. All Zoe could see was the road stretching on forever. All she could hear was the steady thrum of the tyres rolling over black-top. Mile after mile after mile. There wasn't even the distraction of the radio to break the monotony.

She had managed to stop shaking, but the terror was still there, burrowing into her gut. From time to time she would glance over at the driver's seat and wonder what the hell she was going to do. The cell phone stuffed into her waistband was a curse and a blessing. Having it there offered up a slim glimmer of hope, but how the hell was she going to use it when he was watching her like a hawk?

Gabriel had turned up on her doorstep shortly after his mom died. It had been years since they last spoke. This hadn't been a conscious decision; it was just one of those things that happened. After he joined the army, she had seen him a couple of times when he was home on leave, but those visits had gotten further apart, then stopped altogether. By the time she went to college it had been two years since she'd last seen him.

Gabriel had wanted to know why she hadn't been at the funeral; he wanted to know if she was okay. She had come up with some lame excuse that he was never going to buy, but he hadn't called her on the lie. She wanted him to go in case Daniel turned up, but couldn't just send him away without it seeming weird, so they had chatted for a short while at the front door then she'd made some excuse about somewhere she needed to be.

A couple of months later he turned up on her doorstep again. This time she told him outright that these unscheduled visits weren't a good idea. He'd asked why and she'd come up with another bullshit excuse that was as lame as her reason for not going to the funeral. The way he had looked at her, it was like he knew what Daniel was doing, although how he could know, she had no idea. He might not have called her on this lie either, but he had given her his number and told her to call if she ever needed anything.

Anything at all.

The way he said this made her wonder again about what he might have actually known. Even though she had no intention of calling him, she had memorised the number, then burnt the slip of paper it had been written on and gone back to her life of cornflakes and water and dinner smoothies. What could he do anyway? What could anyone do?

Then she had fallen pregnant. Desperate and with no one else to turn to, she had reached out to Gabriel. They had met up and it was as though he had just been waiting for her to call. Like she thought, he had a pretty good idea of what Daniel had been up to. He didn't know the full story. Even after that first meeting, he still didn't know everything, but he knew enough.

After she'd filled him in he had gone quiet for a moment, then admitted that he'd been working as a security guard at Myriadian so he could watch Daniel. Zoe had no idea what to make of that. On the one hand it was reassuring to know that there was someone out there who cared enough to look out for her. On the other, the fact that he would do something like that seemed overwhelming after all her years of being alone. Still, she didn't see that she had any option other than to trust him. The fact she was pregnant changed everything. Whatever it took, she had to get away from Daniel.

Back then she hadn't thought she was in any danger from Gabriel. After all, he was Big Brother, and his job had always been to protect her. Except that had been then and this was now. A lot of water had flowed under the bridge. They had both experienced the harsher side of life, and that changed a person. But what sort of person had Gabriel changed into? That was one of the questions currently preoccupying her. She knew he was capable of killing, but where did he draw the line? Did he actually have any lines? In other words, would he kill her? The Gabriel she had grown up with would never have done anything to hurt her, and he sure as hell wouldn't have shot at her even if he was aiming to miss. She didn't know anything about this new version, though.

They didn't stop again until they reached Montana. Butte was the last place of any note that they had passed, and that had been ten miles ago. The gas tank was almost empty again, Zoe's bladder full. Gabriel pulled into a gas station and stopped at a pump. A Ford Fusion was parked beside one of the pumps. The driver was in the booth paying for his gas. There were no other customers.

'I need to use the restroom,' Gabriel said. 'I take it you need to go too?'

Zoe had spent the last three hundred miles trying to forget what had happened the last time, and now she had been slammed right back into that moment. Somehow she managed to nod her head.

'Okay, here's how this works. I'm going to fill up the car and go pay. When you see me come out, come and join me. We'll go to the restrooms together. Please don't speak to anyone.'

Gabriel reached into the glovebox and took out the baseball cap and the used gloves. The ball cap he handed to her; the gloves went into the trash can at the side of the pump. He filled the car then went to pay. Zoe could feel the cell phone burning into the small of her back, but she couldn't use it because Gabriel kept looking over. She watched him take out his wallet; saw him hand over a couple of bills; saw him put the wallet into his back pocket. Saw him look over yet again. By the time he got outside, she was waiting at the door. They walked to the restrooms hand in hand, just a husband and wife vacationing in beautiful Montana. He held open the men's room door and for a moment she just stood there staring at the open doorway.

'After what happened last time, it's best if we do it this way.'

'I didn't say anything to that woman.'

Gabriel considered this for a moment. 'Whether you did or didn't doesn't really matter. The important thing is that she didn't call the police.' He smiled. 'No damage done.'

*No damage done.* Two people were dead. That mattered.

Zoe went in. There was a cubicle and a urinal, and the smell of piss was only partially disguised by the cleaning chemicals. She walked into the cubicle and pushed the door closed. She was just about to reach for the phone when the door swung open. Gabriel looked over her shoulder at the window. It was big enough for a cat to climb through, but that was about it.

'I want this door left open.'

He turned and walked over to the urinal. Zoe heard a zip go down, then splashing.

'I'd hurry if I were you,' he called out. 'We leave when I'm done.'

Zoe's heart was hammering against her ribs; her hands were shaking again. She didn't know what to do with the cell phone. She couldn't exactly hold it. That would be too risky. All he needed to do was glance through the open door and he would see it. In the end she pushed it into her sock and prayed that it didn't work loose. The solution was far from perfect but it was all she had. Gabriel still hadn't finished, but that wasn't surprising. The last time he went was back at the cabin in Oregon, and that was seven hundred miles ago. They both finished at pretty much the same time. Zoe had just managed to get her leggings back up when his face appeared in the cubicle doorway. The phone would have to stay in her sock.

'All done?' he asked.

She nodded. He held out his hand and she took it.

'If we meet anyone on the way out, just smile like you enjoyed it.'

It took a second to get the joke. Now they were that horny couple who just couldn't keep their hands off of one another; that couple who were so desperate they'd do it in a filthy gas station restroom. Zoe smiled, because that was the reaction he was looking for. That was a lesson she had learnt from her marriage. Life ran more smoothly when they thought you were on the same page. It was incredible, really. When she woke up this morning she had thought that Gabriel was her saviour. Now he was the enemy. How the hell had that happened?

Thankfully, they didn't meet anyone on the way out. The forecourt was empty when they got back to the car, which was another reason to be thankful. The guy in the booth wasn't paying them any attention, and that was a third. The cell phone seemed to be secure enough in her sock, and that was a fourth. All Zoe wanted was to get away from here without anyone else dying. There had been too much death today.

A short while later they were back on the I–90, heading deeper into Montana. Gabriel took the tub of caffeine pills from his pocket, shook two into his hand and dry swallowed them. He brought the car up to seventy and set the cruise control. Full darkness had come down hard and it felt like they were flying through space.

'I'm hungry,' he said. 'Can you get the food bag?'

She reached across to the back seat and grabbed the bag. 'What would you like?'

'Some chips would be good.'

Zoe pulled out a bag of chips, opened it, then passed it over. He wedged the bag between his legs and started to eat.

'How about you?' he asked. 'Aren't you hungry?'

Zoe shook her head. 'Not really.'

'You really should eat something. For the baby.'

She peered into the bag but there was nothing to tempt her. It was all junk. Candy bars, muffins, another bag of chips, Coke. The healthiest thing was the water. She took out a fresh bottle and swapped it for the empty one in the door pocket. The muffins were chocolate chip, and wrapped in cellophane, and packed with enough preservatives to keep them fresh until the end of time. The water aside, this was the healthiest option. She took one out, ripped off the wrapper, and started eating. Gabriel kept stealing glances from the driver's seat, which did nothing for her appetite.

She wanted to demand to know why he was doing this.

She wanted him to stay the hell away from her and her baby.

She wanted to kill him.

# Chapter 30

'Wake up, Zoe.'

In the moment it took her to come around, Zoe was lost in a nightmare where she was running blind through a maze that seemed to have dead ends whichever way she turned. The dream was so real it was like it was actually happening. It was also frighteningly familiar because it seemed to sum up her whole existence. She became aware of the road moving beneath her and the steady pulse of the Cherokee's engine, and, although she'd worked out that she wasn't dreaming, she was all too aware that things were very wrong in her world. Her eyes sprang open. The darkness inside the car was painted red and blue, which did nothing to ease her anxieties. She looked over her shoulder and saw a police cruiser riding their bumper. Her eyes snapped to the front again. The speedometer needle was slowly creeping towards zero.

'It's probably just a routine stop,' Gabriel said. 'Nothing to worry about.'

Zoe said nothing.

'I need you to listen carefully,' he continued. 'As soon as you see the uniform, you might be tempted to shout for help. I'd rather you didn't.'

'I won't shout. I promise.'

Gabriel pressed a finger against his lips and she immediately stopped talking. She couldn't get over how calm he was. Her heart was thundering and her thoughts were twisting like there was a tornado inside her brain, but he was sitting there looking as self-possessed as ever, like this was no big deal. They were off the main highway now, bumping along the verge. The needle fell from ten to zero and the Cherokee rolled to a standstill. The cop car came to a stop ten yards behind them. For a long time nothing happened. The cop was silhouetted in the driver's seat, but she couldn't tell what he was doing.

'Relax,' Gabriel said. 'He's just running our plates.'

Relaxing was impossible. She felt as though the cop's life was in her hands. One slip and Gabriel would kill him. The fact that he was a cop made no difference. His arm moved towards her and his hand came to a rest on hers. She wanted to tell him to back the hell off. Instead, she just sat there, frozen to the seat, her mouth shut tight.

'Relax,' Gabriel whispered again.

Zoe didn't respond. She glanced over her shoulder and saw the cop climb out. She watched him lumbering closer, the beam from his flashlight leading the way. He was overweight and slow, and pushing towards retirement, which was yet another reason to worry. If he had been even halfway competent he wouldn't be stuck out here on his own in the dead hours of morning, he would have had a cushy desk job. The cop tapped the driver's window with his flashlight and Gabriel lowered it.

'Is there a problem, officer?'

The light from the flashlight invaded the car, the beam playing over Gabriel's face, then Zoe's. It was impossible not to squint, which must have made her look guilty. Any second now he was going to step back, draw his gun and tell them to step out of the car. She hoped to God that he couldn't see her fear. At the same time she was hoping he could read her thoughts, because he needed to walk away from here and get back in his car and radio for backup, and he needed to do that now.

'Did you know that one of your tail lights is out?'

'I didn't,' Gabriel replied. 'Thanks for letting me know.'

This was it, she thought. The cop was one of those people who did everything by the book. He was going to ask for papers, then he was going to write a ticket, and at some point things were going to go wrong and Gabriel would decide it was easier to kill him.

'Can I see your licence and registration, please?'

'Sure.' Gabriel turned to face Zoe. 'Honey, can you get them? They're in the glovebox.'

Zoe rummaged around in the glovebox until she found them. If the angles had been different, the cop would have seen the box of latex gloves, and that might have raised his suspicions. It took all her willpower to keep her hands from shaking. She passed the documents to Gabriel, and he passed them to the cop. The beam of the flashlight played over the documents one at a time. When he got to the driver's licence he flashed the light at Gabriel so he could check the photo against the face. The cop handed the papers back and Gabriel passed them to Zoe to put in the glovebox.

'I'm not going to write you a ticket this time. But see and get that light fixed.'

'Thank you, officer. I appreciate it. And I'll make sure that gets done today.'

Zoe was waiting for the cop to go back to his car. He needed to get out of here. He had no idea how lucky he had been.

'So where are you folks headed?' he asked, and she wanted to scream.

'Buffalo. We're visiting family.'

'You're getting an early start, then?'

'I prefer driving at night. Less traffic to deal with.'

'Amen to that. Okay, you'd best be getting on your way. And remember that tail light.'

'I will. And thanks again. I appreciate it.'

Gabriel buzzed the window up and pulled onto the highway. The needle moved lazily towards seventy and the cop car shrank in the rear window. Zoe kept watching until it was out of sight.

'You did good back there, Zoe.'

She stared tight-lipped at the road and said nothing.

'It's okay, you can breathe again,' he added.

# Chapter 31

They passed into South Dakota as the new day broke. The sky was grey and low; rain was on the way. Gabriel looked as though he was flagging. And no wonder. He had been driving for nineteen hours straight. He kept rubbing at his face as though that might be enough to push the sleep away. For a brief moment the sun broke through the clouds and lit the inside of the car golden. She touched her belly. *Looks like we live to fight another day.*

A short while after passing through Spearfish they drove into the Black Hills National Forest. The roads got progressively narrower, the signs of civilisation dwindled to nothing, and then they were bumping along a narrow forgotten dirt track and this could have been the last place on earth. All Zoe could see were trees and that leaden grey sky.

The track went on for about six or seven miles before ending at a small clearing. The small single-storey log cabin looked as though it had been there forever. The wood had weathered so much it appeared black, and there were bright red drapes in the windows. The large satellite dish at the side of the cabin was new. Gabriel parked up and killed the engine. For a short while he just sat with his hands resting on the steering wheel and stared blankly through the windshield like he was still seeing the road. He took a deep breath, let go of a long sigh, then got out. Zoe glanced over to make sure he wasn't watching, then leant forward and quickly checked the cell phone was still snug in her sock.

She caught up with him at the front door. The inside of the cabin was surprisingly homely. The sofa and armchair were covered with coloured throws; the bookcase was filled with paperbacks. The kitchen area was small but functional. There was a stove, a refrigerator, a freezer and a microwave. Everything was different from how she remembered, yet it was somehow the same.

'This way,' Gabriel said, and he sounded infinitely weary. He led her to the bathroom and waited at the door while she peed. There were two toothbrushes in a plastic tumbler on the edge of the sink. She guessed the pink one was hers, and if that was the case, how long had he been planning this for? She turned on the faucet and used the noise to mask the sound of the cabinet opening. She hoped to find something she might use to help her escape – a razor, sleeping pills, anything – but the cabinet was empty.

'What are you doing in there?' Gabriel called through the door. 'I'd like to get to bed sometime this week. If that's okay with you, that is.'

Zoe shut the cabinet door. Quietly and carefully. She turned off the faucet and headed out. Gabriel led her to the small bedroom at the back of the cabin. When she was younger this had been her room. Everything was so familiar. Same bed, same scratched thrift store nightstand, same bureau. Even the smell was the same. Dusty and ancient, yet somehow fresh. The view from the window took in a million trees. There was a roll of duct tape on the nightstand, a water bottle and a straw.

Gabriel picked up the duct tape up and Zoe felt her heart stutter to a halt.

'You don't have to do this,' she said

'Unfortunately, I do. Sit down on the bed.'

'Don't do this.'

'Sit down. Please.'

She sat.

'Give me the cell phone.'

Zoe's mouth went dry. 'I don't have a cell phone.'

Gabriel just stared until she took the phone from her sock and placed it on the bed.

'How long have you known?' she asked quietly.

'Since the gas station. I saw you on the security cameras.'

'You said they were switched off.'

He smiled a tired smile. 'I lied.'

He taped her ankles together first, then her lower legs, then her thighs. When he got to her hands, he asked her to put them behind her back. When he was done, he picked up the cell phone and headed for the bedroom door.

'Why?' she asked. There were a whole load of questions buried in that one word. *Why have you brought me here? Why are you doing this? Why, why, why?* Gabriel hesitated in a way that made her think he was going to answer, then drew in a long, weary breath.

'I'm going to get some sleep, Zoe.'

Before leaving, he removed the cap from the water bottle. Because her hands were bound behind her back, the straw suddenly made sense. He closed the door and she heard his footsteps tapping on the old wooden boards. The door of the main bedroom creaked open, then closed again. The squeaking of the bed was followed by two dull thuds as his boots hit the floor. There were more squeaks as he settled down, then everything went quiet.

Zoe gave it a couple more minutes in case he came back, then lay down on the bed. Having her hands behind her back made it impossible to get comfortable. It was also impossible to free herself. The rain had finally started. It was smacking against the window and getting heavier. Even as she closed her eyes, she knew she wouldn't be getting any sleep. This was not how she'd imagined things turning out. Lying on a hard bed, bound and trapped in the middle of nowhere. That had never been a part of the plan.

With her eyes closed she could disappear into the darkness for a while, and that was the next best thing to sleep. Pretending that none of this was happening proved a step too far, but at least the darkness provided a layer of insulation between herself and this latest nightmare. It wasn't fair. After all those years imprisoned in her hellish marriage she thought she'd finally found a way out, but all she had done was swap one nightmare for another. To kill the time, she told the baby some of the stories her mom used to tell her when she was little, stories of dragons and princesses and magical lands.

Stories that started with 'once upon a time' and ended with the monster being slain.

# Chapter 32

The rain cracking against the window softened then stopped as the last light drained from the day. The wet green smell of the forest seemed to be everywhere. Zoe could hear Gabriel moving around in his bedroom. A door opened and he walked through to the bathroom. The shower came on, and stayed on for a few minutes. When he finally appeared his hair was damp and he was wearing fresh clothes. He looked rested, which was more than Zoe could say. She felt wretched, like she was back at college and had just pulled an all-nighter.

Gabriel took a switchblade from his pocket and popped the blade. He freed her feet and legs first, then her arms, the sharp blade slicing easily through the tape. She rubbed her arms to get the blood flowing again. Pins and needles pricked at her bones and her skin stung from the adhesive. Gabriel folded the knife shut and pushed it into his jeans pocket.

'I need to use the toilet,' she said.

'No one's stopping you.'

With that he was gone. Zoe went through to the bathroom. She peed, then washed her hands and face. The person staring back from the cabinet mirror looked like a survivor from a war zone. Her skin was pale, her eyes tired. There were streaks of red shooting through the whites and dark bags hanging underneath.

Zoe still couldn't get used to the short blonde hair. She opened the cabinet, but it was still empty. She found Gabriel standing at the work surface in the kitchen area. There were chopped vegetables on the board and a frying pan on the stove. He saw her and smiled.

'I take it you still make a pretty mean omelette?'

'We need to talk.'

'First we need to eat.'

'Nobody was supposed to die, Gabriel.'

'Eat first, then we'll talk.'

Zoe stared at him until he stepped aside. Everything she needed was laid out in front of her. A box of eggs, a block of cheese and a grater to her left, and small neat piles of mushrooms, peppers and onion on the board, everything already chopped. There were no knives. She glanced around the kitchen area. Anything that might be used as a weapon had been removed.

She grated the cheese, beat the eggs into a bowl, then got the pan sizzling. Cooking for Daniel had been torture; knowing that she was going to eat too made a whole world of difference. She finished making the omelette, slid it onto a plate and carried it to the table. There were two places set. Gabriel's fork and knife were metal; hers plastic. The plastic cutlery completely wrecked any illusion of normality. She placed the plate in front of him.

'Can I have a drink, please, Zoe? There's a carton of orange juice in the fridge. The glasses are in that cupboard over there.'

Zoe followed his finger to a cupboard near the sink. Like the bathroom, the glasses were actually plastic tumblers. She poured two orange juices, placed the tumblers on the table, then went back to the stove and made an omelette for herself. She carried her plate to the table, placed it between the plastic knife and fork, then sat down and started to eat. Being able to eat like a normal person was still a novelty. The first day she had overdone it and made herself sick. Since then she had paced herself, only eating small amounts of any foods that were richer than she was used to. Hopefully in another week or so she wouldn't have to be so careful. Gabriel finished eating and laid his cutlery on the plate. Zoe laid hers down too. She had only eaten half of her omelette, but that was enough for now.

'You want to talk,' he said. 'Let's talk.'

'Why did you kill Josh?'

'I didn't kill Josh. Your husband did that all by himself. He walked up to him, pressed the gun to his head and blew his brains out.'

'Maybe you didn't pull the trigger, but you allowed it to happen, and that makes you responsible. I was upstairs, remember? I heard the whole thing.'

'And I suppose I'm responsible for Daniel's death too.'

The way he left the sentence hanging, it was clear what he was getting at. 'I did not kill Daniel,' she said quietly.

Gabriel shook his head. 'The way I recall it, you gave the trigger that final squeeze.'

Zoe said nothing. She hadn't wanted Daniel to die. Even after everything he'd done, she hadn't wanted that. She told herself this because it was what she needed to believe, but how many times had she lain awake at night wishing him dead? How many times had she imagined the ways? And how many times had she looked into the fantasy and seen herself doing the actual killing? If there was a God, and a final reckoning, how would those last moments back in Oregon be judged? Because, when all was said and done, her finger had been on the trigger. As to who gave it that final squeeze, maybe it was Gabriel, but it could just as easily have been her.

'You said that the problem with my plan was the lack of a body. Isn't that the problem with your plan too?'

'Don't worry, the cops found a body.'

'Jesus, Gabriel. How many people have you killed?'

'I did what needed to be done to keep you safe.'

'But I didn't want you to kill anyone. So who was she?'

'That doesn't matter. All that matters is that you're safe.'

They locked eyes. Zoe wanted to look away but forced herself to hold his gaze. 'I think I'd like to leave now.'

'That wouldn't be a good idea,' Gabriel replied carefully.

'So, what? I'm a prisoner?'

'Of course you're not a prisoner.'

'In that case, I'd like to leave. I can go and stay with Lizzy in New York.'

Gabriel said nothing.

'So, I am a prisoner. I guess the duct tape should have been a giveaway. The fact that you drugged me back in Oregon, well, I guess that was a bit of a giveaway too.'

'I'm sorry about that. Really sorry. If there had been another way.' He shrugged. 'But there wasn't.'

For a moment the anger eclipsed her fear. Anger at the way Gabriel had been keeping her in the dark and making unilateral decisions; anger at Daniel for pushing her into this situation in the first place.

'Here's an idea,' she said. 'Maybe you could have told me what you were up to.'

'Would you have sanctioned killing Daniel?'

It was Zoe's turn to say nothing.

'The situation back in Oregon was too volatile,' Gabriel added. 'I needed to make sure you kept quiet and didn't get hurt. That's why I restrained you. As soon as the situation was under control I took the tape off.'

'Is that supposed to make me feel better?'

'No. You wanted to know why I did what I did. That's why I did it.'

'So you taped me up for my own good?'

Gabriel nodded. 'I'm sorry, but it was the only way.'

'And I suppose that's your excuse for last night.'

Gabriel nodded.

'So, what? You were worried that I might go walking off into the woods and get lost? Was that it?'

'That was part of it.'

'What was the other part?'

'If you just turned up on Lizzy's doorstep what do you think would happen?'

'I guess I'd stay with her until I got back on my feet and then I'd probably go and find a place of my own.'

Gabriel smiled. 'And that's what I've always loved about you, Zoe. You're a dreamer with a tenuous connection to the real world.'

'What's that supposed to mean?'

'Your husband has been murdered. When the police start connecting the dots they'll discover you have one hell of a motive.'

'I didn't kill Daniel.'

'Good luck convincing them.'

Zoe glared at him. 'You still didn't need to tape me up.'

'And if I hadn't, would you have still been here when I woke up?' Gabriel shook his head. 'No, I would have woken up to find both you and my car gone.'

'So why didn't you just explain what was going on? I would have listened.'

'You might have listened, but would you have complied?'

Zoe said nothing.

'Look, I'd just driven halfway across the country. I didn't have the energy for a conversation like that. It was just easier to use the duct tape.'

'Easier for you, maybe.'

'I've already apologised. You want me to apologise again? Fine. I'm sorry.'

'That doesn't make up for what you've done. Not even close.'

'Remember, you came to me, and you did that because you wanted to get free from Daniel. Is he going to hurt you anymore? No, he's not. Is he going to hurt your baby? Again, the answer is no. You're safe here, Zoe. At the end of the day that's all that matters.'

Without another word, Gabriel walked off down the corridor, heading towards the bedrooms. Once again, Zoe was left wondering who this stranger was. She'd trusted him only to discover he wasn't the person she thought, and hadn't she done the exact same thing with Daniel? *Fool me once, shame on you. Fool me twice, shame on me.* She glanced at his plate. The knife and fork were laid neatly on top. Could she steal them without him noticing? Probably not. Maybe later he would get lazy and she could do that, but not yet. When he eventually returned he was holding an electronic tag bracelet in his right hand and a tube of superglue in his left.

'No way,' she said.

'It's for your own good.'

Zoe snorted a humourless laugh. 'You're seriously going to use that argument again?'

'You've been under a lot of stress lately. You're not thinking straight. It would be crazy for you to get this far only to screw it up by doing something dumb and ending up in prison.'

'No, Gabriel, letting you put that thing on my leg would be crazy.'

'Do you think this is easy for me?'

'I don't care if it's easy. I don't want that thing on my leg.'

'Zoe, when you came to me for help, what was my one and only condition?'

'You said that you would help, but we needed to do things your way.'

'No arguments.'

'No arguments,' she echoed quietly.

'I've risked my freedom for you. The least you can do is uphold your end of our agreement.'

'But this wasn't how it was supposed to play out.'

'No, it wasn't, but this is where we've ended up, and the sooner we adapt to this new reality the better it'll be for both of us.' He held the tag up. 'This is only temporary. Once you're thinking straight, I'll take it off. I promise.'

Zoe responded with a glare.

'Roll up your leggings, please.'

She hesitated, then did what he asked. After fixing the tag to her ankle, Gabriel glued the two ends together.

'You're good for twenty yards all the way around the cabin,' he said. 'Go any further and an alert will be sent to my satellite phone.'

Silence spread slowly between them. It was Gabriel who broke it.

'Whenever you start seeing me as the enemy, please remember that it was Daniel who wanted you dead. He was the real enemy.'

'In that case take this thing off my leg.'

'I can't do that. Not yet.'

'But you will.'

'I promised I would, and I always keep my promises. I didn't rescue you from one prison just to put you in another.'

Zoe said nothing.

'Here's something else to think about. Daniel wanted you dead. He wanted that so bad he risked life and liberty to go looking for a contract killer. Now what do you think would have happened if he had found someone else to do the job?'

Again, she said nothing. This time because she could see exactly where this was going.

Zoe washed the dishes and counted off the seconds until bedtime. She doubted she would sleep; she just wanted to get away from Gabriel. He was on the sofa, reading a battered paperback copy of Stephen King's *The Dead Zone*. He'd always been a big reader. That was something they'd had in common when they were younger. She put the plates away then walked over to the sofa. He finished the page he was on before acknowledging her.

'What is it, Zoe?'

'I'd like to go to bed.'

'You don't need my permission.'

She turned and began walking away. Gabriel let her take two steps before telling her to stop.

'Over time your world will become bigger again,' he said to her back. 'Unfortunately, before that happens there will be a certain amount of boundary-pushing on your part. Right now all you're thinking about is escaping. It's only natural. When things are at their bleakest, just remember that you'd be dead by now if I hadn't brought you here. You can think of this as your prison, or you can think of this as a second chance. I'm hoping you'll opt for the latter.'

She turned slowly to face him. 'Is that supposed to make me feel better?'

Gabriel shook his head. 'That would be too much to expect. It's just something to think about, that's all.'

She turned and started walking away. Gabriel let her take another step before telling her to stop again.

'I'm going to need your sneakers.'

She took them off, handed them over, then headed for her room.

'Goodnight, Little Sis,' he called out softly.

# Chapter 33

The first thing Zoe did when she reached her room was examine the electronic tag. It was loose enough to keep the circulation flowing, but too tight to slip over her ankle. The tough plastic would be hard to cut through, even if she did have access to the right tools; the fact that the lock was glued shut made it impossible to open. Next she tried the window, but it wouldn't budge. The hard clear lumps around the frame made her wonder if this had been glued shut as well. Gabriel could talk all he wanted about her not being a prisoner, but that was bullshit. If she had really been free would she be sleeping in a bedroom where the windows had been glued shut?

The top drawer of the bureau contained underwear. Panties, bras, socks. Everything was made from cotton rather than lace. It was practical rather than sexy, and as far removed from the lingerie Daniel used to make her wear as it was possible to get. Zoe picked up a bra and read the label. It was her size. The panties too. The next drawer contained three T-shirts and three shirts. It came as no surprise to see that these were in her size too. Gabriel must have gone through her stuff at the house on Fairfield Boulevard. The idea creeped her out until she remembered the electronic tag. Going through her underwear drawer was one thing; holding her captive was in a different league altogether.

There were jeans and sweatshirts in the bottom drawer. The pockets of the jeans had been sewn shut, front and back. Gabriel clearly didn't want her hiding anything in them. More than anything, these jeans highlighted what was going on here. She might be free to move through the house, and she might be free to go to bed when she wanted, and there might not be any window bars or door locks or handcuffs, but any freedom she had was an illusion. The roll of duct tape was still sitting on top of the nightstand. If she needed another reminder, that would do it. There were so many parallels to her life with Daniel. That too had been a world built on fantasy, lies and half-truths.

She closed the drawer and sat on the bed. The way she was sitting was uncomfortable, but this was intentional. Her back was aching, and whenever she nodded off her head tilted uncomfortably, jerking her awake again. Gabriel was watching TV in the other room, the sound down low. He needed to hurry up and go to bed, because she didn't know how much longer she could stay awake for.

*Goodnight, Little Sis.*

There was a time when that might have made her smile. Everyone wanted to belong somewhere; everyone wanted to know there was someone out there who loved and looked out for them. She wasn't smiling now, though. Like her life with Daniel, there was the before and there was the after. With Daniel the tipping point had been the Day of Stones. With Gabriel, the point where everything changed was that moment back in Oregon when he had slipped something into her coffee and she had woken up to find herself restrained and gagged. To start with she had been more pissed than scared, but that was because she still viewed Gabriel as family.

After her mom died there had been a couple of long years of grieving, both for herself and her father. Back then it had felt as though the sun would never shine again, but over time the dark clouds had slowly parted. One day her father had taken her out to McDonald's and told her he'd met someone. She could tell straightaway it was serious. After some initial misgivings she had come around to the idea. The fact that her father was smiling properly for the first time since her mom's cancer diagnosis went a long way towards this.

Thankfully the woman he'd met seemed nice enough. She wasn't her mom – no one could replace her – but she treated her well. Gabriel seemed okay too. He was fifteen, so three years older than her. He didn't speak much but that didn't bother her because she didn't speak much either. The Little Sis tag went back to their early days. He started calling her that after their parents had sat them down and informed them that they were getting married. He had turned to her and cracked an awkward teenage boy smile and said, 'I guess that makes you my Little Sis, then.' She had returned the smile and said, 'I guess that makes you Big Brother.' That's how they referred to each other from then on. Little Sis and Big Brother.

After the marriage they had moved to South Dakota and settled in Rapid City. Gabriel's grandmother had been ill and his mother wanted to be close by to help look after her. Zoe hadn't minded too much. She might still be living in the middle of nowhere, but at least there weren't memories of her mom everywhere she looked. The other advantage of Rapid City was that they could get out to this cabin on a regular basis. During the summer months that meant every weekend. Most teenage kids would have hated the solitude, but Zoe had loved it because she could read to her heart's content. And Gabriel had loved it because he liked to hunt and fish. The cabin had been in his family for years. For a while back then it had been their second home.

The last time she had been here was the day her father died. He'd gotten up with the sun and gone hunting with Gabriel, something they'd done countless times. Zoe had been reading in the living room when she heard her stepmom screaming. The first thing she saw when she got outside was her father's body lying in the middle of the clearing in front of the cabin. Gabriel was standing beside him breathing hard, his T-shirt soaked with sweat. They had been hunting at the far side of the lake when the aneurysm had struck. Seemingly he had been dead before he hit the ground. Gabriel had carried him back on his shoulder, a distance of maybe four miles.

The one and only time they had talked about what happened, he told her that he hadn't left him there because the wolves would have got him. The thought of this had given her nightmares for a month. Gabriel hadn't been trying to scare her; he had just been giving a straight, honest answer to her question. Carrying a dead body for four miles on his back had been the obvious solution to the problem. At least it had been obvious to him. In hindsight she could now see that what seemed obvious to Gabriel might not be obvious to anyone else. He would see a problem, and see the answer, and emotion just didn't come into the equation.

She had never asked him about this again.

Zoe had carried on living with her stepmom until she went to college. Within six months of her moving out, her stepmom had met a new man on the Internet and relocated to Hawaii to live with him. Their wedding was the last time Zoe had seen her. Flying out to Hawaii wasn't an option, not when she could barely cover her rent; and because she was too busy with all the distractions that came with being a student, she kept missing her stepmom's calls. When Daniel came into her life those calls had gotten even further apart until they eventually stopped altogether.

Her stepmom had died suddenly from a heart attack almost a year to the day after Zoe graduated. By that point her world had shrunk so much she hadn't been able to make the funeral, something she always regretted. Her stepmom had been good to her. She should have said goodbye properly. It was just one more regret to add to a list that seemed never-ending.

# Chapter 34

By the time Gabriel finally switched the television off, Zoe had resorted to pinching her leg to stay awake. She could feel the places where the bruises were going to appear. Gabriel used the bathroom then went through to his bedroom. Zoe listened to him getting settled, then waited some more. She counted out thirty minutes' worth of seconds then tiptoed to the door. The wooden floor froze her feet; she could make out the joins in the wood through the thin material of her socks.

She pressed an ear against the door, then stepped into the hallway and tiptoed quietly along it. With every step she kept expecting Gabriel to come bursting out of his bedroom. The living room was cloaked in darkness. She could just about make out the slightly darker shapes that marked the furniture. The shadows matched the map inside her head, but she still moved slowly, arms waving from side to side in front of her, searching the empty air for surprises. She reached the door and tried the handle. The front door was locked. There was no sign of the key.

Zoe tiptoed over to the window, carefully, quietly, each step taking her a heartbeat closer to disaster. The window was latched but not locked. It let out the tiniest of squeaks when it opened. She froze to the spot, eyes searching the darkness, ears straining to hear.

No sign of Gabriel.

She pushed the window all the way open and climbed out. For a couple of seconds she stood there acclimatising to the night. This darkness was different. Inside the cabin it had been small and contained; out here it was infinite. The low clouds were spread across the sky, stealing the stars and moon. The damp smell of the forest filled her nose. Her socks were wet and freezing and she could feel every single stone.

Zoe counted out fifteen strides, aiming for the point where she thought the dirt track began. She stopped and glanced over her shoulder. The cabin was dark and still. No sign of Gabriel. She took another step, then stopped and glanced over her shoulder again. Still no sign of Gabriel. She took another, stopped again, glanced back. All quiet. She reached twenty. Nothing. Twenty-one. Still nothing. She could sense the trees in front of her. This was a moving darkness, like eddies of ink swimming through the black. The trees were whispering, sharing their secrets. She counted out her twenty-fifth stride. Maybe the tag was a bluff. She took another step and glanced back. She was about to take another when a light came on in the cabin. Just the one, and it wasn't particularly bright, but it was still an affront to the darkness.

She broke into a run, heading for the trees. Stones cut through her wet socks, slicing and jabbing at her feet; branches and twigs scratched at her face and clothes as the forest closed around her. Within six yards she could barely see the cabin anymore. Zoe stopped running and edged her way back towards the treeline, searching for a place where she could see the door. The lights of the living room came on and the door swung open. Gabriel's silhouette filled up most of the doorway.

'Zoe,' he called out. 'I know you can hear me. There are two ways you can play this. You can keep running or you can come back inside. If you come back, there won't be any repercussions, I promise. Like I said earlier, it's only natural for you to try to escape. If you want to keep running, that's fine too. That's what the tag bracelet is for. I'll wait until morning, then I'll come get you. Alternatively you can head for the road, but if you do that your feet will be ripped to shreds and you're going to end up in a prison cell for your part in Daniel's murder.'

Gabriel stopped shouting and Zoe curled tighter against the nearest tree.

'Another thing to consider should you decide to stay out here is the fact that there are wolves running through these hills.'

Gabriel's silhouette blended with the darkness inside the cabin, then the door banged shut. The wolves in Zoe's imagination were waiting to pounce, but she made herself wait a while longer before heading back. She let herself in and closed the door. There was no sign of Gabriel.

She went to her room, took a T-shirt from the drawer to use as a nightdress and got changed. She placed her hands on her stomach and said a quick prayer. The ultrasound felt like a lifetime ago and there was no way to be sure that her baby was all right. There was a definite swell to her belly these days, which had to be a good sign; and her breasts were a little bigger too. No blood. That was the big one. Every time she used the toilet she would check. She didn't want to think about what she would do if she did find blood. Sometimes denial wasn't just the best way, it was the only way.

As she was pulling the quilt over herself Gabriel called out, 'Goodnight, Little Sis.' She thought she detected a note of triumph in his voice. That worried her more than anything else. Gabriel had been so supportive when she had first asked him for help; she thought he had agreed because of their shared history. It had never occurred to her that he might have his own agenda. And if he did, what was it? All she knew was that she was currently out here in the middle of nowhere with a man who was, to all intents and purposes, a complete stranger. If that wasn't bad enough, as far as the rest of the world was concerned, she was dead. No one would be looking for her. The only person who might remember her was Lizzy, but even her memories would fade in time. When you got right down to it, she might as well never have existed.

Gabriel added a 'sleep well', but she didn't respond because she was trying to pretend that he didn't exist. With the light off and her eyes shut tight, she could be anywhere. She could be back in the apartment she had shared with Lizzy, or she could be in a hotel room somewhere exotic. Or maybe she was back in her childhood bedroom in the days before the cancer had taken her mom and an aneurysm had taken her dad.

The illusion lasted until she heard the distant howl of a lone wolf.

# Chapter 35

The sun had travelled through the first part of the sky by the time Zoe woke up. She couldn't believe she had slept so long. She could hear Gabriel watching TV in the living room; she could smell his coffee. She got dressed, then went through to the bathroom to brush her teeth and get washed. Gabriel looked over when she walked into the living room. The TV was tuned to NWCN.

'Sleep well?' he asked.

Zoe nodded.

'It's getting late. You must have needed it. Would you like a coffee?'

'You think I'd let you get me a coffee after what happened last time?'

'Look, if you don't trust my coffee, make your own. I won't be offended. While you're at it, help yourself to breakfast.'

Zoe found a box of Cheerios in one of the cupboards, bowls in another. The milk was in the refrigerator and there were plastic spoons in one of the drawers. Gabriel was engrossed in the news, so she quickly checked the drawer, but there was nothing she could use as a weapon. She poured a tumbler of water then carried everything to the table and sat down. She scooped up a spoonful of Cheerios and hesitated for a second. Cereal with milk might be an alien concept, but it was something she could easily get used to again. Gabriel turned the volume up and glanced over.

'You might be interested in this, Zoe.'

She stopped eating and looked at the screen. The spoon clattered into the bowl, but she barely noticed. The news anchor was giving the top-of-the-hour roundup, but she couldn't take anything in because her attention was fixed on the picture behind him. *Her* picture. The photograph had been taken at a social function she couldn't remember attending. She was wearing a figure-hugging red dress that Daniel had picked out. He wasn't in the shot, but he would have been hovering close by. He never let her out of his sight for long at those events.

The photograph had caused her to stop short, but the thing that took her breath away was what was written beneath it. There was only one word, in block capitals: MISSING. Not dead. Not wanted for murder. *Missing*. That one word was enough to fuel a whole fantasy, one that ended with the police descending en masse on the cabin.

According to the news anchor, Daniel and Josh's bodies had been found. At this stage their deaths were being treated as a double homicide rather than a murder/suicide. That was the first thing she registered. The second thing: they had concluded that she hadn't died in the fire. The fact that the police thought she was alive changed the whole dynamic of the investigation. Rather than trying to work out how she had died, they would be actively searching for her.

Gabriel had wanted it to look like she had died in the fire; he had wanted it to look as though Daniel had murdered her and Josh, then killed himself in a fit of remorse. But that hadn't happened. She glanced over. He seemed as chilled as ever, which made no sense. His plan had gone completely to shit. How could he be so relaxed?

According to the anchor, the body found at the house had been formally identified as Talya Coles, a twenty-five-year-old prostitute who had gone missing in Salem a week ago. The picture in the background had changed to Talya's. She looked much older than twenty-five. Her skin was sallow and pockmarked with acne scars; the haunted look in her eyes suggested a serious drug habit.

The police had reopened the investigation into an earlier fire that had claimed the life of Carlos Rodriguez. Zoe had no idea who he was, but when the anchor mentioned that he had worked at Myriadian it became clear why the police had done this. Factoring in the two people Gabriel shot dead at the gas station, that brought the death toll up to six. She glanced over at him again. He still didn't seem in the least bit bothered by what he was seeing. Did he not understand what was going on here?

The picture cut from the TV studio to a news conference. The camera was aimed at a podium. The Asian guy standing behind it was in his late thirties. He identified himself as Detective Sergeant Tommy Wang of the Portland PD. Wang started off predictably enough by rehashing what the anchor had just said. There were a couple of new details but nothing earth-shattering.

Wang moved away from the podium and Lizzy stepped in to take his place. Zoe's heart stopped when she saw her. Lizzy looked older. Then again, she was older. They both were. More than three years had passed since they had said their goodbyes at Portland airport. She looked more grown-up too, a woman with responsibilities rather than a student who was just out to have a good time. Her hair was shorter. Black instead of red. She was still wearing black, though, and she still had her piercings. Her clothes hid her tattoos. Zoe was certain that the differences were only cosmetic. Deep down she would still be the Lizzy she knew and loved. Her best friend.

Watching her standing there at the podium, the spark of hope in Zoe's chest grew brighter. Would the police be this far along if Lizzy hadn't been there to kick ass? Probably not. On the downside, seeing Lizzy highlighted how alone she was. It was only when you had someone else's love to measure it against that you got a true understanding of loneliness.

Lizzy cleared her throat, then looked at the cameras and started speaking. Her words had probably been scripted, but the delivery came straight from the heart. Zoe had always known how much Lizzy loved her; even when they weren't talking, she knew.

'This is a message to the person who has taken Zoe,' she began. 'Zoe is my friend and I love her so much. She's the best friend anyone could want. She is funny and warm, and she writes the most beautiful stories. Zoe would never hurt anyone. She's the most generous person I've ever met, and her heart is as big as the sun. Nobody who meets Zoe could ever want to hurt her. How could they hurt someone so precious and beautiful? You have the power to make this right. You have the power to let Zoe go. All I ask is that you can find it in yourself to do that. I'm begging you. Please, please, please let Zoe go.'

She managed to hold it together right up to that final 'please'. The last three words were rushed out on a sob that she caught with her hand. The second she finished she was hit with a barrage of questions. Wang was beside her in an instant. He wrapped a protective arm around her shoulders and led her from the podium. Lizzy's head was bowed and she looked totally devastated. Gabriel switched the TV off, and for a long time sat there saying nothing. Zoe couldn't read his mood. Was he worried? Angry? Pissed? He still seemed unnaturally calm, and that made less sense than ever. He must be able to see what was going on here. When he finally spoke, it was like he was reading her mind.

'So what do you think, Zoe? Are my days numbered?'

She said nothing.

'You must have an opinion,' he prompted.

'The police know I'm alive. They think I've been kidnapped. That means they'll come looking for me.' These statements were antagonistic but she didn't care. It was like she had been infected with a little bit of Lizzy's attitude. 'That means your plan didn't work.'

'Didn't it?'

Those two words were enough to make her pause. Gabriel sounded so sure of himself, like he'd got this whole thing worked out. Zoe could feel her hope draining away like air from a punctured balloon.

'When Daniel was alive it mattered whether you were "dead" because you didn't want to spend your life looking over your shoulder. I don't really care what the police think.' He paused. 'Remember the money we took from the gas station. Why did we do that, Zoe?'

'Because you wanted it to look like a robbery,' she replied quietly.

'Exactly. At some point the police will run their ballistics tests and connect those two dots. But that doesn't matter because I was playing for time. While the police were busy looking for an armed robber, we had all the time we needed to drive here.'

He looked at her as though he expected her to contribute, but she had nothing to offer.

'Same thing with the fire at your house,' he continued. 'I could have faked the dental records to make the police believe that Talya was you, but that sort of thing only ever happens in straight-to-DVD movies. Do you know how difficult it would be to pull something like that off? Tracking down dental records, breaking into the surgery, swapping files. It's a mammoth task. And even if by some miracle you manage to pull it off there are no guarantees that the story is going to hold. One loose thread and the whole thing is going to unravel.'

Without another word, Gabriel got up and walked through to his bedroom. She picked up the plastic spoon and gave the bowl a stir. The Cheerios had gone soft and looked like baby mush. She gave them another half-hearted stir then laid the spoon back in the bowl. It was clearer than ever that he was following his own agenda; and it was equally clear that she still had no idea what that was.

# Chapter 36

'Come with me. There's something I want to show you.'

Gabriel handed Zoe her sneakers and then led the way around to the rear of the cabin. As they walked, Zoe catalogued the bulges in his jeans pockets. The one at the back held his pearl-handled switchblade, the front right contained his satellite phone. She wasn't sure about the front left, but it was probably the key for the Cherokee. By contrast, her pockets were empty, but that was because they were sewn shut.

The small gap in the trees would have been easy to miss if you didn't know it was there. Gabriel walked through and beckoned for her to follow. The trail they were on was narrow but well established. The greenery had been worn away, leaving behind a narrow strip of dirt. Within a couple of dozen yards all the trees looked the same. The trail sloped gently downwards, and a couple of minutes later they reached a small creek. From here the path rose again, following the line of the bank. In the distance, Zoe could hear the rush and gurgle of a waterfall.

The rainclouds from yesterday had all blown away and the sun owned the sky again. The only sign that the rainstorm had ever happened was the layer of dampness that blanketed the ground and the trees. The trail ended at a small clearing. The waterfall was straight ahead. It was about thirty feet high, the water tumbling and frothing into a small pool at its base. The leaves and branches broke up the sunlight, turning it into something magical. This had always been one of her favourite places. She used to come here to read. She had happy memories of sitting by this pool, following Bilbo Baggins as he adventured through Middle Earth.

The two graves in the shade of the trees were new. Zoe followed Gabriel over, giving him plenty of space. Each grave was marked with a simple wooden cross. MICHELLE had been carved neatly into the horizontal bar of the left-hand cross. There was no surname. Underneath were her dates: May 17 1990–January 12 2016. Whoever Michelle was, she had only been twenty-six when she died. The second cross was the one Zoe found really disturbing. Once again there was just a forename carved into it: REBECCA. It was the dates that freaked her out: September 8 2014–January 12 2016. Rebecca had only been sixteen months old when she died.

Gabriel cleared the dead flowers from the graves, then walked a circuit of the clearing, bending down occasionally to pick a wild flower. The way he arranged them on the graves was so tender, so respectful. It was hard to imagine that this was the same man who had shot the gas station attendant in the head. He finished laying the flowers then straightened up. For a while he stood there in quiet contemplation, head bowed. All Zoe could do was watch and wonder.

'January 12,' Gabriel said quietly, finally breaking the silence. He sounded as though he was talking to himself, but the words were for her benefit. 'I was home on leave. We

ordered in Chinese and watched a movie. Later we made love.
I didn't know that would be the last time. You never do. Afterwards we lay there talking for a while. Michelle had always
wanted lots of kids and this seemed like the right time to give
Becca a brother or sister. We'd been married for two years by
that point. Two good years.'

Gabriel fell silent. He was staring at Michelle's cross but not
really seeing it. 'I woke first. Smoke was coming under the bedroom door. Our apartment was on the sixth floor and there was
no fire escape. The only way out was through the flames. Somehow I managed to carry Michelle and Becca from the apartment. By that point all three of us were on fire. A neighbour
put out the flames but I have no memory of that. The next thing
I remember was waking up in the hospital. To start with they
wouldn't tell me that Michelle and Becca were dead. They didn't
have to, though. Some things you just know. I actually died as
well that night. My heart stopped for almost five minutes before
the medics got it going again. Some days I think it would have
been better if they hadn't.'

Gabriel finally looked at her, and she wished he hadn't. There
was too much sadness in his eyes. She looked at the graves and
got a glimpse of a possible future. The way they were laid out
there was plenty of space for a third. And a fourth. In her mind's
eye she could see a cross with her name and dates carved neatly
into the wood.

And next to it, a smaller cross bearing her baby's name and
dates.

That was when she started to run.

She had no idea how long she ran for, or where she was going. She was running completely blind. More than once her foot snagged a tree root and she went crashing to the ground. Each time she fell, she got straight back up and started running again, all the time moving further from those graves and heading deeper into the woods. She had to get away from Gabriel. This was more a feeling than a thought. She was operating at a primal level, survival trumping everything else. She would do whatever it took to ensure that happened.

For her.

For her baby.

The only thing that mattered was staying alive long enough to take the next breath. For both of them. So she kept running until it felt as though she could run no more. She ran until her lungs had shrunk to nothing and her heart was set to explode. Even when it felt like she couldn't go another step, she still kept running.

# Chapter 37

Zoe took another tumble, only this time she couldn't get up. Whatever had carried her this far, it wasn't going to take her any further. For a long time she lay there with her face in the dirt, the stink of the forest floor filling her nose. Dots danced wildly in front of her eyes. She was convinced she was having a heart attack. This was it. Her life was going to end with a lonely death out here in the woods, the birds and trees the only witnesses. Zoe closed her eyes and followed her breaths to the final one. Except each breath was followed by another, and another, until she realised that she wasn't going to die after all.

She still couldn't get up, though. Instead, she lay there in the damp dirt telling herself to get her act together. Her thoughts were slowly starting to feel like her own again. She could once again see the past and the future; she was no longer trapped in the now. Zoe rolled onto her back and stared up through the trees. The branches made it look as though the sky was fractured. Any second now it was going to cave in on her. When it didn't, she took this as a sign. Everything in her life might have shattered into pieces, but somehow those pieces were just about holding together.

She struggled to the nearest tree and sat for a while with her back against the trunk. Her hands found her belly. Hopefully the baby was okay. She had to be. Zoe closed her eyes and imagined the way that her little heart had beaten on the ultrasound; she imagined she could feel it now, fluttering beneath her fingertips.

*Please be all right.*

*God, please be okay.*

Not knowing if she was okay or not was the worst part. As far as she could tell her belly was no bigger or smaller than it had been yesterday. She would have given anything to feel the baby kick, but it was too soon for that.

When her breathing had finally returned to normal, she stood up and turned in a full circle. Every tree looked identical. She turned another circle then started walking, following the slope of the land downhill. Her limbs were heavy and felt as though they belonged to someone else, but somehow she managed to stay upright and keep moving. She walked until she reached the lake. It was roughly two miles from end to end, and a half-mile across. The land sloped steeply on every side, trees stretching as far as the eye could see. The beauty of this place was as breathtaking as she remembered. She sat down on a large rock near the water's edge to wait.

It was the middle of the afternoon before Gabriel appeared. She heard him walking up behind her, but didn't turn around. He sat down on the rock, and for a long time they stared at the lake, neither of them saying a word. It was Gabriel who eventually broke the silence.

'Did you ever love your husband?'

She smiled sadly. 'I did once. The moment we met I knew he was the one. I fell hard. By the time I realised I'd made a mistake it was too late.'

'What about Josh? Did you love him?'

She shook her head. 'Not really.'

'But you liked him enough to risk having an affair.'

'We didn't have an affair. We slept together once. That was all. Daniel was away on business and Josh turned up on my doorstep to drop something off for him. He was feeling lonely after splitting up from his wife; I was feeling lonely and vulnerable because I was married to a complete bastard. It shouldn't have happened, but it did.'

That was the simple version. The reality was way more complicated. She had wanted Josh to leave pretty much from the moment he got there; at the same time she hadn't wanted him to go. Being alone in the big house on Fairfield Boulevard usually didn't bother her; in a lot of ways it was preferable to having Daniel there. On this particular evening, though, the loneliness and isolation had been unbearable. They had chatted for a bit, then Josh had said he needed to get going. They must have hugged each other a hundred times. It happened whenever they said hello or goodbye, but this hug was different. That much was immediately obvious. Zoe could sense how much he needed someone at that moment. She could feel his pain. And maybe he could feel hers too. The hug went on longer than it should have, the kiss on the cheek became a kiss on the lips, and somewhere along the line they had ended up in bed, and for a few golden moments she wasn't thinking about smoothies or padlocks on the refrigerator. For a short while she wasn't even thinking about Daniel.

'It wasn't just once though,' Gabriel said. 'What about the time you got together at the Holly Tree?'

Zoe shook her head. 'All we did was talk. Josh had been trying to contact me because he wanted to see me again. I was worried that he was taking too many risks and that Daniel was going to find out what happened. I figured that if I told Josh in person, he might get the message.'

'So you just talked? Nothing happened?'

Zoe shook her head. 'Nothing happened.'

'You wanted it to, though.'

'Maybe. It was nice to be wanted. And I liked Josh. The problem was Daniel.' She paused and sighed. 'Well, you've seen how things worked out when he discovered that we had slept together.'

'Daniel was an idiot. You know that, don't you?'

She almost smiled at that.

'If you're lucky enough to be loved, you don't destroy that. You do everything possible to protect it. Love is fragile enough without self-sabotage entering the equation.'

'Did you love your wife?'

'I did. Very much. Like you, the first moment I set eyes on her, I knew she was the one.'

'I'm figuring that's where the similarity ends.'

This time it was Gabriel who almost smiled. 'Like all couples we had our ups and downs, but for the most part it was good. I loved her; she loved me. That's all that matters when you get down to it.'

'And Rebecca?'

'I loved her too. More than life itself.'

'What was she like?'

When Gabriel didn't answer, she added, 'If you don't want to talk about it, I understand.'

He waved the comment away. 'She was beautiful like her mother, and she had a smile that would melt the heart of an angel.'

'Why have you brought me here? And I want the truth, Gabriel. Is it because you couldn't save your wife and daughter? Is that it? Do you see this as a way of balancing the books?'

Gabriel shrugged. 'Maybe that's part of it. All I know is that you were in trouble, and I was in a position to help you out.'

She pictured the clearing by the waterfall, with four graves instead of two, and once again wondered if Gabriel was capable of killing her. Or maybe she was destined to be here until her hair turned grey and she died of old age. She wasn't sure which was worse.

'So what happens now? Do we just stay here for the rest of our lives?'

'Would that be such a bad thing? I mean, take a look around and you'll see that the rest of the world is fast turning to shit. Maybe opting out would be for the best.'

'I'm being serious, Gabriel.'

'So am I. What I think is that we should take each day as it comes. When you get down to it, that's all any of us can ever do.'

He stood up and started walking back the way he had come. Zoe gave it a moment, then followed. She couldn't help noticing that he had ducked her question. As she walked back to the cabin, the idea that she had swapped one prison for another was burning brighter than ever inside her head.

# Chapter 38

The rest of the afternoon passed slowly; the evening dragged on even more so. They ate together, but there was no conversation. It was like Gabriel had used up all his words out in the woods. After dinner Zoe cleared up. She didn't mind, because for those twenty minutes she could pretend he wasn't in the room. This was another survival tactic she had learnt during her marriage. It was like a superpower: the ability to make another person invisible through the power of your mind.

She finished tidying up then sat down on the sofa and stared at the TV. It wasn't switched on but that didn't stop her staring at it. The stranger who had stolen her face was reflected in the screen. The ragged blonde hair and the dark-rimmed eyes scared her a little. She wondered if she would ever really know this person. Gabriel put down his book and got up suddenly, making her jump.

'Wait here,' he said. 'I've got something for you.'

He walked through to his bedroom, and when he returned there was a plain brown envelope in his hand. He held it out and waited for her to take it. Zoe didn't want to take it because she didn't want to know what was inside. Plain brown envelopes rarely contained good news.

'Relax,' he told her. 'It's not a bomb.'

'So what is it?'

'I assure you it's nothing bad. In fact, I think you might actually like it.'

Gabriel waved the envelope at her and this time she took it. She turned it over, ripped through the seal and peered inside. Time came grinding to a halt. Despite his assurances, it was a bomb of sorts. She slid the ultrasound picture out and for a long time all she could do was stare at it. The pain in her heart was bigger than she was. It was huge and all-encompassing, threatening to swallow her whole. To anyone else this would be a random series of black, white and grey splodges, but to Zoe these abstract shapes represented her whole future.

This wasn't a hoax. It was too elaborate for that. The rip down the middle had been repaired with Scotch tape. Then there was the name printed on the edge: Eleanor Sanders. That made it real. She remembered standing outside the clinic and ripping the ultrasound picture in two; she remembered how devastated she had been when she had dropped the pieces into the trash. Those memories were so sharp they cut.

'How?' was all she could manage.

'I followed you to the clinic.'

'I didn't see you.'

'That's because you were busy looking for Daniel. And because you were so focussed on that, you were blind to everything else. The president himself could have strolled past and you wouldn't have noticed. You looked so sad when you came out of that clinic. Probably sadder than I've ever seen you.'

'That's because I knew I had to get away from Daniel. The problem was that I didn't know how.'

'Listen to me, Zoe, and listen good: I would never do anything to hurt your baby. That's a promise.'

She was still staring at the scan picture.

'Please look at me, Zoe.'

She didn't move.

'Please,' he said gently.

She looked up and met his gaze.

'I will never hurt your baby,' he repeated.

'Why should I believe you?'

Gabriel considered this for a second. 'I guess that one's a question of faith. Like believing in God, or a kid believing in Father Christmas.'

'So, what? You're God now?'

Gabriel smiled. 'On balance, I'd prefer to be Father Christmas. That sounds like a much better gig.' His face turned serious. 'Have I killed people? Yes, I have. You know that. Have I ever killed a child? No, I have not.'

'And what? I'm just expected to take your word for that?'

'Unfortunately that's all I've got to give.'

Zoe said nothing.

'Do you remember your first week at school after we moved to Rapid City? You were getting a hard time from some of the other kids?'

'Of course I remember. You stood up for me.'

'Because that's what big brothers do. They look out for their little sisters.'

They fell quiet and Zoe found her attention drawn back to the scan. She traced the line of Scotch tape with her fingertip. The scar of the rip would be there forever, but at least it was whole again. If only her life could be fixed so easily, she thought. It was Gabriel who broke the silence.

'Earlier, at the lake, you said that you once loved Daniel. I'm assuming that there was also a time when you trusted him?'

She nodded without looking up.

'And how did he ultimately repay that trust?'

'He abused me, then asked you to kill me,' Zoe said quietly.

'That's right,' Gabriel replied. 'I gave him a copy of the scan because I was curious to see how he would react. Do you know what he did?'

Zoe shook her head.

'He told me to proceed with the hit. Which begs the question: what sort of man would kill a baby? Like I told you last night, I'm not the enemy here.' He paused. 'It's going to take time to rebuild the trust between us, but it can be done. You have to believe that.'

'I know,' she said, not because she believed it, but because that was what he wanted to hear. One look and she knew that he had bought the lie. Before she met Daniel she had been the world's worst liar; marrying him had turned her into an expert.

Gabriel didn't say anything else and Zoe used the silence to memorise every last detail of the ultrasound picture. She could feel his eyes on her, but didn't look up. He reached for his book then settled back on the sofa to read. Zoe gave it a minute then slid the scan picture back into the envelope. She removed her sneakers and put them on the table.

'I'm going to bed,' she said.

Gabriel used his finger to mark his place and smiled up at her. 'Sleep well.'

She went to the bathroom to clean her teeth and get washed. The light was still on in the living room when she came out; it was so quiet she could hear him turn the page of his book. She let herself into her bedroom and closed the door gently behind her. The roll of duct tape was still sitting on top of the nightstand. She pressed her ear against the door. There were no sounds of footsteps; no sounds whatsoever.

It took less than five seconds to find the loose floorboard. It was exactly where she remembered. When she was younger there had been a rug covering it; now it was hidden by the bed. She prised the floorboard up, half expecting to see her childhood diary, but there was only dirt, dust and some ancient cobwebs. She picked up the duct tape, dropped it into the void, then carefully replaced the floorboard.

# Chapter 39

The gunshot sounded like distant thunder. It boomed across the treetops and, for a brief moment, Zoe was back at the gas station watching as first the saleswoman was shot dead and then the old guy in the booth. She looked up at the grey sky and told herself again that it was just thunder.

She walked into the clearing, and stopped when she had taken twenty-three strides. She could probably go another two, but didn't want to push it. This was day five and she wanted Gabriel to think that she was settling into her life out here in the woods. That meant not causing waves or doing anything to make him suspicious. Once again she was struck by the parallels between her life here and her life with Daniel. The electronic tag was chafing her ankle. Last night she'd tried to remove it again, but all she succeeded in doing was rubbing her skin raw.

The first spits of rain touched her face. Right now it was hardly worth noting, but that would change fast. The weather out here could turn on a dime. Zoe stood there enjoying the coolness on her skin, and for a moment she was back in Portland. It had been raining on the day she arrived to start college, but she hadn't cared because this was going to be the start of a great adventure. Her whole future was stretched out in front of her and it looked golden. *If I knew then what I know now,* she thought. Except would she have actually changed anything? Probably not. You make the best decisions you can based on the information you have to hand. By the time you've worked out that those decisions are catastrophically bad it's usually too late.

She turned and went back inside. In no time the cabin was filled with the sound of the rain. There might have been plenty of similarities to her life with Daniel, but there were differences too. The biggest difference was that if she felt hungry, she could get herself something to eat. It was such a small thing, but in its own way it was massive. It had been years since she had experienced freedom like this.

She picked up an apple, took a bite, then walked over to the bookcase. It was filled to overflowing with paperbacks. Thrillers and crime books, for the most part, all with cracked spines and well-thumbed pages. Lee Child, Elmore Leonard, Jeffery Deaver, Michael Connelly, Harlan Coben. There were some Stephen Kings as well, all ones she had read.

Zoe ran her fingertips along the spines and felt the tingle of something long dormant coming alive again. She pulled out one of Deaver's Lincoln Rhyme novels, opened it at a random page, and the words jumped into her head. It had been so long since she had experienced this particular brand of telepathy. Too long. She snapped the novel shut and put it back. Guilt was racing through her heart and stomach.

It was another hour before Gabriel returned. His face and hair were shining from the rain and he was carrying two large bags of meat. He held them out for Zoe to take, but all she could do was stare at the blood on his hands. He shook the bags and that was enough to break her paralysis. She reached out and took them.

'Tonight we eat like kings,' he declared. 'I take it you still like venison?'

'It's been a while since I had any.' She paused, thinking. 'In fact, I haven't had it since I was last here.'

'Seriously?'

'Seriously.'

'Okay, take out two steaks for dinner. The rest can go in the freezer.'

Zoe did what he asked. Having access to the refrigerator and the freezer was another one of those differences, one that felt every bit as alien as having milk on her cereal. Gabriel stripped off his waterproofs, hung them by the door to dry, then moved over to the sink to wash his hands. The way the water turned pink was yet another reminder of how dangerous he was. At heart he was a hunter. Whether the target was a deer or a person, that was what defined him. He caught her staring and smiled.

'What?' he asked.

'Can I read one of your books, please?'

'Of course you can. Books should be read. That's what they're there for. They shouldn't just sit on a shelf gathering dust.'

An uncomfortable silence built between them. Gabriel was staring like he expected more.

'Daniel wouldn't let me read books,' she said.

'That must have been tough. A world without books would be a very empty world indeed.'

Zoe smiled sadly. 'It wasn't the worst thing he ever did, but it was probably the cruellest. The last book I read was *The Storyteller* by Jodi Picoult. I never found out what happened in the end. He burned it before I could finish it.'

'Yeah, well that just about says it all, doesn't it?'

Gabriel dried his hands, and Zoe turned her attention to the bookcase. In the end she chose *The Stand*, even though she had read it before. She figured that if anything happened to her, then at least she knew how it ended.

By mid-afternoon it was raining as heavily as ever. She had forgotten how good this book was. More than that, she had forgotten the simple joy of losing herself totally in a story. Daniel had taken so much from her, but she hadn't been lying when she told Gabriel that this had been one of his cruellest crimes. She turned the page and disappeared back into the book. The plague was well on the way to wiping out most of mankind and, for a short while at least, it was as though the clock had turned back. Her father was still alive, and the long days of summer were stretching ahead of them, and Gabriel was her hero because he'd saved her from the bullies at school.

# Chapter 40

Evening came and the rain still fell. The sound of it hitting the roof echoed through the cabin. The day had been warm enough, but the temperature had dropped with the darkness and there was a fire burning in the grate. Zoe tidied up quickly after dinner because she wanted to get back to *The Stand*. She finished drying the plates and put them into the cupboard. Before she had a chance to pick up her book Gabriel told her to go and sit at the table.

Instead of joining her, he disappeared through to his bedroom. When he returned he was carrying a small box. He put the box on the table and started unbuttoning his shirt. Zoe sat very still. The last button came undone and he slid the shirt off. The scars on his face and neck extended all over his body. His skin was a mess of hard, ridged burn tissue. It was so bad she was left wondering how he'd survived. He sat down, and that was when she noticed the red crosses tattooed on his left arm. There were thirty-six in total. They had been arranged in a neat, grid formation on his biceps, five across and seven down. The way they were laid out made her think of a cemetery.

There was a tattoo gun inside the box. She watched him set it up; watched him use it. The needle dug into his arm again and again, but he didn't flinch. Not once. The sound of the tattoo gun buzzed inside her ears like there was a swarm of insects trapped in there. When he'd finished there were four new crosses on his arm, taking the total up to forty. Gabriel wiped the blood away with a cotton wool ball, admired his handiwork for a moment, then looked across the table and caught her staring.

'It's not what you think,' he said.

'So you didn't kill all those people?'

'Yes, I killed them. Every last one. But that doesn't make me some sort of serial killer.'

'There are forty crosses on your arm.'

'And I remember every single one of those kills like it was yesterday. The thing is, a lot of those crosses came about because I was trying to protect people like you.'

She looked at him and shook her head. 'I don't understand.'

'Do you know what I did in the army?'

Zoe shook her head again.

'I was a sniper. Most of those crosses were earned in Iraq and Afghanistan. They even gave me medals. It turned out I had an aptitude for the work.'

She said nothing. It was easy to imagine him lying belly down in the sun-blasted dirt in some godforsaken corner of the world; easy to imagine him lying there for hours, maybe even days, just waiting for his target to appear; and when the target finally appeared, it was easy to imagine him lining up the crosshairs, squeezing the trigger, then disappearing like a ghost.

Gabriel grabbed his shirt and put it back on. 'Okay, your turn.'

He picked up the tattoo gun, which made it easy to see where this was going. All the same, she didn't understand. She stared across the table, confused.

'Every death should be honoured, Zoe. It's no small thing to take a life.'

'But I haven't killed anyone.'

'What about Daniel?'

She shook her head. 'We've already had this conversation. I didn't kill him.'

He waited for her to meet his eye. 'Okay, I'm going to need an arm. Left or right, you choose.'

Zoe didn't move.

'I'm happy to wait all night.' Gabriel added. 'That was something else I learnt about in the army. Waiting. Turns out I've got an aptitude for that too.'

It was clear that he meant what he was saying. It was also clear that if she said no then she could easily end up antagonising him, and that didn't seem like a good idea. She had to pick her battles carefully. Right now, she couldn't see that there was anything to gain by digging her heels in over this. She stared a little longer, then took off her sweatshirt and rolled back the right sleeve of her T-shirt. Gabriel moved around to her side of the table and picked up the tattoo gun. The needle dug into her arm and she screwed her eyes shut tight. She was trying to keep the pain and noise locked away in a place where it couldn't get at her, but it was impossible when the insects in her ears were screaming so loudly.

'Okay, all done. You can open your eyes.'

Zoe opened her eyes. The tattoo was on the outside of her upper arm. It was an inch high, half an inch across, and identical to the ones on Gabriel's arm. He held out a cotton wool ball. She took it and dabbed the blood away. Looking at it made her think back to the road trip that she had gone on with Lizzy. Despite the pain and discomfort it would have involved, she wished they had gotten tattoos instead of T-shirts. Tattoos were forever; T-shirts were for a season. That was just one of a whole catalogue of regrets she had. Some days there were just too many to count. She looked again at the graveyard of crosses on Gabriel's arm.

'Which was your first?'

Gabriel pointed to the top-right cross.

She hesitated, then said, 'Was that from when you were in the army?'

Gabriel answered with a nod, and for a long time just sat there staring at the cross, lost in thought.

'I never knew their name, but that wasn't unusual. They were just a shape in my crosshairs.' A pause. 'I'd often wondered what it would be like to take a life, but the weird thing was that I didn't feel any different afterwards. I didn't feel older, or more grown up. I didn't feel happy or excited. I didn't feel anything.'

'It must have affected you.'

Gabriel shook his head. 'I woke up that morning one person, and went to bed as the exact same person.'

Zoe was thinking about the gas station again, and the way Gabriel had killed those people. He'd had a job to do, and he had done it. Coldly and professionally. At the moment she seemed to fit into whatever fantasy he was spinning here. If that was to change, if she was to somehow become a problem to him, how would he react?

Or to put it another way, would he really think twice about putting a bullet in her head?

# Chapter 41

'I need to go and get some supplies,' Gabriel said.

Zoe stopped reading and looked up at him. She had noticed they were running low on food, so this wasn't a complete surprise.

'Do I come with you?' she asked carefully.

'I think it might be best if you stayed here,' he replied just as carefully.

Only a handful of words had been shared, but they told a much bigger story, one that started and ended with her being a prisoner here. A week had passed since he tattooed her arm, long enough for them to have fallen into a groove. Zoe had been working hard to convince Gabriel that she was settling into this new life. That seemed to be what he was expecting from her, and he seemed to be buying it. Keeping up the act had been easier than she thought, but then she'd had a lot of practice. Her marriage had been a constant exercise in acting as though the abnormal was normal.

'I'll need your sneakers,' he added.

She had been expecting this too; that illusion of normality only went so far. Get too close to the edges of the reality that had been created here and the cracks started to show. It had been four days since he last took her sneakers. As promised, her world was slowly growing again. What he had conveniently forgotten to mention was that he had the power to shrink it whenever he wanted. Like so much of her marriage, this was something that was understood. Zoe removed her sneakers and Gabriel took them through to his bedroom. She heard the click of the lock being engaged as he was coming out, and then he was back.

'How long will you be gone for?' she asked.

'A couple of hours at least. The good news is that when I get back we'll have fresh fruit and vegetables again.'

For a moment they just stood there staring at each other. Zoe wasn't sure what to do or say. She had the feeling that Gabriel wasn't sure either. This was the first time they had said goodbye since they got here. Before, they might have shared a brief hug, but that no longer seemed appropriate. In the end, he just turned and headed for the door. Zoe followed him outside and watched him climb into the Cherokee. She watched the car bump over the uneven ground and disappear along the dirt track. The sound of the engine faded and then disappeared altogether.

She stood there a moment longer, listening hard in case he decided to come back. The sun warming her face was tempered by the occasional gust of wind. They were already halfway through May. Blink again and it would be June, and she would be in her second trimester. Blink again and another six months would have flown past and she would be giving birth, and that just seemed unbelievable. She still had no idea if the baby was okay. Her belly seemed to be getting bigger, which had to be a good sign. And she was eating healthier than she had done in years, so that was something else to put in the plus column. Feeling her move would go a long way to setting her mind at rest.

Hopefully that would happen soon. The baby had to be okay, otherwise this was all for nothing.

The first thing Zoe did when she got back inside was check the time on the microwave. Gabriel said he would be gone at least two hours. In her head this broke down as thirty to forty-five minutes for him to get wherever he was going, then thirty minutes to an hour to buy supplies, and another thirty to forty-five minutes to get back.

The roll of duct tape was where she had left it, hidden away in her secret place beneath the loose floorboard. She sat down on the bed and used half the roll on each foot. The first few steps felt strange, but by the time she had walked through to the living room she was just about getting used to it. She sat down on the sofa and watched the slow progress of the microwave clock. By her reckoning another thirty minutes would see Gabriel at the furthest point from the cabin.

Those minutes crawled by more slowly than any she had ever known; the last sixty seconds were the longest of all. The number she had been waiting for finally appeared and she headed outside. She counted her strides as she walked towards the dirt track, stopping when she reached twenty-five. This was the point of no return. The patch of dirt directly in front looked no different to the dirt she had walked over to get here; and it was no different from all the dirt she would need to walk over to get to the road. But it was different. The next step would trigger an alert on Gabriel's phone. Then it would be a race against time. If she had got the math right then she should have at least thirty minutes to reach the road.

Zoe took another step, then broke into a jog. She was moving quickly, anxious to get to the road. Every minute was critical. Every second. The track was on a slight downhill gradient that curved gently to the left. Within fifty yards she could no longer see the cabin. Her eyes and ears were wide open, searching for any sign of Gabriel. She was praying that she had enough time to get a lift; praying she had enough time to get to the police. The duct tape seemed to be protecting her feet okay. Every now and then she would stand on a stone and remember she wasn't wearing sneakers. That would slow her down for a few steps, but she would soon find her rhythm again.

The track went straight for a couple of hundred yards before curving to the right. A hundred yards further on it turned sharply to the left. Because of the angles Zoe couldn't see around the corner.

By the time she could see, there was nowhere to hide.

# Chapter 42

The Cherokee was parked twenty yards away. Gabriel was standing with one arm resting on the hood. He looked relaxed. Just a guy hanging out in the woods, enjoying the day. No hurry, no worries. There was no way to get past the car, and the only thing behind her was the cabin. She could run into the trees, but what was the point?

He waved her forward, but she couldn't move because her feet were glued to the ground. He waved again and this time she managed to start walking. Freedom was all around her. It was in the wind and the trees; it was in the wide sky stretching far above her head; it was in the infinity of space that touched all that blue. So close, yet so far, she thought. And then her father's voice came out of nowhere: but close don't get you that cigar, sweetheart, always remember that. *I remember, Daddy*, she thought, and the voice in her head belonged to the little girl she had once been.

Gabriel waited until she was six feet away before moving from the hood. He walked around to the passenger door and held it open. He didn't say a word as she got in; he didn't say a word as he climbed into the driver's seat and started the car. They drove back to the cabin in a silence that was utterly terrifying because it reminded her so much of Daniel. He pulled up in front of the cabin and killed the engine.

'Let's take a walk,' he said.

The order sounded like a request, and this reminded her of Daniel too. The way it was phrased left no room for anything other than total compliance. They walked around to the rear of the cabin and followed the trail to the creek. Zoe was convinced Gabriel was going to turn right towards the graves, and when they got up there he would kill her and bury her body next to Rebecca and Michelle's. She was equally convinced that there was nothing she could do to stop this from happening. Not a single damn thing. If she tried to run, he would come after her, and when he caught up with her he would put a bullet in her head, just like he had done to that woman at the gas station.

He didn't go right, though. Instead, he turned left and followed the creek until they reached the lake. Gabriel didn't talk much at the best of times, but this silence was killing her. She didn't know what he was thinking, and she couldn't read his mood. More than that, her head was filled with loose sand; it was as though she didn't know anything anymore. Gabriel sat down on a rock and beckoned for her to join him. She hesitated, then did what he asked.

'What exactly are you running from?' he asked gently.

Zoe stared at her hands and wished she was invisible; she wished the ground would swallow her whole. The world moved on by a fraction of a degree and she was still sitting there on a rock in the most beautiful place on earth, and Gabriel could still see her.

'Look at me.'

She lifted her head slowly and met his eye.

'First off, I'm not angry you tried to run away. Secondly, this is probably a good time to reassure you again that I have no intention of hurting you or your baby. So I'd like you to answer my question, please. And be truthful. What are you running from?'

'You,' she said and the word was barely audible.

'Why?'

She let out a small laugh and shook her head in disbelief. 'You kidnapped me.'

'That's one way of looking at it.'

'Gabriel, it's the only way of looking at it.'

'I'm the reason you're alive, Zoe. Remember, Daniel wanted me to kill you. He was basically holding you prisoner in that big house back in Portland.'

'I know. But right now it's like I've swapped one prison for another.'

Gabriel looked out over the lake. The breeze was pushing up small waves and the birds were swooping and skimming over them. The sky was reflected in the water, making it seem as deep as the world was high. He turned to face her again. 'Have I ever done anything to hurt you?'

She shook her head.

'Do I leave you to go hungry?'

She shook her head.

'So how can you compare your life here to the life you had with Daniel?'

'Because I'm still a prisoner.'

Gabriel said nothing.

'I just want to be a part of the world again,' she added quietly. 'I want to live in a little apartment that I can call home, and eat when I feel like eating, and if I want to go to a store I'll just jump into my car and drive there. And if I want to go on vacation, I'll head to the airport and catch a flight. And I'll be able to do those things whenever I want because that's what freedom is. It's having the opportunity to make your own choices and your own mistakes.' She stopped talking, then added quietly, 'Is that really too much to ask for?'

'I'm just trying to keep you safe, Zoe.'

'From who? Daniel's dead. He can't hurt me anymore.'

'But you were involved in his murder. Let's not forget that. You talk about being a prisoner, but what you have here is light years from the reality of being held in a real prison. Surely you must see that.'

'I've been thinking about that. After what Daniel did to me, I'm pretty sure that any halfway decent lawyer would be able to argue that there were mitigating circumstances.'

'But "pretty sure" is a long way from being certain. And it's not just you who'll be affected. Who'd look after your baby if you end up in prison?'

Zoe said nothing.

'If you want to go, then go. But the reality of that course of action is that your child might very well end up growing up without a mother. Is that what you want?' Gabriel stopped talking and waited for her to meet his eye. 'You can leave right now if you want. Just start walking. I promise I won't come after you.'

'You're bluffing.'

'And you're still sitting there because you know I'm right.'

He was wrong. She was still here because that poker face didn't fool her for a second. He would probably let her get back to the cabin; he might even let her start walking along the dirt track. But at some point he would come and get her. That was what she told herself because it was what she needed to believe. At the same time there was a tiny dissenting voice at the back of her head whispering that he was right. Because how shitty would that be? To experience a brief moment of freedom and then end up in prison. Like Gabriel had pointed out, who would look after her baby then?

'So, what?' she asked. 'We're going to spend the rest of our lives here? Is that your plan?'

'Of course not. At some point the dust will settle. That would be a good time to join the rat race again. If you want, that is.'

'Exactly how long will it take for the dust to settle?'

'Difficult to say.'

'Because you have no intention of ever letting me go,' she said quietly.

Gabriel stared out over the lake again, watching the birds swoop and dive. 'Okay,' he said, turning back. 'You want me to put a timescale on this. I'd give it at least a year. That should be enough time for everyone to forget about you. That said, if you did decide that you wanted to stay here that wouldn't be a problem.'

'I'll want to leave.'

'You say that now, but it wouldn't surprise me if you changed your mind. I mean, why would anyone want to live cooped up with millions of other people, running around like mice on a wheel, when they could be living out here, breathing fresh air and actually able to hear their own thoughts?'

'When I leave, how will it work? I mean, I can't just walk back into my old life. If I just suddenly turn up out of the blue, the police will still want to talk to me.'

'To start with you'll need a new identity, and you won't be able to contact anyone from your old life. That includes Lizzy.'

'And how exactly am I supposed to get a new identity? That would cost a fortune.'

Gabriel smiled.

'What? Why are you smiling like that?'

'Money won't be a problem. Daniel paid me well to murder you. As for getting hold of false documentation, that won't be a problem either.'

'Okay, so I stay here for the next year. You do realise that at some point I'm going to have a baby.'

Gabriel smiled again. 'Judging by the way your belly keeps getting bigger I'd say that's a foregone conclusion.'

'I'm being serious. Six months from now I'll be giving birth. That means going to a hospital. What will people say when they see the ankle bracelet?'

'Six months from now, you won't be wearing that ankle bracelet. I promised your world will get bigger. That's a promise I intend keeping.'

'You're missing the point. When I turn up at the hospital, they'll want to know who I am.'

'You don't need to go to hospital, Zoe. People have home births all the time.'

She stared at him in disbelief. 'Are you crazy?'

'I'm totally serious. There's no reason you can't have your baby here.'

'Okay, first off, we're in the middle of nowhere. Secondly, there's usually a midwife on hand to help out with a home birth. And thirdly, you're only a short car journey from the hospital if anything goes wrong. So there's three reasons to start with.'

'You'll be fine.'

'So you're going to deliver this baby? Is that what you're telling me?'

'You can do it on your own if you want, but, yeah, I'm happy to help.'

Zoe was still staring. The way he was talking he could have been offering to help carry her groceries. This was insane. They were talking about a baby, for Christ's sake. 'And what do you know about giving birth?'

'What's to know? Women have been having babies for millions of years. The way I see it, the process has been designed to pretty much look after itself.'

'Easy for you to say.'

'Look, Zoe, you're having your baby here, and it's going to be fine.'

The smile he tried for was supposed to be reassuring; Zoe felt anything but.

'Is there anything else you want to talk about?' Gabriel added.

Zoe was sure there must be plenty but her brain had suddenly gone empty. She was stuck on the idea that she would be having her baby out here all alone in the middle of nowhere. She shook her head.

'In that case, let's head back.'

Gabriel got up off of the rock and started walking. Zoe gave it a second then followed. Back at the cabin, he led her through to her bedroom, told her to wait, then headed off to his own room. He returned with a new roll of duct tape and a pair of scissors. He used the scissors to cut the old tape from her feet, then bound her legs and wrists.

'I'm sorry, Zoe, but I don't want you doing something you might end up regretting for the rest of your life. If you think about it, you'll see I'm right.'

Zoe was thinking about it, but all his bullshit rationalisations did was reaffirm the idea that he had no intention of ever letting her go.

'I'm going to go and get our supplies now,' he went on. 'Before I do, I've got one more question. I asked earlier what you were running away from, but maybe you should ask yourself what you're running *to*.'

He held her gaze for a second, then left the room. Zoe listened to his footsteps get quieter as he walked through the living room. The front door closed and the Cherokee started up. For a moment Zoe half expected him to punch the gas pedal like Daniel used to. But that was then and this was now, and even though her life was still being dictated by the whims of a control freak, that was where the similarities ended. Because however dangerous Daniel had been, he wasn't even close to being in the same league.

That last question of Gabriel's was turning over and over inside her mind to the point where it was all she could think about. What exactly was she running to? Her life in Portland, such as it was, was over; the only person who might miss her was Lizzy and they hadn't really spoken in years. So what exactly was out there for her? All the same, whatever fate was waiting out there, it had to be better than this. She listened as the Cherokee's engine faded into the distance; listened to the empty silence that drifted in to replace it.

'You bastard,' she screamed.

# Chapter 43

Gabriel came into the living room carrying a two-inch thick stack of paper. Zoe saw what was printed on the top sheet and her head started to swim. There were only seven words, but they were powerful words: '*The Day of Stones* by Zoe Chapel'. He placed the manuscript on the kitchen table and sat down opposite her.

'How?' was all she could manage.

'How did I get hold of this?'

She nodded.

'I downloaded it from your laptop before I torched your house.'

He stated this like it explained everything, like burning a house to the ground was completely normal. In some ways she supposed it was an explanation; in others it explained nothing.

'I've got a confession,' he went on. 'I've read the first page. It's good, Zoe.'

She shook her head. 'No, it's not. Anyway, you can't tell if something's any good from the first page.'

'I think you can.'

'No, you can't. I've read plenty of books that start off well then run out of steam. Don't tell me you haven't.'

Gabriel went quiet for a moment. 'Okay, I'll give you that. But what you can tell from the first page is whether a book has potential. And I'm telling you, Zoe, this has potential.'

'In your opinion.'

'In my opinion. Look, if you don't want me to read it, just say. I won't be offended.'

'Yeah, right. It doesn't matter what I say, you're going to read it anyway.'

He shook his head. 'No, I'm not. You have my word. This is your work. Your private thoughts. I'm not going to intrude on that unless you give me permission to do so.'

Zoe looked at him and said nothing.

'That's a promise,' he added. 'And why are you so negative about the book anyway?' Gabriel paused, then nodded to himself. 'You let Daniel read it. He told you it was crap.'

'Not in so many words.'

'But he made it clear he didn't like it?'

Zoe nodded. She was back in that moment again. Her Day of Stones.

'I'll understand if you don't want me to read it, but I hope you will.'

Zoe looked across the table at him. The request seemed completely genuine. There was no indication that he was mocking her or being in any way disingenuous. She couldn't understand why, but he really wanted to read the book. She stared for a second longer, then nodded.

'Thank you,' he said.

♦

Gabr
ing its
locked
had neve
looked, G
but the wor

He was al
he was a fast r
hurry up and
they could get b
here. She gave it a
she could take. She

'Would it be okay

'Sure.'

She hovered in fron of him, waiting to be noticed. When it became clear that he wasn't going to be looking up any time soon, she said, 'I'll need my sneakers, please.'

'Sure,' Gabriel said again, and he still wasn't looking up.

She watched his finger follow the words to the bottom of the page. One of the guards had just pushed his gun against Lila's mother's head. When the gun jammed he had hit her in the face with the butt of his rifle, knocking out some teeth. It had been a lucky escape. Zoe remembered writing this passage. She also remembered how happy she had been at the time. She was married to the man she loved, living the life of a writer, and it didn't get much better than that. Gabriel laid the page face down onto the growing pile of ones he had read, then went to fetch her sneakers. By the time her laces were tied he had already sat back down and picked up the next page.

'I'm going to head down to the lake,' sh

'Sure.'

Zoe waited for back

already disappeared

stood, and Gabriel

ers, and Gabriel

her permis

tag,

...e said. 'If that's okay.'

...ay something else, but he had
...nto the story. She walked outside and
...ooking at the dirt track. She had her sneak-
... was engrossed in her novel, and he had given
...sion to go outside the area regulated by the electronic
...nd she was wondering how far she could get before he realised what she was up to. Probably not far enough, unfortunately.
It was so tempting, but she couldn't go off half-cocked at the
first sniff of freedom. If she was lucky, she would get one more
chance to escape. When it came, she had to make it count.

She went around to the back of the cabin and followed the
trail to the creek. The clouds from earlier had blown away and
the sky was high and blue. Back at the cabin the temperature
had been somewhere around seventy; here, in the shade of the
trees, it was much cooler. When she reached the creek, instead
of turning left towards the lake, she turned right and headed up
the hill to the waterfall. She was walking slowly, figuring she had
time to kill.

She reached the clearing, and for a long time just stood there
staring at the graves. What must it have been like for Gabriel
to lose his wife and daughter? You wake up one morning with
your whole future stretching out in front of you, all those plans
and dreams, but by the end of the day the world as you know it
has collapsed into a moment that's going to haunt you for the
rest of your days. Was that why Gabriel had turned out like he

had? Was that the thing that had changed him into this stranger she barely knew? Then there were his experiences in the army to consider. How had they affected him? She didn't care what he said, the act of taking a life had to change a person. Anyone saying otherwise was a liar.

Except it wasn't that simple. It never was. She could see how this version of Gabriel could have evolved from the teenager she had known. He had always been quiet, preferring to spend hours playing video games on his own rather than hanging out with friends. And these were always the eighteen-plus games, the ones where the only objective was to kill and destroy. Then there was his love of hunting. He once told her that he killed his first deer when he was only six years old. At that age she had been playing with dolls and learning to ride her bike. In truth it wasn't the army that turned Gabriel into a killer. That was something he'd been doing since he was old enough to hold a gun. She walked over to the pool, and for a short while the crash and rush of the waterfall numbed her thoughts. Like Novocaine, it wore off too quickly.

She hated Gabriel for keeping her prisoner; hated him for killing all those people to get her here; hated the fact that she didn't even know the names of the two who had died at the gas station. She hated the fact that he could make her hate this much, because hate was like cancer. If she let it get a hold it would end up consuming her, and that wasn't going to help. If she was going to stand any chance of escaping she needed to think logically, not emotionally.

Zoe hunkered down on the bank and started searching through the stones. The water was freezing and in no time she could barely feel her fingers. Still she kept going, moving stones, picking them up, disregarding them. A large stone in the shallows at the edge of the pool caught her eye. She picked it up and studied it. This should do the job. It fitted snugly inside her hand; one edge was flat and smooth. She picked up a second stone, then sat down on the trunk of a fallen tree and ran it along the smooth edge of the first stone. She ran her finger along the edge. It didn't feel any sharper. This was clearly going to take time.

She rubbed the stone against the flat edge, again and again and again. With each stroke she could feel her resolve increase. Somehow, someway she was going to break free from Gabriel. Even if that meant going to prison.

By the time Zoe got back to the cabin it was after six and Gabriel was two thirds of the way through the manuscript. The stones were tucked into the waistband of her jeans and digging uncomfortably into her belly; her T-shirt and sweatshirt were arranged carefully to cover any bulges. In the end, Gabriel didn't even look up when she walked in. All she got was a distracted, grunted 'hi'. She went straight through to her bedroom and lifted the loose floorboard that hid her secret place. The stones went down into the dark shadows, the board went back. She checked to make sure nothing was out of place, then went back through to the living room to fix dinner.

The refrigerator and freezer were full, but nothing tempted her. In the end she went for the easy option: pasta and a jar of sauce. Gabriel ate his on the sofa because he was still reading; she ate hers at the table, and tried to pretend he wasn't there. Back in her room, she took out the stones. The quilt was draped over her hands to muffle the sound of them grinding together. She doubted that Gabriel would be able to hear from the other room but she wasn't taking any chances.

She was working on the assumption that he would restrain her when he did the next supply run. She was also assuming that he wasn't going to allow her access to anything sharp enough to enable her to cut through the tape. She had at least two weeks before they ran out of food; two weeks to get the edge sharp enough.

It was getting late when Gabriel knocked on the door. Zoe was in bed, but sleep had never seemed a more distant prospect. She sat up, pulling the covers with her, and switched on the bedside lamp.

'Come in,' she called out.

The door opened and Gabriel entered. 'I've finished your book.'

The statement prompted a flashback. It wasn't Gabriel standing there, it was Daniel, and this was the end of everything. Despite everything that had happened, she still wanted to know what Gabriel thought. It was crazy, but creative people could be so needy sometimes. They might make out that they didn't care what people thought, they might say that they were creating their art for the sake of it, but that was bullshit. If she ever needed proof of that, all she had to do was think back to this moment, because right now she was hanging on Gabriel's every word.

'Well?' she asked, even though there was a part of her that didn't want to know.

'I loved it. You know, I never saw the end coming, and I always catch the twist. Not this time, though. This one caught me completely by surprise. Did you ever try to get it published?'

She shook her head.

'Because of Daniel?'

She nodded.

'Your husband was an idiot.'

Zoe almost smiled.

'You know it's good enough to get published.' Gabriel touched the left side of his chest. 'You know it here. In your heart. I don't believe anyone who writes this well can't know. You have a rare talent, Zoe. It's a shame Daniel couldn't see that.'

'I appreciate the compliment.'

'But you're going to agree to differ,' Gabriel finished for her.

Zoe nodded and offered up a weak smile.

'And that's the greatest shame of all. Okay, I'm going to bed. Goodnight.'

Gabriel backed out of the room, pulling the door closed gently behind him. The whole exchange had been surreal, and the thing she found most surreal was the fact that she cared what he thought. She switched off the light and the darkness rolled in, reminding her of what was really going on here; reminding her how much she had grown to hate Gabriel. She waited until she heard him climb into bed before going to her secret place to retrieve her stones.

# Chapter 44

'Go to your room, please.'

Zoe turned and looked at Gabriel. This was the first time anything like this had happened. Her mind was running fast, looking for reasons. She must have done something wrong, but what? Each day was much the same as the last. She couldn't see that she had done anything today that she hadn't done yesterday, and certainly nothing that would merit this.

'Please go to your room, Zoe.'

That was enough to get her moving. This was the tone of voice he had used at the gas station, the one that allowed no room for discussion, argument or contradiction. She got up from the sofa and walked to her room. She could hear Gabriel moving around in the living room, and still had no idea why he was so pissed at her. Today really had been as non-eventful as yesterday. She had got up, had breakfast, read for a while, then made lunch. The weather had been beautiful, so they had gone to the lake. Gabriel had gone fishing, while she had sat in the shade of a tree and read.

The minutes dragged by and Zoe's imagination went into overdrive. Somehow Gabriel must have known that she hadn't really been reading. Somehow he knew that she had been dreaming up ways to escape. Somehow he knew about the stones hidden beneath the floorboard. She put the brakes on these thoughts before they had a chance to really get a hold. How could he know? Gabriel might be a lot of things but he wasn't a mind reader. And she had been so careful to make sure he had no reason to suspect her. But she must have done something wrong. If she hadn't, then why had he sent her to her room like a naughty schoolkid?

It had to be getting on for an hour before Gabriel called out for her to come through. She still had no idea what she had done wrong. All she knew was that it had to be something terrible. Gabriel had never hit or kicked her; he hadn't even shown the slightest sign of doing anything like that. Then again, there had been a time when she would have said the same about Daniel. She tried to get up off of the bed but it was impossible. She was convinced that if she went out there then a bad situation was going to get a whole lot worse.

Gabriel called out again and that got her moving. She opened the bedroom door and the first thing that struck her was how gloomy it was. This made no sense. It was somewhere around seven, so sunset was still a couple of hours away. The second thing that struck her was the smell of cooking fish. She walked through to the living room and barely recognised the place.

The table had been set for two. There was a pressed white tablecloth, linen napkins, and metal cutlery at both places. The drapes were drawn and candles flickered in wine bottles; the fire burning in the grate cast a rosy glow on the room. Sinatra was

playing on the stereo, and that just added to the sense of discon-
nection. The whole scene was cosy and intimate, and Zoe was
left feeling like she had slid down Alice's rabbit hole. Gabriel
pulled out a chair for her, and this was the most surreal thing
of all, because he was dressed in his US Army Ranger uniform.
There were medals pinned to his chest and a beret angled on top
of his head.

Zoe sat down, speechless, her eyes not leaving his for a second.
He eased her chair back under the table and poured two glasses
of sparkling grape juice. He held up his glass and waited for her
to do the same.

'Happy birthday,' he said.

All Zoe could do was stare.

'What?' he asked.

'I thought you were mad at me. I thought that's why you sent
me to my room.'

Gabriel's concern gave way to a smile, and then he laughed.
'Yeah, I can see how you might think that. I just wanted you out
of the way so I could surprise you. That's all.'

'Well, it worked. Consider me suitably surprised.'

'It's not too much, is it?'

Zoe surprised herself by laughing. Partly because she hadn't
expected this, but mostly out of relief. If Gabriel was doing
something like this then there was no way he suspected she was
up to anything. She was on familiar territory here. If he needed
her to play along then she could do that with her eyes closed.
She'd had plenty of practice with Daniel.

'It is too much, isn't it?' he asked again.

'Let's just say that if you'd warned me then I might have dressed for the occasion.'

They had Parma ham and melon for their starter; for the main course Gabriel had grilled the fish that he had caught and served it with vegetable rice; dessert was Ben & Jerry's Chocolate Fudge Brownie ice cream. They finished dessert and Gabriel made coffee. He brought the mugs over and placed them on the table. Sinatra was still playing on the stereo, the CD on its third rotation.

'Wait here a second,' he said. 'I've got something for you.'

He went to his room, leaving Zoe alone with her coffee and the music. He returned with two presents. Both were wrapped in shiny red paper and finished off with a pink ribbon. He handed her the smallest one first. From the size, weight and feel, she knew straightaway it was a book. She removed the ribbon carefully and tore off the paper. It was a hardback copy of *The Storyteller*. She opened it to the title page. Gabriel had written:

For Zoe
A copy of The Storyteller for a real-life storyteller.
Happy birthday,
Gabriel

'Now you can find out how it ends,' he said.

'Thank you.'

He held out the second present and waited for her to take it. This one was heavier, and bigger. She knew what it was, but couldn't see why Gabriel would give her something like this. She removed the ribbon and the paper, and placed the laptop on the table. She looked questioningly at Gabriel.

'You're a writer.'

He said this like it was all the explanation that was needed. Maybe in his head it was, but as far as Zoe was concerned this couldn't have been further from the truth.

'I'm not a writer.'

Gabriel raised an eyebrow. 'Because Daniel said so?'

Zoe said nothing.

'*The Day of Stones* was the last thing you wrote, and that was years ago.'

'You don't get it.'

'What's to get? You're a writer, you should write.'

'You wouldn't understand,' she repeated.

'And what exactly don't I understand, Zoe? That you poured your heart into that book, then Daniel came along and ripped it apart?'

Zoe said nothing, because he was right.

'Daniel is dead,' he continued. 'You won. However, if you don't own that victory, it will ultimately be for nothing.'

'What do you want from me?' she asked

'I want you to pick up the pieces and rebuild yourself. You were like a broken bird when you arrived here. But every day you're getting stronger. I reckon you're about ready to fly again.'

'How can I fly when I'm locked up in this cage?'

'I don't remember seeing any locks on the doors.'

*What about the glue on the windows?* she almost asked. She glanced at the tag on her ankle. 'Please take this off.'

Gabriel followed her gaze, but didn't say anything. And that was good because he hadn't said no.

'Please,' she added in a whisper. 'I'm not going to run. I promise. I've been thinking about what you said, and it makes sense to give it a year. It would break my heart to go to prison and not see my baby.'

Gabriel reached for his coffee and took a sip, and still he hadn't said no. Zoe held her breath, hoping, wishing and praying. In the end her wishes came to nothing. Gabriel let out a long sigh, shook his head once, then turned to look at her.

'I'm really sorry, Zoe, it's better if we leave it on for now.'

'So when will you take it off?'

'Soon. I promise.'

Sinatra was singing 'In the Wee Small Hours' and the song ached with a melancholic loneliness that mirrored how she felt. Gabriel might be sitting opposite her but she had never felt so alone. The rest of the world had never seemed further away. Even when she had been imprisoned in the big house on Fairfield Boulevard she hadn't felt this isolated. Right now she might as well have been the last person alive in the universe. That was how lonely she felt. She looked at the laptop and Gabriel followed her gaze.

'What will I write about? I mean, I can't remember the last time I had a good idea.'

'Why not write about your marriage?'

'Who would want to read that?'

Gabriel shrugged. 'I would. And, anyway, what does it matter if no one reads it? Can't you just write it for yourself? Who knows, you might find it cathartic.'

'I guess.'

'Good, so when are you going to start?'

'Tomorrow?' she offered.

His smile indicated that this was the correct answer. Zoe was smiling too. Partly because that was the reaction he was looking for, but mostly because she felt as though she had just scored a small victory. The more he believed she was buying into his fantasy, the more chance he would drop his guard.

Gabriel walked over to the CD player and skipped through the tracks until he found the one he wanted. He walked back to the table and held out his hand. 'It's your birthday. Everyone should dance on their birthday.'

Zoe shook her head, but he just stood with his hand held out until she took it. To start with they moved awkwardly across the floor, slowly finding a rhythm that worked for them. Gabriel's medals were cold against her cheek; his uniform smelled faintly of mothballs. She hated him being so close to her, hated him being so close to the baby, but she was careful to keep these thoughts to herself. Once again, this was familiar territory. How many times had she felt Daniel moving across to her side of the bed and known what was coming next? She had survived by disappearing into a small safe space inside her head. That was where she went now. She was only vaguely aware of the slow movement of her feet; only vaguely aware of Gabriel's touch and smell. She drifted deeper into herself and the thin tether that held her to reality finally snapped, leaving her floating alone in a space that was both infinitely huge and infinitesimally small, a place where nothing and no one could get to her.

It was almost midnight by the time she got back to her room. She shut the door and pressed her forehead against the cool wood, relieved the ordeal was finally over. There had been more dancing, and more talking, and she had done her best to make out that what was happening was normal. The thing was, it wasn't her birthday. That was still a couple of weeks away.

To start with she thought it was a mistake. It was an easy one to make. He had the right time of year. He was just out by a couple of weeks, that was all. It was during their second dance together that the penny finally dropped. Gabriel had pulled her close and asked if she was okay. He had used her name, but there had been a small hesitation before he said it. That hesitation had chilled her heart because it sounded like he was about to call her Michelle. She had tried to tell herself she was mistaken, but then she remembered the dates on the wooden cross that marked Michelle's grave. Out here the days blurred together, but Zoe was pretty sure that it was May 17, Michelle's birthday.

What if Gabriel was looking for someone to take her place? To *become* her. The idea terrified her. If that was what was really going on then Gabriel was even more unstable than she thought, and that meant things were only going to get worse. The countdown until the next supply run had begun. That was her next best chance for getting out of here. Two weeks seemed a lifetime away, though. A lot could happen in that time. Two weeks ago she had been trapped in a nightmare marriage; now Daniel was dead and she was trapped in a whole new nightmare. Gabriel hadn't physically harmed her, but that was no guarantee of anything. He had proved he was both capable and willing to kill. He had also proved that it didn't take much to provoke him into doing that.

Zoe climbed into bed and pulled the quilt over herself. Sleep was a long time coming. Waiting for the next supply run was too risky. The more she thought about it, the more convinced she was that she wasn't going to last another day, never mind two weeks. As to what the hell she was going to do now, she was all out of ideas.

# Chapter 45

The hiker appeared the next afternoon.

Gabriel was out fishing and Zoe was staring at a blank Word document. The second he left she had started hunting for an Internet connection. It hadn't taken long to find one, but it was password protected. She had started with the obvious guesses: names, significant dates, that sort of thing. When she started trying variations of her own name it was clear she was getting desperate. She eventually gave up when she realised she was typing in random strings of numbers, letter and characters. It would take the NSA's computers a month to crack the code this way; if she was lucky she might manage to crack it at some point in the next millennium.

She let out a long sigh of frustration then sat back in her chair. Gabriel was expecting her to write something but she had never felt less inclined to write in her entire life. That said, if she could manage even one page that would show she was at least willing, and it would go a long way to persuading him that she was co-operating. She stared at the blank screen. She hadn't written anything since *The Day of Stones*, and that was years ago. Like any skill, if you don't use it you lose it, and she had lost it big time.

She typed: 'My name is Zoe Chapel and this is my story', then leant back and looked at the words on the screen. It was a beginning. The main character had been introduced, and it worked as brief statement of intent. Who was she trying to kid? It was crap. Total and utter crap. She leant forward and mashed the delete key until the offending words disappeared.

She typed: 'This was what happened.'

When you got down to it, that one statement was at the heart of every story. As a way in, it rarely failed. It wasn't working today, though; it just didn't feel right. She reached for the delete key, held it down until the page was once again a blank white expanse of emptiness, then got up and went through to the bathroom to pee. She might be peeing a hundred times a day at the moment, but for once she didn't need to go. It was just a way to distract herself from the depressing fact that she could no longer write.

She had just sat back at the screen when someone called out. She hurried to the window and moved the drape aside. The hiker was standing next to the Cherokee. He was in his mid-thirties, maybe early forties, and there was a large pack strapped to his back. The long greasy ponytail, dirty denim jacket, tie-dye T-shirt and round John Lennon spectacles marked him as a hippy. She let the drape fall back into place and prayed that he hadn't seen her.

'Hi there,' he called out. 'I'm really sorry to bother you, but I'm lost.'

Zoe flattened herself against the cabin wall and tried to make herself invisible. Judging by the way he was shouting, he knew she was here. He must have seen the drape move. So, what now? Ignore him until he went away? The hiker knocked on the door, and Zoe just about jumped out of her skin.

'Please,' he called out. 'I've been wandering around lost for two days now and you're the first person I've seen. If you've maybe got a telephone I could use? And maybe you could fill up my canteen, please? I'm out of water. I promise not to take up too much of your time.'

Zoe took a deep breath and willed her heart to slow. The water she could help with; the telephone she couldn't. And it would be easy enough to point him in the direction of the dirt track and tell him that it led to the road.

And she could ask him to get help.

The idea died before it had a chance to get going. There was no way she could do that, not after what happened at the gas station. She couldn't be responsible for another death. Gabriel might not be back for hours yet. Then again he could turn up at any second.

She walked over to the door and opened it. The hiker just about melted with relief when he saw her. Up close, he was younger than she first thought. Early thirties, perhaps. He had looked older because his face was filthy and sunburnt. Aside from that, he didn't look any the worse for wear.

'Am I glad to see you,' he said. 'I thought I was a dead man.'

'You said you needed water.'

'Please.' He slid his backpack off, found his canteen and passed it to her. 'Thank you. My name's Jake, by the way.'

She hesitated. 'Mine's Zoe.'

'It's good to meet you, Zoe.'

'Okay, wait here and I'll get your water.'

By the time she got back, Jake had his map out and was spreading it open on the ground. She passed him the canteen and he took a long drink. He paused, took another, then screwed the lid back on.

'Thanks,' he said.

'My pleasure.' Zoe smiled pleasantly and wished he would just hurry up and go. She glanced towards the side of the cabin. There was still no sign of Gabriel, but every second they spent chatting took them a second closer to disaster.

Jake picked up the map, folded it to the section he wanted, and pointed. 'This was where I was when I got lost. I wandered off the trail to go exploring, which was a dumbass thing to do. So, where exactly am I now?'

It took a moment for Zoe to get her bearings. She tapped a road on the map then pointed to the dirt track. 'This track leads to that road. It's not that busy, but you should be able to pick up a lift. It's about a six mile walk.'

Jake looked towards the head of the track; Zoe glanced towards the side of the cabin. She was so tempted to say something. If he started walking now he would be out of sight within a couple of minutes, and Gabriel would be none the wiser. The electronic tag would short-circuit any long explanations. All she had to do was show him it and persuade him that she wasn't a fugitive. Once he realised how serious the situation was he would have to help. If it all worked out, then she could be out of here before nightfall.

She was about to open her mouth when a voice spoke up behind her.

'You didn't tell me we were expecting guests.'

# Chapter 46

Zoe turned slowly and saw Gabriel striding around the side of the cabin. There was a fishing rod in his right hand, a couple of trout in his left, and a wide friendly smile on his face. He leant the rod against the side of the cabin and the fish on the ground, and held out his hand.

'I'm Gabriel.'

'Jake.'

'So what brings you all the way out here?'

Jake shrugged and looked sheepish. 'I'm afraid I got lost. You know, I'm so lucky to have stumbled across you guys. Zoe here was just showing me where I am on the map.'

Gabriel turned to Zoe and his smile was as wide and friendly as ever. 'I'm glad we've been able to help.'

'I don't suppose you've got a phone?' Jake asked. 'I ran my cell battery down trying to get a signal.'

Gabriel shook his head. 'Sorry. No phones. We believe they're partially responsible for the downfall of modern society. We prefer to stay off the grid.'

'Judging by that satellite dish, not all the way off,' Jake said.

Gabriel laughed. 'Being without a phone is one thing; being without ESPN is just a step too far.'

Jake laughed. 'I'm not a sports fan, so I'll have to take your word on that. Look, I've taken up enough of your time. If you could fill up my canteen again, I'll be getting on my way.'

'Why don't you stay here tonight?' Gabriel suggested. 'You could camp down by the lake. It's beautiful down there. Isn't it, honey?'

Zoe nodded but didn't say anything. Her mouth was suddenly full of sand, her head full of dangerous thoughts because she could see where this was headed.

'I'm driving into town tomorrow morning,' Gabriel added. 'I could give you a lift. And there's more than enough fish here to feed the three of us. I'm taking it you're hungry.'

'I couldn't,' Jake said. 'I've already imposed enough.'

'It's no trouble at all. And let's face it, you're in no fit state to walk to the road, and then spend God knows how long waiting for a lift. No, the best thing to do is have something to eat and a good night's rest. Tomorrow you'll feel like a new man.'

'If you're sure it's no trouble.'

'It's not. Okay, I'm going to grab a beer. Do you want one?'

'I'm probably best to stick to water until I'm rehydrated.'

Gabriel laughed. 'Good plan. Okay, give me your canteen and I'll fill it up.'

Jake handed over his canteen and Gabriel went inside. Zoe's mind was racing. She had no idea what to do. She could tell Jake to run, but he'd want to know why and there was no time for explanations.

'Excuse me a minute,' she said.

She didn't hear Jake's reply because she was already moving. She caught up with Gabriel as he was coming out of his bedroom. There was a hunting rifle cradled in his arms. She stopped in the middle of the corridor, blocking his way.

'I didn't say anything. I promise.'

'I know you didn't.'

'So you don't have to kill him.'

'I don't like this any more than you do.'

'Please don't do this, Gabriel.'

'I'm sorry, Zoe, there's no other way.'

'Of course there is. We just let him walk out of here.'

'That won't work.'

'But I didn't say anything.'

'Zoe, whether you said anything or not doesn't matter. He got lost in the woods and survived, and that's a story you can dine on for the rest of your life. Make no mistake, we would play a big part in that story. After all, who saved him? And maybe the story wouldn't get any further than his family and friends, but then again, it might come to the attention of the media. Lost hiker gets saved by forest folk. It's the sort of story they love. And if that happens, don't you think some of those reporters might come looking for us? Then there's the fact that the police are looking for us. What do you think would happen if he's watching the news one day and our faces appear? Don't you think he's going to recognise us?'

'That's not going to happen. My disappearance might have been news for five minutes back in Portland, but no one out here in South Dakota knows I even exist.'

'I can't take that chance.'

'Please don't do this.'

Gabriel shook his head. 'A man has a duty to protect their family, otherwise what sort of man is he? You and the baby, you're my family now, and I will do whatever needs to be done to keep you both safe.'

He turned to leave and Zoe grabbed his arm, pulling him to a stop. 'Please, I'm begging you. Don't do this.'

'Let go of my arm, Zoe.'

She held on tighter, fingers digging into the muscle. 'I don't need you to protect me. Not like this.'

'Yes, you do.'

It didn't matter what she said, Gabriel had made his mind up and nothing was going to change it. She let go of his arm, sprinted to the front door and wrenched it open.

'Run!'

Jake just stared blankly.

'Get out of here!' she yelled. 'He's going to kill you!'

That was enough to break his paralysis. He dropped his map and broke into a stumbling half-run. Zoe heard Gabriel's footsteps getting closer and sprinted into the clearing, aiming to get between the two men. She wasn't sure how much time it would buy, but that didn't matter. Right now she was living from one breath to the next. They both were. In the end, it was all for nothing. The hunting rifle boomed and Jake went down hard, the force of the bullet pitching him into the dirt. The sound of the shot rolled across the treetops and sent birds scattering into the sky.

Jake was dead by the time she reached him. The Lennon spectacles were sitting at an awkward angle and his blank eyes were staring all the way to outer space. The front of his T-shirt was soaked with blood; there was more blood on his beaten-up denim jacket. Gabriel stopped beside her. The rifle was cradled in his arms and he was staring down at the dead body. The hot smell of the gun seemed to be everywhere. It was in her nose and lungs. It was in her stomach, making her want to vomit.

'There wasn't any other way,' he said.

'Yes, there was,' she hissed.

And then she started running.

# Chapter 47

She only managed four steps before Gabriel pulled her to a stop and dragged her into a crushing embrace. She tried to get him with her fists and feet, even her teeth, but it was pointless. He was holding on too tightly, and he was so much stronger.

'Let go.' Getting those two words out was almost impossible because he was squeezing the air from her.

'I need you to calm down, Zoe.'

'Let go,' she repeated, and this time the words were hardly there at all.

Gabriel relaxed his grip a little, just enough so she could breathe again. He still had a tight hold, though, her back pushed hard against his stomach.

'I hate you,' she said.

'In time you'll realise that everything I'm doing here is for you,' he whispered into her ear. 'You and the baby.'

'I don't want to be here. Don't you get it? Even ending up in prison would be better than this.'

'The fact you're saying that proves you're not thinking straight.'

'I'm not thinking straight! What about you? I'm not the one who just killed someone.'

'There was no other way.'

'Is what you tell yourself so you can sleep at night?'

Gabriel didn't reply. Instead, he hoisted her over his shoulder and carried her kicking and punching into the cabin. As they passed through the doorway she caught a last glimpse of Jake's body. The sight of him lying there dead in the dirt knocked the fight out of her. *I'm sorry*, she thought. *I'm so, so sorry.* Gabriel made his way across the living room and down the corridor to her room. He put her down on the bed then left, only to reappear less than a minute later with the duct tape.

'Give me your sneakers.'

'Because I'm not a prisoner here.'

'Just give me your goddam sneakers.'

Zoe glared, then complied. Gabriel taped up her legs and arms. He stopped at the door on his way out, looked at her lying trussed up on the bed, then turned and left. The door closed behind him, leaving her alone with her thoughts and her fear.

It was at least an hour before he returned, which was long enough for Zoe to get her anger under control. Gabriel had been right about one thing. She hadn't been thinking straight. If she had been she wouldn't have said the things she had. She wouldn't have told him that she hated him. Those thoughts were fine when they were locked up inside her head; they weren't okay said out loud. Judging by the fact that he had taken her sneakers *and* used duct tape, she must have really pissed him off. The door swung open and Gabriel entered. He placed her sneakers on the nightstand, then took out his switchblade and popped it open.

'Have you calmed down yet?'

She answered with a nod, but all she could think of was what she would do if she got hold of that knife. Gabriel sat down on the edge of the bed and cut the tape from her arms and legs. It came away with a tearing sound, pulling at the hairs and making her flinch. She sat up and put on her sneakers.

'I'm sorry,' Gabriel said, 'but I didn't know what else to do. I was worried you would do something you might regret.'

'I'm sorry too. I said some things I shouldn't have.'

The apology should have stuck in her throat, but to her ears it sounded completely sincere. This was something else she had learnt from her time with Daniel. She had lost count of the number of times where he had abused her, and she had been the one who apologised.

'I need you to follow me.'

Zoe stood up too quickly, making her head spin. Gabriel was there in an instant, concern in his eyes and in his words.

'Careful,' he said. 'You've been lying down for a while. The blood needs to get flowing again.'

He took her arm and led her through the cabin. Zoe wanted to shake him away, but the fact he was showing some sympathy stopped her. She hated being touched by him, though. Those hands had killed. He let go when they got outside and led the way to the side of the cabin. Jake's body had been moved, but she could see where his blood had soaked into the dirt.

A short while later they arrived at the clearing. Jake's body was lying wrapped in plastic beside Michelle's grave; his backpack and a shovel were next to it. Gabriel picked up the shovel and started digging. He stopped when he'd dug down a couple of feet, removed his shirt, then went back to work with the shovel. He didn't stop again until the grave was almost finished. It was like watching a machine. He dug out a final shovelful of dirt then straightened up and rubbed his back.

'Your turn,' he said as he climbed from the grave.

'Excuse me?'

'Every death needs to be honoured, and you're partly responsible for this one. It's only right that you should help to bury him.'

There were so many ways she could respond. She could tell him that she hadn't pulled the trigger. She could point out that she had done her damnedest to talk him out of murdering Jake. She could tell him that she wasn't the psycho around here. She could tell him to go to hell. And if none of that worked, she could remind him that she was pregnant and shouldn't be digging goddam holes. Instead, she took the shovel and climbed down into the grave.

Gabriel had made it look relatively easy. It wasn't. In no time she was sweating and her muscles were aching. She dug out another shovelful of earth, then took a short breather. Gabriel was drinking from a canteen, the sunlight glinting off his scar tissue. She glanced over at the other two graves. Why couldn't he have died in the fire too?

'Had enough?'

She looked back at Gabriel and nodded. He helped her out of the hole, took the shovel from her and went back to work. Zoe had positioned herself so she didn't have to look at Jake. Seeing his body was one thing too many. So she watched Gabriel dig and tried to separate herself from the situation. If she let reality get hold she wouldn't be able to function. Now more than ever she needed her wits about her.

Gabriel rolled the body over once, twice. The third roll took it to the edge of the grave, where it teetered for a second before gravity took over and pulled it into the shadows. It landed with a sickening thud, a small shower of dirt trailing in its wake. Zoe just stood there wondering how life had conspired to bring her to this moment. The life she had dreamt for herself as a child had not included murder and burials in the woods. Jake's backpack went in next, then Gabriel shovelled the dirt back into the ground. When he was done he patted the earth into a neat, smooth mound.

'Is there anything you want to say?' he asked.

There was plenty, but when you got down to it all those thoughts and feelings could be condensed into two words. *I'm sorry*. She wasn't responsible for Jake's death insomuch as she hadn't pulled the trigger, but she had contacted Gabriel, which meant she had set these events in motion. If she hadn't done that then Jake would still be alive. As would Josh, Daniel, Talya Coles and those two people at the gas station. If she had known that things would turn out like this she wouldn't have approached Gabriel. Not in a million years.

'If there is anything,' he prompted. 'Now's the time.'

Zoe said a quiet *I'm sorry* inside her head. That one was for Jake and God, not Gabriel.

'Can we go?' she said.

'Just a minute.'

One minute ended up being closer to ten. First Gabriel removed the dead flowers from Michelle and Rebecca's graves. Then he went around the clearing collecting fresh flowers. These were sorted into three equal bundles, one for each grave. The last thing he did was stand at the foot of Jake's grave, eyes shut, head bowed. It looked like he was praying, although what he could possibly have to say to God was beyond her. Some sins weighed too heavily to ever be atoned for.

# Chapter 48

They had fish and rice for dinner. Zoe managed to eat a little bit of rice but couldn't stomach the fish. Just looking at it was enough to remind her of Jake. They had only shared a handful of words since getting back and she was glad of the silence.

Gabriel finished eating and placed his fork and knife on the plate. He put them down gently but the sound of metal touching ceramic still set her teeth on edge. He got up without a word and went to his room. While he was gone she cleared the table. She was tempted to take his cutlery but it was too risky. One of the last things he did each night was take his cutlery to his room. She had been monitoring that routine looking for lapses, but so far there hadn't been any. It was unlikely that tonight would be any different. If anything, he would probably be more careful than ever.

Gabriel returned with the tattoo gun. He sat down at the table, removed it from the box and went to work. Zoe carried on cleaning the dishes. She was going as slowly as possible – anything to distract herself from the buzz of the tattoo gun. It wasn't working. The noise was uncomfortable and made her own tattoo itch. He finished inking Jake's cross onto his arm and for a moment just sat there with his eyes closed.

Zoe watched, wondering what was going through his head. Wondering what was going to happen next. His unpredictability was hard to handle. One second he could seem almost normal; the next he was a total psycho. It was like juggling grenades. His eyes suddenly snapped open. Zoe turned away quickly, but not quickly enough. She knew he had caught her staring, knew he must be wondering what she was thinking. She willed her heart to slow and carried on scrubbing the frying pan.

'Come here, please, Zoe.'

She let the pan sink back into the suds, then dried her hands and walked over to the table.

'Sit down.'

Zoe sat. She glanced at him, then quickly looked away, her attention being pulled towards the fire. The days were warming up as summer inched closer, but the temperature still dropped at night. She wondered when they would stop needing to light one. That led her to wonder if she would be around long enough to see that.

'Did Jake give any indication how long he had been lost for?' Gabriel asked her.

'Two days.'

'That should work in our favour. You can cover a lot of ground in that time. Did he say where he was when he got lost?'

Zoe shook her head.

'Are you sure about that? And think hard.'

'I'm sure.'

Gabriel stared past her at the television. The screen acted like a dark mirror, reflecting the room. The flickering of the fire was caught in various shades of grey.

'We need to stick together for the next few days,' he said. 'If anyone comes looking for Jake it would be best if I did the talking.'

Zoe's heart sank. Having Gabriel watching her every move would be a problem. 'What are the chances of that happening?'

'That depends on where he parked his car. The closer he was to the cabin, the more chance there is of someone looking us up. The worst-case scenario is that he's been walking around in circles for two days and is close to where he started.'

*Worst case for you maybe.* Zoe suddenly realised why Gabriel was worried. Killing Jake was one thing. He had been lost. No one knew he had been here. That wouldn't be the case if a cop or a forest ranger dropped by looking for him and went missing. Their colleagues would trace their last movements. How long would it take for them to work out that this had been their last stop?

'You don't have to watch me,' she said. 'If anyone turns up I'll pretend I'm not in.'

'Like you did with Jake?'

Zoe felt the heat rising in her face. There was guilt burning in her gut. 'I made a mistake,' she said quietly. 'I won't make that same mistake again.'

'Okay, but what if someone turns up and sees you?'

'If that happens, I won't say anything.'

'You might not be able to help yourself.'

'You're wrong. Did I say anything to Jake?'

Gabriel shook his head.

'I was tempted. I'm not going to lie. But then I remembered what you said about going to prison. That's why I won't say anything.'

Gabriel went quiet and Zoe waited him out. The part about being tempted was the truth. She had shared this because it wasn't anything he didn't already suspect. Giving that one away hadn't cost her anything, and it would help foster some trust between them. The part about going to prison was a lie. Right now, she would take prison over what was happening here in a heartbeat. At least with prison she would eventually be released. That meant there was the possibility of a future with her baby, which was more than she had here. Gabriel's face suddenly relaxed and she knew he had made his decision. She also knew it wasn't the one she wanted.

# Chapter 49

Gabriel was in her bedroom.

She could hear his breathing. Soft and shallow. Almost inaudible. Zoe lay very still and did her best to control her own breathing. A second ago she had been fast asleep. Now she was more awake than she had ever been, her heart beating so fast it was like it had been shot full of adrenalin. Her first thought was that it was Daniel, but that thought disappeared with the last strands of sleep. For a brief moment she wished it was him, a thought that disappeared just as quickly.

As far as she could tell Gabriel was by the door. That was where the sound originated. She had her back to him, so she couldn't say if the door was closed, but judging by how dark it was she figured it must be. She couldn't turn over because then he would know for certain she was awake. The fact that he was hiding there quietly in the shadows was bad enough, but if he knew she was awake he might want to talk, and she really didn't want to get into a conversation with him right now.

And what if he didn't just want to talk? So far he hadn't shown her any interest in that way, but there was no guarantee that that wasn't playing on his mind. Maybe it had been a slip of the tongue when he almost called her Michelle the other night. Then again, maybe it hadn't been.

Gabriel moved and the floorboards moved with him, letting out a long, low squeak. This was followed by a low creak as he moved again. Zoe forced in another breath and willed herself to relax. There was another creak; this one was definitely closer. One careful footstep was followed by another until he was standing by the bed. He was so close she caught the smell of fried fish on his clothing.

Nothing happened for a moment, then he leant in even closer and ran his hand across her hair, his fingertips gently stroking the strands. Zoe did her best not to flinch, but that was impossible. He had to know she was awake. The only reason he wasn't saying anything was because it suited him to believe she was asleep. If that was the case then that just made what he was doing all the more terrifying.

'You are so beautiful,' he whispered, and Zoe's heart stopped dead in her chest. She lay there frozen to the mattress, her heart thundering in terror. Nothing else happened for a while. No more words, no more touching. All she could do was lie there pretending to be asleep.

It had just reached the point where she was convinced she couldn't take any more when Gabriel turned and walked away. He paused when he reached the door and, although her back was still to him, she knew he was watching her.

It was a long time before he left. She listened to his footsteps fade as he walked back to his room. A switch clicked and the darkness brightened a little, tainted by the light sneaking through the crack at the bottom of the door. Zoe rolled onto her back and stared through the blackness, searching for the ceiling. There was no way she was getting back to sleep again, not after that.

The place where Gabriel touched her still tingled. That was what disturbed her most, the fact that their personal boundaries seemed to be blurring and disappearing. Then there was what he had said. He had never called her beautiful before. Their relationship just wasn't like that. As teenagers they had been brother and sister. Sometimes they hated each other, but mostly they got on. When Gabriel had come back into her life that was where they picked up from. Big Brother and Little Sis. Those roles were set in stone. They knew how to play them. They knew how to act and behave. But they weren't kids anymore, they were all grown up, scarred by the shit that life had thrown at them.

Gabriel had promised that her world would become bigger, but right now it was smaller and more claustrophobic than ever. She had been here before. Daniel used to promise that things would get better too, but they never did. And they weren't going to get better now. Gabriel would keep shrinking the boundaries until they eventually crushed her. It didn't matter what he promised; that was where this was headed. There was a sense of inevitability to what was happening here, a sense of history repeating itself. There had been a time with Daniel where she believed that things might get better. That was a mistake she would never make again.

For a long time she lay there dreaming up one escape plan after the next. Some were elaborate, some ridiculous. The one thing they had in common was that they were all doomed to failure. At some point she realised she was coming at this from the wrong angle. If this had been a plot problem then she would have reached this conclusion a lot sooner. But this was real life. Get it wrong in a book and no one gets hurt; get it wrong out here and there was every chance she and her baby would end up dead.

She couldn't escape from Gabriel. That was where she'd been going wrong. The electronic tag made it impossible. If she tried to run, he would come after her. Even if she headed blindly into the woods he would still find her. Waiting for the next supply run wouldn't work either. The second she passed the twenty-yard mark, the tag would send out an alert. She could probably reach the road before Gabriel got back, but then what? While she was trying to hitch a lift she would be totally exposed. Maybe someone would pick her up before he drove by; maybe they wouldn't.

Either way it was academic, because she probably wouldn't live long enough for that to happen. The way he'd so casually murdered Jake highlighted again how dangerous he was. If someone got in his way, he had no qualms about taking them out. At the moment it suited him for her to be alive, but what happened when that changed?

For a long time she lay in bed, going over every conversation she could remember them having. She was thinking again about the time they had danced together on Michelle's birthday when an idea occurred to her. She chased it around for a while, and the more she chased, the crazier it seemed.

It could work, though.

It had to.

Because right now it was all she had.

# Chapter 50

Gabriel was still awake. She could hear him moving around in his room. His light was on, so he was probably reading. Whatever he was doing she wished he would hurry up and go to sleep. The waiting was killing her. A short while later he got up and went to the bathroom. He let himself back into his bedroom. The light went off. The bed squeaked as he got comfortable. The cabin fell silent and Zoe counted off the minutes in her head. She reckoned an hour would probably be long enough. He should be asleep by then.

The clock in her head eventually hit the hour mark, but she gave it a bit longer just to be sure. She dressed quickly and carefully. The black leggings were the same ones she had worn on the drive from Portland. Her T-shirt was also black. The sweatshirt was grey; it was lighter than she would have liked but it would have to do. Gabriel had taken her sneakers, so she put on every pair of socks she could find.

She took a couple of tentative steps. Her feet felt totally alien because of all the padding. She took another and a floorboard let out the tiniest creak. It was no louder than a sigh, but it sounded like a scream. Everything seemed too loud. The sound of her breathing; the low murmur of the vast forest on the other side of the window.

She reached for the door handle and hesitated. If Gabriel saw her dressed like this there was no telling how he might react. Maybe he would act as though he didn't care. Then again, he might put a bullet in her head. Her hands travelled down to her belly and she said a silent apology. If things went wrong she wanted the baby to know that she had at least tried. She opened the door and paused again. Any second now Gabriel's light was going to come on. She was convinced of it. She gave it a couple of seconds just to be sure, but the light remained off. There was no sound coming from his room. No signs of movement. No signs of life, period.

Zoe reached the living room without Gabriel appearing and that felt like a major victory. Now she had got this far she was moving as fast as she dared. Her socks were shushing gently against the wooden floor and even that seemed too loud. She crossed the dark living room carefully, all the time hoping the map in her head was accurate. The front door was locked, but the window opened as easily as it had done on her first night here. A breath of forest air came rushing in, chilling her skin. Sounds rushed in on the breeze. The whisper of the wind in the trees; the distant calls of the night animals. Everything was still way louder than it should have been, the smells sharper.

She was tempted to make a run for it. The problem was the electronic tag. Gabriel might be fast asleep right now, but that would change the second his phone went off. A sudden noise froze her to the spot. It took a second to establish that it was just the wind blowing over the roof, and another second before she could breathe again. She pushed the window open as far as it would go then stepped back into the room. There was still time to abort. She could shut the window and go back to her room and Gabriel would be none the wiser. So far there had been no real damage done. At that moment there were a hundred reasons why she shouldn't go through with this, and only one why she should. The baby. That was enough to trump all else.

Zoe walked over to where the sofa should be, hands extended. Her foot found it first. She knelt down and felt around for her book. To start with she couldn't find it, and then her fingertips brushed the cover. Before she could change her mind, she opened the book and tore out the first page. The darkness amplified the sound to the point where it sounded like a buzz saw. She froze again and stared in the direction of Gabriel's room.

Still all quiet.

She tore out another page, and another. With each page the evidence against her was mounting; she had now passed the point where she would be able to talk her way out of this. She tore out eight pages in total, separated them into two neat piles, then took each pile in turn and twisted the pages into a tight taper.

The fire was almost out but a couple of logs were still glowing orange at the edges. She pressed the end of a taper to one of them and blew gently. Nothing happened. She blew again. Still nothing. Her hand was shaking. The heat had enclosed it like a glove. She tried again. This time the taper caught and the darkness shrank back, burned away by the flame.

The drapes caught easily. So did the sofa. The breeze coming through the open window fanned the flames. The room revealed itself as the fire took hold. It was spreading so fast she didn't need the second taper. The flames were devouring everything it touched; smoke was swirling around the rafters and getting into her lungs; the heat was a physical presence, pressing against her skin, burning her. This was the point where she should get out. There was still enough time to climb through the window and make a run for it. Give it another thirty seconds and that would no longer be an option.

Instead of climbing out of the window, Zoe turned and hurried back to her room.

# Chapter 51

The voice inside her head was screaming for her to get the hell out, every instinct pushing her towards the open window, but her feet were taking her further away. She reached her bedroom and let herself in. The door slid quietly back into the frame. The latch clicked home. She could smell the fire, which meant that Gabriel would be able to smell it too. She had just managed to jump into bed and drag the quilt over herself when she heard him explode from his room and charge towards the living room. The footsteps stopped suddenly and Zoe knew he was seeing the flames.

The footsteps started up again and a second later her door burst open. Gabriel was standing there in his boxer shorts, back-lit in orange and yellow, his scar tissue shining in the firelight. The self-possession was gone, the confidence. He looked scared. This was the reaction she had been hoping for. When he set fire to the cabin back in Oregon he had been in control. He had lit the match then watched the building burn. Now the fire was in control, just like it had been the night his wife and daughter died. She hoped he was back in the apartment the three of them had shared. She hoped he was reliving everything that happened that night. She hoped he could feel the pain of losing his wife and daughter. Most of all, she hoped he could forget who he was for a few seconds and see her as his saviour.

'The cabin's on fire,' he yelled. 'We need to get out.'

Zoe sat up in bed, quickly but carefully. Her right hand was hidden beneath the quilt. She didn't want him to see the T-shirt that was wrapped around it. She conjured up a panicked expression and glanced around the room as though she was searching for an escape route.

'The window,' she said. 'We can get out the window. Use a drawer to break it.'

Gabriel sprinted to the bureau, wrenched the top drawer out, then ran at the window and slammed it into the glass. The window exploded in a shower of glass and the cool air rushed in. He pulled the drawer back in, dragging more glass with it, then ran it from side to side, breaking off the worst of the pieces that were still attached to the bottom of the frame. Zoe was already out of the bed, heading for the window. The quilt was in her right hand, hiding the T-shirt. She held it out for him to take.

'Drape this over the frame. So we don't cut ourselves.'

He reached for it and she let go a fraction of a second too early. It fluttered to the floor and he followed it down, his arm outstretched, fingers grasping. Zoe had already seen the shard she wanted. It was six inches long and as sharp as a knife. She swooped down and grabbed it, then lunged forward. She had been aiming for his throat, but he moved at the last moment and the shard dug deep into his arm instead. His eyes widened and his hands moved up to cover the wound. Blood was seeping through his fingers.

She glanced at the broken window, then turned and ran to Gabriel's room. The door was wide open when she got there, the lights off. She banged the switch as she ran in and the shadowy yellows and oranges were replaced with bright white light. The room was military neat. No clutter anywhere. There was a large framed photograph of Michelle and Rebecca hanging above the bed. Michelle was blonde and pretty; she looked eastern European, maybe Russian. Zoe recognised the sadness in her eyes because she'd seen the same thing in her own. They said they loved you, and in their hearts they might believe that, but whatever it was they felt, it wasn't love. Real love didn't take the sparks from your eyes; it put those sparks there.

There was a laptop on the nightstand, but no sign of the car key or the satellite phone. Zoe ran over to the bed and wrenched the pillows away, hoping to find his phone, and coming up empty. She could hear Gabriel staggering around in the other room. The fact he hadn't followed her meant she had hurt him. The fact he was still moving meant she hadn't hurt him badly enough. She figured that he must be looking for something to stem the bleeding. That was why he hadn't come after her.

Zoe spun around and saw his jeans folded neatly on the chair behind the door. The second she picked them up she could tell there was something in the pockets. The phone was in the front right, the car keys in the front left, the switchblade in a back one. The knife and phone ended up in the waistband of her leggings; she kept the keys in her hand. She glanced at the open doorway. The fire was burning brighter than ever, and closing in. She wrenched a drawer from the bureau, tipped the contents out, then ran at the window, shattering the glass. She banged the sharpest shards away from the bottom of the frame, dropped the drawer out of the window, then grabbed the quilt from the bed and pushed it into the frame.

'Zoe!'

She turned. Gabriel was standing in the doorway. The top half of his body was smeared with blood and he had a T-shirt wound around the upper part of his left arm to stem the bleeding. Spears of yellow and orange were flashing on the wall behind him, cutting through the darkness. Wisps of smoke snaked all around his body.

'You can't escape, Zoe.'

For a moment she was back in Seattle watching Daniel walk up the aisle of the bus. She could feel every blow he had ever inflicted on her. She could hear him belittling her and making out that she was a piece of shit. She could feel his anger and rage; she could sense all the insecurities hidden behind those emotions. She blinked and it was Gabriel standing there. He was grinning like he had won, although what he might have won, she had no idea.

Zoe launched herself at the window and started climbing through. Gabriel was moving too, his footsteps thumping on the floorboards. He grabbed her by the sweatshirt and started pulling her back in. She tried to shake him off but he was holding on too tightly. She fumbled the knife from her waistband, popped the blade, and slashed one of the arms holding her. He howled in pain and let go.

Before he could grab her again, she climbed all the way through, dropped to the ground and sprinted around to the front of the cabin. She blipped the Cherokee's doors open and climbed in. The engine started first time. Zoe slammed the car into reverse and backed up fast. She pulled the steering wheel hard to the right, sending dirt spinning up from the tyres. A shadow passed across the rear-view mirror. She looked again but it was gone. The shadow passed along the side of the car, then Gabriel was wrenching open the driver's door and trying to drag her out. Zoe stamped on the gas and the Cherokee rushed forward, pulling her away from his grip. She drove on for a dozen yards then hit the brakes. The car skidded to a halt and she slammed it into reverse.

Gabriel tried to jump clear, but wasn't fast enough. The car clipped him, sending him crashing to the ground. She stamped on the brakes and stared at him through the windshield. He was scrabbling around in the dirt and her first thought was that he was struggling to get up. Then she saw the gun on the ground a couple of yards from him. He lunged forward then fell back down again, and now the gun was only a couple of inches away.

Zoe put the car into drive and hit the gas. The wheels spun, sending dirt and stones ricocheting against the arches. She aimed the car at Gabriel. The gun was in his hand and he was standing in a combat stance. The first bullet shattered the windshield and ripped through the passenger seat headrest. The second smashed through the rear window, passing close enough for her to feel it on her face.

There was a loud bang as metal connected with flesh and bone. Zoe drove on for another ten yards and rolled to a gentle stop. Gabriel was lying motionless in the rear-view mirror. The gun had fallen from his hand and was lying on the ground a couple of yards from him. This time he didn't attempt to grab it. The burning cabin filled the rear window. The roof had started to sag and wouldn't last much longer. The heat had fractured the windows and the flames were reaching out, clawing at the night. Her hands slipped off the steering wheel, searching for her belly.

'Everything's going to be okay,' she whispered. 'No one can hurt us now.'

# Chapter 52

Zoe pulled into the hospital parking lot and switched off the Cherokee's engine. In the end she had driven to Spearfish. The facilities at Rapid City were better, but it was that much further. For a long time she just sat there staring blankly. Her plan only extended to getting away from the cabin. She hadn't thought beyond that because she hadn't believed it was ever going to happen.

But it had happened, and here she was. Free at last.

Except she wasn't free. Not really. For that to happen she needed to persuade the police that she hadn't been responsible for Daniel's murder. That was why she was hesitating. If the police believed her then she would be free; if they didn't then she would end up in prison. That was the gamble. That was the risk. The second she stepped through the doors of the hospital, she would be setting a whole host of events into motion, events she had no control over.

No one knew she was alive. She could just turn the key in the ignition and drive. She didn't have to be Zoe Chapel anymore. She could be anyone she wanted; she could go anywhere. It was so tempting, but she was done with running scared. She had been doing that for too long now. A life filled with fear was the only life she knew. She deserved better than that.

Her baby deserved better.

Driving away from the cabin she had become convinced something was wrong with the baby. How could the stress of the last couple of weeks not have affected her? Babies needed to be loved and cherished and cared for, even more so in those precious months before the birth. And wouldn't that be about right? To finally escape from Gabriel only to discover her baby was dead. She grabbed the satellite phone from the passenger seat then got out. The night was cold and dark, but it belonged to her and her alone, and how long had it been since she had been able to say something like that?

At the main entrance she hesitated, but only for a second. Her decision had been made. She was going through with this, whatever the outcome. She needed to make sure her baby was all right. She stepped forward and the automatic doors shushed open. The receptionist did a double take when she saw her. Zoe had caught her reflection in the doors, so the reaction wasn't a surprise. The woman with the wide panicked eyes staring back at her looked like a refugee from a war zone. Her hands, face and clothes were bloodstained and dirty. Her hair was an untidy blonde mess. She had taken off a couple of pairs of socks to make it easier to drive, but the fact that she wasn't wearing shoes must have registered.

'I've been kidnapped and I'm pregnant,' Zoe said. 'I want an ultrasound. I need to know my baby is okay. Please help me. I need to know she's still alive.'

The last sentence came out on a choked sob. She tried to hold back the tears but it was impossible. The receptionist dashed around the desk and guided her by the elbow to a nearby seat. This small act of kindness just made Zoe cry even harder.

'I'm sorry,' she sobbed.

'It's okay,' the receptionist assured her. 'There's nothing to be sorry for. Is there anyone I can contact for you?'

Zoe shook her head.

'Okay, just sit here for a second. I'll go and find someone who can help.'

A short while later Zoe was lying on a bed in a room that was essentially the same as the one where she'd had the ultrasound in back in Portland. She barely noticed when the cold ultrasound gel was smeared onto her stomach. Her attention was fixed on the screen. This time she knew what she was looking at so she was able to locate the heartbeat immediately. A wave of relief washed through her, engulfing every other emotion. All the pain and heartbreak, all the fear, just disappeared as she watched that tiny heartbeat pulsing on the screen. Whatever happened, it was going to be okay. This was the only thing that really mattered; everything else was just details.

'You're baby's okay,' the nurse said.

'Thank God,' Zoe whispered. The tears were back, turning the screen into a grey blur. 'Thank you, thank you, thank you.'

The nurse who treated her wounds talked non-stop, which was fine. By the time she finished Zoe knew everything there was to know about her, and she hadn't had to offer up any of her own history in exchange. Aside from some scratches and scrapes she had come through her ordeal pretty much unscathed. There was a small cut on her left thigh that she had got when she climbed out of the window of the cabin, but that was the worst of her injuries.

After getting cleaned up she was taken to a private room. She didn't have the money to pay for this, but the police had asked for her to be kept apart from the other patients until after they had spoken to her. As soon as the nurse left, Zoe called Lizzy. She had memorised her cell number in case anything happened to the iPhone she'd stolen from Marilyn. Her hands were shaking as she punched it into the satellite phone. Lizzy answered with an urgent 'Hello?' She sounded way more awake than she should have for this time of the morning. She also sounded like she was expecting bad news.

'It's me. Zoe.'

There was a moment of silence, then an explosive 'Is it really you?'

'It's really me.'

'Where are you?'

'I'm in a place called Spearfish. It's in South Dakota.'

'Don't move. I'll be there as soon as I can. Are you staying in a hotel?'

'I'm actually in the hospital.'

'The hospital. Are you okay?'

Zoe sat up a little straighter on her bed and placed a protective hand on her belly.

'We are now.'

# Chapter 53

There was a knock on the door and an Asian man walked in. Zoe initially thought he was another doctor, but he wasn't dressed like one, and he just wasn't giving off that doctor vibe. The confidence was there, but there was an air of calculated distance that didn't fit. His eyes swept across the room as though he was looking for enemies, before settling on hers. He smiled but there was something calculated about that too. He was middle-aged, and good-looking, and vaguely familiar. He introduced himself as Detective Sergeant Tommy Wang of the Portland police, and she finally worked out where she had seen him before. Wang had headed up the investigation back in Portland. He had accompanied Lizzy at the press conference.

He moved a chair to the side of the bed and sat down. 'How are you feeling?'

'Fine.' The reply was quick, and well practised. Zoe was getting fed up with people asking if she was okay.

'I've got a few questions,' Wang said. 'If you're up to it.'

'I've already spoken to the local police.'

'I know, and if you want to do this later, that's not a problem.'

Zoe didn't want to do this, period, but that wasn't an option. At some point Wang would ask his questions, and she would have to answer them. On that basis they might as well get this over and done with.

'I'm fine to do this now.'

'I appreciate it.' He paused. 'The Rapid City police department is looking into what happened at this end. I'm interested in what happened back in Oregon.'

The last sentence was left hanging there. It was a statement filled with questions. Zoe looked past Wang and focussed on the window. The sky was grey and a light rain was tapping at the glass. She had known this would happen, but that didn't make it any easier. Her stomach was suddenly in knots. Her hands were clasped tightly together to try and stop them shaking. She had decided to go with the truth because it was bound to come out eventually. In the long run it would be for the best if it looked as though she had nothing to hide. She turned her attention back to Wang and smiled a sad, lonely smile.

'No one was supposed to die. No one except me, that is. The plan was for me to fake my death. It was going to look like suicide. I just wanted to get away from my husband. I couldn't do that on my own, though. That's why I enlisted Gabriel's help. Gabriel was my stepbrother.' She paused, then added quietly, 'I should never have trusted him. If I hadn't then Josh and Daniel would still be alive. All the others too.'

Wang locked eyes with her. 'Okay,' he said, stretching the word out. 'How about we start at the beginning? And please, take as much time as you need.'

Zoe started with her Day of Stones with Daniel and worked forward from there. It felt good to be getting it out there. It was cathartic, cleansing. Where it got difficult was when she spoke about the deaths. There had been too many of those, and they all weighed heavily on her conscience. All she ever wanted was for Daniel to stop hurting her. She never wanted anyone to die. She finished with a question of her own.

'Am I going to prison?'

'Why would you think that?'

'Because I asked Gabriel to help me.'

'Maybe so, but from what you've told me you didn't actually kill anyone.'

For a split second Zoe was back in Oregon. Her shaking hand was gripping the gun, and Gabriel was holding it steady. Maybe she had pulled the trigger; maybe she hadn't. God knows she had the motive, and Gabriel had provided her with the means and opportunity. This was the one thing she had left out of her account. Maybe Wang would have believed that Gabriel coerced her into pulling the trigger, but if he didn't then a conspiracy to murder charge would turn into a murder charge, and her baby would be all grown up by the time she got released from prison.

Except now that Gabriel was dead she wouldn't have to face a conspiracy charge, she suddenly realised. That threat had only worked when he was alive. Now that he was dead there was no one to point the finger of blame or contradict her story.

'You said you ran your stepbrother over in front of the cabin,' Wang said. 'That was the last time you saw him?'

'That's correct.'

'When the Rapid City police got to the cabin there was no sign of a body.'

Zoe shook her head in disbelief. 'No that can't be right. He was right there in front of the cabin.' She met Wang's gaze. 'Are you sure?'

'Positive. There was no body.'

'Maybe it was taken by wolves,' she said quickly, grasping at the first straw she could find. 'There are wolves in the forest.'

'If something like that had happened there would have been drag marks in the dirt.'

'You think he's still alive, don't you?'

'That's one possibility. Another is that he wandered into the woods and died from his injuries.'

'If that was the case then surely the police would have found his body.'

'Not necessarily. Those woods are massive. A person could easily walk in there and never be found.'

'Even with search dogs?'

'So far the dogs haven't found him. But we'll keep looking.'

Wang was doing his best to reassure her, but it wasn't working. Zoe was thinking back to a conversation she'd had with Gabriel when they first arrived at the cabin. He had pointed out that the lack of a body meant that Daniel would never have bought into the idea that she had committed suicide. The same thing was happening here. Without seeing Gabriel's body for herself, there was no way she was ever going to believe he was dead. From this moment on, she would be constantly looking over her shoulder.

'I should have checked for a pulse,' she whispered to herself. 'I should have made sure he was dead.'

'That's the last thing you should have done. He tried to shoot you. Believe me, you did the right thing by getting away from there.'

'Easy for you to say.'

'Look, your stepbrother is injured, and he doesn't have any transport. Assuming he's still alive, how far do you think he'll get before we catch him?'

'He could have walked to the road and got a lift.'

'You said he was covered in blood and wearing nothing but a pair of boxer shorts. No one's going to give him a lift looking like that.'

Zoe shook her head. 'You have no idea what you're dealing with here. All he needs is for one vehicle to stop. If he's lying on the road playing dead, don't you think someone might stop? Of course they would. If you see someone in trouble, you're going to want to help. And Gabriel's armed. As soon as they walk over to him, he's going to take control of the situation. He'll get them to drive somewhere, then he'll shoot them and take their car.'

'You don't know that's what happened.'

'It would have gone down something like that.'

Wang went quiet, thinking. 'We will find him, Zoe.'

'But will you find him before he comes after me?'

'He's not going to come after you.'

'You're sure of that?'

'We're going to keep you safe.'

'And how exactly do you intend to do that?'

'To start with I'm going to arrange for a police officer to be posted on your door.'

'What about when I get out of here? Are you going to have someone guarding me twenty-four hours a day?'

'If that's what it takes, then that's what we'll do.' Wang offered up a reassuring smile. 'Don't worry, Zoe. We'll keep you safe.'

# Chapter 54

*We'll keep you safe.*

After Wang left, those were the words that stayed with her. She had no doubt he believed what he was saying, and maybe the police could keep her safe in the short term, but they couldn't keep her safe forever. At some point their focus would shift, and all those promises would turn to dust, and Gabriel would be out there waiting. Wang thought that he knew what he was dealing with, but he didn't. Not really. Zoe had thought she knew Gabriel, but she didn't have a clue either. By the time she realised that, it was too late. Too late for Daniel. Too late for Josh. Too late for everyone else who died.

It wasn't too late for her baby, though.

She dressed quickly in the clothes she had worn the previous night. This time she only wore one pair of socks. The hospital slippers were flimsy but they were all she had. She finished dressing and checked her reflection in the window. The best she could say was that she looked more presentable than when she arrived.

She'd gotten as far as the door when the satellite phone rang on the nightstand. She walked over and picked it up. Lizzy's number was on the screen, which meant her plane must have landed. Zoe switched the phone off, placed it on top of the cabinet and walked back to the door. She opened it slowly and looked out. The corridor was empty. It would take time for Wang to arrange a guard, and it would take time for Lizzy to drive here from the airport.

Zoe stepped into the hallway and followed the signs to the stairs. The next left took her into a corridor that was much the same as the one she had just been in. The two nurses walking towards her were chatting and laughing and not paying her any attention. Her heart was thumping, her feet telling her to run, but somehow she kept walking, one unsteady footstep following the next.

The reception area was busy, but everyone was too wrapped up in their own dramas to bother with hers. Zoe hesitated at the main entrance, convinced Gabriel was out there waiting. She stopped again when she got outside, eyes scanning the parking lot. The couple of people she saw seemed more concerned with getting out of the rain.

Thankfully the Cherokee was where she'd left it. The police were no doubt planning on impounding it, but they hadn't got around to it yet. She checked the back seat as she walked around to the driver's door, but there was still no sign of Gabriel. For a moment she sat at the wheel with her hands on her belly, watching the raindrops chase each other down the windshield. In hindsight coming here had been a stupid thing to do. She should have driven to a car dealership and traded the Cherokee for a car capable of getting her as far away from South Dakota as possible, and as much cash as she could get.

She should have just disappeared when she had the chance.

It wasn't too late to do that. She might have lost the advantage that came with people assuming she was dead, but America was a big place. There had to be somewhere out there where she could lose herself. A place where she could build a new life for her and her baby. Coming here was just one more regret to add to the list.

Lizzy would be here soon. She would park in this lot and go inside, and find that her so-called friend had disappeared. Zoe had wanted to write her a letter, but what could she say to make this okay? What words could she find to make Lizzy understand that there wasn't any other way? At that moment she wanted nothing more than to talk to Lizzy. If ever there was a time when she needed a friend that time was now, but she couldn't risk anything happening to her. She had tried making various deals and bargains with herself, but kept arriving back at the same place: if she stayed then Lizzy would persuade her to go back to New York, and that would put her in Gabriel's sights. If anything happened to Lizzy, she would never forgive herself.

A Spearfish PD car cruised past the front of the hospital and parked near the entrance. It was far enough away not to be a threat, but Zoe still sank down in her seat. She peered over the top of the steering wheel and saw a cop walk over to the door. His attention was fixed on getting inside; he didn't look back, not once. Zoe started the car and drove out of the lot. Rapid City would be her first stop. She knew where the car dealerships were; knew which ones to avoid. The Cherokee was only a couple of years old. Even in its current condition someone would be willing to take it with no questions asked. She wouldn't get anywhere near what it was worth, but she'd get enough to buy another vehicle.

As to where she might eventually end up, that one was still in the air. She was thinking a city because that would provide more anonymity than a small town. Another advantage was that a city hospital would have better facilities for when the baby arrived. Whether that city ended up being on the eastern seaboard or the West Coast, or somewhere in between, she couldn't say. Her plan was to keep driving until she felt safe, and then she would drive a bit further just to be sure, and wherever she ended up that would be their new home.

# Epilogue

Emily was eighteen months, and getting so big. It was hard to believe she was walking and talking already, but she was. They said those early years went fast and that you should cherish every moment, but Zoe hadn't realised it would go this fast. Emily was currently fast asleep in the stroller, and that definitely made this a moment worth cherishing. Zoe loved her daughter more than life itself, but being a single parent was tough. On that basis she was never going to turn down the opportunity to have five minutes to herself.

She settled back on the bench and stared out at the Atlantic stretching all the way to the horizon. The sky was blue, the sun burning bright, but the water still managed to look grey. The breeze blowing in from the ocean added a chill to the day. This was her first time in Atlantic City, and her last. It was everything she had expected and more. Tacky, touristy, not her sort of place at all. On the plus side it was a city full of strangers. No one had given her so much as a second look the entire time she had been here. Invisibility was a state of mind. Give the impression that you are a lone island in the middle of a vast ocean and people left you alone. New Orleans was the city she currently called home, but probably not for much longer. They had been there for almost six months now, which had to be some sort of record.

Money was tight but they were just about managing to scrape by. The Internet had been a lifesaver. She spent hours searching eBay, looking for bargains which she would then sell on for a small profit. She was never going to become rich, but she was just about earning enough to keep their heads above water. The beauty of this idea was that she could do it anywhere. All she needed was an Internet connection. When they did eventually move to a new city she wouldn't have the hassle of touring the restaurants and coffee houses looking for work. She had needed to do this to start with, and it had been a pain in the ass. Then there was the fact that she kept thinking about what happened in Seattle. After Emily came along she hadn't been able to work for a while; then she hadn't been able to afford to work because childcare costs were so high. That was when she came up with the Internet idea.

Emily had been born in Orlando, but they hadn't stayed there long. Sitting all alone in the hospital, seeing all the other new mothers being visited by their friends and family, she had felt so vulnerable. She imagined everyone was watching her. They probably weren't. Why would they? Her life and troubles were nothing compared to the excitement of having a new baby. That hadn't made the fear go away, though. As soon as she had recovered from the birth, she had moved on. That was the point where she realised that her life would never be normal. The birth of a baby should be a cause for celebration; it shouldn't be a trigger for her paranoia.

She was currently going under the name Jennifer Smith. Smith because it was the most common surname in the US,

Jennifer because it was the first name that came up on the online random name generator she had logged on to. Jennifer Smith didn't have a passport, but she did have an Arizona driver's licence and a birth certificate. Getting hold of them had been a challenge, but it was so much easier to move around when you existed on paper. Zoe was still toying with getting a passport, but that presented a whole different level of risk. She liked the idea of leaving the US for good and starting a new life in a brand new country; she liked the idea of not having to constantly look over her shoulder. Then again, who was she trying to kid? At some point she would find herself searching the shadows and that urge to move on would become too strong to ignore.

She hated herself for the way she had treated Lizzy. When she arrived at the hospital she must have thought that Gabriel had snatched her. That theory would have been easy for the police to disprove. All they had to do was check the security cameras and they would have seen her walk out of the hospital alone. That didn't make what she had done all right, though. Not even close. She needed to explain her reasons to Lizzy; she needed her to understand. Most of all, she needed absolution. Because if Lizzy could forgive her then maybe she could start to find ways to forgive herself. If she could see herself as worthy through the eyes of another, then just maybe she could find the worth in herself.

Sitting on that bench, the urge to run was stronger than it had been in a long time, her paranoia levels running higher than she had ever known. She must have spotted Gabriel a hundred times since she'd arrived in Atlantic City. Of course, when she looked again, it hadn't been him. She hadn't seen hide nor hair of him since that night at the cabin. That was another reason she was finally doing this. After twelve months, her paranoia had reduced to the point where she could consider reaching out to Lizzy. Even so, she had still waited another six months just to be sure.

Zoe spotted Lizzy walking along the boardwalk and her heart missed a beat. She was at least sixty yards away, her head moving from side to side, checking the faces of the people she passed. All Zoe could do was sit frozen to the seat. The voice inside her head was telling her to leave, but her heart wanted her to stay put, and that was shouting loudest.

Lizzy suddenly stopped dead, did a quick double take and broke into a run. Zoe was on her feet in an instant, moving towards the stroller, ready to flee, but before she knew it Lizzy had dragged her into the fiercest of hugs and was squeezing the life out of her. Zoe wriggled out of the hug and stepped back. Lizzy looked much the same as she had looked at the press conference. Black clothes, black hair cut into a neat fashionista bob, piercings. Her eyes were filled with tears and there were mascara tracks on her cheeks. She wiped her face and her fingers came away grey.

'Oh my God, Zo, it's really you! I've been so worried. I thought I was never going to see you again.'

Zoe smiled. 'It's good to see you too. You have no idea.'

Lizzy laughed and wiped her eyes again. 'Believe me, I have every idea.'

'You weren't followed, were you?'

'No.'

'You're sure?'

'Positive.'

'And no one's been watching your apartment or following you?'

'No one's been watching me, Zo. Relax. You're safe.'

When she called last night, Lizzy had been adamant that she hadn't been followed. Zoe had cross-examined her to the point where Lizzy eventually told her to shut up. Even then she had kept asking. The old Zoe would have backed down, but that Zoe was long gone. She caught a movement out of the corner of her eye and looked down at the stroller. Emily's eyes were wide open and she was gazing around like she had never been asleep. Zoe picked her up before she started screaming her head off and drawing attention.

'She is gorgeous,' Lizzy cooed. 'Can I hold her, please?'

'Since when have you wanted to get within a million miles of a baby?'

'Under normal circumstances that would be true. But this is your baby, and she's gorgeous, so hand her over.'

Zoe handed Emily over and watched amazed as Lizzy fussed over her like she had been dealing with babies her whole life. Zoe could still remember how nervous she had been when Emily was first born. It had taken a while to even get comfortable holding her.

Lizzy caught her looking and smiled. 'I come from a large family, remember? There were always babies around while I was growing up.' She cooed and fussed Emily a bit more then looked back at Zoe. 'How are you doing? And I want the truth.'

'We're doing okay.' Zoe bit her lip, hesitating.

'Whatever it is, spit it out,' Lizzy said.

'I'm so sorry,'

'Sorry for what?'

'Sorry for everything. I've been the worst friend in the world.'

'Shut up, will you? The past is the past and that's where it stays. All that matters is you're here now.'

'You know I'm going to disappear again, don't you?'

'What I know is that you reached out to me once, and when you're ready you'll reach out again, and one day you'll feel comfortable enough to stop running and when that happens you know where to find me.'

Zoe felt the tears pricking at her eyes. She couldn't remember the last time she had cried. She had been too busy running and just trying to survive.

'I'm sorry.'

'Say that again and I'll change my mind about forgiving you.'

Lizzy held Emily out and waited for Zoe to take her. She sat down on the bench and patted the space next to her.

'Okay,' she said. 'Sit your ass down and tell me what you've been up to for the last couple of years. And don't you dare miss anything out. I want everything, girlfriend. Every last detail.'

Zoe watched Lizzy walk away and pushed back the tears. She had talked more than she had talked in ages and her throat was sore. Lizzy hadn't wanted to go; Zoe hadn't wanted her to go either, but it had to be like this. She needed to make sure Lizzy didn't follow her. She had promised she wouldn't, and Zoe trusted her, but you just couldn't be too careful. She bounced Emily on her knees, provoking a chuckle.

'So what do you think of your Aunt Lizzy, then? She's something else, isn't she?'

Emily let out another chuckle and grabbed for Zoe's fingers.

'I really hope you get to know her. You'll love her. And she'll be a good person to go to for clothes advice when you're a teenager. I'm afraid your mom is pretty useless on that score.'

The homeless guy barely registered when he walked past. He was just another face amongst all the other passing faces. She had glanced at him for a millisecond, decided he wasn't a threat, then gone back to fussing Emily. When he sat down at the far end of the bench, that put him firmly on her radar. Without being too obvious, she put Emily back into the stroller. She glanced over as she was fixing the straps. The idea that this was Gabriel had got lodged into her brain, fuelling her paranoia. She was convinced it was him; at the same time it came as no surprise to discover it wasn't.

Zoe saw Gabriel at least two dozen times on the way to the bus station; she saw him another dozen times as she was waiting to board her bus; even when she had taken her seat she still couldn't relax. It was only when the bus pulled away that she was finally able to breathe a little easier. She didn't mind the paranoia, though, because that kept her sharp, and staying sharp was keeping her and Emily alive. Because Gabriel was out there somewhere. That was her first thought when she woke up and her last thought before she closed her eyes, and she didn't mind that either because she couldn't afford to forget. If there was one thing she had learnt from her time with Daniel it was that you couldn't be too careful. Maybe Gabriel was looking for her; maybe he wasn't. But he was out there, and she didn't know what he was thinking, and that was all the reason she needed to be cautious.

Her life was anything but perfect, but for the most part it was hers. That didn't just count for something, it counted for everything. And what was perfect anyway? Once upon a time she'd had the so-called perfect life, and the so-called perfect marriage. She would take what she had now over that any day. When you got right down to it the only thing that really mattered was this little bundle wrapped up in her arms. Emily gave a little chuckle and Zoe smiled down at her.

'Don't worry,' she whispered. 'Mommy's going to keep you safe.'

# Acknowledgements

As always the biggest thanks goes to my family. Karen, Niamh, Finn, you are my world. Love you now and always.

Camilla Wray has been guiding me through the publishing industry for the past five years now and I can't think of anyone else I'd want by my side.

This is the fourth book I've worked on with Katherine Armstrong, and as always it's been a blast. It's so good to have the band back together!

Huge thanks also to Mary Derby, Emma Winter, Kristina Egan and Sheila David at the Darley Anderson Agency. You guys are the best.

Finally, a massive thank you to everyone who has taken the time to read my books. You have no idea how much that means to me.

Want to read
# NEW BOOKS
before anyone else?

Like getting
# FREE BOOKS?

Enjoy sharing your
# OPINIONS?

Discover

# READERS FIRST

Read. Love. Share.

Sign up today to win your first free book:
## readersfirst.co.uk